Sir James Melville

The Memoires of Sir James Melvil of Hal-Hill

Containing an Impartial Account of the Most Remarkable Affairs

Sir James Melville

The Memoires of Sir James Melvil of Hal-Hill
Containing an Impartial Account of the Most Remarkable Affairs

ISBN/EAN: 9783337184155

Printed in Europe, USA, Canada, Australia, Japan

Cover: Foto ©Raphael Reischuk / pixelio.de

More available books at **www.hansebooks.com**

THE
MEMOIRES

O F

Sir James Melvil

Of *HAL-HILL:*

CONTAINING

An Impartial Account

Of the moſt Remarkable

AFFAIRS of STATE

During the laſt Age, not mention'd by other Hiſtorians :
More particularly Relating to the KINGDOMS

O F

England and Scotland,

Under the R E I G N S

Of
{ Queen *Elizabeth,*
| *Mary* Queen of *Scots,*
AND
| King *JAMES.*

In all which Tranſactions the Author was Per-
ſonally and Publickly concern'd.
Now publiſhed from the Original Manuſcript.

By *GEORGE SCOTT,* Gent.

LONDON,
Printed by *E. H.* for *Robert Boulter* at the *Turks-head* in *Corn-hill,*
againſt the *Royal-Exchange,* 1683.

THE
EPISTLE
TO THE
READER.

AS there is scarce any kind of Civil *Knowledge* more *necessary* or profitable than History; (*which is therefore very aptly stiled by the Ancients,* The Mistress of Life,) *so of all sorts of History there is none so useful as that which unlocking the Cabinet, brings forth the* Letters, *private Instructions, Consultations and Negotiations of Ministers of State; for then we see things in a clear light, stript of all their paints and disguisings, and discover those* hidden Springs of Affairs, *which give motion to all the vast* Machines *and stupendious Revolutions of Princes and Kingdoms, that make such a noise on the Theatre of the World, and amaze us with unexpected shiftings of Scenes and daily Vicissitudes.*

Of this latter kind are those Memoires *wherewith we here Oblige the World, being the many Years Transactions and Experiences of an eminent publick Minister in his long and faithful Services under, and Negotiations with several Princes, and at as ticklish a Juncture and important Crisis of Affairs as could almost happen in any Age : for having upon the perusal not only found the same to contain many remarkable passages, not met with in any Histories of those times, and in such Occurrents as they have touched upon, to be much more exact and full in divers considerable Circumstances ; But observed it likewise to be furnisht with much excellent, plain, honest advice (delivered by the By) which might be of great advantage to Princes, and both Examples and Precepts whereby their Councellors and Favourites may be Caution'd what just, free and generous Measures they ought to take, if they would not tread the same Precipices, whereby others have Shipwrackt both their Masters and themselves, I could not but apprehend my self obliged to Communicate such a Treasure to the Publick, as well for a ge-*

a 2

neral

neral good, as in fome meafure to difcharge my Devoir to the memory of the worthy Author, from whom I have the honour to be defcended.

Three things there are Effential to any Hiftory, and which chiefly recommend it to the efteem of judicious Readers.

1. That the fubject matter be real, and of confiderable moment.
Women and Children may be delighted with, and dote upon Romances,
and filly Legends ; or liften with attentive Admiration to the Wars
of the Pigmies, and Adventures of the Faiery Land. But men of
fence always expect folid Tranfactions, and fuch fubftantial Examples as may be of advantage to improve their judgment in Civil Wifdom, and the neceffary conduct of Life.

2. That the Author be capable of knowing what he fpeaks, and
have Opportunities to difcover the Certainty, and full Circumftances of thofe Affairs, whereof he undertakes to Treat.

3. And laftly, His Honefty, That he be a man of impartial
Veracity, and firm Refolution to obferve inviolable that prime Law
of Hiftory, Ne quid falfi audeat dicere, ne quid veri non
audeat. Not to dare deliver any falfhood, nor to conceal any
Truth.

All which Characters are happily met in thefe Memoires.
The matters contain'd, are both Lofty and Weighty, for they
Treat of the Actions and Sufferings of Princes, and perfons of the
firft Rank : Open the clofe Confultations and Intrigues of feveral
of the ableft Minifters of State at that time in Chriftendom, and
fhew on what Hinges the greateft Affairs were turned, and by what
Artifices managed, fo as to be either accomplifht or Defeated.

Nor could any Gentleman have better Advantages to be acquainted with the moft private and referved Scenes of thofe Paffages
which here he delivers to the World, fince in general of all that he
writes, he may properly fay, Quorum pars magna fui, They are
matters within his own Circle, and declare fuch as muft of neceffity
fall within his own notice, fince through his hands, and he himfelf
had a principal part in the manage and tranfacting of them ; being
a perfon concern'd in the moft knotty Affairs (efpecially relating to
Scotland) during his time : And therefore as Ocularis Teftis,
his work may Challenge that Credit which many other Authors do but
begg from the Charity of their Courteous Readers ; at leaft deferves

as

as much or more efteem as any other Writers of that time, who in refpeƈt of him were but Auriti.

The Author was defcended of one of the moft honourable Families of the Kingdom of Scotland, *as being Third Son to the Lord of* Kaeth, *and at Fourteen years of Age was fent by the Queen Regent to be Page of Honour to her Daughter* Mary *married to the Dauphin of* France. *But by her allowance he entred into the Service of the Duke of* Montmorance (*Great Conftable of* France, *chief Minifter to* Henry *the Second) who earneftly defired him from her Majefty, having a fancy for the Youth's promifing parts ; he was* Nine *years Entertain'd and Imploy'd by him, and when he grew up to riper Years and try'd Abilities in matters of greateft Importance, an honourable Penfion for his greater encouragement was fetled upon him by that* King.

Then being defirous for his further Accomplifhment to Travel, *having his Queens leave and his Mafters permiƒion for that purpofe :* But paffing through Germany *he was detain'd by the perfuafion of the Eleƈtor* Palatine, *and at his earneft intreaties neceffitated to condefcend to attend at his Court, where he* Refided *Three years, being by him imployed on feveral Embaffies. After which, obtaining his confent to profecute his former intentions of further Travel, he vifited* Venice, Rome, *and the moft famous Cities of* Italy. Returning through Switzerland *to the Eleƈtors Court, he there found a Call from Queen* Mary, *then returned to her Kingdom of* Scotland, *after the death of her Husband King* Francis, *to attend her Service.*

The Queen Mother of France *at the fame time had offer'd him a large Penfion, and profitable Offices, to engage him to wait upon her Service at the Court of* France ; *fhe finding it her intereft at that Junƈture to keep good Correfpondence with the Proteftant Princes in* Germany, *and knowing him to be moft acceptable to all of them. But though it appeared moft advantagious to his private Fortunes to have accepted of her noble Offers ; yet in this and at all other times he prefer'd his Loyalty to his Intereft, and efteem'd himfelf engag'd in Duty to ferve his natural Princefs rather than a Stranger.*

Upon his arrival in Scotland *he was admitted a Privy Councellor, and Gentleman of her Chamber, being continually imploy'd by her Majefty in matters of her greateft concernments, till her unhappy confinement in* Lockleven : *All which he difcharged with an exaƈt fidelity, and had fhe taken his found Advice, many of her misfortunes might have been avoided.* He

He was afterwards Noticed by all the Four ſucceſſive Regents in a ſpecial manner, and intruſted by them with Negotiations of greateſt moment, Though after the Queens impriſonment he had ever owned the King's ſide.

When his Majeſty King James came to the Government, he was eſpecially recommended by the Queen, then Priſoner in England, to him as one moſt faithful, and capable of doing him Service. Whereupon he was likewiſe by his Majeſty admitted a Member of his moſt Honourable Privy Council, and of his Exchequer ; as alſo made Gentleman of his Chamber, continuing ever in favour and Imployment till his Majeſties paſſage into England, to receive his Hereditary Right, the Crown of that Kingdom, upon the death of Queen Elizabeth.

The King would gladly have taken him along with him thither, offering him conſiderable advancements there : But being now ſtricken in years, and deſirous to Retreat from the troubles of the World to ſpend the remainder of his days in Contemplation, begged his Majeſties permiſſion thereto. However, after the King's going for London, he found himſelf in Duty engag'd once to wait upon his Majeſty in that Kingdom, and accordingly went thither, and was graciouſly received ; and having attended there ſome weeks, humbly giving his Majeſty his beſt advice, no Court allurements (whereof he had great ſtore) could prevail with him to alter his former Reſolutions of privacy ; So that he return'd to his own Houſe, where, as in Harbour, reflecting on the paſs'd Voyage of his Life, and all the various Weather, and difficult Storms of Publick Affairs, wherein he had been concern'd ; to inform the World of the true State of thoſe Tranſactions, and to direct others (eſpecially his Children) how to conduct themſelves if call'd to ſuch Services, he with his own hand drew up the following Memoires. How far he deduced them I cannot certainly determine ; 'tis very probable he had given an account of all till the going of the King to England, though this Copy extend not ſo far : However thou haſt all that I have, and nothing more then what is the Author's, for I ſhould eſteem it impiety to obtrude any thing of my own under his Name. And I hope the Reader will rather accept kindly what is here happily Retriev'd, than be offended at me for not furniſhing him with more than the injuries of time and ill men have left us.

And indeed I was not a little encouraged to this Publication by Reflecting on the wonderful preſervation of ſo much of it, after ſo many Years, and its then coming ſo Providentially to my hand, it

having

The Epiſtle to the Reader.

having found the Caſtle of Edinburgh *an Aſylum till the Year* 1660, *which yet had not been able to afford ſhelter to the* Publick Records *of the* Kingdom, *from the hands of Tyrannical Uſurpers : Though I have not met with any Information by what way it came thither, far leſs how ſecured ſo long a ſpace, and amidſt ſo many Confuſions, being there recommended to no Man's particular Care, but expoſed to the mercy of the* Rabble : *Whence it was wonderfully reſcued by* Mr. Robert Trail *late Miniſter of the* Gray-Fryars Church *in* Edinburgh, *when Impriſon'd there, to whom the Author's hand-writing was exactly known. This Mr.* Trail *counting it an happineſs to have lighted on ſo great a* Rarity, *knowing the Worth and Abilities of the Author, remitted it to Sir* James Melvil *of Hal-hil, the Author's Grand-Child : From whence it was derived to me, and having peruſed it, and thought I ſhould be highly injurious to the* Publick, *if I did not Communicate it to the World ; together with the Author's following* Epiſtle *to his Son in the nature of a Dedica-tion, wherein as he ſhews his deep inſight into the Intrigues of* Princes Courts; *ſo it likewiſe gives an evident Demonſtration of his ſincerity in what he has herein Delivered ; and of his firm Affection to ver-tue and honeſty, and deteſtation of vice, and thoſe flattering Arts whereby evil and Self-ſeeking Councellors have often abuſed the beſt of* Princes.*

This is all I thought neceſſary to Advertiſe thee of, touching this Publication, *and ſo leave it to thy Candid peruſal.*

George Scott.

T H E

THE

AUTHOR

TO HIS

SON.

Dear S O N,

SEeing thou haft fhewn they felf fo willing to fatisfie my expectations of the following, and obferving many of my former *Precepts* during thy younger years, I grant now unto thy requeft the more gladly, to put in writing for thy better memory, feveral paffages which thou haft heard me rehearfe concerning the life I did lead during my peregrination through the moft part of *Europe*, from the Age of fourteen years till this prefent hour ; together with the profperous fuccefs, and hard accidents hapned to me, hoping that thou wilt be fo wife as to help thy felf in time by my faults, and not wait upon the hurtful experience of the common fort, feeing no man can fhew the right way better than he who hath oft-times chanced upon By-rodes ; affuring thee, that, next unto the fpecial favour of God, nothing ftood me in fo much ftead as the early embracing of *unbought experience*, by obferving the ftumbling Errours of others.   Neither did I ever find any thing more dangerous than the frequent flighting to notice any feen example, which was always accompanied with over late Repentance.

The moft part of things which I purpofe to fet down prefently, are certain old written Memorials which were lying befide me in fundry parcels, treating of matters wherein I have been imployed my felf by fundry Princes, or which I have feen, or obferved being in their Countries (as the purpofes of themfelves will declare) to ferve for an example of life, and better behaviour to thee and thy Brother, concerning the Service of Princes, and medling

ling in their Affairs; which I could not efchew, for I fought not them, but they me. I enforced my felf to ferve them more carefully, diligently and faithfully than any of my Companions, whereby I won greateft favour with thofe who were *Wife, Grave, Aged* and *Experimented*; as with the Prince *Elector Pallatine*, and the old Duke of *Momorancie,* Conftable of *France,* who had the whole Rule and Government of the Country under King *Henry* the Second, his Mafter and mine; who were fo conftant, that their favour lafted fo long as I remained in their Service; not without extream and dangerous *Envy* of fuch of my Companions as were naturally inclined to that vile Vice, whom I took great pains by patience, prefents and humility to gain; obliging them by that carriage to lay afide part of their malice. But when it chanced me after to ferve Princes of *Younger Years,* and of lefs Experience, at the firft by the like diligence, care and fidelity, I obtained their favour above the reft of their Servants; yet at length they were carried away by the craft and envy of fuch as could fubtilly creep into their favour, by flattery and by joining together in a deceitful bond of fellowfhip, every one of them fetting out the other, as *meeteft* and *ableft* for the Service of their Prince, to the wrack of him and his Country; craving the Prince to be fecret, and not to Communicate his Secrets to any but their Society. Thus the Princes good qualities being fmother'd with fuch a Company, were commonly led after the *Paffions* and *Particularities* of thofe, who fhot only at their *own marks*: Some of them continually poffeffing his *Ear*, and debarring there-from all honeft, true and plain fpeakers; fo that no more hope could be left of a gracious Government, nor place for good men to help their Prince and Country, where-through fell out many foul, ftrange and fad *Accidents,* as may be afterward feen and read: Princes mifufed, and abufed, their Country robbed, their beft and trueft Servants wracked, and the wicked inftruments at laft perifhed with all their high and fine pretences; others, ay fuch-like, fucceeding in their place, never one taking example to become more temperate and difcreet, becaufe of the deftruction of thofe who went before them; but as highly and fiercely following their greedy, vain and ambitious pretences, obtaining

the

the like Tragical reward. For my part, albeit I had feen, and oft-times read of the wrack and backward rewards of all fuch true, faithful Servants and Councellours, as were moft careful of the Weal and Safety of their Prince, in refifting and gainftanding the devices of the *wicked fort*, and fometimes minding the Prince not to fuffer himfelf to be led by thofe who commit fo many wrongs, and errours at their Appetite, yet I left not off from what I thought my *Duty*, neither for *Fear*, nor *Danger*, to op-pofe my felf continually to the *falfe fetches* of fuch Mi-nions, until, I muft confefs rather following the *Extremi-ty* than the right *Midft*, I loft my Credit with the Prince, and Tint my reward, repofing over-much truft upon their conftancy and my good Service, which hath been oft an hurtful opinion unto honeft Men ; with over-late Repentance I was compelled to lament, as did Mon-fieur *de Bouffie* when he was left and mifliked by his Ma-fter, crying out, *Alas, wherefore fhould Men be earneft to furpafs their Neighbours in worthinefs and fidelity, feeing that Princes, who get the fruits of our Labours, like not to hear of plainnefs, but of pleafant Speeches, and are eafily altered without occafion upon the trueft Servants ?* I perceive well that to continue in their favour they fhould not be ferved with Uprightnefs, but with Wylinefs ; and inftead of ufing free Language for their Honour and Prefervation, their Ser-vants fhould frame and accommodate themfelves to their *Pleafure* and *Will* ; which may be eafily done by the dul-left fort of Men ; but my *daft opinion* was, that I might ftand by *Honefty* and *Vertue*, which I find now to be but a Vain Imagination, and a Scholaftical Difcourfe, unmeet to bring Men to any profitable *Preferment* : And yet my nature will not fuffer me to proceed by any other means, I being of the fame Mind and Nature, and by a juft Call and Command, firft of the *Queen* his Majefty's Mother, and afterward of himfelf, having more Matter and grea-ter Warrant then many others, as well to admonifh, ad-vertife and reprove the Prince to gain-ftand all evil In-ftruments, took the more freedom, finding my felf there-to in Duty obliged, againft the Rule given by *Seneca* to *Lucullus*, faying, *If thou defireft to be agreeable to Great Prin-ces, do them many Services, and fpeak to them few words.* *Plato*

was

was of the fame opinion, the favour of Princes being
obtained with great pain, and travel, and retained with
great difficulty; therefore fhould the wife Courtier be
careful of offending them, either by gefture, word or deed;
for being once in *difgrace* with them, they may well forgive, but they fhall never be fo great with them again
do what they will. Sometimes a Man man difcreetly
put the Prince in remembrance of his long and good Service, but caft not up thy Service, nor be importunate in
demanding rewards; therefore be not fo audacious as to
find *fault* with thy Prince's proceedings, nor to give advice
unrequired, or advertifements without good grounds of
being credited; for Princes notice not any thing but what
is told them by their *Favourites* and *Minions*, who commonly feem to allow and take pleafure of whatfomever
Recreation they find the Prince inclined to, not as by way
of *flattery*, but as by way of yielding, and leaving their
own pleafure to take pains to pleafe the Prince; they
never appear mifcontent although he do not *Reward* them
in due time, they never challenge him of *breach of Promife*
in cafe he break it. In many of thefe Rules I confefs I have
over-fhot my felf, for too great fervency towards the Princes Service, having never minded my own particular advancement and profit: For otherwife I fhould have at the
earneft defire of the Houfe of *Guife*, my old and great ac-
quaintances while I was refiding at the Court of *France*,
titled in the Queens Ear, that her Rebellious Subjects,
who had at their own hands, without her Authority,
changed Religion, fhould have been exemplarily punifhed as Rebels and Trayters: That if fhe condefcended
to acquiefce to the eftablifhing the *Reformed Religion*, it
would be conftructed as meannefs of Spirit, and that fhe
wanted Authority to curb fuch a mutinous People: That
it was below her at the arrogant defire of her Nobility,
and to remove the idle jealoufies of her other Subjects, to
lay afide *Rixio*, as being derogatory from her honour, that
fhe could not have liberty to keep about her what Servants fhe pleafed, feeing hence there might be ground to
alledge, there were other bad defigns to follow, when in
the firft place they defired to feparate from her, fuch as they
knew would be moft trufty to her, and in whom fhe could
most

moſt confide. This kind of Language would probably have moſt ſuited her Majeſties humour, and would have procured to my ſelf great Bribes, from *Rixio* and his Po=piſh friends for my reward. But I thought it was more the part of a *True Friend* to her Majeſty, to acquaint her, that ſeeing her Subjects had now imbraced the Proteſtant Religion, looking upon the Popiſh Principles as *Damning*, it was not her intereſt to do any thing that could give them any jealouſie that ſhe intended to alter their Religion ; that as the Entertaining of *Rixio* gave to all ſuch, ſome apparent ground of harbouring ſuch appre-henſions, he being a known Enemy to their *Religion* ; that having ſo much of her favour, he would undoubtedly uſe his endeavours to perſwade her to Re-eſtabliſh that Reli-gion, which ſhe her ſelf profeſſed ; ſo it gave juſt ground of diſcontent to the *Nobility*, who would look upon any extraordinary honour confer'd by her Majeſty upon a *Stranger*, as highly prejudicial to them, who were as wil-ling and able to ſerve her as he could be ; and reflecting upon their *Loyalty*, as if ſhe had more truſt to place in a Stranger then in her own native Country-men, and born Subjects. Had I not more regarded my Princeſs her Intereſt, then mine own, I ſhould have accepted the large offers made me by the Earl of *Bothwel*, when he deſired me to ſubſcribe with the reſt of his flatterers that Paper where-in they declared it was her Majeſties intereſt to Marry the ſaid Earl, but I choſe rather to lay my ſelf open to his hatred and revenge, whereby I was afterward in peril of my life, and tell her Majeſty, that thoſe who had ſo ad-viſed her, were betrayers of her honour for their own ſel-fiſh ends, ſeeing her marrying a Man commonly judged her Husbands murtherer, would leave a Taſh upon her name, and give too much ground of jealouſie, that ſhe had conſented to that *foul deed*: I wanted not fair offers from *Randolph* and *Killegrew*, Reſidents here from the *Court of England*, if I would have in ſo far complied with their deſigns, as not to have divulged what I perceived to be their drifts, which I could not conceal, finding them ſo deſtructive to the Kingdom. I had the fair occaſion of making a large fortune to my ſelf, if I would have gone along with the Earl of *Arran*, by Counſelling the King's

Majeſty

Majefty to follow his violent advices; but finding them fo far contrary to his intereft; I did think my felf ingaged to warn his Majefty that he was a dangerous man, who gave him fuch advices ; that if he followed the fame, he would run himfelf upon inevitable Precipices; that his Majefty's hearkening to the Duke of *Lennox* and him, the one a Papift, the other a wicked and ungodly man, would breed jealoufies in his Subjects minds, which might produce dangerous effects. This freedom, and many times the like, I took ; which though his Majefty accepted in good part, yet I thereby contracted me ftore of Enemies : But it was always my Principle, rather to hazard my felf by plain fpeech, when 'twas neceffary, than to expofe my Mafter to danger, by filence or bafe flattery. And though the Common Practice which I mention'd e're while, may feem to thrive beft in fome Courts for a time, yet under Grave and Wife Princes, and at long-run, the honeft Maximes will prove moft acceptable and fafe. Therefore I willingly opened thefe things to thee, that thou mayft as well know what is ufually done, as what ought to be. There is a certain difcretion to be ufed, that is free both from Sawcynefs and Affentation ; and a man may many times, if he skill it aright, give his Prince good Counfel, contrary to his inclinations, yet without incurring his difpleafure. This thou oughteft to ftudy, if ever thou be called to publique Affairs, and though thou mayft bend with the neceffity of fome Accidents, and yield to the times in fome things, though not going juft fo as thou would have matters to go ; and humour the Prince in an ordinary bufinefs, to gain opportunity of doing greater good to him and thy Country at a more lucky Seafon ; yet be fure that thou never Engage in any Difloyalty, Cruelty, or Wickednefs, nor fuffer any thing to pafs that thou feeft will tend to his Ruine or grand Prejudice, without noticing it to him in fome humble manner; and though for that time it be dif-relifhing or flighted, yet when he fees the Effects follow that thou admonifhedft him of, he will love thee the better, and rather hearken to honeft Advice for time future : And withal thou wilt obtain the Favour and Bleffing of Almighty God, whom thou muft at all times endeavour

faithfully

faithfully and uprightly to ſerve, if ever thou expecteſt
Bliſs in this or the other World ; To whoſe Gracious
Providence I Commit thee, with the hearty well Wiſhes
and Beniſon of

Thy Dearly Loving Father

JAMES MELVIL.

SIR

MELVILS MEMOIRS:

In reference to

MARY Queen of SCOTS

AND

JAMES VI.

K Ing *Henry* VIII. of *England* being difcontent with the Pope, for refufing to grant the Divorce from his wife Queen *Katharine* of *Caftile*. For revenge he looked through his fingers at the Preachers of the Reformed Religion, who had ftudied in *Dutch-land* under *Martin Luther*, and were lately come to *England*. In procefs of time the hatred betwixt the King and the Pope came to fo great a length, that he proclaimed himfelf *Head of the Kirk of England*, and difcharged S. *Peters* Pennies to be paid from that time forth ; with a ftrict command to all his Subjects, no manner of way to acknowledge the Pope. He obtained the faid Divorce from his own Clergy, marrying another, which occafioned to him the hatred of the Pope, Emperour and King of *Spain*, and all their Affiftants. . He again defiring to ftrengthen himfelf at home, conjecturing the probability of a Combination againft him, found it his Intereft to entertain a ftrict Amity with *James* V. of *Scotland* his Nephew, for he was determined to Unite this whole Ifle in one Religion, and in one Empire, failing of Heirs male procreate of his own body : Having then but one Daughter called *Mary* with the divorced Queen ; which Daughter he declared to be a Baftard. Upon which confideration Ambaffadors are fent thither, inviting that King to a Conference at *York*, whither *Henry* offered to come and meet him. Alledging by fuch an Interview, matters might be more effectually condefcended upon conducing for the mutual Interefts of both Kingdoms, then could be expected from the endeavours of Ambaffadors to be imployed in that Affair.

King *James* having ferioufly confidered the Overture, and advifed thereabout with his Council ; upon their deliberation and advice, returns his refolution to attend his Uncle, Time and Place appointed. With which anfwer the Ambaffadors highly fatisfied, return to their Mafter who rejoiced exceedingly at fo happy a Succefs of that matter. Whereupon great preparations are made at *York*, for the Entertainment of his Nephew with the greater Solemnity.

The Clergy of *Scotland*, fworn Clients to the Pope having had feveral Confultations hereanent, were alarm'd with this Propofal, and

King his Father had for making War againſt the King of *England* his
good Brother, was too manifeſtly felt by the whole Subjects. And
little better to be looked for, in caſe a new unneceſſary War be made,
for your Majeſties ſtaying away from the intended Meeting at *Tork.*
The King took ſuch delight in this language, that he determined to
follow the advice given therein. And at his firſt meeting with the
Prelates, who had then very great rule in the Country, he could not
contain himſelf any longer, when they came hoping to ſee their Plots
put in execution. After many ſore reproofs, that they ſhould have
adviſed him to uſe ſuch cruelty upon ſo many Noble men and Barons,
to the peril of his own Eſtate. *Wherefore,* ſaid he, *gave my Predeceſſors
ſo many Lands and Rents to the Kirk? Was it to maintain Hauks, Dogs,
and Whores to a number of idle Prieſts? The King of* England *burns,
the King of* Denmark *beheads you;* I ſhall ſtick you with this *Whingar.*
And therewith he drew out his Dagger, and they fled from his preſence
in great fear. The King reſolved fully to keep his promiſe with his
Uncle the King of *England,* thinking it both his honour and advancement ſo to do.

The Prelates of *Scotland,* thinking themſelves far out-ſhot, and thereby in a dangerous condition, conſulted together how to bring the
King again to their opinion. They reſolved in the firſt place to offer
to pay him yearly out of the Rents of the Kirk, fifty thouſand Crowns,
to maintain hired Souldiers, beſides the ordinary Subjects which obey
the Proclamation, in caſe the King of *England* ſhould make Wars againſt
Scotland, becauſe of the Kings not keeping the appointment at *Tork.*
They thought this would be an allurement to the King who liked
well to be rich. Yet they concluded, that unleſs the matter were proponed and favourably interpreted to his Majeſty by ſuch as had his ear, that
would not do the buſineſs. They beſtowed therefore largely of their
Gold to his familiar Servants, and further promiſed unto *Oliver Sinclar* ,
that they ſhould cauſe him to be advanced to great Honours, and to be
made Lieutenant of the whole Army againſt *England,* in caſe that King
Henry would intend Wars againſt *Scotland.* Which they affirmed he
would not, nor durſt not, having already ſo many Irons in the Fire.

This was communicated by the Prelates to the Minions at Court, and
chearfully condeſcended to by them, who had by flattery gained greateſt favour. And chiefly by drawing of fair Maidens to the King, and
ſtriving to be the firſt advertiſers whoſe Daughter ſhe was, and how
ſhe might be obtained ; and likewiſe of mens Wives. They waited
a convenient time when the Treaſurer ſhould be abſent, who was a
ſtout bold man; therefore they durſt not ſpeak in his preſence. For he
always offered by ſingle combat and at the point of the Sword, to maintain what he ſpoke. At this time he was abſent from Court, for the
King had given the Ward and Marriage of *Kelley* in *Angus* to his ſecond
Son ; and he was gone there to take poſſeſſion thereof. In his abſence
then this was proponed to the King, and ſo backed by *Oliver Sinclare,*
and ſuch of the Clergy as had been beſt acquainted with his Majeſty, as
he was induced to give ear thereto. They having added ſeveral other
perſuaſions, at ſuch times as they brought unto him fair Maidens, and
mens Wives. Then they took occaſion in the next place, to ſhew his
Majeſty that the Laird of *Grange* his Treaſurer, was alſo become a He-
retick

retick,and that he had always a NewTeftament in Eng i hin hisPoutch.
And likewife that he was become fo proud,and pult up by his Majefties
favour, that no man might abide him. And that he was fo extream
greedy, that he was unmeet to be Treafurer : and too told to have
procured for his fecond Son the rich Ward and Marriage of *Kelley* worth
Twenty thoufand pound. The King anfwered, *That he efteemed him to
be a plain frank Gentleman, that he loved him fo well, that he would give-
him again the faid Ward and Marriage for a word of his mouth.* The
Prior of *Pittenweem* replied and faid, *Sir the heir of Kelley is a lufty fair
Lafs, and I dare pledge my life, that if your Majefty will fend for her prefently, that he fhall refufe to fend her to you.*

The King affirming ftill the contrary, there was a Miffive written.
And the Prelates and their Faction devifed,that the faid Prior of *Pittenweem* fhould carry the Letter, and bring over the Maiden-heir of *Kelly*
to the King. But the Treafurer, who knew him to be his deadly enemy,
refufed to deliver her to him. Alledging the faid Prior to have been all
his days a vile Whoremafter,having deflowred diversMaidens,therefore
he thought him an unfit Meffenger. Who was fo glad as he, to return
with this backward anfwer. He and his Affociates kindled up the King
in fo great choler againft the Treafurer,handling the matter fo finely
and hotly, that they obtained a Warrant to charge the Treafurer to
Ward within the Caftle of *Edinburgh*. Which they forgot not to do,at
his firft coming to Court. He again gheffed that leefings would be
made againft him, therefore ufed great diligence to be with the King.
And notwithftanding of their charge, paft peartly in to his Majefty,
who was at his Supper in *Edinburg* ; but the King looked down upon
him, and would not fpeak to him, nor know him. He neverthelefs
fteps forward, and faid, *Sir what offence have I done,who had fo much of
your favour when I parted from you with your permiffion ?* The King anfwered, *Why did you refufe to fend me the Maiden whom I wrote for, and
gave defpiteful language to him I fent for her ?* Sir, faid he, *there is none
about your Majefty dare avow any fuch thing in my face.* As for the Maiden, *I faid to the Prior of* Pittenweem, *that I was well enough to be the
Meffenger my felf to convey her to your Majefty; but thought him unmeet,
whom I knew to be a forcer of Women, and the greateft deflowrer of Wives
and Maidens in* Scotland. The King faid, *Haft thou then brought the
Gentlewoman with thee ? Yes Sir,* faid he. *Alafs,* faith the King, *they
have fet out fo many leefings againft thee, that they have obtained of me a
Warrant to put thee in Ward ; but I fhall mend it with a contrary command.* Then faid the Treafurer lamentingly, *My Life, Sir, or Warding
is a fmall matter ; but it breaks my heart that the World fhould hear of your
Majefties facility.* For he had heard that in his abfence they had caufed the King to fend to *England*, and give over the intended Meeting
at *York*. Whereat the King of *England* was fo offended, in that he had
been fo publickly fcorned and affronted, that he fent an Army to
Scotland to deftroy it with Fire and Sword. Albeit the King liked nothing of this War, he was ftill kept in hope that it fhould tend to his
great honour and advantage. And that *England* had fo much to do
as would bufie them elfewhere;fo that they would foon repent them,
and be compelled to fue for Peace ere it was long. In the mean time
their Gold was made ready the more to encourage the King, and large
promifes of much more, in cafe the War continued. The

The King was engaged to raife an Army to defend his Country and Subjects, who went to that War, to fhew their obedience much againft their hearts. But when they perceived *Oliver Sinclare* raifed up upon mens fhoulders, and proclaimed Lieutenant over the whole Army at *Salway Sands*; the Lords, in difpight that the Court and Country fhould be governed by fuch mean men as were Penfioners to the Prelates, refufed to fight under fuch a Lieutenant, but fuffered themfelves all to be taken Prifoners. So the whole Army being overthrown, the King took thereat great difpleafure. There was great murmurings in the Country, that for pleafuring the Prelates the Kingdom fhould be thus endangered. The report whereof, and the juftnefs of the complaint, made the King burft out with fome language againft them who had given him fo bad advice. Which was carried over foon to their ears, and they fearing the effects of his difpleafure, caufed him to be poifoned, having learned that Art in *Italy*, called an *Italian Poffit*. The Cardinal *David Beaton* was with his Majefty in the time of his death, and caufed to be written the Form of a Teftament at his own pleafure, being dictated by himfelf, which upon that re fon was afterward annulled

The King of *England* could not forget this injury and difpleafure done him of the Kings breaking of his promife. He was much troubled at his death, his Wars were rather to have moved the Eftates of *Scotland* to know that his favour and friendfhip had been better for them than his feud. He was ftill in hope to have gained him with confent and advice of the beft of his Subjects to have joined in a Bond Offenfive and Defenfive. For he had received information of the Kings worthy qualities, and rare natural endowments, and entertained a marvellous great love and liking of him. Thinking he could not have left the Kingdom in a better hand, than to his own Sifters Son, neareft in bloud unto him, and meeteft of any to build up a fair Monarchy to be firft begun in a manner in his own perfon. In refpect that for his time, which he looked would be but fhort, his Nephew would have been but his Coadjutor, and Lieutenant under him, and after him poffefs the whole under one Religion, one Law, and one Head. And thought that thereby *France* fhould never afterward have the occafion of ftirring up the one Country againft the other ; and that the Pope fhould be fecluded from gathering up fuch fums of Silver from his Subjects, for Confirmation of Benefices, or for Bulls or Difpenfations. For his wrath and vengeance againft the Pope was exceeding great, who had made him many promifes, and had broken them all, fearing as faid is, to offend the Emperour, who was fo great and mighty a Prince. Therefore the King of *England* feeing he had now altogether loft the hopes of the *Scots* alliance and concurrence, he compelled the Gentlemen of *England* to exchange their Lands, with the Lands of Abbies, Cloifters, and other Temple Lands, giving them more than their own, that fo the faid Lands fhould never return to the Kirk without a manifeft Rebellion, or a dangerous fubverfion of the whole ftate of the Kingdom. And to be revenged upon the faid Cardinal *David Beaton*, who he thought had difappointed him of all the hope he had of *Scotland*, he dealt with Sir *George Douglafs*, and the Earl of *Angus*, who were but lately returned out of *England*, where they had refided during the time of their banifhment, till the death of King *James* V.

Thefe

Thele two Brothers appearing to be of the Reformed Religion, perfuaded *Norman Lefly* Mafter of *Rothes*, the young Laird of *Grange*,and
John Lefly of *Parkhill* , who had been perfecuted by the faid Cardinal
for Religion, after he had taken their Preacher, Mr. *George Wifhard*,
and burnt him at St. *Andrews*. Thefe I fay were eafily ftirred up
to flay him whom they were perfuaded to be an Enemy to the true
Religion, to the welfare of the Country, and to themfelves in particular.

This proud Cardinal was flain then in his Caftle at S. *Andrews*, and
fo ended all his practices, having obtained nothing but vain travel
for his pretences, and fudden death. Having been the occafion of the
death of a worthy King, who was inclined to Juftice, and gave no credit to his Officers in their two fpecial points, to reward and punifh.
For whoever did him good fervice, he would fee them rewarded, yea
albeit they chanced to be abfent ; and as to punifhing of Evil Doers,
fo foon as he had heard the complaint, he leapt upon his Horfe, and
did ride to the parties himfelf, with a few company, 'ere they could be
aware of him, and he would fee fharp execution. So that he was de-
fervedly both loved and feared. He was very couragious,well favoured and fhapen, of a middle ftature, very able of body. But evil
company fell about him,entering out of Child-hood into furious Youth
enticing him to Harlotry, ftriving who fhould fpie out for himthe
faireft Maidens, and likewife at length mens Wives ; with them he
abufed his body, to the offence of God and divers good Subjects. For
which he was not left unpunifhed, for he had but two young Sons and
they died both within eleven hours ; fo that at his deceafe he had
but one Daughter called *Mary*, born when he was upon his Death-
bed.

King *Henry* VIII. of *England*, having onely one Son called *Edward*,
he and the Eftates of both Countries, defiring ftill this whole Ifle of
Britain to be united in one Monarchy, made a contract ofmarriage
between the faid two, which was afterward broken upon ourpart, her
Majefty being tranfported unto *France* by the Weft Seas. Whereupon
enfued great War between the two Kingdoms, which was afterwards
agreed upon this condition,that *Edward* fhould marry *Elizabeth* eldeft
Daughter to *Henry* II. of *France*, and *Francis* his Son fhould marry our
Queen. My Lord *Hamilton* was advanced to the Government of
the Country by the Laird of *Grange* Treafurer,Mr. *Henry Balnears*,and
others that were of the Reformed Religion, when as he appeared to be
a true Gofpeller. But he had been afterward foon altered by the Abbot
of *Pafly* his Baftard-brother, and became a great Perfecuter of Gods
Word, and had been by the perfuafions of the faid Abbot and Cardinal
eafily drawn tobreak thefaid Contract ofMarriage made between King
Edward and our Queen.

After that the young Queen came to *France*, there was great difpu-
ring whether the Marriage with the Dauphine fhould take effect or
not. For at that time there were two Factions in the *French* Court,
firft the Brethren to the Houfe of *Guife*, as the Duke of *Guife* and the
Cardinal of *Lorrain*, brothers to our Queen Dowager,and uncles to our
young Queen *Mary*, preffed earneftly to fetforward the faid Marriage
with *France* ; the old Conftable Duke of *Montmorancy*, was of opinion
that

that it was meeteſt to give her in marriage to ſome Duke or Prince in *France*, and to ſend them both home to *Scotland* to keep that Country in good obedience. Becauſe when Princes are abſent, and far from their own, ruling their Countries by Lieutenants, moſt commonly the Sub-jeͨ of ſuch Countries uſe to rebel : which if *Scotland* ſhould do, it would be hard and coſtly to get them reduced. And thereby in ſtead of making *France* the better of the Marriage with the Dauphin, it might make it to be in a far worſe caſe. The Houſe of *Guiſe* again deſiring to have their Siſters Daughter Queen of *France* to augment their re-putation and credit, alledged it would be both honourable and profi-table to the Crown of *France* to have this addition, · And that there were Revenues in abundance to maintain Gárriſons within the King-dom, to hold the Subjeͨs under obedience, building Citadels, and ha-ving the whole ſtrength in their hands. Herein they prevailed, ſhe being married unto the Dauphine.

John de Monluck Biſhop of *Valence*, was ſent Ambaſſador from *France* to the Governour and Queen mother Siſter to the Duke of *Guiſe*. And when the ſaid Ambaſſadour was to return to *France*, it pleaſed the Queen-mother to ſend me with him, to be placed Page of Honor to the Queen her Daughter, I being then 14 years of Age. But the ſaid Biſhop went firſt to *Ireland*, commanded thereto by the K. his Ma-ſters Letter, to know more particularly the motions and likelihood of the Offers made by *Oneel, Odoneel, Odocart,* and *Callock*, willing to ſhake off the Yoke of *England*, and become ſubjeͨ to the King of *France* ; providing that he would procure the Popes gift of *Ireland*, and then ſend to their help 2000 Hacbutiers, 200 Light Horſemen, and 4 Cannon.

We ſhipped for *Ireland* in the Month of *January*, and were ſtorm-ſted by the way in a little Iſle called *Sandiſle* before *Kintire*, where we were compelled to tarry 17. days, by reaſon of the Storm. Thence we hoiſed Sail toward *Ireland*, but the Storm was yet ſo extreamly violent, that with great danger of the Ship and our lives, we entered in at the mouth of *Loghfeul* in *Ireland* upon Shrove-tueſday in the year 1545. for the Skipper and Marriners had loſt all hopes of ſafety, having left their Anchors behind them the night before. 'Ere we landed we ſent one *George Paris* who had been ſent to *Scotland* by the great *Oneel* and his Aſſociates, who landed at the houſe of a Gentleman who had mar-ried *Odocarts* Daughter, dwelling at the ſide of a Lake, who came to our Ship, and welcomed us, and convoyed us to his houſe, where we reſted that night.

The next morning *Odocart* came there, and convoyed us to his houſe, which was a great dark Tower, where we had cold chear, as Herring and Bisket, for it was Lent. There finding two *Engliſh* Gray Friars who had fled out of *England* (for King *Edward* VI. was yet alive) the ſaid Friars perceiving the Biſhop to look very kindly to *Odocarts* Daughter, who fled from him continually, they brought to him a Woman who ſpoke *Engliſh* to lie with him. Which Harlot be-ing kept quietly in his Chamber, found a little Glaſs within a Caſe ſtanding in a window, for the Coffers were all wet with the Sea Waves that fell into the Ship during the Storm. She believing it had been ordained to be eaten, becauſe it had an odoriferous ſmell, therefore ſhe

lickt

licked it clean out, which put the Bifhop into fuch a rage, that he cried out for impatience, difcovering this harlotry, and his choler in fuch fort as the Friars fled, and the Woman followed. But the *Irifh* men and his own Servants did laugh at the matter, for it was a Viol of the moft pretious Balm that grew in *Egypt*, which *Solyman* the Great Turk had given in a Prefent to the faid Bifhop, after he had been two years Ambaffador for the King of *France* in *Turkey*, and was efteemed worth 2000 Crowns.

In the time that we remained at *Odocarts* houfe, his young daughter who fled from the Bifhop, came and fought me, where-ever I was, and brought a Prieft with her who could fpeak Englifh, and offered, if I would marry her, to go with me where-ever I pleafed. I gave her thanks, but told her that I was but young, and had no Eftate, and was bound for *France*.

Now the Ambaffadour met in a fecret part with *Oneel* and his Affociates, and heard their Offers and Overtures. And the Patriarch of *Ireland* did meet him there, who was a Scotchman born called *Wachop*, and was blind of both his eyes, and yet had been divers times at *Rome* by Poft. He did great honour to the Ambaffadour, and conveyed him to fee S. *Patricks* Purgatory, which is like an old Coal-pit which had taken fire by reafon of the fmoke that came out of the hole.

From *Odocarts* houfe we went to a dwelling place of the Bifhop of *Roy*, not far from the narrow Firth that runs thorough *Loghfeul* to the Sea, The faid Irifh Bifhop had been alfo at *Rome*. and there we refted other three weeks, waiting for a Highland Bark, which *James Machonel* fhould have fent from *Kintire* with his Brother *Angus*, to carry us back to *Dunbarton*. Which being come for us, we parted to a Caftle which the faid *Machonel* had in *Ireland*; and from that we imbarked and refted a night in the Ifle of *Jura*, and the next night in the Ifle of *Bute*. But by the way we loft our Rudder, and were in great danger when we came to *Kiltire*. *James Maconel* did treat us honourably, and told the Bifhop that he was the welcomer for my fake, becaufe he had been kindly ufed by my Father when he was warded in the Caftle of *Dumbar*, during the time that my Father was Captain thereof, of whom he made an honourable report to the Bifhop. Which occafioned him the more kindly to notice me. After he had caufed us to be landed at *Dumbarton*, we went ftreight to *Sterling*; where after eight days, the Ambaffadour took leave of the Queen, and went again to *Dumbarton*. where there were two French Ships (that had brought Siver to *Scotland* to pay the French Souldiers in Service, there ready to recive us. So failing by the *Ifle of Man* along the South Coaft of *Ireland*, we landed at *Conquet* in *Brittany* eight days after our Embarking, not without fome danger by the way both from Englifh Ships, and a great Storm; fo that once at Midnight the Mariners cried that we were all loft. At *Breft* in *Brittany* the Bifhop took Poft toward the Court of *France*, which was in *Paris* for the time. And becaufe I was young, and he fuppofed I was not able to endure the toil of riding Poft, he directed two Scottifh Gentlemen, whofe Fathers he had been acquainted with in *Scotland*, to be careful of me by the way. And we bought three little Nags to ride to *Paris*. He defired the two Brothers to let me want for nothing by the way,

which

which he would recompenſe at the next meeting. He left with me as much money as would buy a Horſe and bear my expenſe upon the Road to *Paris.*

Now we three enquired after other company, and found other three young men, the one a French man, the other a Brittain, and the third a *Spaniard*, who were to ride the ſame way. We were all ſix lodged in one Chamber at the firſt Inn we did quarter at, in which were three Beds, the two French men had one Bed, the two Scots another, the Spaniard and my ſelf the third· I over-heard the two Scotſh men diſcourſing together, that they were directed by the Biſhop to let me want for nothing, therefore ſays the one to the other, we will pay for his Ordinary all the way, and ſhall accompt twice as much to his Maſter as we disburſe, when we come to *Paris*, and ſo ſhall gain our own expence. The two French men not thinking that any of us un-derſtood that Language, were ſaying to themſelves, Theſe Strangers are all young, and know not the Faſhion of the Hoſtlaries, therefore we ſhall reckon with the Hoſt at every Repoſe, and ſhall cauſe the Strangers to pay more than the cuſtom is, and that way ſhall ſave our own charges. And accordingly the next day they went to put it in execution; but I could not forbear laughing in my mind, having un-derſtood ſo much French as to know what they were aiming at, wherewith I acquainted the young Spaniard; and ſo we were upon our guard: yet the two Scotch men would not conſent that I ſhould pay for my ſelf hoping that way to beguile the Biſhop : but the Spa-niard and I wrote up every days accompt. By the way riding tho-rough a Wood, the two French men lighted off their Horſes, and drew out their Swords, having appointed other two to meet them. But beholding our countenance, and ſeeing that we were making for our defence, they made a Sport of it, alledging that they had done it to try if we would be afraid, in caſe we ſhould be aſſaulted by the way. But theſe two Rogues that met us, left us at the next Lodging; and when we came to *Paris*, the two Scotch men never obtained payment of the Biſhop, for that they had disburſed, becauſe of their intended fraud. We were 13 days in riding betwixt *Breſt* and *Paris*, where we arrived in the Moneth of *April.*

Within a Moneth after our arrival at *Paris*, the Biſhop of *Valence* was ſent to *Rome* ; and becauſe he took Poſt, he left me behind him, having tabled me in a very good Ordinary, and agreed with Maſters to teach me the French Tongue, and to Dance, Fence and play upon the Lute. I know not why he did not preſent me to the Queen, as he had engaged ; albeit afterward he ſaid that he was minded to make me his Heir. ·

The cauſe why he was at this time ſent to *Rome*, was this: Pope *Paul* the Third had exchanged ſome Lands belonging to the Church, for *Parma* and *Placentia*, two Towns appertaining formerly to the Dutchy of *Milan*, and gave them to his Son *Piere Luis Farnes*, who married his eldeſt Son *Octavio* to the Baſtard Daughter of the Empe-rour *Charles* the Fifth. The ſaid *Piere* ιLuis being murthered for his deteſtable Vices, the next Pope *Julius* pretended to bring again the ſaid two Towns to the Church, in ſtead of the Church Lands that had been exchanged for them ; compelling the Duke *Octavio* (finding himſelf

felf unable to withſtand the Popes forces) to put the ſaid Towns into
the King of *France* his cuſtody: for he was in as great fear of the Emperour his Father-in-Law, who had gotten poſſeſſion of the Dukedom
of *Millan.* And for that effect he ſent his Brother the Duke of *Caſters*
to *France*, to whom King *Henry* of *France* gave his Baſtard Daughter
in marriage. The King of *France* being as earneſt to have an Eſtate
in *Italy*, as the Emperour was to hinder him from it, by reaſon of *Millan* and *Naples*, to which the King claimed a right, though the Emperour
had them in poſſeſſion. Therefore ſo ſoon as he did ſee the French Garriſon within the Town of *Parma*, he took part with the Pope. Which
made the K. of *France* endeavour to make a Peace with K. *Edward* VI. of
England, by the means of the Duke of *Northumberland*, who had a
ſtrict Friendſhip with *France*, having a hidden mark of his own that
he ſhot at, as his Proceedings afterward declared. The Peace with
England being concluded, that King *Edward* ſhould marry *Elizabeth*
Eldeſt Daughter to *Henry* the Second of *France* ; and that he ſhould
give his conſent that the Queen of *Scotland*, who was betrothed to him
ſhould be married with *Francis* Dauphin of *France*, in which Peace
Scotland was alſo comprehended. The Biſhop of *Valence* was ſent to
Rome to endeavour to oblige the Pope to deſert the Emperour, but he
returned without obtaining ſucceſs in his Expedition : which was the
cauſe that the dealing betwixt the King of *France* and *Oneel* in *Ireland*
ceaſed. And in the mean time the King of *France* emits a Proclamation forbidding his Subjects to ſend to *Rome* for any Bulls, or Confirmation of Benefices; which together with the agreement with *England*,
put the Pope in great fear that *France* would become Proteſtants in deſpight, as *Henry* the Eighth had lately done before. He was the more
confirmed in this opinion, becauſe an Army was ſhortly after made
ready to paſs into *Germany*, to the aid of the Proteſtant Princes; where
King *Henry* himſelf did in perſon lead thouſand men. For then
many of the *Germans* were become Proteſtants, occaſioned at firſt by
the inſolent avarice of the Pope, and the ſhameleſs proceedings of his
ſelling of Pardons, and by the zeal and boldneſs of *Martin Luther*, who
being perſecuted, was maintained and aſſiſted by the good Duke *Frederick* the of *Saxony*, Landgrave of *Heſſe*, and other Princes of the Empire. Whereupon the Emperour *Charles* the Fifth took occaſion under
pretext of maintaining the Catholick Roman Religion, to pretend to
bring the Empire and all the Dominions thereof, as Patrimony to him
and his poſterity. And therefore abandoned his Son-in-Law the Duke
Octavio to the Popes diſcretion, for to obtain the greater aſſiſtance from
him againſt the *Germans*. Which deſign the Emperor had once brought
near to paſs. For after that he had vanquiſhed the Proteſtants in Battle,
and taken Priſoner Duke *John Frederick*, he paſſed thorough the moſt
part of the Provinces and Free Towns of Dutchland, and took from
them their Liberties, placing Officers at his pleaſure, and receiving from
them of Gifts and Ranſoms, Sixteen hundred thouſand Crowns, and
Five hundred Piece of Artillery. Yet the doubted the Landgrave, who
was a valiant Prince, and chanced to be abſent from the ſaid Battle ;
therefore he dealt with *Duke Maurice*, Godſon to the ſaid Landgrave,
to perſwade his Godfather to come in, under aſſurance and promiſe,
which the Emperour broke, retaining the ſaid Landgrave captive upon
the ſubtlety of a Syllable.   C 2   This

This Duke *Maurice* was Coufin to the Captive Duke of *Saxony*, and had obtained the Electorat of *Saxony*, which the Emperour took from his Coufin and gave to him. Whereupon he, as a fine Courtier affifted the Emperour, helping him greatly in his Victories againft his Country and Friends for his own promotion. But when the Landgrave called him Shelm, Pultroon, Traitor, and deceiver of him whofe Daughter he had married, he made earneft fuit to the Emperour, for the Liberty of his Godfather, though in vain. The Emperour alledging no promife to have been broken to the faid Landgrave, caufing the Letter of Promife and Pacification to be read in his prefence in the Dutch Tongue, wherein was a written word which admitted of two divers interpretations: to wit, this word *Enig* was interpreted by the Emperour *Perpetual*, and by the Landgrave and Duke *Maurice* it was taken for *Null* or *Nane*. But they could not help themfelves, for the Landgrave was two years fo ftraitly kept by the Spaniards, that oft in the night they held a light Candle to his face, to be affured that he was fleeping; and vexed him fo, that through defpight he would fpit in their faces, crying out continually againft *Maurice* who was not fleeping: But had fent fecretly to the King of *France*, declaring how not onely his Godfather and he were fo abufed and deceived by the Emperour; but that he had begun already to rob the Empire of its Liberties, to change the State thereof to a Monarchy, againft the Oath and Promife made at the Election and his Coronation. And that under pretext to fupprefs Herefie, he was fo affifted by the Pope, that he was like to prevail. Intreating the King not to fuffer them who were his Friends to be fo oppreffed, feeing it was no ways his Intereft that his Competitor fhould grow fo great, feeing thereby he fhould be the more in a capacity to annoy him at his pleafure. Whereupon the faid King took occafion to levy an Army, and to convoy the fame into *Almaign*, and appearing to feek their Liberty, he poffeffed himfelf in his way of *Metz*, *Towl*, and *Verdun*, three great Imperial Towns and Bifhopricks.

In the mean time Duke *Maurice* lying at the Siege of *Magdeburg* Lieutenant for the Emperour, giving not the leaft ground of fufpecting him difcontent for the Landgraves retention, but rather endeavouring to make appear how far he was obliged to the Emperour, who had fo highly advanced him, like a fine Courtier, evidencing publickly his refolutions of fetting forward his Mafters intereft, and executing all his Commands, whether they fhould be right or wrong.

Yet the Duke of *Alva* alledged in fecret Counfel with the Emperour, that *Maurice* lingred too long at the Siege of the faid Town And that it was to be fufpected, that he was offended at the ufage his Godfather did meet with. But *Granvil* Bifhop of *Arras*, on the contrary, faid, that fuch drunken Dutch heads needed not be fufpected. Efpecially feeing two of the faid Dukes Counfellours were Penfioners to his Sacred Majefty; and advertifed him continually of all the Dukes moft fecret deliberations. Yet they thought expedient to fend for the Duke, to fee if he would prefently obey, or pretend fome excufe.

But Duke *Maurice* had as much fubtilty as any Spaniard of the Emperors Council, having had intelligence that the Emperor had bribed

two

two of his Secretaries, yet he gave not the leaft ground to conjecture that he knew any thing thereof, appearing to do nothing without them, deliberating all his Enterprifes in their prefence, whereby the Emperour was deluded fo as to expect no harm from him. And when the Duke was fent for, he took Poft immediately for the Court, taking in his Company one of the Secretaries whom he knew to be the Emperors Penfioner, whom he fent before to fhew the Emperor that he was following at leifure, by reafon of a pain he had taken in his fide occafioned with riding Poft.

But the Duke had fecretly commanded his Lieutenant to bring up the whole Army with all diligence, and to march night and day. So that he furprifed the Emperour ere he had received the leaft notice thereof: for he was compelled to rife from Supper, and fly forth of *Isbrugh* with Torch-light; and fo clearly out of Dutchland, that he never fet foot within it again.

This done he fent to the King of *France*, who was with his Army befide *Strasburgh*, giving him great thanks for his pains, advertifing him of the Emperors flight, intreating him to return home with his Army: for *Maurice* was disfatisfied that he had taken three of the Imperial Towns, and in the mean time he hafted through the whole Country, reftoring the Free Towns to their former Liberty and Priviledges.

The Emperor again fearing to be compelled, fet at liberty the Duke of *Saxony*, and the Landgrave of *Hefs*. Finding himfelf fruftrate of his expectation, and underftarding that Duke *Maurice* had a great grudge againft the King for taking fraudulently the three aforefaid Towns from the Empire, he dealt with *Maurice* fecretly, allowing all that he had done. And fo both being reconciled, they together laid Siege to the Town of *Metz*, though in vain. Whereby may be obferved how dangerous it is in Civil Diffentions, to bring in great companies of Strangers to fupport any of the Parties. It may appear impertinent for me, to write thus much of the Affairs of *Dutchland*, being my felf but young for the time, and not prefent in the French Army. But afterward when I was in *Germany*, I had this accompt from the good Elector Palatine, fo that none could attain to more certain Information thereof.

The Bifhop of *Valence* was at this time at *Paris*. He was defirous to have fome knowledge in the Mathematicks; and for that effect he found out a great Scholar in divers high Sciences, called *Cavatius*. This *Cavatius* took occafion frequently in conference, to tell him of two familiar Spirits that were in *Paris* waiting upon an old Shepherd, who in his youth had ferved a Prieft, and who at his death left them to him. The Bifhop upon the Kings return from *Germany*, introduced the faid *Cavatius* to the King. Who to verifie what he had faid, offered lofe his head, in cafe he fhould not fhew the two Spirits to his Majefty, or to any he fhould fend, in the form of Men, Dogs, or Cats. But the King would not fee them, and caufed the Shepherd to be burnt, and imprifoned the faid *Cavatius*.

The Bifhop had another learned man to his Mafter, called *Taggot*, who had been curious in fundry of the faid Sciences, and knew by the Art of Palmeftry, as he faid to me himfelf, that he fhould die before he
attained

attained to the age of 28. years. Therefore, said he, I know the true Religion to be exercised at *Geneva*, there will I go and end my life in Gods service. Whither accordingly he went, and died there, as I was afterwards informed.

At this time the Bishop of *Valence*, being at Court in *St. Germans*, he was resolved to have presented me to the Queen. But in the interim, Captain *Ninean Cockbourn* then one of the Scots Guard, had obtained liberty to visit his Friends in *Scotland*, and was lately returned. This man was a Busie Medler, and had been sometimes entertained about my Fathers house. He finding that I could speak French, told me that he had a matter of consequence to impart to the Constable; and intreated that I would go along with him to be his Interpreter, because he had not the French Tongue. But he would not acquaint me with the matter, till he was in the Constables presence.

We attended till one day after dinner, when he was to give audience to divers Ambassadors. He commanded us to wait at his Chamber door till two Afternoon, which hour he failed not to keep, after he had heard the Ambassadors, and made report to the King of their demands, and advised him what to answer. We two were brought in to his Cabinet, where he was alone with a Secretary. Then the Captain began to declare, how that in his late being in *Scotland*, Bishop *John Hamilton*, whole Guider of the Governour his Brother, had been dangerously sick, so that his Speech was lost without all hope of recovery. That the Queen Dowager of *Scotland* had taken occasion hereof, to prevail with the Governour so effectually, that he had resigned the Government to her, she being made Queen Regent, and willing me to shew the same to the Constable. But I required to know what further he had to say; Then he proceeded to shew that when the Bishop of S. *Andrews* had recovered his Speech and health, by the help of *Cardanus* an Italian Magician, he cursed, and cried out, that the Governour was a very Beast, for quitting the Government to her, seeing there was but a Skittering Lass between him and the Crown. But I blushed, when the Captain pulled upon me to tell these very words to the Constable. He perceived how loath I was to rehearse it, at last he pressed me. I told him I did not think it worthy to be communicated to his Lordship. He asked my name, and caused his Secretary to write it up, and enquire if I was of Kin to the Captain. Who said in bad French, that I was his Sisters Son. The Constable enquired of me, if that was truth. I told him I had no relation to him at all. Then he desired to know with whom I was in that Country. I answered his Lordship, that the Bishop of *Valence* had Commission from the Queen Regent of *Scotland*, to place me her Daughters Page. He desired to know if I would remain with him, in case he procured the Bishops consent. I answered, that I should think my self much honoured, by being in the company of a Person so famous in *Europe* as he was: but that I believed he durst not dispose of me, in respect of the Promise he had given to the Queen Regent. He answered, that he could present me when he pleased to the Queen; but if I would be satisfied to stay with him, he would not fail to advance me. I exprest my self much obliged to his Lordship, that he had so far taken notice of me, and willing if he procured the Bishops consent.

The

The Conftable failed not at his firft rencounter with the Bifhop, to enquire concerning me, and expreffed his defire to have me in his Service. To which the Bifhop acquiefced, and acquainted me therewith that fame night, that the Conftable was the beft Mafter in *France*, and would not fail to promote me. Whereupon I entered into his Service, in the Year 1553.

I grant thefe Trifles are not worthy to be here inferted, were it not to teftifie Gods gracious goodnefs to the pofterity of the Faithful. As *David* obferves in his Pfalms, *I have been young, and now am old, yet did. I never fee the Juft abandoned.* For it was God that moved the Queen Regents heart to take two of my Brothers into her Service, and to fend me into *France* to be placed with her Daughter our Queen. Who alfo moved the Bifhop to be fo kind to me, that if I had been his own Son, he could not have had more affection for me : and the fame God moved the Conftables heart to defire me.

In the Year 1553. in the Moneth of *May*, the Conftable of *France* raifed a great Army. And being the Kings Lieutenant, led them firft to *Amience* in *Picardy*. For when the King of *France* was in *Dutchland* with his Army, as he gave out, to help the Princes of the Empire, *Mary* Queen of *Hungary* then a Widow, Sifter to the Emperour, and Regent of *Flanders*, entered with an Army into *Picardy*, and burnt the Kings Palace of *Fontanbrey*, with divers other little Towns and Villages. Thinking thereby to divert the King, that he fhould have come back to defend his own bounds. Thus they entered into hot Wars, and the King in his return befieged feveral Towns and took them.

Therefore the Emperour in the Spring time of that fame Year, entered in perfon with a great Army into *Picardy*, and won *Turuam*, and *Sedan*, and burnt divers Burghs and Villages: which caufed the Conftable to go with his Army to refift him. The two Armies being incamped feven leagues afunder, the Conftable was advertifed by a Spie, that all the Emperours Horfemen were to come in the night to affault the French Camp. Therefore he to fhun that furprife, marched all night forward toward the Enemy, with all his Forces Horfe and Foot, whereby he furprifed thofe who thought to have found him in bed, and gave them the overthrow. Many were killed, and fome taken ; among the reft the Duke of *Arefcot*, Leader of thofe defigned for that Enterprife, was taken Prifoner.

After this Victory, King *Henry* the Second came to the Camp himfelf. The Emperour retiring toward the Town of *Valencien*, the Kings Camp following always upon his Wing, making divers days journeys before he came to the faid *Valencien*. where the Emperour had fet down his Camp without the Town upon an Hill, making Trenches round about the fame. Where the King prefented him battle, waiting in vain a whole day, to fee if he might be provoked to come forth. And for that effect fent a number of Infantry Perdews to his Trenches, to bring on the Skirmifh, where the Emperour fent out fome Companies of Horfemen, who were foon beat back within their Foot. In the mean time the Emperour caufed his whole Artillery to fire at our Camp, though not much to our prejudice. We were advertifed that the Emperour was determined not to hazard Battle, for he began to

believe

believe that Fortune favoured no more his old age. Therefore when night drew near, the King retreated to *St. Quintine*, where the Conftable fell deadly fick, being then in his great Climacterick. Then both the Armies were fent to their Winter Garrifons, the Emperour went for *Bruxels*, and the King to *Paris*, and the Conftable to his Palace at *Chantilly*, to recover his health.

During this Winter there was a great Convention between *Calis* and *Ardrefs*, where Cardinal *Pool* was appointed Mediator by the Pope, to agree the two great Princes, but without any effect. Therefore the next Spring the King went firft into the Field with his Army, in the Year 1554. as the Emperour had done the Year before. At which time I was made his Penfioner, by the Conftables means. His Majefty befieged and took firft *Marianbrugh*, a gallant Town, and of great ftrength. He took alfo *Bovineand*, and at length *Dyvan*. But the Caftle of *Dyvan* fituated upon a high Rock, was ftoutly defended by a Spanifh Captain, who at length coming forth to fpeak with the Conftable about Compofition, was retained; and the men of War came forth with their Bag and Baggage. Few or none of the Souldiers who came forth of *Dyvan*, but were hurt either with fhelves of ftaves, by the force of our Battery, or were burnt with the Fire-brands, that they did roll down the fteep hill whereupon the Wall was built. And thrice they repulfed our *French* Footmen, Eleven Banner-bearers whereof went up to the breach ; *to wit*, Firft one with the Enfign in his hand, not followed with his Company, who was killed, and fell tumbling down the Hill. Then another Souldier to win the Office, took up the Enfign, and went up likewife to the head of the Wall, who was alfo killed. Then the third, and all the eleven one after another, loft their lives, not at all affifted by their Companies. Notwithftnding that the Conftable, my Mafter, ftood by crying and threatning in vain ; for which he degraded their Captains, and brake their Companies. There was a Scotch-man, Brother to *Barnbougle*, called *Archibald Moubray*, who with his drawn Sword ran up to the head of the Wall, and returned fafe. But he got no reward, though I ufed all my endeavours for him. Thus many are readier to punifh faults, than to reward good deeds.

After this the King entered far in the Low-Countries, burning and carrying away great Booties. But fo foon as the Emperour could convene any Forces together, our Army began to retire homeward. Then the Emperour fent five thoufand Horfemen, to fee if they might perceive any occafion of advantage. Which they frequently affayed, affailing our Rear-guard at the paffing over a little Water. At which time the Conftable ftaid behind himfelf, and turning his face toward them, he withftood their charge ftoutly, with the *French* Footmen, and fome Light-horfemen, until the whole Army had paffed over the faid Water, not far from *Cambray*. So the Emperours Horfemen followed no further at that time : believing that the King was refolved to return to *France*, and difmifs his Army for that year. But the King drew along the Frontier toward a place of great ftrength, called *Kenty*, where he planted his Camp, and befieged the faid place: which I heard the Conftable promife to deliver to the King in eight days. Which promife was not performed, for the Emperour came in perfon with his Army

for

for the relief thereof. Which Army the Conſtable rode out to meet
with the whole *French* Horſemen, leaving the Foot at the Siege. For
he had great intelligence, and had heard where the Emperour was reſolved to encamp, marching along a great Hight which had a Steep
towards the part where our Camp lay. But it was eaſie to ride, up
and down at the ſide thereof. Where our Horſemen did ride, and the
Emperour ſent down ſome on Horſeback to skirmiſh. At which time
Normand Leſly Maſter of *Rothes* won great reputation ; for with
thirty Scotchmen he rode up the Hill, upon a fair Grey Gelding.
He had above his Coat of black Velvet his Coat of Armour with two
broad white Croſſes, the one before and the other behind, with Sleeves
of Mail, and a red bonnet upon his head, whereby he was known and
ſeen afar off by the Conſtable, the Duke of *Anguion*, and Prince of
Conde. Where with his 30 he charged upon 60 of their Horſe-men
with Culverines, followed but with ſeven of his number. He in our
fight ſtruck five of them from their Horſes with his Spear before it
brake. Then he drew his Sword and ran in among them, not valuing
their continual ſhooting, to the admiration of the beholders. He ſlew divers of them, and at length when he ſaw a company of Spear-men coming down againſt him, he gave his Horſe the Spurs, who carried him
to the Conſtable, and there fell down dead: for he had many ſhots,
and worthy *Normand* was alſo ſhot in divers parts, whereof he died
fifteen days after. He was firſt carried to the Kings own Tent, where
the Duke of *Anguien*, and Prince of *Conde* told his Majeſty that *Hector* of
Troy was not more valiant than the ſaid *Norman* : Whom the ſaid King
would ſee dreſſed by his own Chirurgions, and made great moan for
him. So did the Conſtable, and all the reſt of the Princes, but no man
made more lamentation than the Laird of *Grange* , who came to the
Camp the next day after, from a quiet Road whither he had been commanded.

Now the Emperour ſet down his Camp two miles from *Renty*, and
in an inſtant entrenched the whole Camp round about, ſave onely the
face of the ſteep Hill that looked towards our Camp.

All that night there were many upon the Watches of both Armies,
for every man looked for a Battle the next day following. And therefore the Emperour, like an old experienced Captain, ſeiſed upon a
Wood in the night time, that lay upon a Hill ſide between the two
Camps; which was not onely a great advantage to him, but compelled
the moſt part of our Army to ſtand in arms all night ; whereby they
were rendered the more unable againſt the next day, wanting the refreſhment of reſt, and then the place of Battle was a plain Valley that
lay under the ſaid Wood. The next morning early, after every man
had ſaid their prayers, and taken a little refreſhment, we placed our
Army in good order of Battle, under the ſaid Hill and Wood. The
King himſelf that day commanded the Battle, but he deſired the Conſtable to abide with him, to give Counſel as occaſion would fall out.
The Duke of *Guiſe* led the Vant-gard, and the Marſhal of *St. Andre*
the Rearguard. Firſt ſo many of our *French* Foot, as are called In-
fant Perdews, were led along the Hill and Wood, beginning to skirmiſh with the Spaniards, who were within the Wood ; who had ſo
great advantage, being covered with Buſhes and Trees, that they com-

D
pelled

pelled our Foot to retire fearfully. Which well favoured beginning, the
Emperour might well perceive from the Hill whereon he was encam-
ped. Therefore like a skilful Captain, he took the occafion to hazard
a good part of the Vant-guard with feven Field-pieces, who by his direction came forward. The *Spaniards* with their Fire arms through the
Wood, a thoufand Lance-Knights with bright Corflets, along the Hill
fide, with long Pikes. The Count of *Swertfenburg* with all his Reiters
at the Hill Foot, and the whole Light-horfemen of the Emperours
Army upon his right hand. At which time, our Foot, who were appointed to skirmifh with the *Spaniards*, retired more and more, as alfo our Light-horfemen in the Valley, drew afide, and gave too great
place to the Emperours Vant-guard. Which when it came where
Monfieur *D' Tavanes*, and Monfieur *D' Lorge* ftood with their Companies, feeing them make for defence, they marched more coldly. The
Duke of *Guife* in the mean time faid, that he would ride back to the
Battle, and obtain the Kings Command before he would charge upon
the Enemy. But Monfieur de *Lorge* who was an old Captain, alledged
that there was no time to take Council, fort he Enemy, faid he, will be
as foon at the King as you. Therefore it was refolved, to charge couragioufly upon the Enemy ; which being done, and a little rencounter
made, the Reiters fhot off all their Piftols, and finding themfelves not
backed, nor followed with the reft of the Emperours Army, as they alledged was promifed unto them, they gave back and fled, being pur-
fued by our Horfe, who flew feveral of the Dutch Foot, and fome of
the Spaniards, for the Wood was their relief, but the Horfe all efcaped, within the Ramparts of the Emperours Camp. Their Field-pieces
were taken, and many Spaniards made Prifoners. Therefore we called it a won Battle, and marched forward, poffeffing the ground where
the Fight was, and fet down our Camp the fame night hard befide
the Emperours. Who feemed not that he had loft any thing, but remained ftedfaftly within his Trenches. All that night the Army for
the moft part was upon the Watch, and the next day the Armies looked
peaceably one upon another. For we would not hazard to charge
them within their Foot, and they ftaid for twelve thoufand frefh men
that were coming to their aid. But in the Evening, they difcharged
all their Canons, which overthrew part of our Tents ; and we again
difcharged all our Cannon at them, and did laugh to fee the bullets
light and rebound among them. Yet the fame night, without Trum-
pet or beating of Drum, we raifed our whole Army, and retired home
to our own Town of *Montreal*, and left *Renty* unwon, alledging that
we had won a battle, which was better ; and that we wanted Horfe-
meat in the beginning of Winter. But the Emperour fuffered us patiently to pafs away, not appearing to underftand that he knew any
thing of our retreat, being content that he had preferved *Renty* from
being taken.

After this, the Emperour being aged, and finding himfelf vexed
with the Gout and Gravel, he thought fit to leave the World,
and retire himfelf to a Monaftery of Monks in *Spain*. But firft he
made means with the Princes of the Empire, to elect his Son
Philip to be Emperour, which they altogether refufed, thinking
him too mighty, and the more in a capacity to fubdue their Liberties,

as his Father had attempted to do before. But they were content to chuse his Brother *Ferdinand*, who was King of *Bohemia*, and Archduke of *Austria*, which Dominions lay nearest the *Turks*. The said *Ferdinand* having also some Lands in *Hungary*, would be compelled to defend his own Lands, and that way would be content with less Contribution from the Estates of the Empire. He gave over to his Son *Philip* his other Kingdoms and Dominions that he had in *Spain*, *Italy*, and the *Low Countries*. And for the establishing his said Sons Estate, he drew on a Treaty of Truce for the space of five years with *France*. Which was agreed upon, and sworn between the Parties. But the said Truce was soon broken at the persuasion of Pope *Paul* the Fourth, who intending to bring back again to the Church, some Church Lands that his Predecessors had disposed to their Friends. As the common custom of Popes is, the one Pope dispones to his Bastards or Nephews, the next Pope revokes the Lands, pretending the same to be for the good of the Church, and gives them again to his Kindred and Friends. But those who had the Lands that Pope *Paul* the Fourth claimed, were a great Clan in *Italy*, called *Collonois*, who were dependers upon the King of *Spain*, and were under his Protection, and would not grant to give over any of their Possessions unto the Pope, neither for his Cursing, Threatning, or Bragging, but stood in their own defence. Whereof the Pope impatient, put on by two of his Nephews, sent the one of them to *France* called the Cardinal *Caraff.* The said Legat had born before him a Hat upon the point of a Sword, both Hat and Sword to be presented to the King of *France*. The Sword as an assured token of Victory, and the Hat as a token of triumph : requiring the King as eldest Son of the Catholick Church of *Rome*, to send an Army to *Italy*, to help the Popes Holiness recover again to the Kirk, such Lands as were wrongfully with holden from the same, by the said race of the *Collonois*. And for to take away all scrupulosity from the Kings Conscience, by reason of his Oath and Sacrament at the closing up of the Truce with the King of *Spain*, he the said Cardinal as Legat from Gods Vicar, having power, would give him full absolution, he having power to bind and loose. Alledging moreover that in doing so dutiful an Office for the Kirk, the King should reap a great advantage to himself, seeing he might thereby be put in possession of the Kingdom of *Naples* by the Forces of the Pope. Who should join with the Kings Army, after he had helped the Kirk to recover her Lands from them, who were maintained in the possession thereof, by his Competitor the King of *Spain*.

The Duke of *Guise* and the Cardinal of *Lorrain* his Brother, imbraced this Proposition very earnestly. For the Duke expected to be made Vice-Roy of *Naples*, whereby he might the more easily sometime make his Brother Pope. But the old Constable my Master, was utterly against the breaking of the Peace. Yet the two ambitious Brothers prevailed, persuading the King, that as the Constables age required rest, so the King being in the flower of his years, ought not to let slip so fair an occasion to recover again the Kingdom of *Naples*, to the Crown of *France*.

Thus a great Army was prepared and sent into *Italy*, under the Conduct of the Duke of *Guise*, and likewise the Kings Lieutenant in *Piccardy*

cardy entered in upon the King of *Spains* Dominions with Fire and
Sword, fo unexpected by thofe of the *Low Countries*, that fome of the
French Light-horfemen entered upon Horfeback, within one of their
Kirks upon a Sunday, and fnatched the Chalice out of the Priefts hands
when he was mumbling his Mafs.

The King of *Spain* took this breach of the Peace heavily to heart,
and both affifted the *Collonois* againft the Popes Forces more earneftly
than he would have done ; and alfo prepared a great Army againft the
next Spring to invade the Frontiers of *Piccardy* in *France*.

In the mean time that the Duke of *Guife* with his *French* Army was
in *Italy*, the Pope took occafion haftily to compound with the *Collonois* ; who finding themfelves like to be ftraitned, before the King
of *Spains* Forces could be ready to fupport them, gave the Pope part of
his defire, he fecuring to them the reft.

But the Duke of *Guife* judged himfelf greatly difgraced by the Popes
guile, and difappointed as to the expectations he had of the preferment
to the Kingdom of *Naples*, when he underftood that the Pope was a-
greed without him, and that in ftead of concurring and helping him to
conquer the Kingdom of *Naples*, according to his engagement, he
plainly refufed ; pretending that the Winter was near at hand, and
that it was, by far more fitting , that all Chriftian Princes were agreed
among themfelves, to make War againft the Great Turk. So that all
the favour the Duke of *Guife* had, by undertaking this Journey into *Italy*, was to get a Kifs of the Popes Foot ; which occafioned great anger
in the King of *France*, both at the one and the other. Then for the
fpace of two Moneths, every man at the Court of *France* had liberty to
fpeak ill of the Pope, who at that inftant agreed with the King of *Spain*
by the mediation of that fame Cardinal *Caraff*, who had carried the
Sword and Hat a little before to the King of *France*. Which Cardinal
was afterwards ftrangled by the next Pope *Pius* IV. for practifing to
bring, the Great Turk into *Italy*, againft the Chriftians. Which he
at his death confeffed he had, for his own greatnefs. This I underftood
afterward, being at *Rome*.

Now to return to the Duke of *Guife* his Army, abandoned by the
Pope. He returned to *France* with the lofs of the moft part dead for
hunger, and weakned by ficknefs, and flain by the *Spaniards*, who
waited at their heels all the way. Before the Duke of *Guife* his coming home to *France*, the King of *Spain* was entered upon the Frontiers
of *France* with a great Army of . . . . . . thoufand men. Whom to re-
fift, the Conftable, my Mafter, was fent with fixteen thoufand. The
day before he took leave of the King at *Rhemes* in *Champaigne*, riding
to the hunting, there came a man in grave apparel following him on
Foot, crying for audience for Gods fake. Whereupon the Conftable
ftaid, willing him to fpeak. Who faid, *The Lord fays, feeing that thou
wilt not know me, I fhall likewife not know thee, thy glory fhall be laid in
the duft*. This ftrange language put the Conftable in fuch a rage, that he
ftrook the poor man into the face with the horfe rod which was in his
hand, and threatned to caufe him to be hanged. The man anfwered,
he *was willing to fuffer what punifhment he pleafed, feeing he had performed his commiffion*. The Duke of *Nevers* perceiving the Conftable
troubled, drew near, defiring to know the caufe. The Conftable told
                                                                      him

him that fuch a Knave had been preaching to him of God. Then the Duke did alfo threaten the poor man. But as they did ride forward after the King, I ftaid behind, and asked the man what had moved him to ufe fuch ftrange language towards the Conftable ; he anfwered, *That the Spirit of God gave him no reft till he had difcharged his mind of that Commiffion given him by God.*

Now the Spanifh Army above mentioned, was led by *Emanuel* Duke of *Savoy,* along the Frontiers of *France,* who at laft planted his Camp about the Town of *St. Quintin.* Whither the Conftable fent the Admiral of *Chaftillion,* his Sifters Son, to defend the fame, and lodged his Camp at *La Ferr,* five Leagues from the Town of *S. Quintin :* which was not fufficiently furnifhed with Men and Munition, wherefore he affayed the next day, in vain, to put in it more Companies, under the Conduct of *Mounfieur d' Andelot,* Brother to the faid Admiral. After the preparation of two days, he marched forward with his whole Army toward *St. Quintin,* carrying with him eighteen Cannons, with fome Boats that are commonly in Camps, to pafs the Army over Rivers and Waters. For there was a little Logh upon the South-weft fide of the Town, in the which the faid Boats were fet. And Monfieur *D' Andelot,* firft with three hundred, entered the Town that way ; but fo foon as it was perceived, the Enemy ftopped the reft from entering.

But fo foon as the Duke of *Savoy* was coming with his whole Army towards us, the Conftable alledging that he had furnifhed *St. Quintin* fufficiently, drew homewards towards *La Ferr* in good order, intending to efchew Battle if he could, the other being more powerful than he. His intention was to pafs and befiege *Calis,* but the whole Horfemen of the Enemy were hard at us, againft the time we had travelled four miles ; where the Conftable ftopped a little time. At length he faid that thefe Horfemen came to ftay us till the Foot were advanced; Therefore he thought beft to pafs forward to a narrow Poft betwixt a Wood and a Village, there to give them Battle if he could not efcape them. In the mean time the Marfhal *D' St. Andre,* a great Man for that time gave unhappy advice, that all the French Servants who were on Horfeback fhould retire from among the men at Arms, jeft they fhould be an impediment to them who were to fight. there bei g as many Servants as there were Mafters. They were glad to get them out of the Preafe, fpurring their Horfe with fpeed homewards, intending to ftay upon fome Hill to behold the Combat. The Enemy perceiving fo great a number of Horfemen, as they thought flying, in the very inftant, took occafion to charge upon our Light-horfemen. Whereupon the Conftable being in a Valley between two Hills, marching toward the ftrait part where he intended to ftay, fpurred forward up the little Hill that he might fee how to refift, and put order to the Battle : which gave an hard apprehenfion to others that he was flying. But when he turned on the top of the Hill to behold the Onfet, no man would tarry with him for any command. Though he always cried return, return, their heads were homewards, and their hearts alfo, as appeared. Then his Mafter of the Horfe bringing him a Turkey fpeedy Horfe to run away with the reft, he anfwered in anger, *That it was againft his Profeffion and Occupation to fly* ; addreffing himfelf fearlefly

lefly againſt the greateſt Troop of Enemies, ſaying, *Let all true Ser-*
vants to the King follow me : though onely threeſcore Gentlemen accompanied, him, who were all overthrown in an inſtant. The Conſtable deſired to be killed, but the Maſter of the Horſe cried continually,
It is the Conſtable, kill him not. But before he was known, he was
ſhot thorough the thigh, and then was taken priſoner. I being hurt by
a ſtroke upon the head, was again mounted by my Servant upon a
Scotch Gelding, which carried me through the Enemies, who were
all betwixt me and home. Two of them ſtruck at my head with
Swords, becauſe my Head-piece was ſtrucken off in the firſt rencounter. Theſe two were ſtanding betwixt us and home, to catch Priſoners in a narrow ſtrait. But my horſe ran through them againſt my
will, and through the Village, for the Field between it and the Wood
was full of ſmoke of the Culverins. There moſt of our Foot were ſlain.
The leaping over a Dike ſeparated me from the two, and ſo being paſt
the ſaid Village there was room enough to eſcape. So I came ſafe to
La Ferr, where I did meet with Mr. *Henry Killegrew* an Engliſh Gentleman, my old Friend, who held my horſe, till I ſate down in a Barbers
Booth to be dreſſed of the hurt in my head. In the mean time a Proclamation was made that no man ſhould remain within the Town, but
the ordinary Garriſon, becauſe the Governour thereof looked for a
Siege.

By the loſs of this Battle, the Town of *St. Quintine* and ſeveral other
Towns were loſt. Whereby the King of *France* found himſelf reduced
to ſo great ſtraits, that he was compelled to accept of a very hurtful Peace
at *Cambray* ; where I was for the time with my Maſter the Conſtable, yet a Captive.

With the ſaid Conſtable, was adjoined in Commiſſion the Cardinals
of *Lorrain* and *Chaſtillion,* the Marſhal of *St Andre,* the Biſhop of *Or-*
leance, and the Secretary *Anbapin* : For the King of *Spain,* were the
Duke of *Alva,* Prince of *Orange,* and Cardinal *Granvel* : for Queen
Mary of *England,* were Commiſſioners, *William* Biſhop of *Ely,* and Do-
ctor *Wotton.* The Commiſſioners made peace betwixt *France, Spain,*
England and *Scotland.* The Conſtable was much for the Peace, the
Cardinal of *Lorrain* deſired the continuance of the Wars. For by the
Peace, the Conſtable would get leave to come home, to guide the King
and Court again, as he had formerly done. By the continuance of the
Wars, he would remain ſtill Priſoner, leaving the Government of the
King and Court of *France* to the Cardinal and the Duke of *Guiſe,* his Brother. *Spain* that was victorious, took advantage of their ſtrife and
emulation. *France* and *England* loſt by the ſaid Peace. The King
inclined moſt to the Conſtables Counſel. *England* appeared deſirous
that *Calis* ſhould be reſtored, believing that the King of *Spain* would
not agree till they had ſatisfaction of their demands. Yet they were
fruſtrate of their expectations. At length perceiving the two great
Kings careleſs of their ſatisfaction, they appeared content with a ſcornful mean (albeit it was not) caſt in by the Cardinal of *Lorrain* : to wit,
that *Calis* ſhould be reſtored to them at the end of eight years, or elſe
five hundred thouſand Crowns. And for payment of the ſaid ſum, in
caſe the ſaid Town was not rendred unto them at the end of the time
ſpecified , that in the mean time they ſhould have three great men of
France

France, to be kept as Pledges for the reſtitution of the ſaid Town.
Now the Engliſh Commiſſioners knew that nothing of this would be
kept, nevertheleſs they appeared content finding themſelves abandoned by *Spain*. So the Peace being concluded, *Spain* obtained all
their deſires, the *Conſtable* obtained liberty, the Cardinal of *Lorrain* could not mend himſelf, no more than the Engliſh Commiſſioners.

However the ſaid Cardinal took this advantage of the ſaid Peace,
that the firſt Article of the Peace obliged all of them to leave their
partialities, and join together to ſuppreſs the great number of Hereticks, who were ſo increaſed through all their Dominions, that
it was thought hard enough to the Pope, the Emperour, the Kings
of *Spain* and *France*, together with the Queen of *Scotland*, to reduce
them again to the Catholick Faith. The ſaid Cardinal propoſed to
himſelf another advantage, wherewith to recompence his loſſes: for
he thought at the end of eight years, when *England* would look either
to get *Calice* reſtored again to them, or elſe the ſum above ſpecified, he
would cauſe his Siſters daughter, the Queen of *Scotland* to be proclaimed righteous Queen of *England*, and alledge that Queen *Elizabeth*
was but a Baſtard. And that way he thought not onely *Calice*, but
all *England* ſhould appertain to the Queen of *Scotland*. As for the
Pledges, he reſolved ſuch men ſhould be choſen that *France* would make
little account of.

After the concluding of this Peace, Ambaſſadors were ſent to *Flanders* and *England*. The Cardinal of *Lorrain* out of *France*, to take
the King of *Spains* Oath, and to ſwear for the King of *France* his ob-
ſervation thereof. The Secretary *Dardois* alſo was ſent out of *France*,
to do the like in the name of the *Dauphin* of *France* and the Queen
of *Scotland* his Spouſe, giving them this new ſtile, In the name of
Francis and *Mary* King and Queen of *Scotland*, *England*, and *Ireland*,
Dauphin and Dauphinois of *Viennois*. Whereat the Duke D' *Alva*
and Cardinal *Granvel* ſmiled, ſaying this will breed ſome buſineſs ere
it be long. The Cardinal of *Lorrain* ſhortly after cauſed to be renewed
all the Queen of *Scotlands* ſilver Veſſels, and engraved thereon the
Arms of *England*. The Marſhal *Montmorancy* my Maſters eldeſt Son,
was ſent to *England* to ſwear the Peace, and to take the Queen of
Englands Oath. So ſoon as Sir *Nicholas Throgmorton* underſtood of
this new Stile and Arms uſurped by the Queen of *Scotland*, to which
he ſaid ſhe had no right, he being Ambaſſador from the Queen of *England* to *France*, complained thereof to the King and Council of *France*,
though he got but Dutch excuſes; alledging that in *Dutchland* all the
Princes Brothers, Couſins, or Children, are ſtiled Princes or Dukes of
that ſame Houſe. The Conſtable adviſed the King to Commiſſion me
to ſwear the Peace in *Scotland*. But the Cardinal of *Lorrain* alledged
Mounſieur *Bettancourt* Maſter of the Houſhold to the Queen Regent
was meeter; becauſe the Inſtructions tended to declare unto the
Queen Regent, how that the firſt and principal Article of the Peace,
was that the Pope, the Emperour, the Kings of *Spain* and *France*, ſhould
join together to reduce again the moſt part of *Europe* to the Roman
Catolick Religion, and to purſue and puniſh with Fire and Sword
all Hereticks, who would not condeſcend to the ſame; deſiring the
Queen

Queen Regent to do the fame in *Scotland*; and to begin in time, before the Herefie fhould fpread any further ; which was already too far fpread by her gentle forbearance, as had been reported to the King of *France*. Praying her diligently to take courfe therein without fear, or refpeft of perions, feeing that no Country of it felf was able to withftand the whole Forces of fo many confederate Catholick great Princes.

It is above declared, that all thofe Prelats who had great Rule and Authority for the time, had affifted the Queen Regent in breaking the Contraft of marriage with *England*, and tranfporting the young Queen to *France*. But the Archbifhop of *S. Andrews* began to think that in cafe the young Queen died without fucceffion to her body, that the Earl of *Arran* his Nephew might the eafilier be Crowned, the Governour his Father being already in poffeffion, was againft the tranfporting the Crown matrimonial to *France*. And he having for the time, the guiding both of the Governour his Brother, and of the Country, drew eafily the moft part of the Clergy upon his fide. Whereupon the Queen Dowager was compelled to addrefs her felf to a contrary Faction, to be the more in a capacity of compaffing her defign; to wit, to the Nobility and Barons, who were become Profeffors of the Reformed Religion, conniving at their fecret Preaching, for further ingratiating her felf with them : whereby the Proteftants fo increafed, that the moft part of the Country became Profeffors of the Reformed Religion. And fuch as had upon that accompt been formerly banifhed, as upon account of the flaughter of the Cardinal, were called home to fortifie the Faction that moft furthered her defigns. In the mean time the Bifhop of *St. Andrews* fell fick, fo that he loft his Speech and was given over for dead. The Queen Dowager looks upon this as a fit opportunity of wrefting the Government out of the Lord *Hamiltons* hands, having the concurrence of the Lords that were Proteftants, and their dependents, who were not a little incenfed at the faid Governour, becaufe he had been fo influenced by his Brother, as by his Council to endeavour the ruine of their Religion. And the ways they took became effectual, he having been at laft induced to refign the Government into the Queens hands, who thereupon was declared Regent.

The Proteftants were thus at this time her beft friends, and by the diligent preaching of the Preachers, they were increafed to fo great a number, that fhe judged it would prove a dangerous and difficult matter to compel them to defert their Principles. But the inftructions which *Bettancourt* brought to her, and to Monfieur *Dofel* Lieutenant in *Scotland* for the King of *France*, and to all others who had greateft credit about her Majefty were fo ftrict, and mixed with fome threatnings, that fhe determined to follow them. She therefore iffued out a Proclamation a little before Eafter, commanding every man great and fmall to obferve the Roman Catholick Religion, to refort daily to the Mafs, that all fhould make Confeffion in the ear of a Prieft, and receive the Sacrament. By word of mouth fhe acquainted feveral of the Proteftant Lords, that they behoved to defert their Principles, fhe fhewed to them the Commiffion, that was fent her out of *France*, and the danger that would follow thereupon, if not obeyed.

When the Nobility and States of the Country perceived her to be in earneft,

earneft finding themfelves alfo threat'ned by Monfieur *Defel*, they left the Court : And confulting together what was meeteft f or them to do, they fent unto her Majefty the Earl of *Argile*, and Lord *James* Prior of *St. Andrews*, to fhew her Majefty, in name and behalf of the reft, how that they had been permitted by her Majefty, to keep their own Minifters of a long time, fometimes fecretly, and fometimes openly. That by her tolerance, their Religion had taken fuch root, and the number of the Proteftants fo increafed, that it was a vain hope to believe, they could be put from their Religion, feeing they were refolved, as foon to part with their lives, as to recant.

The Queen Regent did as much difrelifh this kind of Language, as they had done her Proclamation, fo that fhe began to perfecute, and they to ftand to their own defence, binding themfelves together, under the name of the Congregation. Therefore they brake down Images, Kirks, and Cloifters.

The Queen Regent fent to *France*, advertifing her Daughter, and her Husband of thefe diforders, requiring help and Forces to fupprefs this in time, or elfe all would be loft : Declaring that fhe had ground of fear, that my Lord *James* Prior of St. *Andrews*, natural Son to *James* the Fifth, would under pretext of this new Religion, ufurp the Crown of *Scotland*, and pluck it clean away from the Queen her Daughter, unlefs fudden remedy were applied thereto. Upon this advertifement, fome of the Council of *France* advifed, prefently to raife a great Army for reducing of *Scotland*; but the Conftable counfelled the King, whofe Penfioner I was for the time; to fend me unto *Scotland*. The King firft gave me his Commiffion by word of mouth, and then the Conftable his chief Councellor, directed me at length in his Majefty's prefence, as followeth.

Your Native Queen, faith he, is married here in *France* unto the *Dauphine*, and the King is informed by the Cardinal of *Lorrain*, that a Baftard Son to *James* fifth, called *Prior de St. Andre*, pretends under colour of Religion, to ufurp the Kingdom unto himfelf; his Majefty knows that I was ever againft the faid marriage, fearing thereby to make our old Friends our new Enemies, as is like to come to pafs this day. But I gave too great place to the Houfe of *Guife*, to deal in the affairs of *Scotland*, becaufe the Queen Regent is their Sifter. But now feeing their violent proceedings, are like to occafion the lofs of the Kingdom of *Scotland*, I muft needs meddle, and put to my helping hand, as having better experience of the nature of that Nation, then apparently they have. I affure you that the King is refolved to hazard his Crown, and all that he hath rather then that your Queen be robbed of her right, feeing fhe is now married unto his Son. And he refolves to fend an Army to *Scotland* for that effect, though he would gladly fhun the trouble thereof, if it were poffible. For now after his Majefty hath had Wars long enough with his old Enemies, and hath agreed with them upon very rational confiderations, he is loath to enter again into a new unneceffary War, with his old Friends. Seeing there is probable ground of conjecture, that it is not their default, but that the fame is occafioned by the harfh ufage they meet with. I hear that Monfieur *Defel* is cholerick, hafty, and too paffionate. Such are not qualified to rule over remote, and form'd Coun-

know not the reason why they followed it not, though I conjecture,
that the variance which fell out between the Two Kingdoms hindered it. The *Englifh* man and I, by the way, entered into great familiarity, fo that he fhewed me funsdry fecrets of the Country, and of
the Court. Among other thing he told me, that King *Henry* the
Eighth, had in his life-time been fo curious, as to enquire at Men called *Diviners*, or Negromancers, what fhould become of his Son King
Edward the Sixth, and of his two Daughters, *Mary* and *Elizabeth*.
That anfwer was made unto him again, that *Edward* fhould dye, having few days, and no Succeffion; and that his Two Daughters fhould
the one fucceed the other. That *Mary* his eldeft Daughter fhould
marry a *Spaniard*, and that way bring in many ftrangers to *England*,
which would occafion great ftrife, and alteration. That *Elizabeth*
fhould Reign after her, who fhould marry either a *Scottifh* man, or a
French man. Whereupon the King caufed to give poifon to both his
Daughters, but becaufe this had not the effect, he defired (for they
finding themfelves altered by vehement vomitings, and purgings, having fufpected poifon, had taken remedies) he caufed to proclaim them
both baftards. But the Women that attended about Queen *Mary*, alledged that her matrix was confumed. For fhe was feveral times fuppofed to be with Child to King *Philip* of *Spain*, yet brought forth
nothing but dead lumps of flefh. Therefore to be revenged upon
her Father, the *Englifh* man told me, that fhe had caufed, fecretly in
the night to take up her Father's bones, and burn them. This the honeft Gentleman affirmed to be truth, though not known to many.
He was a Man of great gravity, about fifty years of age. When he
came to *London*, he fhewed me great kindnefs, and made me a prefent
of fome Books.

Upon my return to *France* I found a great change, King *Henry* the
Second being hurt in the head with a fhiver of a Spear, by the Count
of *Montgomery*, at the Triumphal Juftings of his Daughter's marriage
with the King of *Spain*, dyed Eight days after at *Paris*. And the
Conftable my Mafter was commanded to retire him from Court, to
his Houfe, by the new King, *Francis* the Second, Husband to our Soveraign: who was wholly guided by the Duke of *Guife*, and the Cardinal *Lorrain*, competitors to the faid Conftable in Court emulation.
Which occafioned, that my Voyage, and the anfwer I had got, was all
in vain: for the Houfe of *Guife*, were the chief inftruments of all the
troubles in *Scotland*.

When I did fhew the Conftable at his Houfe the anfwer, of my Commiffion, which was according to his hearts defire, the Tears came over
his cheeks, crying alack for the lofs of the King my good Mafter, that
he fhould not have feen before his death, *Scotland* recovered again,
which he efteemed loft: feeing you are thereby alfo fruftrate of a good
reward, which this your fervice merited. Now I have not fuch intereft as I formerly had to advance you, but if you will take fuch part
as I have, you fhall be very welcome. I anfwered, that as I had
been with him in his profperity, I would not defert him in his adver-
fity.

Now there was no more appearance of concord betwixt the Queen
Regent, and the Congregation in *Scotland*. For the King of *France*
was

was raifing Men to fend thither: The Congregation again fought help from *England*, which they obtained, the rather becaufe the *Englifh* Ambaffadour refident in *France*, had advertifed his Miftrefs, how that the Queen of *Scotland*, and her Husband had taken the Style of *Egnland* and *Ireland*, and alfo had ingraven the Arms thereof upon their Silver Plate.

The Queen Regent, and Mounfieur *Dofel* with his *French* men, inclofe themfelves within *Leeth*, which they did fortifie to receive the *French* fupply, which was daily expected. At length thofe who were befieged made a falley, caufed the Congregation to fly, and took their Artillery, till an Army from *England*, came under the conduct of the Duke of *Norfolk*. At which the Queen Regent being indifpofed by the Sea Air at *Leeth*, retired her felf to the Caftle of *Edinburgh*; where fhe took ficknefs and dyed, during the time that *Leeth*, was befieged, both by *Scotland* and *England*, regreting that fhe had occafioned to her felf, and the Kingdom, fo much unneceffary trouble, by following the advice of her *French* friends.

During the Siege of *Leeth*, all *Scotch* men who were in *France*, were detefted; and divers of them upon fufpicion made Prifoners. Which obliged me to repair from the Conftable's Houfe, to the Court, to require Licenfe from the Queen my Soveraign, to vifit other Countries, whereby I might be rendered more able afterward to do her Majefty agreeable fervice. Which fhe granted, and prefenting me to the King her Husband, I had a kifs of his hand, and fo took my leave.

The Conftable my good Mafter, recommended me to the *Elector Palatine*, advifing me to remain at his Court, to learn the *Dutch* Tongue. I was courteoufly received by the faid Prince Elector, and obtained fuch favour at his hands, that he obliged me to attend at his Court, as one of his Servants. So foon as he heard of the death of King *Francis* the Second, King of *France*, who dyed at *Orleance*. I was fent to condole for the faid King's death, as the cuftom of Princes is, and rejoice with the new young King *Charles* the Ninth, alfo to comfort our Queen, and the Queen Mother. The King's death made a great change, the Queen Mother was glad at the death of King *Francis* her Son, becaufe fhe had no guiding of him, he being wholly councelled by the Duke of *Guife*, and the Cardinal his Brother, the Queen our Miftrefs, being their Sifter Daughter. So that the Queen Mother was much fatisfied to be freed of the Government of the Houfe of *Guife*, and for this caufe fhe entertained a great grudge at our Queen. In the mean time the King of *Navarr*, and Prince of *Conde*, who were imprifoned, and fhould have been executed three days after, the Scaffold being already prepared, were by the Queen Mother fet at liberty. The Conftable alfo having been charged to come to Court, expected no better meafure;he therefore gave it out that he was fick, being carried in a Horfe-Litter, and making little Journeys, he drew out the time fo long by the way, that in the mean time the King dyed. Whereof being informed he leapt on a Horfe, and came frankly to Court, and like a Conftable commanded the Men of War, who were upon the Guards. The Duke of *Guife* and his Brother, were commanded out of the Town. The Queen Mother

was

her Mother, who was King *Chriſtiernus* Daughter of *Denmark*, begotten
upon the Emperour *Charles* his Siſter, who alſo loſt the Kingdom of
Denmark, pretending to make it Hereditable, whereas it was Elective.
The ſaid King *Chriſtiernus* was kept in Priſon, till his death. This
Dutcheſs his Daughter, alledged that the Kingdom of *Norway* appertained unto her, as Heir unto her Father, and that the ſaid Kingdom
was Hereditary unto her Father, albeit *Denmark* was not, and intended then to marry her eldeſt Daughter unto *Frederick* King of *Denmark*, and to give over with her ſaid Daughter the Kingdom of *Norway*. But the ſaid Dutcheſs offered unto Duke *Caſimir* her ſecond
Daughter, which he refuſed, and dealt with his Father to ſend me
unto *England*, to propoſe Marriage for him unto the Queen of *England*. But I refuſed to undertake that Commiſſion, having ground
to conjecture, that ſhe would never marry, upon the reflection I
made upon that ſtory, one of the Gentlemen of her Chamber had
told me, ſeeing ſhe knowing her ſelf unable for ſucceſſion, I ſuppoſed
ſhe would never render her ſelf ſubject to any Man. The ſaid Duke
was very much diſpleaſed at me, becauſe I refuſed.

About this time the *Cardinal of Lorrain* being at *Trent*, took occaſion to viſit the old Emperour *Ferdinand* at *Iſbrack* his dwelling place,
not far from *Trent*. And there the ſaid *Cardinal* propoſed two marriages, firſt the King of *France*, *Charles* the Ninth, to the eldeſt Daughter of *Maximilian* Son to *Ferdinand*, lately choſen King of the *Romans*,
and co-adjutor to the Empire. Then he propoſed the Queen of *Scotland* Dowager of *France*, to *Charles* Arch-duke of *Auſtria*, brother to
the ſaid *Maximilian*.

The Queen was by this time returned to *Scotland*, and apparently
had been advertiſed by the ſaid *Cardinal*, that he had propoſed the ſaid
marriage, and it ſeems ſhe had reliſhed the Overture.

Her Majeſty returning was gladly welcomed by the whole Subjects. For at firſt, following the counſel of her friends, ſhe behaved
her ſelf humanely to them all, committing the chief handling of her
affairs unto her Brother the Prior of St. *Andrews*, whom afterward
ſhe made Earl of *Murray*, and to the Secretary *Lidingtoun*, as meeteſt,
both to hold the Countrey at her devotion, and alſo to beget a ſtrict
friendſhip between her Majeſty, and the Queen of *England*. For my
Lord *Murray* had great credit with my Lord *Robert Dudly*, who was
afterward made Earl of *Leiceſter*. And the Secretary *Lidingtoun* had
great credit with the Secretary *Cecil*. So that theſe four made a ſtrict
and ſiſterly friendſhip, between the two Queens, and their Countries.
So that there appeared outwardly no more difference, but that the
Queen of *England* was the Eldeſt Siſter, and the Queen of *Scotland* the
Younger, whom the Queen of *England* promiſed to declare ſecond
perſon, according to her good behaviour. So that Letters and correſpondence paſt weekly betwixt them, and at firſt there appeared nothing more deſired by either of them, then that they might ſee one
another, by a meeting at a convenient place, whereby they might alſo declare their hearty and loving minds each to other: For our
Queen was ſo nettled with the hard uſage ſhe had met with from the
Queen Mother of *France*, who had likewiſe hardly uſed all her friends
of the Houſe of *Guiſe*, that ſhe was the more earneſt to make friendſhip

fhip with her, and with fuch whom fhe knew that *Queen* liked worſt;
The two Queens this way keeping on their outward friendſhip for a
while, with the plain and honeſt meaning of our Queen, as I afterward
did perfectly know. There came a Letter to me out of *Scotland*, from
the Secretary *Lidingtoun*, at the Queens command, defiring me to
make my felf acquainted with the *Arch-duke Charles* of *Auſlria*, youn=
geſt Brother to *Maximillian*, then King of the *Romans*, and Emperour
in effect, for the Emperour *Ferdinand* his Father had nothing but the
Name, by reafon of his Age. I was defired to inform my felf concerning his Religion, his Rents, and his Qualities, his Age, and Stature, and
defired to fend home word, and therewith to fend his Picture, if it
could be done. It was thought I might obtain the occaſion thereof,
by means of the *Elector Palatine* my Maſter, for the time greateſt in
favour with the Emperour *Maximillian*.

Now my Lord *Elector* being at an Imperial Convention holden at
Ausbrugh, had of his own head inquired of *Maximillian*, what the *Car-*
dinal of *Lorrain*'s bufinefs had been with his Father *Ferdinand*, when
he came to fee him from *Trent*. For the good *Elector* was afraid, it
had been about fome matters of Religion. For *Ferdinand* was a devout Catholick, and *Maximillian* appeared to be a zealous Proteſtant.
For he was but lately chofen King of the *Romans* at *Francford*, not
without difficulty. Being himfelf one of the *Seven Electors* as King
of *Bohemia*, he was to fue fix *Electors* for their Votes: To wit, the
Elector Palatine, the Duke of *Saxony*, and the Duke of *Brandenburgh*,
three Proteſtant Princes; and three Biſhops *Mentz*, *Triers*, and *Collain*,
Catholicks. Both thefe Factions were put in hope, that being *Empe-*
rour he would declare himfelf of their principles. In the mean time
he ufed fecret preachings to pleaſe the Proteſtants, but he went openly to the *Maſs*, whereby the Biſhops thought themfelves affured of him.
But the good *Elector Palatine* believed firmly, that after his Fathers
death, he would declare himfelf a plain Proteſtant. Thus he won
both parties to make him *Emperour*. He told the *Elector Palatine* at
the Convention in *Ausbrugh*, that the *Cardinal* of *Lorrain* had propofed two marriages to the Emperour his Father. The one was *Charles*
young King of *France*, to his own Eldeſt Daughter; the other was
the Queen of *Scotland* Dowager of *France*, to his Brother the *Arch-*
Duke Charles. The *Elector* inquired how he reliſhed thefe two marriages; he anfwered he could not but like well of them, feeing he
was not to expect a better match to his Daughter then the King of
France, nor to his Brother then the Queen of *Scotland*, who the *Car-*
dinal alfo alledged had right to the Crown of *England*. The *Elector*
faid, that fince he was pleafed with the Overture of marrying his
Brother to the Queen of *Scotland*, that he had a *Scottiſh* Gentleman
with him, who could be a good inſtrument to bring forward the faid
marriage.

Whereupon *Maximillian* defired to fpeak with me, and becaufe for
the time I was in the Countrey of *Hefs*, he defired him to fend me
to him upon my return. Which the *Elector* did, and fent with me
one of his Councel, called Monfieur *Zuleger*, joining us in one Commiffion. When we had given accompt of our faid Commiffion, my
companion told the *Emperour*, that I had a particular with his Ma-

jefty, and fo retired himfe'f, leaving me alone in the Chamber. Where
I prefented a Letter to him, written with the *Elector's* own hand,
in *Dutch*, fignifying that I was the *Scotfman*, whom he promifed to
fend unto him. After he had read the writing, he did fhew methe
part wherein the *Elector* affured him, that I would fhew im the
truth of all fuch things as I knew, which he would ask of me, faying
You are much obliged to the *Elector Palatine*, for he hath given me
a very good Character of you. I pray you, fays he, tell me how long
you have been in his company. I faid more then three years : he
inquired why I did not anfwer in *Dutch*; I anfwered, becaufe I had
the *French* more familiar, and knew that no Language could come
wrong to his Majefty. For he could very promptly fpeak good *La-*
tine, Italian, Spanifh, Sclavonian, and *French.* Then he inquired again
in *French*, how I came to the *Elector Palatine.* I told him, that being
brought up at the Court of *France* with the *Conftable*, there had fallen out fome variance between *France* and *Scotland*, partly occafioned
from difference in Religion, and partly from other particulars, whence
proceeded a general diflike at the Court, of all *Scots-men* at that time
in *France*, fome being upon fufpicion imprifoned, others lookt down
upon. The confideration whereof, haft'ned my profecuting a former
intention I had deliberated upon, of vifiting other Countries. That
being minded to begin at *Dutchland*, the *Conftable* of *France* had by
his Letter addreffed me to the *Elector Palatine.* He inquired how
long I had remained with the *Conftable*; I anfwered, nine years. He
faid I was happy who had been fo long in company with two of the
wifeft Men in *Europe*, and was pleafed to fay that he was glad of the
occafion of being acquainted with me. He began more particularly
to fhew unto me the caufe why he defired to fpeak with me, inquiring concerning the Eftate of *Scotland*, of the late troubles with *France*,
of the agreement new made, what great Men had the greateft intereft, and all the Noblemens Names who had affifted both parties. He
proceeded to inquire further, what help *England* had made unto *Scot-*
land, during the troubles with *France*, if they were bandied together, if their friendfhip continued, and of the Queen's title to *Eng-*
land, if the Nobility of *Scotland* would concur to advance her to the
Crown of *England*, if they would think it the intereft of *Scotland* to
have the two Kingdoms joined in one : feeing it was to be fuppofed,
that the Queen or Prince would certainly chufe to dwell in the beft
Country, and thereby would be further from them. Thefe, and feveral other things he inquired, and I anfwered as I thought moft pertinent. When he had heard my returns, he was pleafed to fay it was
not the leaft good office that my Lord Elector had done him, in fending me to him, and gave me thanks that I had been at the pains to
come. If *Charles* my Brother, fays he, were fo happy as to obtain your
Queen in marriage, no Man fhall have more credit with him then
you. He defired me to abide with him fome time, that he might difcourfe with me at more length. So I tarried with him twenty
days, with very favourable entertainment and difcourfing with me
feveral times, he put me in hope that his Brother *Charles* would be
fhortly at home : And gave me an accompt of fuch news as came to
him from all Countries. It was he who firft told me, of the death
of

of the Duke of *Guise*, killed by *Poltrot*, at the Siege of *Orleance*. He
appeared to be very glad at the death of that gallant Warriour, though,
I could not conjecture for the time what could move him. By frequent conference with him, I suspected that he would be an Enemy
to the marriage of his Brother with our Queen, but to get some further tryal thereof, I requested my companion Monsieur *Zuliger*, to
drink himself merry with some of his Secretaries, and then to cast in
the purpose of the marriage of our Queen with Duke *Charles*, whether or no it was desired or relished by the Emperour. The said Secretary shew'd him plainly, that he was against any such preferment
to his Brother, whereby he might become King both of *Scotland*, and
England, by reason of an Essay that the Emperour *Charles* the Fifth
had made once, to divide his Dominions among the three Sons of *Ferdinand* his Brother, failing Heirs of King *Philip* his Son, who then
had but one Son, Don *Carlo*, sickly, and of a tender, weak complexi-
on, whom he afterwards himself killed secretly in Prison, suspecting
him to be of the Reformed Religion, and to keep intelligence with
the Princes of *Flanders*, who professed the same. And *Maximillian*
hoped to succeed to the whole, failing Heirs of the said King *Philip*
as having married the said *Philip*'s Sister, and having by her many
Children of his own, whom he rather desired to be preferred, then his
own Brother. For in case the Arch-duke *Charles* had been made King
of *Scotland* and *England*, he thought thereby he would have the fitter
occasion of usurping the Low-Countrys, upon the pretext of some
old right.

Having understood this I would wait no longer, but pressed daily
for my dispatch, that I might return to my Lord *Elector*: And the
Emperour again used great intreaties to oblige me to stay with him,
promising to advance me if I would enter into his service, but finding
no inclination in me to comply with his desire therein, he at length
willed me to stay with him but half a year. But I humbly excused my
self, pretending that I behoved to be shortly in *Scotland*, which moved
him the more earnestly to desire me to stay with him, which because
I would not grant to do, I found he was discontent. One night late
after Supper, he parted in a Boat towards the Town of *Lintz*, and sent
his Secretary unto me, excusing himself, that he did not meet with
me before parting, seeing an urgent occasion called for his speedy departure ; and seeing I was to return to *Scotland*, he had written a Letter to the Queen in my favour, which the Secretary delivered unto me.
I told the Secretary, that I had not yet seen *Italy*, and that I was pur-
posed first to visit *Rome*, *Venice*, *Florence*, and the most remarkable
Cities there, e're I returned to *Scotland*, upon which account, at first
I refused the said Letter, but answered, there was no danger how
long it was undelivered, seeing there was no thing therein contained,
but what concerned my self.

The Town of *Ausbrugh* being the nearest Port of *Germany* to *Venice*, I agreed with Mounsieur *Euliger* to return toward my Lord *Elector*, and thence I took my Journey towards *Venice* and *Rome*. And
came back through all the fairest Cities of *Italy*, and through
Switzerland, to *Heidlberg*, where the Prince Elector kept his
Court.

I have

I have above declared how that the Duke of *Guife* was flain by *Poltrot*, at the Siege of *Orleance*; It was after the battel of *Drues*, in the which baoth the chieftains were taken. The Prince of *Conde* for thofe of the Religion, and the *Conftable* for the King. The Queen Mother incontinently made the Peace, far againft the mind of Madam de *Guife*, who earneftly requefted her, not to make the Peace fo fuddenly, left it fhould be thought that the Duke of *Guife* had only had hand in the Wars. But neverthelefs the Queen Mother went forward with the Peace, changing the Prince of *Conde* for the *Conftable*, making them both good inftruments of the agreement.

The Peace being made, the Queen Mother began to think upon a Wife for her Son King *Charles*. For that effect, fhe fent unto the Prince Palatine, a Secretary called Monfieur *Wyllot*, fhewing unto him, that the King her Son, was very defirous to marry *Maximilian*'s Eldeft Daughter intreating him as a trufty friend, to propofe the matter as of his own head, as a fteadable Alliance, conducing for the weal of the Empire, and to fend her the picture of the Princefs, which fhe thought fit to be done upon fome confiderations, before fhe would proceed more publickly. Which affair he went about moft diligently, and he was pleafed to fend me with the anfwer and picture, with a congratulation of the late made Peace.

At my coming to the Court of *France*, which was at *Paris* for the time, the *Conftable* would needs be my convoy, to the young King, and Queen Mother, who had a mifliking of the faid *Conftable* for the time, becaufe he had brought in the *Admiral* to *Paris* againft her will, who was accufed to have promifed reward unto the forefaid *Poltrot*, to kill the Duke of *Guife*. The *Admiral* again defired to come before the Privy Council to purge himfelf, offering to undergo his tryal. But the Queen Mother defired not thefe animofities among the great Men to be removed, but rather wifhed that their hatred might continue, and their contentions increafe, as having laid her Plot to fecure her own greatnefs, by the means of their ftrife, as was after manifeftly feen. For during their divifions, the Duke of *Guife*, King of *Navarr*, Prince of *Conde*, the *Conftable*, the Marfhal *de St. Andre*, with the moft notable great Men of *France* were all flain, and becaufe the faid *Admiral* efcaped during the Wars, the Peace was made for the third time, and under the covert of marriage of the young King of *Navarr*, who was afterward King of *France*, the faid *Admiral* was barbaroufly murdered with all that remained of the wor thieft Noblemen, and Captains of *France*. But to return to the purpofe the *Conftable* and *Admiral* were at Court at that time, againft the Queen Mother's will, where the *Admiral* was declared innocent of the Duke of *Guife* his flaughter. And at that time the *Conftable* determined to abide at Court, and to maintain himfelf in his Office of great Mafter by the authority of his great Office of the *Conftablry*, affifted by the force of his friends. For he fufficiently underftood the Queen Mother's *Italian* tricks, therefore to win credit, he prefented me to the young King, and fate down upon a Stool by him, and the Queen his Mother, and held his Bonnet upon his Head, taking upon him the full authority of his great Office, to the Queen Mother's great difcontent whereat fhe was fo impatient, that fhe turned away her

face

face, when I was declaring my Commiſſion, after the delivery of my
Letters of Credence to the King, and her, which the King was very
glad to hear, being thereby put in hope, that the marriage would take
effect. He was ſo deſirous to ſee the picture of that young Princeſs,
that he cut the thread himſelf, that bound on the Wax-cloth about the
ſaid picture. In the mean time I retired me forth of the Chamber;
and was earneſtly ſought after the reſt of the day, but could not be
found until the *Conſtable* and *Admiral* came to their Chamber, at
Even, who inquiring of me the cauſe of my retiring, I remembred
the *Conſtable*, in what a rage the Queen Mother was, when I delivered my Commiſſion, and that I found my ſelf obliged in honour to
ſtand upon the reputation of my Maſter, who was a free Prince.
Whereupon they appeared well ſatisfied, approving what I had done,
but withal they told me, that they were the cauſe of that bad humour, the Queen Mother had been in, and that ſhe had made a Proclamation, that all Ambaſſadours ſhould Addreſs themſelves to the
King, and her as Regent. Therefore they adviſed me, to go the
next day to ſee her at Dinner, aſſuring me that ſhe would not fail
to call for me, and inquire the cauſe of my abſenting, before I had
told out my Commiſſion, and he inſtructed me what I ſhould ſay in
anſwer. So ſoon as her Majeſty perceived me, ſhe deſired me to ſtay
till ſhe had Dined, telling me that ſhe would ſend for her Son the
King, to come to her Chamber, to hear out the reſt of my Commiſſion.

The King being come, the Chamber was voided, and her Majeſty
firſt inquired, why I told not out the reſt of my Commiſſion the day
before. I anſwered, as I had been inſtructed, how that it appeared to
me, for the time, ſhe deſired not ſo many auditors, and that I ſtayed
upon her better opportunity, which anſwer ſhe appeared much to re-
liſh, deſiring me when at any other time I ſhould be ſent again, to Addreſs my ſelf only to the King, and to her, and to no other. I anſwered, that among all the King's Servants, I was beſt acquainted with
the *Conſtable*, and therefore had made him my Convoy to both their
Majeſties. No, ſays ſhe, I find no fault that you Addreſſed your ſelf to
him; yet I knew ſhe entertained a mortal hatred againſt him. So after
I had ended the Declaration of my whole Commiſſion, firſt concerning the Congratulation of the Peace, and then made excuſes in Name
of the Confederate Princes of the Empire, for ſending help to the
Prince of *Conde*, during the Wars for Religion, with a requeſt to keep
the ſaid Peace inviolate, and to make ſuch Laws of Oblivion, as were
wont to be done among the *Greeks* and *Romans*, after ſuch Civil Diſ-
ſentions. And then I gave a full account, how my Lord *Elector* had
proceeded with *Maximilian*, and what his anſwer was. All the time
that I ſpoke ſhe remembred the King to take good notice, ſaying he
was much obliged to that good Prince, that took ſuch pains for his
marriage, and the weal of his Kingdom. Then ſhe drew me aſide
entering into a particular diſcourſe with me, telling me that ſhe hoped
I would not make too long ſtay in *Dutchland*, but reſolve to ſpend
ſome of my time in the Court of *France*, ſeeing it was there I had been
brought up. For albeit, ſhe ſaid ſhe had ſeveral who could ſpeak *Dutch*,
yet there was none about her, who were ſo familiar with the Princes
of

of the Empire as I was, or had fuch favour and credit, as fhe underftood I had, to do the King and her fervice. Therefore fhe offered to
make me a Gentleman of the King's Chamber, to provide me with
an honourable Penfion, to advance me to Offices and Honours, as if
I had been a *French-man* born; and that fhe would imploy me not
only to *Germany*, but alfo to *England* and *Flanders*. I gave her Majefty many thanks, taking her offer to my confideration. In the
mean time that I was waiting upon my difpatch, the *Admiral's* death
was confpired by the Brother and Friends of the Duke of *Guife*, to be
executed by Captain *Charry*, in great favour with the Queen Mother,
as Chief Captain of her Guard, Commanding fix hundred *Hagbu-
tiers Gafcons*. The faid enterprife being difcovered to the *Conftable* by
the old Dutchefs of *Farrara*, Daughter to King *Lewis* the Eleventh,
Mother to the Widow Dutchefs of *Guife*. The *Conftable* went to his
Houfe, four Leagues from *Paris*, and the next day after, the faid Captain
Charry was flain upon the ftreets of *Paris*, by Mounfieur *Chattelier* the
Admiral's friend. Which put the Queen, and all the Court into a
fear, and firm opinion that the deed wsa done by the *Conftables's* and
Admirals direction. But the *Admiral* purged himfelf; the *Conftable*
was fent for, and many requefts-made to him, to fettle, and eftablifh
quietnefs in the Court and City.
      While I was yet at *Paris* undifpatched, I received Letters from the
Earl of *Murray*, and *Lidingtoun* at the Queens Command, calling me,
home, to be imployed in her Majefties fervice, in fome of her affairs
of confequence; which I prefuppofed to be concerning her marriage.
Whereupon I determined to obey my Queens Commands, and immediately after my return to *Germany*, to prepare for a Journey to *Scotland*. Though this refolution of mine, was far contrary to the mind
of the *Conftable*, *Admiral*, and Prince *Palatine*. But his Son Duke *Cafimir*, took occafion to defire me to prefent his picture to Queen *Elizabeth*. I have faid already that he was very diffatisfied, becaufe I
refufed to go to *England*, to propofe marriage for him to the Queen,
he having been incouraged thereto by the *Vidam* of Charters, lately
come hither from the Court of *England*, who thought himfelf fo familiar with that Queen, that it fent an *Italian* Gentlemen of his, to
propofe that marriage, as he alledged, at the inftance of the Elector
Palatine, to whom the Queen gave a general anfwer, defiring the
young Prince to come unto *England*, either openly, or privately dif-
guifed, and declaring that fhe would never marry Man, till fhe might
firft fee him. Notwithftanding hereof, I ftill diffwaded his Father
from fending him, alledging that he would be very chargeable to
him, and that he would reap nothing but fcorn in recompence. Whereat the young Prince was fo moved, that he let the Court for three
days. But the good Prince his Father fent for him, threat'ning to
difcountenance him, if he became not my friend, Whereupon we
agreed, that at this time I fhould carry with me his picture, and prefent it to the Queen of *England* in my return to *Scotland*, feeing I was
fo averfe from his going thither in perfon. Which I was fatisfied to
do, providing that I might alfo carry along with me, the picture of
his Father and Mother, and of all the reft of his Brothers and Sifters,
together with a familiar Letter from the Elector, whereby I might have
                                                            the

the more eafie accefs, and fitter opportunity to bring in the purpofe
of the pictures, as by accident, hoping that fhe would defire to fee
them, efpecially the picture of the faid young Duke.

So having obtained my defire, I parted from *Heïdlberg*, where the
Elector held his Court for the time, who gave me a Commiffion to
the Queen of *England*; to wit, an anfwer to her demanded Alliance,
offenfive, and defenfive, with the Proteftant Princes of *Germany*, which
formerly had been but obfcurely anfwered unto her Ambaffadour,
Sir *Henry Knolls*, at the Dyet Imperial, holden at *Francfort*, in the
year 1562. Excufing himfelf, and the reft of the Princes his confederates, who had but lately chofen *Maximillian* to be King of the *Romans*, and Co-adjutor to the Emperour his Father, feeing he had promifed unto them, to declare himfelf openly a Proteftant, fo foon as he
durft, after the deceafe of his old Father *Ferdinand* : and in the mean
time had their promife to keep correfpondence with him, and to make
no League with any foreign Prince, without his confent and knowledge. And that if they had done otherwife, he might perchance
have taken occafion thereupon, to lay the blame upon them, in cafe
he did not as he had promifed. For they began to fear and doubt of
his upright meaning in reference to Religion, and yet thought not
fit upon their part, to give him any ground to lay the blame upon
them; but in cafe he kept not his promife after the deceafe of *Ferdinand*, they fhould then prefently make fuch Alliance with her, as fhe
had required, which they durft not for the time difcover unto her
Ambaffadour, requefting her Majefty to keep this fecret to her
felf.

She appeared fatisfied with this excufe, promifing to difcover it to
none of her Council ; but fhe lamented that the Princes of *Germany*
were fo flow and tedious in all their deliberations. Whereupon I began to praife them for their Truth, Conftancy, Religion, Ardour, and
quick execution, after they had concluded any weighty matter. But
I fet out moft fpecially the Elector Palatine's humanity, his treating
of Strangers, upholding of Univerfities, and how he was the mouth
of his confederates, to deal with all other neighbour Princes. She anfwered, that I had reafon to fpeak fo concerning him, for he had written very much in my favour, regretting that the inclinations I had to
ferve my native Queen, had obliged me to leave him, though he
would gladly have retained me with him a longer fpace. I told her
Majefty, what a great trouble it was to me, to refolve to leave the fervice of fo worthy a Prince, that no confideration could have engaged
me thereunto, other then that duty I owed to my Soveraign, who had
commanded me to attend her affairs. That for the better remembrance of him, I defired to carry home with me his picture, and the
pictures of all his Sons and Daughters. So foon as fhe heard me mention the pictures, fhe inquired if I had the picture of the Duke *Cafimir*,
defiring to fee it. And when I alledged I had left the pictures in *London*, fhe being then at *Hampton-Court*, and that I was ready to go forward on my Journey, fhe faid I fhould not part till fhe had feen all the
pictures. So the next day I delivered them all to her Majefty, and
fhe defired to keep them all night, and fhe called upon my Lord *Robert Dudly* to be judge of Duke *Cafimir's* picture, and appointed me to
meet

meet her the next morning in her Garden, where she caused to deliver them all unto me, giving me thanks, for the fight of them. I
again offered unto her Majesty all the pictures, so she would permit
me to retain the Electors, and his Ladys, but she would have none of
them. I had also fure information, that firft and laft she defpifed the
faid Duke *Cafimir*. Therefore I did write back from *London* to his
Father, and him in Cypher, diffwading them to meddle any more in
that marriage. And received great thanks afterward from the faid
young Duke, who immediately married the Elector of *Saxony*'s Eldeft
Daughter. Albeit this may appear fomething from the purpofe of the
Queen our Sovéraign, yet it brings me home to her Majefty with
fome propofals of marriage to her felf. For the Queen of *England* entertained me very familiarly, fhewing me the Sifterly love that was
betwixt her and the Queen our Soveraign, how careful she was of her
well-fare, how defirous to fee her well fetled in her own Country with
her Subjects, and alfo well married. That she was refolved to propofe two perfons for fit Husbands unto her, whereby their amity
might beft ftand and increafe, hoping that she would not marry without her advice, promifing upon her faith to write to me, fo foon as I
was arrived at *Scotland*, with her own hand, that I might be a good
inftrument to move the Queen my Miftrefs to accept either the one
or the other. Now though she forgot to write unto me about it, yet
she fent inftructions to Mr. *Randolph*, to propofe my Lord *Robert*
Dudley as a very meet Husband for our Queen. I fuppofed that my
Lord *Robert*, afterward Earl of *Leicefter*, had diffwaded her from imploying me in that matter, feeing Mr. *Randolph* was there already, her
Majefties Agent.

Now the Queen my Miftrefs, to keep promife and correfpondence
with the Queen of *England*, had fent and advertifed her, of the propofal made to her of a marriage with the Arch-duke *Charles*, requiring
her friendly advice and confent therein.

The Queen of *England* anfwered her by her Agent Mr. *Thomas Ran-*
dolph, as followeth, for after a little Preface, he declares, and gives in by
writing, this to be the Queen his Miftrefs's mind.

The Queen my Soveraign, faid he, hath not only deeply advifed
about that propofal of marriage with your Majefty, but hath alfo
thought it neceffary, by me to fhew you, what she thinketh both
meet and unmeet to be confidered, and feemingly to her by way of
friendfhip, to declare as a dear Sifter, who intends your Majefties honour, and as a loving Friend, who is careful of your well-fare.

Three fpecial things her Majefty thinks fit to be confidered in marriage.

Firft, The mutual contentment betwixt both parties in refpect of
their private perfonages, fo that their love each towards one another,
may continue as well before God as Man.

Secondly, That the perfon may be fuch as your Majefty, being a
Queen of a great Realm, and multitude of People, may be fure of an
advantageous Alliance, fuch as cannot be prejudical to your Countries
interest.

Thirdly, She thinks fit that the choice be fuch, that the amity which
is now fo ftrict betwixt the Queens Majefty, and your Highnefs, not
only

only for your own perfons, but with both Realms, may be continued, and not diffolved nor diminifhed. Then he declares at length,
how that he doubts not, but that her Majefty, who was once already
married, will know how confiderately to ponder the match, that it
may be meet for her felf, and her Subjects; but as to what belong-
ed unto the Queen his Sovereign, it merited to be well confidered.

It is true, that the feeking out a Husband to your Majefty, is honourable, and expedient ; a thing that her Majefty rellifheth much in
your Highnefs, albeit hitherto fhe hath not found fuch difpofition in
her felf, remitting her heart and mind in that affair to be directed by
the Almighty God.

But this herein her Majefty confidereth, that to feek out fuch a
Husband, as is fought for by your friends, in the Emperours Linage,
will certainly procure at laft fome mifunderftanding, and give apparent occafion of diffolving the Concord, that is now betwixt the two
Nations, and an interruption of fuch a courfe, as otherwife might be
taken, to further and advance fuch a Title as your Highnefs hath to
fucceed to her Majefty, to the Crown of *England*, if fhe fhould depart
without iffue of her Body.

Then he ufeth fome unfit perfwafions and menaces, threat'ning that
fome in *England* were going about with practices to fet forward their
pretended right, to her Majefties prejudice, which fhe by her difcreet
behaviour and conformity to his Miftreffes pleafure, might prevent,
by moving her thereby, not only to proceed in the inquifition after
your Majefties right, and with her power to further the fame, but
alfo to hinder that which appears to be to the contrary.

And now if your Majefty would know, what kind of marriage
would beft content her, and her Realm, fuch a one as would breed
no jealoufie, nor trouble betwixt your Majefties, and your Countries,
as did the marriage with the *French* King. But rather it is to be
wifhed, that there might be found out fome Nobleman of great birth
in *England*, who might be agreeable to you ; with whom her Majefty would more readily, and more eafily declare, that fhe inclines, that
failing of Children of her own Body, you might fucceed to her Crown;
otherwife I do plainly tell you, that my Soveraign can promife nothing
in that matter, tending to your fatisfaction.

Thefe were Mr. *Randolph's* firft inftructions, and propofitions, unto the Queen, concerning her Marriage with the Arch-duke *Charles.*
But he had a fecret Commiffion to my Lord of *Murray*, and Secretary
Lidingtoun, to propofe my Lord *Robert Dudley* ; and he defired me
alfo, to fet forward his marriage with the Queen, as meeteft of all
other.

By this kind of procedure it was apparent, that the Queen of *England* did not relifh this propofal of marriage, of the Arch duke *Charles*
to our Queen. She gave a farther, and more clear demonftration
thereof a little after, by fending the Earl of *Suffex* to the Emperour's
Court, as well to congratulate his Coronation, as indirectly to draw
on the marriage of the Arch-duke *Charles* with her felf. And fhe
was put in hope, that it would take effect : Yet this defign was not
fo fecretly managed, but our Queen was thereof advertifed, by fome

G of

of her friends in *England.* And from hence arose inward griefs and
grudges between the two Queens, which within a little time burfted
forth, occafion thereof being given by the Queen of *England:* For in
a familiar Letter to our Queen, fhe appeared therein to give her, as
formerly, a friendly advice: which our Queen thought but double
dealing, remembring as well her late diffwading anfwer from the marriage of the Arch-duke *Charles,* as her late practifes in the Emperours
Court. The Queen of *England*'s Letter was written at the defire of
fome of the Houfe of *Hamiltoun :* For after that Mr. *Randolph* had fpoken, as is above mentioned, againft the marriage of the Queen with
the Arch-duke *Charles,* and he alledged that fome Noblemen in *England* would be fitter matches for her, he proceeded fo far with my
Lord of *Murray,* and Secretary *Lidingtoun,* as to fay, What would you
think of my Lord *Robert Dudly* for your Queen? But finding fmall
account to be made of him, he advertifed the Queen his Miftrefs thereof. Whereupon liberty was granted to *Matthew* Earl of *Lennox,* who
dwelt then in *England;* to go to *Scotland,* as defirous to fee the Queen,
and take courfe in fome of his own affairs. Now his Eldeft Son, my
Lord *Darnly,* was a lufty young Prince, and apparently was one of the
two that the Queen of *England* had told me that fhe had in her head, to
offer unto our Queen, as born within the Realm of *England.* But to
return unto the Letter written by the Queen of *England* unto our
Queen, fhe would appear therein to be very careful for the Queen her
Sifters quiet Eftate and Government, defiring her to take heed that
in fhewing pleafure to the Earl of *Lennox,* fhe did not difpleafe the
Houfe of *Hamiltoun,* feeing thereby trouble and ftrife might arife in
her Country. Sundry other fuch purpofes fhe had, which at fome
time would not have been taken in ill part; but now all advices given by the Queen of *England,* were mifconftructed, partly becaufe of
her being inftrumental in hindring the marriage with Prince *Charles,*
and partly becaufe *David Rixio* lately admitted to be her French Secretary, was not very skilful in inditing *French* Letters, which fhe did
write over again with her own hand. The anfwer then that our
Queen did write unto the faid Letter, declared fome fufpicions and anger to have been taken, and thefe fhe manifefted in fome harfh expref-
fions, which were conftructed by the Queen of *England,* as a violati-
on of their former familiarity, and Sifterly correfpondence, which had
been ever kept up fince the Queens return out of *France.* Whereupon enfued fo great a coldnefs, that they left off for a confiderable
time from writing each to other, as they had formerly done weekly
by Poft. So that the Queen refolved to fend me to *England,* to renew their outward friendfhip; for in their hearts from that time forth
there was nothing but jealoufies and fufpicions. The Queen my Miftrefs thought that if their difcord continued, it would cut off all correfpondence between her and her friends in *England:* and that
Queen had no inclination for War, but by all means poffible defired
to fhun trouble, or any occafion of expences, the King of *Spain* and
fhe being already entered into controverfie. For he judged her a fo-
menter of the troubles in *Flanders,* and the Low Countries, and not
without reafon. For fhe thought her felf abandoned by the King of
Spain, at the late Peace made at *Cambray,* and her chief Councellers
                                                              thought

thought it. convenient for the interest of *England*, that Factious should
be nourished in *France, Flanders, Scotland*, and *Spain.*

At my home-coming to *Scotland*, I found the Queen's Majesty, at
St. *Johnstoun*, in the Year of God 1564, the fifth day of *May.* I was
very favourably received by the Queens Majesty, and presented unto
her Letters from the Emperour *Maximilian*, the Elector *Palatine*, the
Duke of *Lorrain*, and Cardinal of *Lorrain*, and Duke of *Aumale*, all in
my favours. After that I had at length informed her, that I found
Maximilian was against the marriage of his Brother *Charles* ; she likewise understanding the Queen of *Englands* part therein, as is above
specified, she altogether laid aside any further thoughts of the marriage
with the Arch-duke *Charles.* And whereas she had once resolved to
have sent me to *Germany*, she takes another resolution, intending that
I should be sent to *England.* Though I was not yet resolved in setling my self in *Scotland*, seeing small probability of advantage, and
greater appearance of troubles and disorders, then I could ever imagine to find at my home-coming. And I was somewhat loath to lose
the occasion and offers of great preferment, that had been made to
me in *France*, and other parts. But I found the Queen my Sovereign,
so urgent, and of her self well inclined, and indued with so many
Princely vertues that I could not find in my heart to leave her, requiring so earnestly my help and assistance, to draw the hearts of her
Subjects to her, which were alienated upon account of difference in Religion. I knew she stood in need to gain friends, and that it was much
her interest to keep correspondence with the Queen of *England* ; so
that I resolved rather to serve her my native Queen for little profit,
then any other Prince in *Europe* for great advantage. I found her
naturally more liberal then her Revenues allowed her. For she not
only setled upon me in pensions, one thousand Marks yearly, out of
her Revenues in *France*, but she also offered me her heritage of her
Lands in *Aghtermughtie*, which I refused to accept, alledging I could
better want it then she. Though another hearing of so liberal an offer, a little after fought and obtained it.

Thus I was engaged to resolve to wait upon her commands, and to
lay aside all hope of any other preferment in *France*, and other Countries, albeit, for the time, I had no heritage but my service. So within a few weeks I was dispatched to *England*, with these following Instructions out of the Queens own mouth, to deal with the Queen of
England, with the *Spanish* Ambassadour, and with my Lady *Margaret,
Douglas*, and with sundry friends she had in *England* of different opinions. The general Instructions were written with the Secretary *Lidingtoun's* own hand, subscribed by her Majesty as follows:

Inſtructions to our familiar Servitor James Melvil
*preſently directed to our deareſt Siſter the Queen
of* England. *Given at* Edinbrugh *the* 28th *of*
September, 1564.

IN the firſt, after that you have preſented our Letters, and our commendations, in moſt hearty manner, you ſhall declare unto our good
Siſter. That having been upon my progreſs towards the Northmoſt
parts of our Realm this two months, during which time we have had
neither Letter nor other Advertiſement from our good Siſter. Therefore for continuation of the mutual Intelligence betwixt us, by all good
Offices of amity, we reſolved to direct you towards her, to viſit her
on our behalf, to inform her of our health and good eſtate, that, at
your return you may be able to report the like of her unto us, ſhe
being the perſon in the World, to whom next our ſelf, we wiſh moſt
good luck and proſperity.

Item, That by Letters of my Lord *Robert* to *Lidingtoun*, as alſo of
her Secretary to Our Brother *Murray*, and to *Lidingtoun*, We have perceived that Our ſaid good Siſter finds ſome fault with Our Letters
written to her in anſwer of hers in the Earl of *Lennox*'s matter, as if We
had taken her motion therein in evil part. We are moſt ſorry that
Our Letters have been ſo interpreted, for of a truth We had no other
meaning of her in that matter, then that her Advertiſement came
from a friendly mind, and was both worthy of thanks, and to be anſwered with the like good will, as We believe We did in Our Letter,
albeit We remember not preſently the very words or ſubſtance thereof. For We uſe not to reſerve any Copy of Our familiar Letters
written with Our own hand, whereof We now repent becauſe of that
Letter. For if We had any Copy thereof, We might now clear Our
ſelves of that doubt, *viz.* What words therein could give her ground
of offence. Therefore you ſhall pray her in Our Name, to let you ſee
in that Letter, what words they are which have offended her; that you
thereupon declaring my meaning, may put her out of any ſuch ſuſpicion. It is true, at the receipt of the Letter, We were ſomewhat
offended, and judged We had good cauſe, ſeeing it appeared that Our
Nobility were grieved with Our Licenſe granted to the Earl of *Lennox*, that his coming was like to diſturb the peace and quiet of Our
Realm. Our *Brother* and *Lidingtoun*, ſhew unto Us, that they perceived by their Secretaries Letters, that they were alſo thought partakers
in this matter; and that they miſtaking alſo his coming, deſired the
ſtay thereof to be procured by theſe undecent means. Though they
proteſted the contrary unto Us, and indeed We have better proof of
their fidelity toward Us, then that We can ſuſpect any ſuch double
dealing from their hands, they being ſo far obliged to Us, and ſo much
intruſted by us. We thought Our ſelves little indebted to that perſon, whoſoever he was, that made ſuch report of Our Subjects, that
they

they would make known their grievances to any other then Our
felves.

Thefe, and the like confiderations, moved Us to great choller, which
probably might have occafioned Us to write the more freely, and that
We were not curious to cover Our paffions, writing, to her with-
whom We efteemed Our Selves fo familiar, that We had ground to
believe fhe would take all in good part that procceded from Us, efpecially what was no ways defigned for her offence. Therefore you
fhall pray her to put away all fuch opinions, if fhe have conceived
any, and if there be any word in Our Letter having two fenfes. fo that
any one may be mifconftrued, and fo give to her occafion of offence ;
intreat that fhe will rather interpret the fame to the gentleft fignifica-
tion, and not take it in the worft fenfe. And then I doubt not but the
whole Letter, fhall appear to her as it was by Us conceived and dire-
fted, that is from one dear friend to another.

We have further hereupon, imparted Our mind to you by mouth,
which you may enlarge as occafion requires.

You may defire her to give you an anfwer conform to the fub-
ftance of *Lidingtoun*'s Letters, written to my Lord *Robert*, and Mr. *Cicil*.
Efpecially concerning the drawing on another meeting of Men of credit; fully inftructed with both Our minds, and to deal fo plainly, and
frankly as all fufpicion may have an end.

You muft alfo inform your felf diligently concerning the proceedings,
and intentions of this prefent Parliament, of all fuch as can give you
any knowledg therein, for what caufe it is called, what is to be treated in
it, how long it will fit. Endeavour to inform your felf, if any thing touching Us, will be therein handled. You may fay to that Queen, as out of
your own head, that your Miftrefs expects that fhe will fuffer nothing to
be treated therein, that may directly or indirectly tend to Our prejudice, We not being by her forewarned thereof. She knows that as
well Our felf, as our Minifters whom We have at any time directed
to thefe parts, have ever depended upon her only advice, and followed
the fame in all points. And feeing the fpecial matter moved, in the
beginning of the laft Parliament, was the eftablifhing of the Succeffion, and that it was probable, that the Subjects would yet be earneft
to be at a certainty in that point. And if fhe omits fo good an occafion, of doing fomething for Us, whereby the World may underftand
that fhe ufeth Us, and efteems Us, as her next Coufin, and only Sifter,
the World will think that her amity is not fo great, as We take it to
be. And fuch as envy our familiarity, and would have it broken, will
hence take occafion to fpeak, that our friendfhip is rather in words, then
deeds:

Mary R.

Being arrived at *London*, I lodged near the Court, which was at
Weftminfter. My Hoft immediately gave advertifement of my coming,
and that fame night her Majefty fent Mr. *Hatton*, afterward Governour of the Ifle of *Wight*, in her name to welcome me, and to fhew
me, that the next morning fhe would give me Audience in her Garden at eight of the Clock. She had been advertifed by the Eral of *Bedford* Governour of *Berwick*, that I was upon the way. That fame
night

night I was vifited by Sir *Nicholas Throgmorton*, one of my old and
deareft friends, by long acquaintance. Firft during his banifhment in
France, in the Reign of Queen *Mary*; and afterward while he was Ambaffadour in *France* for this Queen, where I was, for the time, Penfioner to King *Henry* the Second, and Servant to the Conftable. This
Sir *Nicholas* was my dear friend, and had procured a Penfion for me
from his Miftrefs, to help to entertain me on my Travels, when I had
willingly banifhed my felf the Court of *France*, fo long as there were
Civil Wars between *France* and *Scotland*. He was a devout friend
to the Queen my Miftrefs, and to her Right and Title to the Succeffion to the Crown of *England*. From him I had full information of
affairs, and friendly advice how to proceed with the Queen, and every Courtier in particular. For he was a fpecial inftrument of helping
my Lord of *Murray*, and Secretary *Lidingtoun*, to pack up the firft
friendfhip betwixt the two Queens; and betwixt the Earl of *Murray*
and Lord *Robert*; and between the two Secretaries. Albeit he had no
great kindnefs either for my Lord *Robert* or Secretary *Cicil*, yet he
knew that nothing could be done without them. Among other coun-
fels, he gave me advice to ufe great familiarity with the Ambaffadour
of *Spain*, in cafe I found the Queen his Miftrefs hard to be dealt with,
alledging that it would be a great Spur to move the Queen of *England*, to give our Queen greater, and more fpeedy contentment in her
defire, then yet fhe had done.

The next morning Mr. *Hatton*, and Mr. *Randolph* late Agent for the
Queen of *England* in *Scotland*, came to my Lodging, to convoy me to
her Majefty, who was, as they faid, already in the Garden. With
them came a Servant of my Lord *Robert's*, with a Horfe and Foot-
mantle of Velvet laced with Gold, for me to ride upon. Which Servant, with the faid Horfe, waited upon me all the time that I remained there. I found her Majefty walking in an Alley. And after I had
kiffed her hand, and prefented my Letter of Credence, I told her Majefty in *French* the effect of my Commiffion, as near to the aforefaid Inftructions as I could, and fometimes being interrupted by her demands,
I anfwered as I judged moft pertinent. The reafon why I fpoke
French, was, that being but lately come home, I could not fpeak my
own Language fo promptly as was requifite. Her firft demand was
concerning the Letter, that the Queen had written to her with fuch
defpiteful Language, that fhe thence conjectured all friendfhip and familiarity to have been given up. Which had made her refolve never
to write any more, but another as defpiteful, which fhe took out of
her pocket, to give me to read, fhe having had it already written to fhew
it me. She told me fhe had hitherto delayed to fend it, becaufe fhe
thought it too gentle, till fhe had written another more vehement, for
anfwer to the Queens angry Bill. For my part I appeared to find fuch
hard interpretation to be made upon the Queen's loving and frank
dealing, very ftrange. I told her Majefty that my Miftrefs could
not call to mind, what words they were which had given her fuch
offence. Whereupon fhe brought forth the Queens Letter, giving it
me to read. Which when I had perufed, I faid I could find therein no
offenfive word, when I confidered the familiarity had formerly been
betwixt them. Alledging, that albeit her Majefty could fpeak as good
French;

French, as any who had not been out of the Country, that yet she was out of use of the *French* Court Language, which was frank and short, and had frequently two significations, which familiar friends took always in the best part. Intreating her Majesty to tear the angry Letter, which she thought to have sent in answer. And in revenge of the Queens, I protested that I should never let her Majesty know that her true plain meaning had been so misconstructed. Having tossed some words upon this matter, she being desirous of an honest colour or pretext, she appeared the more readily satisfied in that point. For the fear she had that friendship and correspondence should altogether break off, our Queen being the first seeker to renew and continue the same, by sending me thither, thereby evidencing that she did not stand upon Ceremonies with her Eldest Sister, in my presence then she did rent her angry Letter, with promise of such friendly and frank dealing in times coming, as all her good Sister's dealings and proceedings should be interpreted to the best.

Thus the old friendship being renewed, she inquired, if the Queen had sent any answer to the proposition of marriage made to her by Mr. *Randolph*. I answered, as I had been instructed, That my Mistress thought little or nothing thereof, but expected the meeting of some Commissioners upon the Borders, with my Lord of *Murray*, and the Secretary *Lidingtoun*, to confer and treat upon all such matters of greatest importance, as should be judged to concern the quiet of both the Countries, and satisfaction of both their Majesties minds. For seeing your Majesty cannot so soon find the opportunity of meeting betwixt your selves, so much desired, which in it self is not so expedient until all other jealousies be first removed, and all former doubts cleared by your most trusty and familiar Councellors, the Queen my Mistress, as I have said, is minded to send for her part my Lord of *Murray*, and the Secretary *Lidingtoun*, and expects that your Majesty will send my Lord of *Bedord*, and my Lord *Robert Dudley*. She answered, It appeared that I made but small account of my Lord *Robert*, seeing that I named the *Earl* of *Bedford* before him, but said, that e're long she would make him a far greater Earl, and that I should see it done before my returning home. For she esteemed him as her Brother, and best friend, whom she would have her self married, had she ever minded to have taken a Husband. But being determined to end her life in Virginity, she wished that the Queen her Sister might marry him, as meetest of all other with whom she could find in her heart to declare her second person. For being matched with him, it would best remove out of her mind all fears and suspicions, to be offended by any usurpation before her death. Being assured that he was so loving and trusty, that he would never permit any such thing to be attempted during her time. And that the Queen my Mistress might have the higher esteem of him, I was required to stay till I should see him made Earl of *Leicester*, and Baron of *Denbigh* ; which was done at *Westminster* with great solemnity, the Queen her self helping to put on his Ceremonial   he sitting upon his knees before her with a great gravity. But she could not refrain from putting her hand in his neck, smilingly tickling him, the *French* Ambassadour and I standing by. Then she turned, asking at me, *How I liked him ?* I answered
ed

ed, that as he was a worthy Servant, so he was happy who had a Princefs, who could difcern and reward good Service. Yet, fays she, you like better of yonder long Lad, pointing toward my Lord *Darnly*, who as neareft Prince of the Blood, did bear the Sword of Honour that day before her. My anfwer was, That no woman of fpirit would make choice of fuch a Man, who more refembled a Woman then a Man. For he was handfom, beardlefs, and Lady faced. And I had no Will that she fhould think that I liked him, or had any eye or dealing that way. Albeit I had a fecret charge to deal with my Lady *Lennox*, to endeavour to procure liberty for him to go to *Scotland* (where his Father was already) under the pretext of feeing the Countrey, and conveying the Earl his Father back again to *England*. Now I found the Queen of *England* was determined to treat with my Sovereign, firft concerning her marriage with the Earl of *Leicefter*, and for that effect she promifed to fend Commiffioners unto the Borders. In the mean time, I was very favourably, and familiarly ufed. For during nine days that I remained at the Court, it pleafed her Majefty to confer with me every day, and fometimes thrice in a day, in the morning, after Dinner, and after Supper. Sometimes she would fay, that feeing she could not meet with the Queen her good Sifter, to confer with her familiarly, that she was refolved to open a good part of her inward mind to me, that I might shew it again unto the Queen. She told me she was not fo much offended with the Queens angry Letter, as that she feemed fo far to difdain the marriage of my Lord of *Leicefter*, which she had caufed Mr. *Randolph* to propofe to her. I anfwered, That it was probable he had let fall fomething thereof to my Lord of *Murray*, and *Lidingtoun*, but that he had never propofed the matter directly to her felf, and that as well her Majefty, as thofe who were her moft familiar Councellors, could conjecture nothing thereupon, but delays and driving off time concerning the declaring of her to be fecond Perfon, which would be clearly tryed at the meeting of the Commiffioners above fpecified. She replied, That the tryal and declaration thereof, would be hafted forward according to the Queens good behaviour, and applying her felf to follow her pleafure and advice in her marriage. And feeing the matter concerning the faid declaration was fo weighty, and of fo much import, she had ordered fome of the beft Lawyers in *England*, diligently to fearch out who had the beft right, and she heartily wisht it might be found to be her dear Sifter, rather than any other. I faid I was very confident that her Majefty was ingenuous in that Declaration, and that my Miftrefs expected no other at her hand. But I lamented, that even the wifeft Princes, did not fufficiently pry into the hidden defigns of their familiar Councellors, and Servants, except it were fuch an honourable and rare Prince as *Henry* the Eighth, her Majefties Father of happy memory, who of his own head was determined to declare his Sifters Son, King *James* the Fifth, Heir apparent to the Crown of *England*, failing Heirs to be gotten of his own Body, while her Majefty was not yet born, but only her Sifter Queen *Mary*, and that for the earneft defire he had to unite this whole Ifland. She faid she was glad he did it not. I faid, that then he had but one Daughter, and expected no more Children, and yet he had not fo many fufpicions in his head

as

as your Majefty hath, though you are certainly convinced you will never have any Children, feeing your Majefty declares your felf refolved to dye a Virgin. Yes, fays fhe, I am refolved never to marry, if I be not thereto neceffitated by the Queen my Sifter's harfh behaviour toward me. I know the truth of that Madam, faid I, you need not tell it me. Your Majefty thinks if you were married, you would be but Queen of *England,* and now you are both King and Queen. I know your fpirit cannot endure a Commander. She appeared to be fo affectionate to the Queen her good Sifter that fhe expreffed a great defire to fee her. And becaufe their fo much, by her, defired meeting could not be fo haftily brought to pafs, fhe appeared with great delight to look upon her Majefties picture. She took me to her Bed-chamber, and opened a little Cabinet, wherein were divers little pictures wrapped within Paper, and their Names written with her own hand upon the Papers. Upon the firft that fhe took up was written, *My Lord's Picture.* I held the Candle, and preffed to fee that picture fo named, fhe appeared loath to let me fee it, yet my importunity prevailed for a fight thereof, and found it to be the Earl of *Leicefter's* picture. I defired that I might have it to carry home to my Queen, which fhe refufed, alledging that fhe had but that one picture of his. I faid, your Majefty hath here the Original, for I perceived him at the fartheft part of the Chamber, fpeaking with Secretary *Cicil.* Then fhe took out the Queens picture and kiffed it, and I adventured to kifs her hand, for the great love therein evidenced to my Miftrefs. She fhewed me alfo a fair Ruby, as great as a Tenis Ball, I defired that fhe would either fend it, or my Lord of *Leicefter's* picture, as a Token unto the Queen. She faid, if the Queen would follow her counfel that fhe would in procefs of time get all fhe had; that in the mean time fhe was refolved in a Token to fend her with me a fair Diamond. It was at this time late after Supper, fhe appointed me to be with her the next morning by Eight of the Clock, at which time fhe ufed to walk in her Garden. She inquired feveral things of me relating to this Kingdom, and other Countries wherein I had travelled. She caufed me to dine with her Dame of Honour, my Lady *Strafford* (an honourable and godly Lady, who had been at *Geneva* banifhed during the Reign of Queen *Mary*) that I might be always near her, that fhe might confer with me. I had formerly been acquainted with my Lady *Strafford,* as fhe paffed through *France.* I had good intelligence from her and my Lady *Throgmorton.* At divers meetings we had divers purpofes. The Queen my Miftrefs had inftructed me to leave matters of gravity fometimes, and caft in merry purpofes, left otherwife I fhould be wearied, fhe being well informed of that Queens natural temper. Therefore in declaring my obfervations of the cuftoms of *Dutchland, Poland,* and *Italy,* the Buskins of the Women was not forgot, and what Countrey Weed I thought beft becoming Gentlewomen. The Queen faid fhe had Cloths of every fort, which every day thereafter, fo long as I was there, fhe changed. One day fhe had the *Englifh* Weed, another the *French,* and another the *Italian,* and fo forth. She asked me which of them became her beft ? I anfwered, in my judgment the *Italian* drefs, which anfwer I found pleafed her well, for fhe delighted to fhew her golden coloured

H

hair,

hair, wearing a Caul and Bonnet as they do in *Italy*. Her hair was more reddifh then yellow, curled in appearance naturally. She defired to know of me, what colour of hair was reputed beft, and whether my Queens hair or hers was beft, and which of them two was faireft. I anfwered, the fairnefs of them both was not their worft faults. But fhe was earneft with me to declare, which of them I judged faireft? I faid fhe was the faireft Queen in *England*, and mine the faireft Queen in *Scotland*. Yet fhe appeared earneft. I anfwered, they were both the faireft Ladies in their Countries; that her Majefty was whiter, but my Queen was very lovely. She inquired which of them was of higheft ftature? I faid, my Queen: Then, faith fhe, fhe is too high, for I my felf am neither too high nor too low. Then fhe asked what kind of exercifes fhe ufed? I anfwered that when I received my difpatch, the Queen was lately come from the High-land hunting. That when her more ferious affairs permitted, fhe was taken up with reading of Hiftories: That fometimes fhe recreated her felf in playing upon the Lute, and Virginals. She asked if fhe played well? I faid reafonably for a Queen.

That fame day after Dinner my Lord of *Hunfdean* drew me up to a quiet Gallery, that I might hear fome Mufick, but he faid that he durft not avow it, where I might hear the Queen play upon the Virginals: After I had hearkned awhile, I took by the Tapiftry that hung before the door of the Chamber, and feeing her back was toward the door, I entered within the Chamber, and ftood a pretty fpace hearing her play excellently well, but fhe left off immediately, fo foon as fhe turned her about and faw me. She appeared to be furprized to fee me, and came forward, feeming to ftrike me with her hand, alledging fhe ufed not to play before Men, but when fhe was folitary to fhun melancholly. She asked how I came there? I anfwered, as I was walking with my Lord of *Hunfdean*, as we paft by the Chamber door, I heard fuch melody as ravifhed me, whereby I was drawn in e're I knew how, excufing my fault of homelinefs, as being brought up in the Court of *France*, where fuch freedom was allowed; declaring my felf willing to endure what kind of punifhment her Majefty fhould be pleafed to inflict upon me for fo great an offence. Then fhe fate down low upon a Cufhion, and I upon my knees by her, but with her own hand fhe gave me a Cufhion, to lay under my knee, which at firft I refufed, but fhe compelled me to take it. She then called for my Lady *Strafford* out of the next Chamber, for the Queen was alone. She inquired whether my Queen or fhe played beft? In that I found my felf obliged to give her the praife. She faid my *French* was good, and asked if I could fpeak *Italian*, which fhe fpoke reafonably well. I told her Majefty I had no time to learn the Language perfectly, not having been above two Months in *Italy*. Then fhe fpake to me in *Dutch*, which was not good; and would know what kind of Books I moft delighted in, whether Theology, Hiftory, or Love matters? I faid, I liked well of all the forts. Here I took occafion to prefs earneftly my difpatch, fhe faid I was weary fooner of her company, then fhe was of mine. I told her Majefty that though I had no reafon of being weary, I knew my Miftrefs her affairs called me home, yet I was ftayed two days longer, till I might fee her Dance, as I was afterward informed. Which being over, she inquired of me whether she or my Queen Danced beſt? I anſwered, the Queen Danced not ſo high, and diſpoſedly as ſhe did. Then again ſhe wiſhed, that ſhe might ſee the Queen at ſome convenient place of meeting. I offered to convey her ſecretly to *Scotland* by Poſt, clothed like a Page, that under this diſguiſe ſhe might ſee the Queen as *James* the Fifth had gone in diſguiſe to *France* with his own Ambaſſadour, to ſee the Duke of *Vendom's* Siſter, who ſhould have been his Wife. Telling her that her Chamber might be kept in her abſence, as though ſhe were ſick; that none needed to be privy thereto except my Lady *Strafford*, and one of the Grooms of her Chamber: She appeared to like that kind of Language, only anſwered it with a ſigh, ſaying, alas if I might do it thus. She uſed all the means ſhe could, to oblige me to perſwade the Queen of the great love ſhe did bear unto her, and that ſhe was fully minded to put away all jealouſies and ſuſpicions, and in times-coming to entertain a ſtricter friendſhip then formerly. She promiſed that my diſpatch ſhould be delivered to me very ſhortly at *London*, by Secretary *Cicil*: For now ſhe was at *Hampton Court*, where ſhe gave me my anſwer by mouth her ſelf, and her Secretary by writing.

The next day my Lord of *Leiceſter* deſired me to go down the River in his Barge with him to *London*. He had in his company Sir *Henry Sidney* Deputy of *Ireland*. By the way my Lord entered familiarly into diſcourſe with me, alledging that he was well acquainted with my Lord of *Murray*, *Lidingtoun*, and my Brother Sir *Robert*, and that he was by report ſo well acquainted with me, that he durſt upon the Character he had heard of me, deſire to know what the Queen my Miſtreſs thought of him, and the marriage that Mr. *Randolph* had propoſed. Whereunto I anſwered very coldly, as I had been by my Queen commanded. Then he began to purge himſelf of ſo proud a pretence, as to marry ſo great a Queen, declaring he did not eſteem himſelf worthy to wipe her Shoes, declaring that the invention of that propoſition of marriage proceeded from Mr. *Cicil* his ſecret Enemy. For if I, ſays he, ſhould have appeared deſirous of that marriage, I ſhould have offended both the Queens, and loſt their favour. He intreated me to excuſe him at her Majeſties hands, and to beg in his Name, that ſhe would not impute that matter to him, but to the malice of his Enemies.

Being landed at *London*, our Dinner was prepared by the Earl of *Pembroke*, who being great Maſter, yet humbled himſelf ſo far as to ſerve the ſaid Table, as Maſter of the Houſhold himſelf. He was a devout friend to my Queens Title of ſucceeding to the Crown of *England*.

After Dinner, I took leave of the *French* Ambaſſadour, and the *Spaniſh*, having received divers advertiſements from them. My Lord of *Leiceſter*, beſide what he had ſpoke to me, did write to my Lord of *Murray* to excuſe him at the Queens hands. The day appointed I received my diſpatch from Secretary *Cicil*, together with a Letter of Credit and a more ample Declaration of the Queens mind, touching the ſame anſwers ſhe had made me her ſelf. He gave me alſo a Letter to Secretary *Lidingtoun*. For as is above ſaid, Secretary *Cicil*, and

Leicefter, my Lord of *Murray,* and Secretary *Lidingtoun* ruled both Queens, and as yet kept good correfpondence together. When I took my leave, Secretary *Cicil* conveyed me through the Clofe, to the outer Gate of the Palace, where he himfelf put a fair Chain about my Neck. My Lady *Lennox,* and Sir *Nicholas Throgmorton* fent many good advices to the Queen, to be followed according as occafion offered. My Lady *Lennox* fent alfo Tokens, to the Queen a Ring with a fair Diamond ; fhe fent an Emerauld to my Lord her Husband, who was yet in *Scotland*; a Diamond to my Lord of *Murray* ; a Watch fet with Diamonds and Rubies to the Secretary *Lidingtoun* ; a Ring with a Ruby to my Brother Sir *Robert.* For fhe was ftill in good hope, that her Son my Lord *Darnly,* would come better fpeed concerning the marriage of our Queen, then the Earl of *Leicefter.* She was a very wife and difcreet Matron, and had many favourers in *England* for the time.

At my return, I found the Queens Majefty ftill at *Edinbrugh.* To whom I declared at large my manner of proceding with the Queen of *England,* and gave her Majefty her anfwers to the fpecial heads of my inftructions in writing.

Her Majefty anfwered to the firft, that whereas the Queen thought the time very long fince fhe received either word or writ from her, whereby fhe might underftand of her good eftate, and had fent me thither to vifit her in her behalf, that she thought the time as long, albeit fhe had conceived fome difpleafure concerning the angry Letter. Which was the greater, in refpect it appeared that fhe difdained the offer of the beft good fhe had to give, to wit, the Man whom fhe efteemed as her Brother. And whereas fhe had fent me to vifit her, fhe was more fatisfied with my coming, then fhe would have been with any other, being formerly of her acquaintance, with whom fhe could the more familiarly declare her inward mind to the Queen my Miftrefs; feeing fhe could not meet with her felf, fo foon as fhe defired. As I might declare how familiarly fhe had conferred with me, acquainting me with all her inward griefs and defires, and how well fhe was fatisfied, and how willing to continue all good offices of amity, and that fhe would for that effect, fend fhortly down to the Border, Commiffioners, who were named by her felf, to meet with my Lord of *Murray* and *Lidingtoun.*

As for the Parliament, it was yet in doubt whether it held or not. If it held, the Queen fhould get no hurt in her Right, neither directly nor indirectly, but fhe fhould be forewarned in due time.

Then I fhewed her Majefty at length, of all other purpofes that fell out occafionally betwixt that Queen and me, together with the opinions and advertifements of divers of her friends in *England,* as well Catholicks as Proteftants. I gave her, at the defire of the *Spanifh* Ambaffadour, the intimation of his Kings good will toward her.

Her Majefty was very glad that matters were brought again to this pafs, between her and the Queen of *England,* having thereby occafion of getting intelligence from a great number of Noblemen, and others her friends in *England.* For fhe was alfo afraid, that the blame of the difcord, would have been laid upon her if it had continued.

After

After that her Majefty had at great length underftood all my management and proceedings in *England*,. fhe inquired whether I thought
that Queen meant truly toward her inwardly in her heart, as fhe appeared to do outwardly in her fpeech. I anfwered freely, that in my
judgment, there was neither plain dealing, nor upright meaning, but
great diffimulation, emulation and fear, left her Princely qualities
fhould over foon chace her from the Kingdom, as having already hindered her marriage with the Arch-duke *Charles* of *Auftria*. It appeared likewife to me, by her offering unto her with great appearing
earneftnefs my Lord of *Leicefter*, whom I knew at that time fhe could
not want.

Shortly after my Lord of *Murray* and *Bedford* met near *Berwick*; to
treat concerning the marriage with *Leicefter*, with flenderer offers,
and lefs effectual dealing then was expected. But the faid Earl of *Lei-*
cefter had written fuch difcreet and wife Letters unto my Lord of *Mur-*
ray for his excufes, that the Queen appeared to have fo good liking to
him, as the Queen of *England* began to fufpect that the faid marriage
might take effect. Her apprehenfions of this, occafioned the Lord
Darnly his getting more readily licenfe to come to *Scotland*, in hope
that he being a handfome lufty youth, fhould rather prevail, being
prefent, then *Leicefter* who was abfent. Which licenfe was procured
by the means of the Secretary *Cicil*, not that he was minded that any
of the marriages fhould take effect, but with fuch fhifts to hold the
Queen unmarried fo long as he could. For he perfwaded himfelf, that
my Lord *Darnly* durft not proceed in the marriage without confent
of the Queen of *England* firft obtained to the faid marriage, his Land
lying in *England*, and his Mother remaining there. So that he
thought it lay in the Queen his Miftrefs her own hand, to let that
marriage go forward, or to flay the fame at her pleafure. And in cafe
my Lord *Darnly* fhould difobey the Queen of *Englands* command,
to return upon her call, he intended to caufe for fault him whereby
he fhould lofe all his Lands, Rights, and Titles that he had in *Eng-*
land.

The Queens Majefty, as I have faid before, after her returning out
of *France* to *Scotland*, behaved her felf fo Princely, honourably, and
difcreetly, that her reputation fpread it felf in all Countries. She was
determined, and of her felf inclined to continue fo unto the end of
her life, defiring to entertain none in her company, but fuch as were
of the beft converfation, abhorring all vice and vicious perfons. In
this her refolution fhe defired me to affift her by affording her my
good counfel, what way was moft effectual to ingratiate her felf with
her Subjects. And in cafe fhe (being yet young) might forget her
felf by any unfeemly gefture or mif-behaviour, that I would warn her
thereof, by admonifhing her to forbear and timoufly reform the fame.
Which Commiffion I did at firft altogether refufe to accept of, faying.
That her vertuous actions, her natural judgment, and the experience.
fhe had learned in the Court of *France*, had inftructed her fo well, and
qualified her fo abundantly, to be an example to all her Subjects and
Servants, that fhe needed none to admonifh her. But fhe would not
leave it fo, but faid fhe knew fhe had committed divers errours, upon
no ill meaning, only for want of the admonition of loving and con-

cerned friends. Becaüse that the greateſt part of Courtiers commonly flatter Princes, to infinuate for their favour, and will not tell them
the truth, fearing thereby to diſoblige them. Therefore ſhe adjured
and commanded me to accept that charge, which I ſaid was a very
ruinous Commiſſion, begging her Majeſty to lay that burthen upon
her Brother my Lord of *Murray*; and the Secretary *Lidingtoun*. She
anſwered, ſhe would not take it in ſo good part from them, as from
me. I ſaid, I was afraid that through proceſs of time, it would cauſe
me to loſe her favour. She ſaid, it appeared I entertained an ill opinion of her conſtancy and diſcretion: which opinion ſhe doubted not
but I would alter, after I had undertaken, and praĉtiſed that friendly
and famiiliar charge. In the mean time ſhe made me privy to all her
moſt urgent affairs, but chiefly to her dealings with any foreign
Nation. She ſhewed unto me all her Letters, thoſe which ſhe received from other Princes. She deſired me to write in her favour, to
ſuch Princes as I had been acquainted with, and to ſuch forreign Councellors as I knew to be eminent Men. In which Letters, I did not
omit to ſet out her vertues. I uſed to ſhew to her their returns, which
ordinarily gave me an accompt of the moſt remarkable occurrences of
thoſe Countries, to her Majeſties great contentment. For ſhe was of
a quick ſpirit, curious to know and get intelligence of the ſtate of other
Princes. She was ſomething ſad when ſolitary, and was glad of the
company of ſuch as had travelled to other Kingdoms.

    Now there came here in company with the Ambaſſadour of *Savoy*,
one *David Rixio* of the County of *Piedmout*, who was a merry fellow, and a good Muſician. Her Majeſty had three Valets of her
Chamber who ſung three parts, and wanted a Baſs to ſing the fourth
part. Therefore they told her Majeſty of this Man, as one fit to make
the fourth in Conſort.

    Thus he was drawn in to ſing ſometimes with the reſt, and after-
ward when her *French* Secretary retired himſelf to *France*, this *David*
obtained the ſaid office. And as he thereby entered in greater credit,
ſo he had not the prudence how to manage the ſame rightly. For
frequently in preſence of the Nobility, he would be publickly ſpeaking to her, even when there was greateſt Conventions of the States.
Which made him to be much envied and hated, eſpecially when he
became ſo great, that he preſented all ſignatours to be ſubſcribed by
her Majeſty. So that ſome of the Nobility would frown upon him,
others would ſhoulder and ſhut him by, when they entered the Queens
Chamber, and found him always ſpeaking with her. For theſe who
had great Aĉtions of Law, new inteſtments to be taken, or who deſired to prevail againſt their Enemies at Court, or in Law Suits before
the Seſſion, addreſſed themſelves to him, and depended upon him,
whereby in ſhort time he became very rich. Yet he wanted not his
own fears, therefore he lamented his eſtate to me, asking one day my
counſel how to behave himſelf. I told him that ſtrangers were commonly envied, when they medled too much in the affairs of other
Countries. He ſaid he being Secretary to her Majeſty in the *French*
Tongue, had occaſion thereby to be frequently in her Majeſties company, as her former Secretary uſed to do. I anſwered again that it
was thought that the greateſt part of the affairs of the Countrey paſt
through

through his hands, which gave offence to the Nobility. I advifed him
in their prefence to retire from the Queen, giving them place. And
that he might defire the Queen to permit him to take that way, I
told him for an example, how I had been in, fo great favour with the
Elector Palatine, that he caufed me to fit at his own Table, and that
he ufed frequently to confer with me in prefence of his whole Court;
whereat divers of them took great indignation againft me : Which fo
foon as I perceived, I requefted him to permit me to fit from his own
Table with the reft of his Gentlemen, and no more to confer with
me in their prefence, but to call me by a Page to his Chamber, when
he had any fervice to command me. Seeing otherwife he would prejudge himfelf and me, both by giving ground of difcontent to his
Subjects, in too much noticing a ftranger, and fo expofe me to their
fury. Which I obtained, and that way my Mafter was not hated, nor
I any more envied. I advifed him to take the like courfe, if he was
refolved to act as a wife Man. Which counfel he faid he was refolved
to follow, but afterward told me that the Queen would not fuffer
him, but would needs have him carry himfelf as formerly. I anfwered, that I was forry for the inconveniencies that might follow thereupon. And afterward finding the envy againft *Rixio* ftill to increafe,
and 'that by his ruine which I did forefee to be inevitable, her Majefty might Incur difpleafure, and her affairs be prejudged, feeing I clearly perceived that the extraordinary favour fhe carried to that Man,
did much alienate the hearts of her own Subjects from her. I remembred her Majefties' command lately laid upon me, when fhe particularly injoined me, to forewarn her, of any circumftance to be obferved
in her carriage, which I thought could tend to her prejudice. I had
before this time taken fome fuch freedom, in defiring her to defift
from fome things which I knew were diffatisfactory to her Subject,
and upon my acquainting her Majefty therewith, fhe had been pleafed to reform them. The reflection hereupon, incouraged me the
more cheerfully, in hope of the like fuccefs, to forewarn her Majefty
of the inconveniencies I did clearly forefee would inevitably follow, if
fhe in time did not alter her carriage to *Rixio*. Therefore upon the
firft opportunity, I took occafion to enter with her Majefty upon
this difcourfe, in moft humble manner reprefenting, what I did upon
rational confiderations conjecture would be the confequences, of
the too publick demonftrations of favour, fhe gave to *Rixio*, a ftranger,
and one fufpected by her Subjects to be a penfioner of the Pope. That
though they were refolved not to challenge her Majefties Religion,
though contrary to theirs, allowing her Liberty of Confcience, yet
it was not to be fuppofed, but the too much owning of *Rixio*, a known
Minion of the Pope, would give ground of fufpicion, that fome defign to the prejudice of the Eftablifhed Religion, would be by him
contrived. That to prevent this; her Subjects would find themfelves
obliged, to ufe all their endeavours to ruine a Man, and a ftranger,
from whom they could expect no good office, as being a known
Enemy to their Religion. For the Nobility would certainly take it
as an high affront upon them, to fee her fo vifiby more countenance
a ftranger, then them her native Subjects. I told her her Majefty very
freely what advice I had given to *Rixio*. She anfwered me, that he
medled

medled no further then in her *French* writings, and affairs, as her
other *French* Secretary had done formerly. And that whoever found
fault therewith, she would not be so far restrained, but that she might
dispence her favours to such as she pleased. I remembred her Majesty what displeasure had been procured to her, by the rash mis-behaviour of a *French* Gentleman called *Chattellier*, who transported to
miscarry himself by her affability, had thereby highly injured her Majesty. I told her Majesty that a grave and comely behaviour toward
strangers, not admitting them to too much familiarity, would bring
them to a more circumspect and Reverend carriage. I told her, how
necessary it was, that she particularly noticed all her actings, seeing
those of her Subjects who were not of her Religion, were easily allarumed with any thing which could be therein misrepresented. That
if their hearts were once lost there would be great difficulty of re-
gaining that place in their affections, which yet they found her due
as their Sovereign Princess. She thanked me for my continual care,
evidenced in this free advice, and ingaged to take such order in reference thereto, as the case required.

I have already told, how that my Lord *Darnly* was advised to ask
License to come unto *Scotland*. At his first coming he found the
Queen at *Weems*, making her progress through *Fiffe*. Her Majesty
took very well with him, and said, That he was the properest and
best proportioned long Man that ever she had seen ; for he was of a
high Stature, long and small, even and straight. He had been from
his Youth well instructed in all honest and comely exercises. After
he had haunted Court some time, he proposed marriage to her Majesty, which proposal she at first appeared to disrelish, as that same day
she her self told me, and that she had refused a Ring, which he then
offered unto her. I took occasion freely hereupon to speak in his favours, and to convince her Majesty, that no marriage was more her
interest then this, seeing it would render her Title to the Succession
to the Crown of *England* unquestionable. I know not how he came
to fall in acquaintance with *Rixio*, but I found he also was his great
friend at the Queens hand, so that she took ay the longer the better
liking of him, and at length determined to marry him. This being
made known to the Queen of *England*, she sent and charged him to
return. She also sent her Ambassadour Sir *Nicholas Throgmorton* to
Scotland, to disswade the Queen from marrying him, and in case the
Queen would not follow her advice, to perswade the Lords, and so
many as were of the Protestant Religion, to withstand the said marriage, till the said Lord *Darnly* should subscribe a Bond to maintain
the Reformed Religion, which he had ever professed in *England*.

The Queen again perceiving the Queen of *Englands* earnest opposition to all the marriages that offered unto her, resolved to delay no
longer. But my Lord Duke of *Chattellerault*, my Lords of *Argile*,
Rothes, *Murray*, *Glencairr*, and divers others Lords, and Barons, with-
stood the said marriage. Who after they had made an Essay to take
the Lord *Darnly* in the Queens company at the Raid of *Baith*, and as
they alledged, to have sent him to *England*, Failing in this their enterprise, they took them to the fields to her Majesties great dissatisfaction, and heart-breaking. Her Majesties Forces were sooner ready
than

then theirs, so that she persued them here and there, whereby they were so straitned that they could never have the opportunity of drawing together. And at length, they were compelled to flee unto *England* for refuge to her, who by her Ambassadours had promised to hazard her Crown in their defence, in cafe they were driven to any strait, because of appearing against the said marriage. Though this was expresly denyed them, when coming to demand help. For when they sent up my Lord of *Murray* to that Queen, the rest abiding at *New-castle*, he could obtain nothing but disdain and scorn, till at length he and the Abbot of *Kilwinning* his Companion in that message, were perswaded to come and confess unto the Queen upon their knees, and that in presence of the Ambassadours of *France* and *Spain*, that her Majesty had never moved them to that opposition and resistance against their Queens marriage. For this she had desired to satisfie the said Ambassadours, who both alledged in their Masters names, that she had been the cause of the said Rebellion, and that her only delight was to stir up dissention among her Neighbours. Yet by this cunning, she overcame them. For she handled the matter so subtilly, and the other two so cowardly, in granting her desire contrary to what was truth, being put in hopes relief, if they would so far comply with what was judged her interest for the time, that she triumphed over the said Ambassadours for their false allegiance. But unto my Lord of *Murray*, and his neighbour, she said, now you have told the truth, for neither did I, nor any in my Name stir you up against your Queen. For your abominable Treason, may serve for example to my own Subjects to rebel against me. Therefore get you out of my presence, you are but unworthy Traytors. This was all the reward they procured at her hands, and had not some of the Protestants in her Kingdom, who favoured them upon accompt of their Religion, interposed what they could with her, they would not have been permitted, during their banishment, to have remained within her dominions. Although a little before, she had promised to give them what assistance they demanded to the uttermost of her power, upon condition that they would please her so far, as to sit down upon their knees in presence of the said Ambassadours, and make the foresaid false confession. And as for secret help, she gave them none, only they obtained a small contribution among some of their own Religion there, who were their friends, which was distributed among them at *New-castle*, where they remained comfortless, and in great trouble.

The Queen finding the shifts the Court of *England* made to delay her marriage with any Man proposed, hasted forward her marriage with my Lord *Darnly*, which was solemnized in there Palace of *Haly-rood*-House, within the Queens Chappel at the Mass, wherein *Rixio* was no small instrument. *Scotland* being by this time almost wholly of the Reformed Religion, took a dislike of the King, because of this, he having formerly professed the Reformed Religion in *England*. Hence were occasioned rumours, that there was some design on foot, for planting again in *Scotland* the Roman Catholick Religion, there being ground of suspicion, that *Rixio* was a Pensioner of the Popes. And at this same time, the Pope sent Eight Thousand Crowns in Gold

I   to

to be delivered to our Queen, which augmented thefe fufpicions. But
the Ship wherein the faid Gold was, did Ship-wrack upon the Coaſt
of *England*, within the Earl of *Northumberland's* bounds, who alledged the whole to appertain. to him by juſt Law, which he caufed his
Advocate to read unto me (when I was directed to him for the demanding reſtitution of the faid Sum) in the old *Norman* Language.
Which neither he nor I underſtand well, it was fo corrupt. But all
my intreaties were ineffectual, he altogether refuſing to give any part
thereof to the Queen, albeit he was himſelf a Catholick, and otherwife profeſſed fecretly to be her friend.

After that the Queens Majeſty had married my Lord· *Darnly*, ſhe
did him great honour her felf, and defired every one who expected
her favour, to do the like, and to wait upon him. So that for a little
time, he was well accompanied; and fuch as fought favour by him,
fped beſt in their Suits. But becaufe he had married without advice
of the Queen of *England*, my Lady *Lennox* his Mother was committed to the Tower of *London*, where ſhe was kept for a long time.

All this time I attended ſtill upon the Queen, but with lefs familiarity then formerly. And feeing my ſervice for the time no more
needful, humbly begged liberty of the Queen to return to *France*, and
other places, where I had fpent the greateſt part of my life. But this
her Majeſty abfolutely refufed to grant, expreſſing fome defire to know
what could move me to defert her fervice. I faid the time was full of
fufpicions, and that I was confident I could do her more fervice abroad
then at home as matters had fallen out. She anfwered, that ſhe knew
I could do her more fervice at home, then any Servant ſhe had if I
pleafed, but that I had left off ufing my wonted freedom with her in
giving her my opinion of her proceedings. I told her Majeſty I was
fomewhat apprehenfive that my opinions would be unpleafant to her,
but ſhe affirmed the contrary, telling me that I had Enemies, who
ufed their endeavours to imprint a bad Character of me in the King,
as if I had been a favourer of the Earl of *Murray*, which ſhe had put
out of the King's head, as being better acquainted with my nature
and conditions: Saying, that ſhe knew well that I had a liking to the
Earl of *Murray*, but not to his actings of taking up Arms againſt her.
That ſhe was affured that I loved her ten times better then him. She
faid moreover, that if any did endeavour to mifreprefent her as much
to me, that ſhe wiſht I ſhould give them no more credit againſt her,
then ſhe had done, or ſhould do againſt me. She advifed me to wait
upon the King, who was but young, and give him my beſt counfel,
as I had formerly done to her, which might help him to ſhun many
inconveniencies. And ſhe gave me her hand, that ſhe would take all
in good part whatever I did fpeak, as proceeding from a loving and
faithful Servant. Defiring me alfo to befriend *Rixio*, who was hated
without a caufe. The King alfo told me, who they were who had
fpoken to him in my prejudice. And faid they were known to be
fuch common lyars, as their tongue was no ſlander. By thefe and fuch
like means, the Queens Majeſty obliged me more and more to be careful, to be ferviceable to her. And I judged my felf ingaged as the
greateſt demonſtration I could give of my being faithful to her, to
give her my opinion, what ufe ſhe might make for her own advantage,

of

of the harfh ufage the Earl of *Murray* and his affociates had received
in *England.* How uncourteoufly that Queen had ufed them before the
French and *Spanifh* Ambaffadours, fhe having broken all her fair promifes unto them.

Firft, I told her Majefty that ever fince her return to her own
Countrey, fhe had been endeavouring to get her Nobility and whole
Subjects, intirely affected to take part with her in all actions whatfoever, and chiefly againft *England* in cafe fhe might have occafion of
imploying them. Though fhe could never hitherto obtain her defire,
becaufe of the fecret bond and promife was made among them, when
the *Englifh* Army was at the Siege of *Lieth,* helping to put the *Frenchmen* out of *Scotland.*

Now, faid I, Madam the occafion is offered, whereby your Majefty
may bring your defired intention to pafs, if you could find in your
heart either to pardon the Earl of *Murray,* and his affociates, or at
leaft to prolong the Parliament, wherein they are to be forfaulted untill your Majefty may duly advife, and fee whether it will be more
your intereft to forfault them, or give them ground of hope of obtaining your pardon, according to their carriage for the future. To this
fhe anfwered, now when they could do no better, they fought her ; but
when fhe fought their concurrence, fuch as Subjects owe to their native Prince, they would not hear her, no more would fhe now notice
their Suits. I faid, whenfoever they were to make their Suits it
fhould not be by me, but this I propofe of my felf to your Majefty,
who can choofe the beft, and leave the worft in all accidents. Seeing
it is no little matter to gain the whole hearts of all your Subjects, and
alfo of a good number in *England,* who favour them and their Religion, who would admire fuch Princely vertues. When they fhould
fee fo pregnant a proof of your Majefties being able to Mafter your
own paffions and affections, all will then conclude, that you were moft
worthy to reign over Kingdoms, finding you fo ready to forgive, and
fo loath to ufe vengeance, efpecially againft Subjects already vanquifh-
ed, and not worthy of your wrath. If your Majefty confider ferioufly, clemency at fuch a time will be found moft convenient, and that
part of Juftice called Equity, more profitable then rigour. For extremity frequently brings on defperate enterprifes. At this her Majefty entred into choller, faying, I defie them, what can they do or
what dare they do ? Madam, fays I, with your Majefties pardon, my
propofition is in obedience to your own Commandment; to fhew you
my opinion at all times for the weal of your affairs. Then fhe faid
fhe thanked me, granting that it was a good advice, and neceffary to
be done, if fhe could in fo far command her felf. But that yet fhe
could not find in her heart to have to do with any of them upon divers confiderations, intreating me neverthelefs to continue giving her
my advice at all occafions. For albeit fhe did not follow this, fhe
might perchance do better at another time. I anfwered, that it was
only the confideration of her intereft, that made me appear fo concerned. Many Noblemen being banifhed, and fo near as *Newcaftle,* having many other Noblemen at home, of their kindred and friends, fo
malecontent, as I knew them to be for the time, made me fear fome
attempt towards an alteration. For I told her, I had heard dark fpee-

ches, that we fhould hear news e're the Parliament was ended. Her Majefty anfwered, that fhe likewife wanted not advertifements of the like rumours, but that our Countrey-men were talkative. I ufed the fame freedom with *Rixio*, for then he and I were under great friend-fhip. But he evidenced a difdain at all danger, and defpifed coun-fel, fo that I was compelled to fay, I feared over late Repen-tance.

You have heard that Sir *Nicholas Throgmorton* was one of the two *Englifh* Ambaffadours who were fent hither to ftay the marriage, and to make many promifes in his Miftreffes Name, to fo many as would re-fift the fame, which promifes were afterward denied by the Queen of *England*, and by Mr. *Randolph*. But Sir *Nicholas Throgmorton* ftood neither in awe of Queen or Council, to declare the verity, that he had made fuch promifes to them in her Name, whereof the Coun-cellors and craftieft Courtries thought ftrange, and were refolving to punifh him for avowing the fame promife to be made in his Miftreffes Name, had not he wifely and circumfpectly obtained an Act of Coun-cil for his Warrant, which he offered to produce. And the faid Sir *Nicholas* was fo angry that he had been made an inftrument to de-ceive the *Scots* banifhed Lords, that he advifed them to fue humbly for pardon at their own Queens hand, and to ingage never again to offend her for fatisfaction of any Prince alive. And becaufe as they were then ftated they had no intereft, he penned a perfwafive Letter, and fent unto her Majefty as followeth.

" **Y**Our Majefty hath in *England* many friends of all degrees, who
" favour your Title, but for divers refpects. Some for very
" Confcience fake, being perfwaded, that in Law your Right is beft ;
" fome for the good opinion they have conceived, by the honourable
" report they have heard of your vertues and liberality, the confidera-
" tion whereof ingageth them to efteem your Majefty moft worthy to
" Govern ; fome for factions, who favour your Religion ; fome for the
" ill will they bear to your competitour, feeing their own danger if
" Lady *Katharine* fhould come in that place.

" Of thefe, fome are Papifts, fome Proteftants, and yet however they
" differ among themfelves, in Religion or other particulars, they are
" both of one mind for the advancement of your Title. Your Ma-
" jefty hath alfo divers Enemies for various refpects, not unlike to the
" other, whofe ftudy hath always been, and will be, unlefs they be
" made friends, to hinder any thing that may tend to your advantage.
" In one point all concur, both Friends and Enemies, yea the whole
" People, that they are moft defirous to have the fucceffion of the
" Crown declared and affured, that they may be at a certainty, only the
" Queen her felf is of a contrary opinion, and would be glad the matter
" fhould always be in fufpence.

" Your un-friends have done what they could, to take the ad-
" vantage of the time, to your prejudice. And for that end, preffed
" the holding of the Parliament, which was before continued till *Octo-*
" *ber* laft. Knowing affuredly, that if the Parliament held, the Suc-
" ceffion of the Crown would be called in queftion. And they thought
" the time ferved well for their purpofe, when there was divifion and
" trouble

" trouble in your own Realm, and no good underſtanding betwixt
" you and the Queen of *England*. And her Subjects your friends, for
" eſchewing that inconvenience and winning of time to give your
" Majeſty place to work, and remove all impediments, ſo far as wiſdom
" may have found the means to drive it oft till the next ſpring. Now
" their advice is, that in the mean time your Majeſty indeavour by
" wiſdom to aſſure your ſelf of the whole Votes, or at leaſt of the beſt
" and moſt conſiderable of the Parliament, when ever the matter ſhall
" be brought in queſtion. Which may be done, by retaining the hearts
" of thoſe you have gained already, recovering of thoſe who are bran-
" gled, winning of the neutrals, and ſo many of your adverſaries as
" may be gained; for it is not to be ſuppoſed that all can be won who
" are already, ſo far addicted to the contrary Faction, but when the cauſe
" of their averſion is removed the effect will ceaſe.
" Generally your Majeſty will do well to forbear any act that will
" offend the whole people, and uſe ſuch means as will render you moſt
" acceptable to them. Strangers are univerſally ſuſpected to the whole
" people, againſt which your Majeſty hath in your marriage wiſely
" provided, by abſtaining to match with a forreign Prince. So do they
" adviſe your Majeſty to abſtain from any League or Confederacy, with
" any forreign Prince that may offend *England*, till you have firſt eſ-
" ſayed what you can purchaſe by the benevolence of the born Sub-
" jects thereof. Not that they would deſire your Majeſty to forfeit
" your friendſhip with *France*, and *Spain*, but rather that you ſhould
" wiſely entertain them both to remain at your devotion, in caſe at-
" terward you have need of their favour. Nevertheleſs it is their wiſh
" that the ſame may rather remain in generalterms as heretofore, then
" that you proceed to any ſpecial act which may offend *England*,
" which you cannot with honour bring back again when you would.
" As many of oour acverſaries as are addicted to the contrary Faction
" for hatred of your Religion, may be gained when they ſee your Ma-
" jeſty continue in the temperance and moderation you have hitherto
" uſed, within your own Realm in matters of Religion, without inno-
" vation or alteration. As many as by miſreports have been carried
" to the contrary Faction, may by true report be brought back again,
" when they ſhall hear of your clemency uſed towards your own Sub-
" jects, which vertue in Princes, of all others, moſt allures the hearts of
" people to favour, even their common Enemies. As many as can
" deal warily and diſcreetly with your friends of both the Religions,
" and are only addicted for Conſcience ſake to my Lady *Katharine*,
" being perſwaded of the preference of your Title in Law, may be gai-
" ned to your Majeſty by contrary perſwaſions, and by adducing of
" ſuch reaſons and arguments, as may be alledged for proof of your
" good cauſe, whereof there are abundance to be had. Some your
" Majeſty will find in *England*, who will hazard as far as they dare,
" to ſerve your turn in this behalf. But becauſe it is ſo dangerous to
" Men to deal in, and may endanger Lives and Lands, if they be ſeen
" earneſt medlers, travelling in that point ſo as would be neceſſary, it
" will require ſuch inſtruments of your own when time comes, who
" may boldly ſpeak without danger, and with whom the Subjects of
" *England* dare freely communicate their minds, and enter into con-
" ference.

" ference. If any be afraid of your Majefty, thinking that you have
" an ill opinion of them, the affurance by a trufty Minifter of your
" good will, whom they may credit, will quickly put them out of
" doubt and make them favourable enough. They who are conftant-
" ly yours, are eafily retained at your devotion : Thofe who hereto-
" fore have born any favour, and by the late occurrences are any way
" brangled, will be brought home again, when they fhall fee your
" Majefty, now when it is fallen in your hands to ufe rigour or mer-
" cy, as you pleafe, rather incline to the moft plaufible part, in fhew-
" ing your magnanimity, when you have brought your Subjects to
" fubmiffion and gentlenefs, as the good Paftour to reduce his Sheep
" that were gone aftray home again to the fold. Thofe who are yet
" neutrals, by the fame means, and true information of your intereft
" by Law, may all be won to your fide. This done, when the mat-
" ter comes in queftion, your friends will earneftly prefs your intereft
" at this Parliament, and you will without controverfie bear it a-
" way.
" This device, in fo far as concerns your reconciliation with your
" Subjects, is not a fetch for their favour, but is thought expedient for
" your fervice by many who have no favour for them, and are dif-
" ferent from them in Religion. For it will bring the Queen of *Eng-*
" *land* greatly to favour you, when fhe fhall fee fuch an Union in your
" own Kingdom, of the Head and whole Members together. She will
" not know how to difturb your Majefties eftate, efpecially when the
" Reconciliation takes effect in the hearts of the Subjects in *England*,
" who will think themfelves in an happy condition, if they fhould
" come under the Government of fo benign a Princefs who can fo rea-
" dily forgive great offences. For albeit it muft be acknowledged that
" my Lord of *Murray*, hath by his inconfiderate carriage given your
" Majefty great ground of offence, yet it is hard to perfwade the Pro-
" teftants, that your quarrel againft him hath any other foundation,
" then that he differs from you in Religion. Upon this ground, they
" find themfelves engaged to efpoufe his quarrel. If then they per-
" ceived your Majefty gracioufly inclined to take him again unto fa-
" vour, and forgive what is by paft, the Proteftants in *England* would
" doubtlefs declare themfelves more affectionate to your intreft, when
" they fhall fee more of their own Religion fo clemently handled.
" And that your Majefty may have experience, that it is your advance-
" ment your friends would by this means procure, and not the advan-
" tage of thofe with whom your Majefty is offended, a middle way
" may be followed, as is frequently ufed in fuch like cafes, where not
" only the multitude is fpared, but the chief authors are preferved. It
" may pleafe your Majefty to caufe a Letter to be pen'd in good terms
" and form, and publifh the fame by Proclamation, declaring the juft
" caufe of your anger againft all of them ; and that yet for declaring
" your own good nature above their defervings, you are content to re-
" mit the whole, except fuch principles as you pleafe to referve and ex-
" cept by name from the general Pardon. And that with whom you
" will not take fuch fevere order as you might in Law, till you have
" further tryal and experience of their Penitence. The perfons fo to
" be nominated and excepted fhall depart out of *England*, to what Coun-
" trey

" trey pleafeth your Majefty; there to remain during your pleafure.
" In this mean time, if your Majefty find that this benign ufage of
" yours, fhall produce fuch fruit as is here fpoken, your Majefty may
" further extend your favour, as you find convenient and profitable for
" your felf. For your Majefty hath ftill the crimes lying above their
" heads. In the mean time all who favour them in *England*, will
" plead in their caufe with your Majefty, fo far as their power extends
" as if they were Agents for your Majefty. They will in no ways, if
" they can efchew it, be again in the Queen of *Englands* debt, neither
" by obtaining of any favour at your hand by her intervention, nor yet
" for any fupport in the time of their banifhment. But rather it may
" pleafe your Majefty, that their charges be allowed them of their own
" Lands. By following this advice, which in no ways can be prejudi-
" cial to your Majefty, but will much conduce for your intereft, you
" may recover the greateft part of the Bifhops of *England*; many of
" the greateft Nobility and Gentlemen, who are yet Neutral.

Their Names were declared to her Majefty in Cypher, by whofe
means he alledged her Majefty fhould obtain fo great rn intereft in
England, that albeit that Queen would appear againft her, fhe needed
not to care. For in fending but one thoufand Men of her own, out
of four parts of *England*, a fufficient number fhould join with them;
by whofe forces, without any ftrangers, her Majefty fhould obtain the
thing which is wrongfully refufed and retained.

When her Majefty had ferioufly pondered this difcourfe, it had
great influence upon her, to move her to follow the defire thereof, as
well for the good opinion fhe had of him who fent it, as being of her
own nature more inclined to mercy then rigour; fhe being alfo wife,
and being convinced that it tended to the advancement of her affairs
in *England*. She was therefore fully refolved to have followed the
advice thereof, and to prolong the Parliament which had been called
to forfault the Lords who had fled. *Rixio* appeared alfo to have been
gained for counfelling her hereto. My Lord *Murray* had fued to him
very earneftly, and more humbly then could have been believed, with
the prefent of a fair Diamond inclofed within a Letter, full of repentance and fair promifes, from that time forth to be his Friend and Protector. Which the faid *Rixio* granted to do with the better will,
that he perceived the King to bear him little good will, and to frown upon him.

Following this advice and advertifement given by Sir *Nicholas Throg-*
morton, the Queens Majefty fent my Brother, Sir *Robert Melvil*, to remain her Ambaffadour in Ordinary at the Court of *England*, to be
ready at all occafions in cafe any thing were treated at the Parliament
concerning the Succeffion, and to purfue the Defign laid down by Sir
Nicholas, and her other friends in *England*.

In this mean time, there was a *French* Gentleman fent home here ;
called Mounfieur *d' Villamonte*, with a Commiffion to treat with the
Queen, that in no wayes fhe fhould fhew any favour to the proteftant
banifhed Lords. Becaufe that all Catholick Princes were bandied to
root them out of all *Europe*. Which was a device of the *Cardinal* of
Lorrain lately returned from the Councel of *Trent*. He had caufed
                                                                    the

the King of *France*, to write earnesty to that effect. Which unhappy Message, occasioned divers tragical accidents. For the Queen was loath to offend her friends in *France* of the house of *Guise*, albeit she would have done little at that time by her own pleasure to satisfie the King of *France* who was but young and only guided by his Mother whom she had no good cause to like well of. But *Rixio* was thought also not to think fit to offend so many Catholick Princes confederated, and especially the Pope with whom he had secret intelligence. Hereby the Queen was again induced to hold the Parliament to forfault the banished Lords, against her own intention and her former deliberation. Now there were a number of Lords at home, friends to the Lords who were banished, as the Earl of *Mortoun*, the Lord *Ruthven*, the Lord *Lindsay*, and divers other Gentlemen who favoured them only for their Religion, some of them were discontent, that their friends should be fortaulted, others had special reasons inducing them to fear the Sitting of that Parliament. Especially the Earl of *Mortoun*, and his dependers feared a revocation that was alledged to be made at the said Parliament, to bring back again to the Crown divers great dispositions given out during the Queens minority, and some benefices which had been taken by Noblemen at their own hands during the Civil-Wars under pretext of Religion. These and such considerations, moved them to consult together how to get the Parliament stayed, and to make a change at Court. The Earl of *Mortoun* had a crafty head, and had a Cousin called *George Douglass;* the natural Son to the Earl of *Angus*, who was Father to Dame *Margaret Douglass* Countess of *Lennox*, the King's Mother. The said *George* was continually about the King, and by his Mother, and Brothers means, put in his head such suspicions against *Rixio*, that the King was prevailed with to give his consent to his slaughter. This the Lords of *Mortoun*, *Lindsay*, *Ruthven*, and others had devised, to become that way Masters of the Court and so to stop the Parliament.

The King was yet very young, and not well acquainted with the nature of this Nation. It was supposed also, that the Earl of *Lennox* knew of the said design. For he had his Chamber within the Palace, and so had the Earl of *Athol*, *Bothwel* and *Huntly*, who escaped, by leaping over a Window toward the little Garden where the Lyons were lodged. This vile act was done upon a *Saturday* at six a-Clock at night, when the Queen was at Supper in her Closet. A number of Armed Men entered within the Court, before the closing of the Gates, and took the Keys from the Porter. One part of them, went up through the Kings Chamber, conducted by the Lord *Ruthven* and *George Douglass;* the rest remained without, with drawn Swords in their hands, crying, *A Douglass, A Douglass.* The King was before gone up to the Queen, and was leaning upon her Chair, when the Lord *Ruthven* entered with his Helmet upon his Head, and *George Douglass,* and divers others with them, so rudely and irreverently, that the Table, Candles, Meat and Dishes were overthrown. *Rixio* took the Queen about the waste, crying for mercy, but *George Douglass* plucked out the Kings Dagger and stroke *Rixio* first with it, leaving it sticking in him. He making great shrieks and cryes, was rudely snatcht from the Queen, who could not prevail either with threats or

intreaties,

intreaties, to fave him. But he was forcibly drawn forth of the Clofet and flain in the outer Hall, and her Majefty kept as a Captive. That fame night the Earl of *Athol*, the Laird of *Tullibardine*, and Secretary *Lidingtoun*, and Sir *James Balfour* were permitted to retire themfelves out of the Palace, and were in great fear of their lives. The next morning being *Sunday*, I was let forth at the Gate, and paffing through the outer Clofe, the Queen being looking forth at a Window, cryed unto me to help her. I drew near, and affured her of all the help that lay in my power. She defired me with all hafte to go to the Provoft of *Edinbrugh*, and defire him to convene the Town to relieve her out of thefe Traytors hands. But run faft, fays fhe, for they will ftay you. As this word was fpoken, one Mr. *Wisbet*, Mafter of the Houfhold to the Earl of *Lennox*, was fent with a Company to ftay me. To whom I gave good words, faying, that I was only going to Sermon at St. *Giles's* Church. But I went in hafte to the Provoft, and told him my Commiffion from the Queen. He anfwered, That he had another commandment from the King, but that he fhould draw the people to the *Tolbooth*, and fee what they would do, though he expected no help from their hands, becaufe the moft part of them were fo difcontent with the prefent Government, that all defired a change. Yet he convened them, though in vain. Which backwardnefs of theirs, I did intimate to her Majefty, by one of her Ladys, whom fhe fent again unto me, to tell me that fhe fuppofed my Lord of *Murray* and his affociates, who were yet banifhed, remaining at Newcaftle, would be fent for by thofe who were about her. Willing me at his coming, to perfwade him not to join with thofe who had fo highly affronted her, but to hold himfelf free, and be her friend in this ftrait, which doing fhould be his great advantage and purchafe her love and favour for ever. Which commiffion I did not fail to execute at his coming upon *Monday*, but he was more moved at his meeting with her Majefty, who imbraced and kiffed him, alledging that if he had been at home he would not have fuffered her to have been fo uncourteoufly handled. Which fo much moved him, that the Tears run from his eyes. He knew fufficiently well that it was not for his caufe, but for their own particular ends, that the greateft part who had made that enterprife had therein ingaged, which made him the lefs concerned in them. Yet he and his Company refolved to keep the day, againft which they were fummoned to the Parliament.

In the mean time, the King repented himfelf of his acceffion to that affair, whereupon her Majefty took occafion to perfwade him to abandon thofe Lords, who had committed fo odious a crime, as to hazard her life, together with her Child which was in her Belly. That neverthelefs fhe was refolved to forgive them, and give them what fecurity thereupon they would demand. The Lords feeing the King drawn from them, and my Lord of *Murray* not fo frank for them as they expected, were neceffitated to do the next beft, and confented that a pacification fhould be penned, which was divers times written over, to put in and out certain heads and claufes, to drive time until the writing might appear plaufible. Her Majefty caufed the King to advife tnem, to difcharge the Guard that kept her, that fo the fecurity might be fubfcribed, fhe being at liberty. Seeing otherwife it

K would

would not avail them in Law, if there were the leaft appearance of re-
ftraint upon her, during the time thereof. So upon *Tuefday* they went
all to their reft, but the Queen, King, *Traquair*, and *Arthur Areskin*
Mafter of the Horfe for the time, went out of *Halirood*-Houfe at midnight toward the Caftle of *Dumbar*, and left word with one of her Ladies to me, that I fhould be earneft to keep the Earl of *Murray* from
joining with the other Lords. Who the next morning found themfelves greatly difappointed being left without any appearance of a pacification. In the mean time, I ufed my endeavours very effectually
to keep my Lord *Murray* from joining with the late offenders. I ingaged to him, that in fo doing, I fhould procure a pardon to him, and
all his followers. They on this manner being deftitute of all affifters,
were compelled to flee unto *England* to *Newcaftle*, where in a manner
they might find the other Lords nefts yet warm.

A few days before, my Lord *Duke*, my Lords of *Glencairn* and *Rothes* had obtained their pardons. For they were divided during their
banifhment, and her Majefty found it not her intereft to have fo many Lords againft her. She had alfo now again indeavoured to draw
the Earl of *Murray* from the Earl of *Mortoun*, and his accomplices, becaufe he had for the time a great friendfhip and many dependers, that
fhe might be the more eafily revenged upon that moft deteftable deed
of murthering her Servant in her prefence. For fhe being big with
Child, it appeared to be done to deftroy both her and her Child.
For they might have killed the faid *Rixio* in any other part, at any
time they pleafed. My Lord *Murray* and his dependants, defired me
to carry their humble thanks unto her Majefty, and to fignifie unto
her, how willingly they acquiefced to her Majefties defire, and how
they had difcharged themfelves to fuch as had committed that vile
act. And that they promifed her Majefty never any more to have to
do with them, or intercede for them.

I rencountred her Majefty coming from *Dumbar* to *Hadingtoun*,
and was very favourably received with great thanks for my care of
her honour and welfare. That night in *Hadingtoun* fhe fubfcribed divers remiffions for my Lord *Murray* and his dependers, lamenting unto me the King's folly, ungratitude, and misbehaviour. I excufed the
fame the beft I could, imputing it to his youth, which occafioned him
to be eafily led away by pernicious Councel, laying the blame upon
George Duglas and other bad Councellors, praying her Majefty for many neceffary confiderations, to remove out of her mind any prejudice againft him, feeing that fhe had chofen him her felf againft the
opinion of many of her Subjects. But I could perceive nothing from
that day forth, but great grudges that fhe entertained in her heart.
That night in *Hadingtoun*, the King inquired of me, if the Lord of
Murray had written to him. I anfwered, That his Letter to the Queen
was written in hafte, and that he efteemed the Queen and him but one.
He faid, he might have alfo written to me. Then he enquired what
was become of *Mortoun*, *Ruthven* and the reft of that Company. I
told him, I believed they were fled, but I knew not whither. As they
have Brewed, fays he, fo let them drink. It appeared to me that he
was troubled he had deferted them, finding the Queens favour but cold.
The next day they came to *Edinbrugh*, and lodged within the Caftle
　　　　　　　　　　　　　　　　　　　　　　　　　　　　where

where fome were apprehended and executed, who had been in the Court of the Palace, and had kept the Gates that night wherein *Rixio* was flain.

Her Majefty was now far gone with Child, and went to *Sterling*, intending to ly in there. Thither the King followed her, and from that to *Allway*. At length fhe came back to the Caftle of *Edinbrugh*. It was thought that fhe fled from the King's company. I travelled earneftly to help matters betwixt chem, and was therein fo importunate, that I was thought troublefome. So that her Majefty defired my Lord of *Murray* to reprove me, and charge me not to be any more familiar with the King : Who went up and down all alone, feeing few durft bear him company. He was mifliked by the Queen, and by all fuch as fecretly favoured the late banifhed Lords : So that it was a great pity to fee that good young Prince caft off, who failed rather for want of good Counfel and Experience, then from any bad inclinations. It appeared to be fatal to him, to like better of flatterers and ill Company then plain fpeakers and good Men : Which hath been the wrack of many Princes, who by frequenting good Company would have proved gallant Men.

About this time the Queen of *England* was taken with a great Fever, that none believed fhe could live : All that Kingdom was thereby in great perplexity. But a ftrange thing is to be marked, that two contrary Factions there, had both determined, unknown to other, to fend for our Queen, and fet the Crown of *England* upon her head. My Brother Sir *Robert Melvil* was then Ambaffadour there refident, and I ferved in place of Secretary here at home, becaufe Secretary *Lidingtoun* was abfent under fome fufpicion. He fent home continual advertifements how to proceed, and I again returned the anfwers at her Majefties direction.

Now began the Earl of *Rothvel* to be in great favour, to the great diffatisfaction of many. He and the Earl of *Huntly*, and the Bifhop of *Roffe*, envied the favour that the Queen fhewed unto the Earl of *Murray* ; for they were upon contrary courfes. The Queen on the other hand, knew how generally he was well liked of both in *England* and *Scotland*, and that fhe would be the better liked of in both Kingdoms that fhe fhewed favour to him. And as fhe refolved to follow the former advice and information fent her by Sir *Nicholas Throgmorton*, fo fhe forgat not the late help he had made her at his home-coming Thefe two Earl with the forefaid Bifhop, took occafion when the time of her Majefties delivery drew near, to perfwade her to imprifon my Lord of *Murray* ; to remain no longer then fhe fhould be delivered, alledging that they were affuredly advertifed, that he and his dependers were refolved to bring in the banifhed Lords, even at the very time of her Child-bearing : For they thought, if once he were warded, they fhould find devices enough to caufe him be kept, and difgraced, efpecially when he fhould be abfent, and not have opportunity of anfwering and refifting their Calumnies. Whereof her Majefty gave me an accompt, defiring me to mind her of their fecret defigns againft *Murray*, without any juft caufe, flowing only from their own hatred who had devifed his ruine.

The Earl of *Mortoun* was now in a hard condition, though many of the Barons of *Lauthran* were his friends, they could be little ſtedable to him. Among the reſt the Laird of *Elphingſtoun*, my Brother-in-law, whoſe Mother was a *Duglas* of the Houſe of *Whittengem*. Upon accompt of this friendſhip, the Earl of *Mortoun* cauſed to write unto my Siſter the Lady *Elphinſtoun*, deſiring her to perſwade me to write in his favours to the *Elector Palatine*, and other Princes of my acquaintance in *Germany*, to ſuffer him to live in their Country. For my Brother, by her Majeſties direction, preſſed the Queen of *England* to put them forth of her Kingdoms. And they durſt not go to *France*, where the Queen had ſo many friends. This I did ſhew unto her Majeſty that ſhe might be the more confirmed how groundleſs that report was, made by the aforeſaid Lords againſt *Murray*. Wherewith ſhe appeared well ſatisfied, reſolving to continue her kindneſs for my Lord *Murray*, but that withal ſhe charged me not to write in favours of *Mortoun*.

In the mean time, Mr. *Henry Killegrew* was ſent hither Ambaſſadour from the Queen of *England*, who was in great ſuſpicion of her eſtate, finding ſo many of her Subjects favourers of our Queen. The ſaid Ambaſſadour complained againſt one Mr. *Ruxbie*, who was harboured in *Scotland*, being a Rebel and a Papiſt : Declaring how that the Queen his Miſtreſs had commanded *Mortoun* and his Complices forth of her Country : Which was done by open proclamation, to pleaſe the Queen and her Ambaſſadour, who cryed out continually for her ſuffering them to abide ſo long in *England* : Yet as we afterward underſtood, they were ſecretly over-lookt, upon condition that they would keep themſelves quiet. Mr. *Killegrew* alledged alſo that the Queens Majeſty had been practiſing with *Oneel* in *Ireland*, who had his Ambaſſadour preſently in *Edinbrugh*, in company of the Earl of *Arguile*. And Thirdly he complained of ſome diſorders upon the Borders, made by *Scottiſhmen*. But the principal pretext of his Commiſſion, was to comfort the Queen over her late troubles, to congratulate her freedom, and good ſucceſs over her wicked and rebellious Subjects.

It may appear ſufficiently by that Queens former proceedings, that all the Siſterly familiarity was ceaſed, and in place thereof nothing but jealouſies, ſuſpicions and hatred. And yet they kept an outward correſpondence, for keeping up Neighbourhood and Intelligence. The *Scots* Ambaſſadour for the time in *England*, had ſo good hap that his credit was great, for he was eſteemed ſure and ſecret. Which cauſed a great number of the Nobility, Proteſtants and Papiſts to Communicate their inward minds, and ſecreteſt intentions unto him. Mr. *Randolph* had not the like credit in *Scotland*, but only with ſome of the ſimpleſt ſort of the Miniſters. For this *Ruxbie* was ſent in hither to appear to be a zealous favourer of her Majeſties Right and Title to the Crown of *England*. He was to endeavour to ſpeak with the Queen, and to take an occaſion of informing her Majeſty of the great friendſhip divers of the Catholicks had for her, who durſt not deal with the *Scots* Ambaſſadour being a Proteſtant ; but that he would deal himſelf betwixt her Majeſty, and them. All this was to eſſay what he could draw out of her Majeſty to give advertiſement thereof to Secretary *Cicil*. He addreſſed himſelf unto the Queens Majeſty
by

by the Bifhop of *Rofs*, who was a Catholick. The faid Bifhop defire-
ing her Majefty to be fecret. What he learned for the time I cannot
tell, but he did write fundry intelligences unto the Secretary *Cicil*,
which did prejudice. But this fine contrivance was not fo fecretly
kept, but my Brother Sir *Robert* had knowledge thereof, and alfo of a
Letter that the Secretary *Cicil* wrote again unto *Scotland*, to the faid
Mr. *Ruxbie* promifing to fee him rewarded, and defiring him to continue in his diligence. Of all which my Brother by his good intelligence was fo well advertifed, that in due time he gave her Majefty
and me information thereof. He gave his advice, how to carry for
the future in that affair. So that when Mr. *Killegrew* made his complaint upon the receit of Mr. *Ruxbie*, her Majefty incontinently caufed
him to be apprehended, and all his Cyphers and Writings, among the
which was found the Letter written by Secretary *Cicil* above-mentioned. *Ruxbie* finding himfelf difcovered, fell immediately upon his
knees, granting himfelf worthy of a thoufand deaths, humbly craving
pardon. Her Majefty caufed him to be fo fecretly and ftraitly kept,
that the *Englifh* Ambaffadour could get no intelligence for what caufe
he was apprehended, until that the Queen did fhew him her felf, that
upon his complaint to fatisfie the Queen her good Sifter, fhe had caufed to apprehend the faid *Ruxbie*, who fhould be delivered fo foon after his return as it fhould pleafe her Sifter to fend for him.

But as this Mr. *Ruxbie*, was fecured, fo was the complaint made
againft him kept fecret. For her Majefty was advifed, to appear altogether ignorant of any of his practifes againft her devifed by Secretary *Cicil*, it not being thought her intereft to put that fhame upon
one who profeffed fo much to be her friend. Nor was it time to caft
off intelligence, fo long as it was found profitable to entertain it, as it
would have indeed proved, had not fuch unhappy chances fallen out
fhortly after,

The Queens Majefties reckoning being near run out, fhe caufed me
to difpatch for *England*, to be in readinefs to give an accompt of the
news of her delivery to that Queen; leaving a Blanck in her Letter
to be filled up either with a Son or a Daughter, as it fhould pleafe God
to grant unto her. And to require the Queen of *England* to fend hither in her name, fuch of hers as fhe knew to be beft inftruments for
entertaining good love and friendfhip betwixt them, to be Goffips, as
alfo to fatisfie her concerning the moft part of *Killegrew*'s demands.

All the while I lay within the Caftle of *Edinbrugh*, praying night
and day for her Majefties good and happy delivery of a fair Son. This
prayer being granted, I was the firft who was thereof advertifed by
the Lady *Boin* in her Majefties Name to part with diligence the 19 *th.*
of *June* 1555 betwixt Ten and Eleven in the morning. By Twelve
of the Clock I took Horfe, and was that night at *Berwick*. The
fourth day after, I was at *London*, and did firft meet with my Brother
Sir *Robert*, who that fame night fent and advertifed Secretary *Cicil*
of my arrival, and of the Birth of the Prince, defiring him to keep
it quiet till my coming to Court to fhew it my felf unto her Majefty, who was for the time at *Greenwich*, where her Majefty was in
great mirth, dancing after Supper. But fo foon as the Secretary *Cicil* whifpered in her Ear the news of the Prince's birth, all her mirth
was

was laid fide for that night. All prefent marvelling whence proceeded fuch a change, for the Queen did fit down putting her hand under
her Cheek, burfting out to fome of her Ladies, That the Queen of *Scots*
was Mother of a fair Son, while fhe was but a barren ftock. The next
morning was appointed for me to get Audience, at what time my
Brother and I went by Water to *Greenwich*, and were met by fome
friends who told us how forrowful her Majefty was at my news, but
that fhe had been advifed to fhew a glad and cheerful countenance:
Which fhe did in her beft Apparel, faying, That the joyful news of
the Queen her Sifter's delivery of a fair Son, which I had fent her by
Secretary *Cicil*, had recovered her out of a heavy ficknefs which fhe
had lyen under for fifteen days. Therefore fhe welcomed me with a
merry volt, and thanked me for the diligence I had ufed in hafting
to give her that welcome intelligence. All this fhe faid, before I had
delivered unto her my Letter of Credence. After that fhe had read
it, I declared how that the Queen had hafted me towards her Majefty as one whom fhe knew of all her friends, would be moft joyful of
the glad news of her delivery, albeit dear bought with the peril of her
life, fhe being fo fore handled that fhe wifhed fhe had never been married. This I faid by the way to give her a little fcare from marriage.
For fo my Brother had counfelled me, becaufe fometimes fhe boafted
to marry the Arch-duke *Charles* of *Auftria*, when any Man preffed her
to delare a fecond perfon. Then I requefted her Majefty to be a Goffip to the Queen, to which fhe gladly condefcended. Your Majefty,
faid I, will now have a fair occafion to fee the Queen, whereof I have
heard your Majefty fo oft defirous. Whereat fhe fmiled, faying, fhe
wifhed that her eftate and affairs might permit her In the mean time.
fhe promifed to fend both honourable Lords and Ladies to fupply her
room.   Then I gave her Majefty, in my Queen's name, moft hearty
thanks, for her friendly vifiting and comforting her by Mr. *Henry
Killegrew*. She inquired if I had left him in *Scotland*, and what was the
caufe of his long ftay. I anfwered, That the Queen took her Chamber
fhortly after his arrival, which was the chief caufe of his delay. But
I had in Commiffion to tell her Majefty fomething thereabout, to fatisfie her mind in the mean time, and to thank her Majefty for the putting away of the *Scots* Rebels out of her Country, albeit there were
fome Reports that they were yet fecretly entertained by fome of her
Subjects, though I hardly believed that any of her Subjects durft be fo
bold, or fo difobedient. She affirmed they were out of her Dominions, and if it might be otherwife tryed out it fhould not pafs without rigorous punifhment. I told her Majefty, that upon her defire, and
Ambaffadours complaint, the Queen had caufed to apprehend Mr. *Ruxbie*, and had ordered him to be delivered to her Majefty whenever fhe
fhould pleafe to fend for him. And as concerning *Oneel*, fhe had no
dealing with him, nor knew that there had been any Servant of his
fent to my Lord *Arguile*, until Mr. *Killegrew*'s coming that fhe caufed
to enquire at the faid Earl, who acknowledged that *Oneel* had fent one
unto him about private purpofes betwixt themfelves, but that fhe did
neither fee nor fpeak with that Man, nor had any dealing with any
Man in *Ireland*.

Her

Her Majefty feemed to be well fatisfied with the matters of *Ireland*, and concerning Mr. *Ruxbie*, but fhe forgot to fend for him. Before I took my farewell in order to my return, I entered with her Majefty concerning the Title. For my Lord of *Leicefter* was become my Queens avowed friend, and had been twice in hand with the Queen of *England* a little before my coming, defiring her to declare my Miftrefs next Heir : Alledging it would be her greateft fecurity, and cried out in anger that *Cicil* would undo all. Likewife the Duke of *Norfolk*, the Earl of *Pembroke*, and feveral others, fhewed themfelves openly her friends, after they underftood the birth of the Prince. So that her Majefty's matters in *England* were hopeful ; and therefore I was advifed to fay unto her Majefty, That I was affured fhe had. formerly delayed the declaring the Queen fecond perfon, only till fhe might fee fuch Succeffion of her body as now God had gracioufly granted : intreating her Majefty to embrace that fair offered opportunity of fatisfying the minds of many, as well in *England* as in *Scotland*, who defired to fee that matter out of doubt. And the rather becaufe that the Queen my Miftrefs, would never feek any Place or Right in *England*, but by her Majefties favour and furtherance. She anfwered, That the birth of the Prince, was a great Spur to caufe the moft skilful Lawyers in *England*, to ufe greater diligence in trying out that matter, which fhe efteemed to belong moft juftly to her good Sifter, and that fhe wifhed from her heart that it fhould be that way decided. I replied, That at my laft being with her, I found her Majefty upon the fame tearms, but that as I had brought her good news from the Queen, I was very defirous to be fo happy as to carry home with me unto her Majefty, the good tydings of that fo long delayed Declaration. She anfwered, fhe was refolved to fatisfie the Queen in that matter, by thofe Noblemen fhe was refolved to fend unto *Scotland*, for the Baptifm of the Prince. All this I perceived to be but fhifts, and fo took my leave, becaufe my Brother was to remain there. The next day her Majefty fent unto me her Letter, with the Prefent of a fair Chain.

My Brother gave me the advice of her Majefties friends, together with his own inftructions how to proceed after my coming home as followeth.

Firft, that he is in fuch fufpicion for his handling there, by the advertifements of Mr. *Ruxbie*, and practifes of her Enemies, that her Majefty muft fignifie to Mr. *Killegrew* that fhe is minded fhortly to call him home, elfe he fears he fhall be commanded to return.

Secondly, That her Majefty require the Earl of *Leicefter* and Secretary *Cicil* to be fent to be her Goffips, as fitteft inftruments to perfect all Articles and good Offices of Amity betwixt them.

- *Item*, That Mr. *Killegrew* be well treated and rewarded, that he may make good report to hold off difcord, that intelligence may continue; and defire him to declare unto the Earl of *Leicefter*, and Secretary *Cicil*, that it cannot ftand with good friendfhip, to be fo long fed with fair woods without effect.

Item, That her Majefty caft not off the Earl of *Northumberland*, albeit as a fearful and facile man he delivered her Letter to the Queen of *England* ; neither appear to find fault with Sir *Henry Pearcie* as yet, for his dealing with Mr. *Ruxbie*, which he doeth to gain favour at
Court

Court, being upon a contrary faction to his Brother the Earl.

Item, That Mr. *Ruxbie* be well kept, and fent far North to fome fecure part that he give no hafty intelligence, for he hath already written unto Secretary *Cicil* by Sir *Henry Pearcy* his convoyance, that he can difcover all your practifes and fecrets.

Let my Lord *Arguile* entertain *Oneel* as of himfelf, the Queen not appearing to know thereof.

The Secretary *Cicil* devifed ftrange practifes againft the meeting, which becaufe my Lord of *Leicefter* difcovered unto the Queen his Miftrefs, *Cicil* ftirred up the Earl of *Suffex* to forge a quarrel againft him, but the Queen took the Earl of *Leicefter's* part, and finally agreed them, and alfo *Leicefter* and *Ormond.*

Item, That her Majefty fhould write two Letters with Mr, *Killegrew* to my Brother, the one that he might fhew unto the Queen of *England,* the other that he might fhew unto the Secretary *Cicil.*

Item, To advertife my Brother what he fhould do more for my Lady *Lennox,* whofe liberty might do much good.

Now to conclude, feeing the great mark which her Majefty fhoots at, let her Majefty be more careful and circumfpect that her defires being fo near to be obtained, be not all over-thrown for lack of fecrecy, good management, and Princely behaviour, having fo many factious Enemies lying in wait to make their advantage of the leaft appearance that can be made.

Shortly after my coming home Mr. *Killegrew* the *Englifh* Ambaffadour obtained his difpatch, with a friendly anfwer to his contentment, and a fair Chain ; and with him her Majefty fent thefe two Letters following to my Brother by his own advice that he might take occafion to let the Queen of *England* fee the one, and Mr. *Cicil* the other, partly to ferve to put fome doubts out of their minds ingendered by Mr. *Ruxbie's* advertifements, for, as I have faid, the Bifhop of *Rofs* made the faid *Ruxbie's* addrefs to the Queen, for neither he nor the Earl *Bothwel* defired her Majefties affairs to profper under my Brother's management, becaufe he was not of their Faction, fo that by their means *Ruxbie* got that intelligence as put all her Majefties affairs once in a venture, until my Brother's extraordinary intelligence from fuch as were moft intimate with the Queen of *England,* made him caufe to apprehend the faid *Ruxbie* with his whole Letters and Memoires ; as faid is, fo are many good Princes handled, and commonly their trueft Servants d court ed by the envy and craft of their factious Enemies, for wicked men who have loft their credit by trumpery and tricks, whereby they get no place to do good fervice to Princes, effay to creep unto their favour by wiles, flattery, and other unlawful means, whereby they may decourt fuch as furmount them in vertue, and honeft reputation, her Majefties Letter to my Brother was as followeth.

" TRufty and well-beloved, We Greet you well , Whereas your
"   Brother *James* hath told Us of the friendly and faithful advice
" given unto you and him, by Mr. Secretary *Cicil,* toward the conti-
" nuation of the amity betwixt the Queen Our good Sifter and Us, ten-
" ding alfo to Our own particular advantage ; We thought meet to fend
                                                                    " thefe

" thefe few lines to you, that you may thank him heartily in Our
" Name, and declare unto him our meaning and intention, as you find
" opportunity touching the three Points that he did mention at that
" time. ·

" The firft, as we underftand, touching our towardlinefs to them of
" the Religion. The fecond touching ftrict juftice to be obferved upon
" the Borders. The third,that we will endeavour by no other means to
" come to the Succeffion of the Crown of *England*,but by the favour and
" forth-fetting of our good Sifter.

" As to the firft, you fhall anfwer in Our name, That fince Our
" return out of *France* We have neither conftrained hor perfecuted any
" for caufe of Religion, nor yet minds to do ; their credit with Us be-
" ing fo manifeft, that they are intrufted with the principal Offices,
" and bear the chiefeft charges in the Kingdom, and principally imploy-
" ed in our moft urgent Affairs before all others : Sir *Nicholas Throg-*
" *morton* can teftifie what he hath feen and heard at his being here
" thereanent, howbeit that contrary Brutes are blown abroad by the
" malice and practifes of our Enemies. To the fecond , concerning
" the borders, it is moft certain that the principal Officers on both the
" fides are fpecial inftruments of all the diforders, taking occafion up-
" on Our late troubles, when as they perceived that we might not fo
" well take order with them, as We were willing ; as now when it
" hath pleafed God to grant unto Us more quietnefs. Defiring him
" alfo to procure at the Queen his Sovereign's hands that the like di-
" ligence be taken for her part as fhall be feen ufed by Us ; and then
" we doubt not but that both he, fhe and all other who complain
" fhall be fatisfied. As to the third and laft head, you fhall fhew unto
" him the tenor of Our other Letter, for fatisfaction to the Queen and
" Our other Friends in thefe parts. So with my friendly commenda-
" tions to him and his wife, I commit you to the protection of the Al-
" mighty. From the Caftle of *Edinbrugh* this Year 1566.

" TRufty and Well-beloved, We Greet you well. We have recei-
" ved great comfort and contentment by the Declaration your
" Brother hath made to Us, of the Queen Our good Sifter's continu -
" al affection and conftant love towards Us ; which fhe hath now
" fhewn unto you, and your Brother at his coming ; as alfo by her
" Letters unto Our Self : Likewife for the grant fhe hath made to
" be Our Goffip, and promifes to fend fo honourable a Company of
" Lords and Ladies, for folemnizing the fame in her Name ; for which
" in Our behalf you fhall give her Majefty moft hearty thanks, and
" fhew unto her that We defire nothing to be done therein, but as may
" conduce beft for her advantage, and leaft to her expence ; praying
" her always that the principal Man, whom it will pleafe her to fend,
" be fuch a one as We have by long experience known to have been
" moft familiar with her, to whom We may the more freely open
" Our mind, and fignifie divers things which We intended to have fpo-
" ken by mouth unto her felf if God had granted Our defired meeting.
" As concerning *Oneel, Ruxbie* and all other matters, We hope that Mr.
" *Killegrew* will fatisfie her fufficiently, and alfo how that We defire to

have

" have no advancement in that Country, but by her only means and
" help, hoping and intending fo to direct our courfe and behaviour
" toward her, as fhe fhall have caufe more and more to procure ear-
" neftly and carefully her felf, all things that may further Our Weal
" and Advancement, in this Country, that Kingdom, or any other. In
" the which hope We will do our beft to follow fuch meafures as may
" plea fe her, and to avoid all things that may offend her; and We
" give our moft ftrict command unto you to do the like, fo long as
" you remain there ; And wherever you be about Our fervice even as
" I gave you Commandment of before, neverthelefs in the mean time,
" entertain moft kindly and difcreetly all thofe in that Country who
" profefs to bear good will unto Us, and to our Title, yet in fuch fort
" as neither you nor they offend the Queen Our good Sifter: And
" if there chance to come to you any hafty or feditious perfons, ad-
" monifh them gently to ceafe, and if they forbear not, fhew unto
" them, that We have promifed to the Queen to declare the Names
" and Practifes of fuch unto her ; and that we will not fail to do it in-
" deed if they ceafe not: So fhall it be known, that fuch as are about
" to fow difcord between the Queen our good Sifter and Us, doth it
" rather upon particular refpects and for their own advantage, then for
" any defign to advance her Affairs or Ours.

Thefe kind of Writings were for that time devifed to overthrow and
caft down fome intelligences, which were difcovered by *Ruxbie*, and
fome reports raifed by Enemies, that my Brother by his practifes and
perfwafions had kindled a great fire, and had raifed a great faction in
England ; he did not deny but he had dealt with many to win what favour he could to his Miftrefs, but that he had done nothing that
could offend the Queen of *England*, and that he had no Commandment to enterprife any thing which could be difpleafing to her ; by this
means *Ruxbie's* intelligence was fuppreffed, and my Brother fuffered
to ftay ftill in *England*, whereby the Queens friends fo increafed, that
many whole Shires were ready to Rebell, and their Captains already
named by the Election of the Nobility.

About this time her Majefty was advertifed by my Brothers Letters, that the Earl of *Bedford* was upon his journey toward *Scotland*
with an honourable Company : As alfo the Ambaffadour of *France* and
Savoy for the Baptifm of the Prince, which moved her Majefty to pafs
to *Sterling* with the Prince, for the folemnizing thereof, but fhe was
ftill fad, and penfive for the late foul act committed in her prefence fo irreverently, fhe being their born Queen, and thereby in hazard of lofing the fruit of her Womb, fo many great fighs fhe would
give that it was pitty to hear her, and few there were to indeavour to
comfort her.

Sometime fhe would declare part her of grief to me, which I effayed the beft I could to affwage, by telling her that I thought the greater
multitude of friends that fhe had got in *England*, fhould caufe her
to forget in *Scotland* the leffer number of Enemies and unruly offenders, unworthy of her wrath, and that her excellent qualities in Clemency, Temperance, and Fortitude fhould not fuffer her mind to be
                                                                    poffeft

poſſeſt or ſuppreſt with the remembrance of offences, but that rather
ſhe ſhould bend up her ſpirit by a Princely and Womanly behaviour,
whereby ſhe might beſt gain the hearts of the whole people, both here
and in *England*, humbly requeſting her Majeſty firſt to conſult with
her God, next with her honour, and thirdly with her intereſt in the
eſtabliſhing of her ſtate, and in joining the two Kingdoms in a happy
Monarchy, which ſhe knew to be ſo near effectuate in her perſon, ſeeing alſo the baniſhed eſtate of the offenders ſo miſerable, they not having a hole to hide their head in, nor a peny wherewith to buy their
Dinner ; that the moſt noble natures would think them ſufficiently
puniſhed ; that it was a comely thing for a woman to be pitiful, and
to want vengeance. I leave it, ſaid I Madam, to your own judgment,
whether preſently it be more for your honour, and advancement of
your intereſt, to ceaſe from any deſire or purſuit of any further revenge, whereupon may enſue more deſperate enterpriſes, or to give
place unto neceſſity and reaſon to rule over the beaſtly paſſions
of the mind. For as Princes are called divine perſons, ſo no Prince
can pretend to this Title but he who draws near the nature of God
by godlineſs and good Government, being ſlow to vengeance and ready to forgive. It is manifeſtly known that wiſe Princes entertain no
longer feud at their Enemies, then they ſee it may be needful for the
weal of their Affairs and State ; and they change their favour and hatred according to time and occaſions. Your Majeſty may remember
that many things might have been better managed, I ſpeak this with
love and reverence. Your Majeſty might have been as well obeyed
as ever was any King in *Scotland*, if you had taken ſuch Princely care
as was requiſite. You know how that by your Majeſties own expreſs
Commandment, I did ſhew you long before what inconveniencies were
like to fall out upon the grudges I perceived before the ſlaughter of
Rixio, and God is my witneſs I did what lay in my power to have
them eſchewed, and prevented. And ſince that time your Majeſty
hath repented that my advice was not followed : I pray God that the
like repentance fall not out again too late. At my being in *England*,
your adverſaries were beginning to vaunt upon vain reports, that our
Weſterly winds had blown Eaſt among them ; ſo that my Brother
and I had enough to do to beat it out of the heads of divers, who were
devotedly addicted to the advancement of your Title.

This communing began at the entry of her Supper in her Ear in
French, when ſhe was caſting up great ſighs, refuſing to eat upon any
perſwaſion that my Lord of *Murray* and *Mar* could make to her. The
Supper being ended her Majeſty took me by the hand, and went down
through the Park of *Sterling*, and came up through the Town, ever
reaſoning with me upon their purpoſes. And albeit ſhe took hardly
with them at the firſt, ſhe began to alter her mind, thinking fit that my
Lord of *Bedford* ſhould intercede for her Rebels ; they to be baniſhed
out of *England* and *Scotland* during her pleaſure, ſo to be by time
reconciled to them according to their future deportments, and for her
part ſhe purpoſed to proceed with ſuch a gracious Government, as
ſhould win the victory over her ſelf, and all her Competitours, and
Enemies in time coming : which ſhe could have done as well as any
Prince in Europe. But, alas, ſhe had bad Company about her, for

the Earl of *Bothwel* who had a mark of his own that he fhot at, as foon as he underftood of her wife and merciful deliberations, he took occafion to bring in the Earl of *Mortoun* and his affociates, thereby to make them his friends, and by them to fortifie his faction. For apparently he had already in his head the refolution of performing the foul murther of the King, which he afterwards put in execution, that he might marry the Queen. Both which he brought to pafs to his own utter wrack and confufion, and thereby great trouble and mifchief upon the Country ; and was alfo at laft the Queens wrack, and the hinderance of all our hopes in the hafty obtaining of all her defires concerning the Crown of *England*.

The Queens Majefty being advertifed that the Earl of *Bedford* was come to *Berwick* on his Journey to the Baptifm, fent me well accompanied with diligence to meet him at *Coldingham* to be his firft Convoy, and to inform him rightly of all her proceedings, and to overthrow all evil brutes invented by the malice of her adverfaries. For as I have faid, it was a perverfe time, and the more that the number of her friends increafed in *England*, the more practifes her Enemies made, and the more lyes were invented againft her. But the good Earl gave me more credit, then he did to any wrong report that was made. For he was at this time become one of the fureft and moft affectionate friends fhe had in *England*.

There came with him Mr. *Cary* eldeft Son to my Lord of *Hufdean*. Mr. *Hattoun* greateft in favour with the Queen of *England* for the time, and one called Mr. *Lignifh* greateft in favour with the Duke of *Norfolk*, and a good number of Knights and Gentlemen of *York-fhire*. with the moft part of the Captains of *Berwick*. Her Majefty was fufficiently informed by my Brother's writing to her and me, what kind of language and entertainment was moft proper for the Earl, and each of them.

When all the reft of the Ambaffadours were come, they repined to fee the *Englifh-men* more friendly and familiarly ufed then themfelves. For then we had more to do with *England* then with *France*. And the *French* Earl who was fent, was no Courtier, but a fimple Man. And *Monfieur de Morat* the Duke of *Savoy* his Ambaffadour being far off, came after the Baptifm. During their abode at *Sterling*, there was daily Banqueting, Dancing, and Triumph. • And at the principal Banquiet there fell out a great grudge among the *Englifh-men* ; for a *French-man* called *Baftien* devifed a number of Men formed like *Satyrs* with long Tails, and whips in their hands, running before the meat which was brought through the great Hall upon a Machine or Engine marching as appeared alone, with Muficians clothed like Maids, finging and playing upon all forts of Inftruments. But the *Satyrs* were not content only to make way or room, but put their hands behind them to their Tails, which they wagged with their hands in fuch fort as the *Englifh-men* fuppofed it had been devifed and done in derifion of them, weakly apprehending that which they fhould not have appeared to underftand : for Mr. *Hattoun*, Mr. *Lignifh*, and the moft part of the Gentlemen defired to Sup before the Queen and great Banquet, that they might fee the better the Order and Ceremonies of the Triumph. But fo foon as they perceived the *Satyrs* wagging their Tails, they all
                                                                    fate

fate down upon the bare floor behind the back of the Table, that they
might not fee themfelves derided as they thought. Mr. *Hatton* faid
unto me if it were not in the Queens prefence he would put a Dagger
to the heart of that *French* knave *Baftien*, who he alledged had done it
out of defpight that the Queen made more of them then of the *Frenchmen*. I excufed the matter the beft I could, but the noife was fo
great behind the Queen's back, where her Majefty and my Lord of
Bedford did fit, that they heard and turned about their faces to enquire
what the matter meant. I informed them that it was occafioned by
the *Satyrs*, fo that the Queen and my Lord of *Bedford* had both enough
to do to get them appeafed. It fell out unhappily at fuch a time, and
the *Englifh* Gentlemen committed a great overfight to notice it as
done againft them. But my Lord of *Bedford* was difcreet and interpreted all things to the beft.

My Lord of *Bedford* was rewarded with a rich Chain of Diamonds,
worth two thoufand Crowns ; Mr. *Cary* with a Chain of Pearl, and a
Ring with a fair Diamond; Mr. *Hattoun* had a Chain with her Majefties Picture, and a Ring ; Mr. *Lignifh* and five other of Quality had
each of them Chains. I was commanded with many others to attend
them towards the Road. They parted all very well content and fatisfied with the Queens Majefty, but lamented that they perceived the
King fo much flighted. My Lord of *Bedford* defired me to requeft
her Majefty to entertain him as fhe had done at the beginning, for her
own honour and the advancement of her affairs, which I forgot not to
do at all occafions.

After the Baptifm and parting of the Ambaffadours, her Majefty
defirous to put good order upon the Borders, fent the Earl of *Bothwel*
before, who in the purfuit of Thieves was hurt. Her Majefty paft afterward to *Jedbrug* her felf, where the Earls of *Bothwel* and *Huntly*
enterprifed the flaughter of the Earl of *Murray*, but the Lord *Hume*
came there with forces and prevented that enterprife. Her Majefty
returned by the *Merfe*, and defired to fee *Berwick* afar off, where fhe
was honoured with many fhots of Artillery, and Sir *John Fofter* Warden upon the *Englifh* Border came and conferred with her Majefty for
keeping of good order. And the mean time while he was fpeaking
with her Majefty on Horfe-back, his Courfer did rife up with his
formoft Legs, to take the Queens Horfe by the Neck with his Teeth,
but his Feet hurt her Majeftie's Thigh very ill. Incontinent the Warden lighted off his Horfe and fate down upon his knees craving her
Majefties pardon. For then all *England* did much reverence her ; her
Majefty made him to rife, and faid that fhe was not hurt, yet it compelled her Majefty to tarry two days at the Caftle of *Hoome* until fhe recovered again. The King followed her about whitherfoever fhe rode,
but got no good countenance. So that finding himfelf flighted, he
went to *Glafcow*, where he fell fick, it being alledged that he had got
poifon from fome of his Servants.

In the mean time the Earl of *Bothwel* ruled all at Court, having
brought home the banifhed Lords, and packed up a quiet friendfhip
with the Earl of *Mortoun*. After her Majefties return to *Edinburgh*,
fhe reconciled the Earls of *Huntly, Bothwel, Arguile* and others. From
that her Majefty went to *Sterling*, to fee the Prince, and returned again

to

to *Edinbrugh* whither the King was afterward brought, and lodged
in the Kirk-field, as a place of good Air, where he might beſt recover his health. But many ſuſpected that the Earl of *Bothwel* had
ſome enterprife againſt him, few durſt advertife him becauſe he told all
again to ſome of his own Servants, who were not all honeſt. Yet
Lord *Robert* Earl of *Orkny* told him that if he retired not haſtily out of
that place, it would coſt him his life,which he told again to the Queen;
and my Lord *Robert* denied that ever he ſpoke it. This advertiſement moved the Earl of *Bothwel*, to haſt forward his enterprize : he
had before laid a train of Powder under the Houſe where the King
did lodge, and in the night did blow up the ſaid Houſe with the Powder ; but it was ſpoken that the King was taken forth, and brought
down to a Stable, where a Napkin was ſtopped in his mouth, and he
therewith ſuffocated.

Every body ſuſpected the Earl of *Bothwel*, and thoſe who durſt
ſpeak freely to others, ſaid plainly that it was he. Whereupon he drew
together a number of Lords of his dependers to be an Aſſize, which
cleanſed and acquitted him ; ſome for fear, ſome for favour, and the
greateſt part in expectation of advantage. This way being aſſailed, he
remained ſtill the greateſt favourite at Court, My Lord of *Murray*
was retired from the Court ſeveral days before. Her Majeſty kept
her Chamber for a while. I came to the door the next morning after the murther, and the Earl of *Bothwel* ſaid that her Majeſty was
ſorrowful and quiet, which occaſioned him to come forth. He ſaid
the ſtrangeſt accident had fallen out which ever was heard of, for
Thunder had come out of the sky, and had burnt the King's Houſe,
and himſelf was found dead lying a little diſtance from the Houſe under a Tree. He deſired me to go up and ſee him, how that there
⸿was not a hurt nor a mark on all his Body. But when I went up to
ſee him he had been taken into a Chamber, and kept by one *Alexander Durham*, but I could not get a ſight of him.

The bruit began to riſe that the Queen would marry the Earl of
Bothwel, who had ſix months before married the Earl of *Huntly's* Siſter, and that for this deſign he was reſolved to part with his own Lady. Whereat every good Subject who loved the Queens honour, and
the Prince's ſafety, had ſore hearts, thinking thereby her Majeſty
would be diſhonoured, and the Prince in danger to be cut off by him
who had ſlain his Father. But few or none durſt ſpeak in the contrary ; yet my Lord *Herreis* a worthy Nobleman came to *Edinbrugh*
well accompanied, and told her Majeſty what reports were going
through the Country, of the Earl of *Bothwel's* murthering the King,
and how that ſhe was to marry him, requeſting her Majeſty moſt
humbly upon his knees to remember her honour and dignity, and
the ſafety of the Prince, which all would be in danger if ſhe married
the ſaid Earl, with many other great perſwaſions to ſhew the utter
wrack and inconveniencies would be thereby occaſioned. Her Majeſty appeared to wonder how theſe reports could go abroad, ſeeing,
as ſhe ſaid, there was no ſuch thing in her mind. He beg'd her Majeſties pardon, and prayed her to take his honeſt meaning in a good
part. And immediately took his farewell, fearing the Earl of *Bothwel* ſhould get notice thereof. He had fifty Horſe with him for the
                                                            time

time, and caufed each of them to buy a new Spear at *Edinbrugh* and
fo rode home.

I was refolved to have faid as much to her Majefty, but in the mean
time there came a Letter to me from one *Thomas Bifhop* a *Scottifhman*,
who had been long in *England*, and was a great perfwader of many
in *England* to favour her Majefties Title. He ufed oft to write unto
my Brother and me, informations and advertifements. At this time
in his Letter to me, he ufed even the like Language that my Lord
Harreis had fpoken, but more freely becaufe he was abfent in another
Country. He adjured me to fhew the faid Letter unto her Majefty,
declaring how it was bruited in *England* that her Majefty was to marry the Earl of *Bothwel*, who was the murtherer of her Husband, who
at prefent had a Wife of his own, a Man full of all Vice, which reports
he could not believe, by reafon that he judged her Majefty to be of far
greater knowledge, then to commit fuch a grofs overfight, fo prejudicial every way to her intereft, and the noble mark he knew fhe fhot
at : Seeing if fhe married him, fhe would lofe the favour of God, her
own reputation, and the hearts of all *England, Ireland* and *Scotland*,
with many other diffwafions and examples of Hiftory, which would
be tedious to rehearfe. I had been fome days abfent, but upon receipt
hereof I went to Court to fhew this Letter to her Majefty, protefting
that fhe would take it in good part.

After that her Majefty had read the faid Letter, fhe gave it me again
without any more fpeech, but called upon the Secretary *Lidingtoun*,
and told him that I had fhewed her a ftrange Letter, defiring him alfo
to read it. He asked what it could be. She anfwered, a device of his
own tending to the wrack of the Earl of *Bothwel*. He took me by
the hand and drew me afide to fee the faid Letter, which when he
had read he asked what had been in my mind, for, fays he, fo foon as
the Earl *Bothwel* gets notice hereof, as I fear he will very fhortly, he
will caufe you to be killed. I faid it was a fore matter to fee that good
Princefs run to utter wrack, and no body to be fo far concerned in her
as to forewarn her of her danger. He faid I had done more honeftly
then wifely , and therefore I pray you, fays he, retire diligently before the Earl of *Bothwel* comes up from his Dinner. Her Majefty
told him at her firft meeting, having firft ingaged him to promife to do
me no harm. Notwithftanding whereof, I was inquired after , but
was flown and could not be found till his fury was flaked : For I was
advertifed there was nothing but flaughter in cafe I had been gotten.
Whereat her Majefty was much diffatisfied, telling him that he would
caufe her be left of all her Servants, whereupon he renewed his ingage-
ments that I fhould receive no harm, whereof I being advertifed I
went again unto her Majefty, fhewing her that fhe had never fo much
injured me as by thinking that I had invented the faid Letter, affuring her that it came from the faid *Thomas Bifhop*, and that albeit it
had not come from him, I thought it my duty to have freely told her
Majefty my opinion in all reverence and humility, which was contained in the faid Letter, but I found fhe had no mind to enter upon
this fubject.

Shortly after her Majefty went to *Sterling*, and in her back-coming
betwixt *Lithgow* and *Edinbrugh*, the Earl of *Bothwel* rancountered her
with

with a great Company, and took her Majesties Horse by the Bridle, his men took the Earl of *Huntly*, the Secretary *Lidingtoun* and me, and carried us Captives to *Dumbar* : All the rest were permitted to go free. There the Earl of *Bothwel* boasted he would marry the Queen, who would or who would not; yea whether she would her self or not. Captain *Blachater* who had taken me, alledged that it was with the Queens own consent. The next day in *Dumbar* I obtained permission to go home. Afterward the Court came to *Edinburgh*, and there a number of Noblemen were drawn together in a Chamber within the Palace, where they all subscribed a paper, declaring that they judged it was much the Queens interest to marry *Bothwel*, he having many friends in *Louthian* and upon the Borders, which would cause good order to be kept. And then the Queen could not but marry him, seeing he had ravished her and lain with her against her will. I cannot tell how nor by what Law he parted with his own Wife, Sister to the Earl of *Huntly*.

A little before this the Earl of *Murray* had desired liberty to go to *France*, the Secretary *Lidingtoun* had been long in suspicion absent from Court, and was brought in again by my Brother *Sir Robert*'s perswasion, for the great credit and handling he had with many Noblemen in *England* favourers of her Majesties Title, albeit that he had as great credit himself yet he would not follow the custom of ambitious Courtiers who would ingross all to themselves, unwilling to suffer a Companion. He knew also that he was suspected, because the Earl *Bothwel* was not his friend. Thus *Lidingtoun* was again brought in ; but not long after the Earl of *Bothwel* thought to have slain him in the Queens Chamber, had not her Majesty come betwixt and saved him : but he fled the next day and tarried with the Earl of *Athol.* As for me I was not oft at Court but now and then, yet I chanced to be there at the marriage. When I came that time to the Court, I found my Lord Duke of *Orkny* sitting at his Supper who welcomed me, saying, I had been a great stranger, desiring me to sit down and Sup with him : the Earl of *Huntly*, the Justice, Clerk and divers others being sitting at Table, with him. I said I had already Supped, then he called for a Cup of Wine and drank to me, saying, you had need grow fatter, for, says he, the zeal of the Common-wealth hath eaten you up, and made you lean. I answered, that every little member should serve for some use, but the care of the Common-wealth appertained most to him, and the rest of the Nobility, who should be as Fathers of the same. I knew well, says he; he would find a pin for every bore. Then he fell in discoursing with the Gentlewomen, speaking such filthy language, that they and I left him, and went up to the Queen who expressed much satisfaction at my coming.

The marriage was made at the Palace in *Halyrood-house*, after Sermon by *Adam Bothwel* Bishop of *Orkny*, in the great Hall where the Council useth to sit, according to the order of the Reformed Religion, and not in the Chappel at the Mass as was the King's marriage.

After the marriage he who was Earl of *Bothwel* now Duke of *Orkny*, was very earnest to get the Prince in his hands, but my Lord of *Mar*, who was a true Nobleman, would not deliver him out of his custody, alledging

alledging that he could not without confent of the three States : Yet he was fo frequently croft by fuch as had the Authority in their hands; that he was thereby put to a great ftrait. And after that he had made divers refufals, among others he made his moan to me, praying me to help to fave the Prince out of his hands who had flain his Father, and had already made his vaunt among his familiars, that if he could get him once in his hands, he fhould warrant him from revenging his Father's death. I affured his Lordfhip he fhould want no affiftance I was capable to give : He defired to know if I could propofe any out-gate: I anfwered, That I was intimately acquainted with Sir James Balfour, and that I knew how matters ftood betwixt Bothwel and him, namely, there were fome jealoufies arifen betwixt them, which I thought if rightly managed, might be improved for the Prince's fafety. I alfo told him that the Earl intended to have the Caftle out of his hands, for the Earl and he had been great Companions; and he was alfo very great with the Queen, fo that the cuftody of the Caftle of Edinbrugh was committed to him : But afterward he would not confent to be prefent, nor take part with the murtherers of the King, whereby he came in fufpicion with the Earl of Bothwel, who would no more credit him, fo that he would have had the Caftle out of his hands, to have committed the charge thereof to the Laird of Beenftoun. I told his Lordfhip he might make this one of his excufes, That he could not deliver the Prince till he fhould fee a fecure Place to keep him in. And upon the other hand, when I returned to Edinbrugh, I dealt with Sir James Balfour not to part with the Caftle, whereby he might be an inftrument to fave the Prince and the Queen, who was fo difdainfully handled, and with fuch reproachful language, that in prefence of Arthur Aroskine, I heard her ask for a knife to ftab her felf, or elfe, faid fhe, I fhall drown my felf. Now, fays I, to Sir James Balfour, there is no fecurity for you to be out of fufpicion, but to keep the Caftle in your own hands, and fo to be the good inftrument both of faving Queen and Prince, and in affifting the Nobility who are about to Crown the Prince, and to purfue the Earl of Bothwel for the King's murther; I told him that unlefs he took part with them, he would be holden as guilty of the faid murther, by reafon of his long familiarity with the Earl of Bothwel : That it was a happy thing for him that the faid Earl was in fufpicion of him, affuring him that I had intelligence by one who was of the Earl of Bothwel's Councel, to wit, the Laird of Whitlaw, Captain of the Caftle of Dumbar, that the Earl of Bothwel was determined to take the Caftle of Ebinbrugh from him, and make the Laird of Beenftoun one Hepburn Captain thereof, and then to put the Prince there in his keeping.

Sir James Balfour gave ear to my propofition, and confented to help to purfue the murtherers, upon condition that the Laird of Grange would ingage upon his honour to be his Protector, in cafe afterward the Nobility fhould alter upon him, for he and moft of them had formerly run contrary courfes, fo that he durft not credit them.

The Earl of Mar being hereof from me advertifed, by his Brother Alexander Areskine, who was true and careful of the Prince's fafety, coming fecretly to me at midnight, for the days were dangerous for all honeft Men. Now my Lord of Mar being continually required,

M   and

and threat'ned to deliver the Prince out of his hands, at length granted
(only to drive off time) upon condition, that an honeft refponfible
Nobleman fhould be made Captain of the Caftle of *Edinbrugh*, the only fecure place of keeping the Prince in.   This anfwer was thought fit
to affwage the prefent fury, until the Nobility might convene to purfue the Murtherers, and to Crown the Prince, as they had already
concluded at a fecret meeting among themfelves, which was not kept
fo private but that one of the faid Lords gave advertifement thereof to
the Earl of *Bothwel* how that they were minded to inviron the place
of *Halirond-houfe*, and therein to apprehend him : Whereupon he forgot inquiring after the Prince, being only now concerned how to fave
himfelf : therefore he fled out of *Edinbrugh* to the Caftle of *Borthwick*;
from that to the Caftle of *Dumbar*, taking always the Queen with him
wherever he went.

All *Scotland* cryed out upon the foul murther of the King, but few
of them were careful how to revenge it, till they were driven thereto
by the crying out of all other Nations, againft all *Scotifhmen* wherever
they travelled, either by Sea or Land.   Among other Princes, the
King of *France* fent hither to his Ambaffadour *Monfieur de Crook*, a grave,
aged, difcreet Gentleman, advanced by the houfe of *Guife*, a Letter,
therein expreffing his wonder that fuch a foul murther being committed upon the perfon of a King, fo few honeft Subjects were found
to find fault with the fame, for lefs to feek after any tryal, or fee the
fame punifhed.   Whereupon the Lords who had the enterprife in
hand, were hafted forward, to take Arms, and in the mean time they
obliged themfelves by a writing under their hands, which they delivered to the faid *Monfieur de Crook* to fend to the King his Mafter, that
they fhould do their outmoft diligence to try out the Authors of that
foul murther of their King; and in the mean time convened to the
number of 3000 men, and came to *Edinbrugh* and there fet out a Proclamation of their juft quarrel.   Alfo fundry Libels were fet out both
in Rime and Profe, to move the hearts of the whole Subjects to affift
and take part in fo good a Caufe.

The Earl of *Bothwel* having the Queen in his Company, convened a
greater number out of the *Merfe*, and *Lauthian*; and out of all parts
where he had intereft or friendfhip.   Her Majefties Proclamation was
not well obeyed, and fo many as came, had no hearts to fight in that
quarrel.   Yet the Earl of *Bothwel* marched forward out of *Dumbar* toward *Edinbrugh*, taking the Queen with him.   The Lords again with
their Company went out of *Edinbrugh* on foot, with an earneft defire
to fight.   Both Armies lay not far from *Carberry*; the Earl *Bothwel's*
men Camped upon the Hill, in a ftrength very advantageous, the
Lords incamped at the foot of the Hill.   And albeit her Majefty was
there, I cannot call it her Army : for many of thofe who were with
her, were of opinion that fhe had intelligence with the Lords, efpecially
fuch as were informed of the many indignities put upon her by the
Earl of *Bothwel* fince their marriage.   He was fo beaftly and fufpici-
ous, that he fuffered her not to pafs one day in patience, without making her fhed abundance of Tears.   Thus part of his own Company
detefted him, other part of them believed that her Majefty would
fain have been quit of him, but thought fhame to be the doer thereof
directly her felf.   In

In the mean time the Laird of *Grange* did ride about the hill with two hundred horſe-men, who came there with *drumlanrig*, *Ceſſoord*, and *Couldinknows*, thinking to be betwixt the Earl of *Bothwel* and *Dumbar*, and was minded to make an onſet that way, which was plain, and that in the mean time that the Lords ſhould come up the Hill to the part where their adverſaries were Camped.

When the Queen underſtood that the Laird of *Grange* was chief of that Company of horſe-men, ſhe ſent the Laird of *Ormiſtoun* to deſire him to come and ſpeak with her under ſurety, which he did after he had acquainted the Lords with her deſire, and had obtained their permiſſion. As he was ſpeaking with her Maieſty, the Earl of *Bothwel* had appointed a Soldier to ſhoot him, until the Queen gave a cry, and ſaid that he would not do her that ſhame, ſeeing ſhe had promiſed that he ſhould come and return ſafely. He was declaring unto the Queen that all of them were ready to honour and ſerve her, upon condition that ſhe would abandon the Earl of *Bothwel*, who had murthered her Husband, and could not be a Husband unto her, who had but lately married the Earl of *Huntly's* Siſter. The Earl of *Bothwel* hearkened, and heard part of this language, and offered the Combat to any who would maintain that he had murthered the King. The Laird of *Grange* promiſed to ſend him an anſwer ſhortly thereunto. So he took his leave of the Queen, and went down the Hill to the Lords, who were content that the Laird of *Grange* ſhould fight with him in that quarrel. For he firſt offered himſelf, and acquainted *Bothwel* that he would fight with him upon that quarrel. The Earl of *Bothwel* anſwered, That he was neither Earl, nor Lord but a Baron, and ſo was not his equal. The like anſwer made he to *Tullibardine*. Then my Lord *Lindſay* offered to fight him, which he could not well refuſe, but his heart failed him, and he grew cold in the buſineſs. Then the Queen ſent again for the Laird of *Grange* and ſaid to him, that if the Lords would do as he had ſpoken to her, ſhe ſhould put away the Earl of *Bothwel*, and come unto them. Whereupon he asked the Lords if he might in their name make her Majeſty that promiſe, which they commiſſioned him to do. Then he rode up again, and ſaw the Earl of *Bothwel* part, and came down again and aſſured the Lords thereof. They deſired him to go up the Hill again, and receive the Queen, who met him, and ſaid, Laird of *Grange* I render my ſelf unto you, upon the conditions you rehearſed unto me in the name of the Lords. Whereupon ſhe gave him her hand, which he kiſſed, leading her Majeſties Horſe by the bridle down the Hill unto the Lords, who came forward and met her.

The Noblemen uſed all dutiful reverence, but ſome of the Raſcals cryed out againſt her deſpightfully, till the Laird of *Grange* and others who knew their duty better, drew their Swords and ſtruck at ſuch as did ſpeak irreverent language, which the Nobility well allowed of. Her Majeſty was that night convoyed to *Edinbrugh*, and lodged in the midſt of the Town in the Provoſts Lodging. As ſhe came through the Town, the common people cryed out againſt her Majeſty at the Windows and Stairs, which was a pity to hear. Her Majeſty again cryed out to all Gentlemen and Others, who paſſed up and down the ſtreets, declaring how that ſhe was their native Princeſs, and that ſhe doubted not but all honeſt Subjects would reſpect her as they ought to

do,

do, and not suffer her to be abused. Others again evidenced their malice, in setting up a Banner or Ensign, whereupon the King was painted, lying dead under a Tree, and the young Prince upon his knees
praying, *Judge* and *Revenge my Cause, O Lord.* That same night it
was alledged that her Majesty did write a Letter unto the Earl of *Both-*
wel, and promised a reward to one of her keepers to convoy it secure-
ly to *Dumbar* unto the said Earl, calling him her dear heart whom
she should never forget nor abandon, though she was necessitated to
be absent from him for a time, saying, that she had sent him away only for his safety, willing him to be comforted, and be upon his guard:
Which Letter the Knave delivered to the Lords, though he had promised the contrary : Upon which Letter the Lords took occasion to
send her to *Lockleven* to be kept, which she alledged was contrary to
promise. They on the other hand affirmed, that by her own hand
writing she had declared that she had not, nor would not abandon the
Earl of *Bothwel.* *Grange* again excused her, alledging she had in effect abandoned the said Earl, that it was no wonder that she gave him
yet a few fair words, not doubting but if she were discreetly handled,
and humbly admonished what inconveniencies that Man had brought
upon her, she would by degrees be brought, not only to leave him, but
e're long to detest him : And therefore he advised to deal gently with
her. But they said, that it stood them upon their Lives and Lands,
and that therefore in the mean time they behoved to secure her, and
when that time came that she should be known to abandon and detest
the Earl *Bothwel,* it would be then time to reason upon the matter.
Grange was yet so angry, that had it not been for the Letter, he had
instantly left them : and for the next best he used all possible diligence
to make her and them both quit of the said Earl, causing to make ready two Ships to follow after him, who had fled to the Castle of *Dum-*
bar, and from thence to *Sheatland.* In the mean time her Majesty
sent a Letter to the Laird of *Grange* lamenting her hard usage, and
shewing him that promises had been broken to her. Whereunto he
answered, that he had already reproached the Lords for the same, who
shewed unto him a Letter sent by her unto the Earl of *Bothwel,* promising among many other fair and comfortable words, never to abandon
or forget him; which had stopped his mouth, marvelling that her
Majesty considered not, that the said Earl could never be her Lawful
Husband, being so lately before married with another, whom he had
deserted without any just ground, although he had not been so hated
for the *murther of the King* her husband. And therefore he requested
her Majesty to put him clean out of mind, seeing otherwise she could
never get the love or respect of her Subjects, nor have that obedience
payed her, which otherwise she might expect. It contained many
other loving and humble admonitions, which made her bitterly to
weep. For she could not do that so hastily which process of time
might have accomplished.

   Now the laird of *Grange* his two Ships being in readiness, he made
sail toward *Orkney,* and no man was so Frank to accompany him as the
Laird of *Tullibardin,* and *Adam Bothwel* Bishop of *Orkney,* but the Earl
was fled from *Orkney* to *Sheatland,* whither also they followed him, and
came in sight of *Bothwel's* Ship, which moved the Laird of *Grange* to
caufe

caufe the Skipper to hoife up all the Sails, which they were loath to do, becaufe they knew the fhallow water thereabout, but *Grange* fearing to mifs him, compelled the Marriners, fo that for too great hafte the Ship wherein *Grange* was did break upon a Bed of Sand, without lofs of a man, but *Bothwel* had leafure in the mean time to fave himfelf in a little Boat, leaving his Ship behind him, which *Grange* took, and therein the Laird of *Tallow*, *John Hepburn* of *Bautoun*, *Dalgleefh*, and divers others of the Earl's Servants. Himfelf fled to *Denmark*, where he was taken, and kept in ftrait Prifon, wherein he became mad and dyed miferably. But *Grange* came back again with *Bothwel's* Ship and Servants, who were the firft who gave information of the manner of the murther, which the Lords thought fit to let the King of *France* underftand, and of their diligence according to the promife made by them.

My Lord of *Murray* had obtained liberty to pafs unto *France*, fhortly after the murther of the King, for he did forefee the great trouble like to enfue. The reft of the Lords enterprifers after they had fecured the Queen in *Lockleven*, began to confult how to get her Majefty counfelled to demit the Government to the Prince her fon, and for that effect they dealt firft with my Brother Sir *Robert*, becaufe he was fome times allowed accefs to her Majefty. And after that he had refufed flatly to meddle in that matter, they were minded to fend the Lord *Lindfay*, firft to ufe fair perfwafions, and in cafe he could not fpeed that way, they were refolved to enter in harder terms. The Earls of *Athol*, *Mar*, and Secretary *Lidingtoun*, and the Laird of *Grange* who loved her Majefty, advifed my Brother to tell her the verity, and how that any thing fhe did in Prifon could not prejudge her, being once again at liberty. He anfwered, he would give no fuch advice as coming from himfelf, but he fhould tell it as the opinion of thofe he knew to be her true friends. But fhe refufed utterly to follow that advice, till fhe heard that the Lord *Lindfay* was at the new Houfe at the fhore coming in, and in a very boafting humour ; and then fhe yielded to the neceffity of the time, and told my Brother that fhe would not ftrive with them, feeing it could do her no harm when fhe was at liberty. So at my Lord *Lindfay's* coming, fhe fubfcribed the fignature of Renunciation, and Demiffion of the Government to the Prince, and certain Lords named in the faid fignature, to be Regents to the Prince and Country ; her Majefty defiring my Lord *Murray* who was abfent in *France* to be the firft Regent.

This being paft, the Lords concluded to Crown the Prince, and fent Letters to *France* to the Earl of *Murray* to come home. In the 'mean time there were a number of Lords convened at *Hamiltoun*, as my Lord *Hamiltoun*, my Lord *Pasby*, *John Hamiltoun* Bifhop of St. *Andrews*, my Lord *Fleeming*, *Boid*, and divers others, to whom the Lords who were to Crown the Prince would have fent me Commiffioner. Which Commiffion at the firft I refufed, but afterwards I accepted thereof at the advice of Secretary *Lidingtoun*, the Laird of *Grange*, and other fecret favourers of the Queen, who judged it very fit that the whole Country fhould be joined together in quietnefs : fearing that in cafe Civil Wars entred among them, it might endanger her Majefties life : For it was judged that thofe who were at *Hamiltoun* appeared to lean to the Queen.

At

At my coming to *Hamiltoun*, I told them my commiſſion, in the
name of the other Lords, how that the King being murthered, all
neighbour Nations cryed out upon the whole Kingdom, but eſpecially the King of *France*, and the Queen of *England* ſollicited them to inquire after, and puniſh the murtherers. How that they had found
that it was the Earl of *Bothwel*, and ſome of them who had aſſiſted him,
who were puniſhed. And what was paſt ſince thereupon, was known
to the whole Country. That the Queens Majeſty had demitted over
the Government to the Prince her Son, whom they were minded to
Crown ſhortly, whereof they thought fit to warn all the Nobility,
as being reſolved to prejudge no Nobleman of his Rights, Titles or
Prerogatives, requeſting them who were there Convened, to come to
Sterling, and be preſent at the ſaid Coronation, for retaining their own
priviledges, the peace and quiet of the whole Country. Some of the
younger Lords anſwered, and ſaid that they would not believe, that
the Queens Majeſty had demitted the Government, and if ſhe had done
it, it would be found for to ſave her life. But the Biſhop who had
more experience then they, reproved them, and ſaid that thoſe Noblemen had dealt very reaſonably and diſcreetly with them, ſo he drew
the reſt aſide to adviſe, and then returned and gave me this anſwer.

We are beholden to the Noblemen who have ſent you with that
friendly and diſcreet Commiſſion, and following their deſire we are
ready to concur with them, if they give us ſufficient ſecurity of that
which you have ſaid in their name, and in ſo doing, they give us occaſion to conſtruct the beſt of all their proceedings, paſt and to come.
So that if they had acquainted us with their firſt enterpriſe of puni-
ſhing the murther, we ſhould heartily have taken part with them.
And whereas now we are here convened, it is not to purſue or offend
any of them, but to be upon our own guards, underſtanding of ſo great
a concourſe of Noblemen, Barons, Burroughs, and other Subjects. For
not being made privy to their enterpriſe, we thought fit to draw our
ſelves together, till we ſhould ſee whereto things would turn.

When I returned back to *Sterling*, and declared this anſwer, it was
judged ſatisfactory by all wiſe and honeſt hearted men. But others
ſaid, That however they minded to do, I had painted out a fair ſtory
for them, and in their favours. So that I perceived them already divided in Factions and Opinions: For ſo many of our Lord as leaned
to *England* deſired not the ſtability of our ſtate, others had particular
prejudices and deſigns againſt the *Hamiltouns*, and expected to get them
ruined, to gain advantage to themſelves by fiſhing in troubled waters.
So that the *Hamiltouns* were ill uſed, for they would fain have agreed
with the reſt, but their friendſhip and Society was plainly refuſed at
this time, and they not permitted to come to the Coronation, nor yet
to take inſtruments that they ſhould not be prejudged in any ſort,
which occaſioned great trouble afterward in the Country. For they
perceiving themſelves caſt off, and their friendſhip and aſſiſtance refuſed, endeavoured for their own ſecurity and defence to draw in other
Noblemen, and Barons to join with them, who had not as yet joined
with the other Lords, and therefore were the more eaſily drawn upon
that ſide : and theſe were afterward called the Queens Lords, whey
then

they were convinced of the bad usage the *Hamiltouns* had received. I have before related that my Lord *Murray* was written for, to come home, and so soon as he came to *London* the Lords were thereof advertised, who desired me to ride and meet him at *Berwick*, and shew him, how that the Office of Regent was appointed for him. Which Journey I accepted with the better will, in that some friends who were best inclined, thought meet to give him good counsel in due time: My Commission from the Lords was to inform him of all their proceedings, and of the present Estate, and to desire him to do nothing without their knowledge with the Queen. For they feared that he might carry himself with that mildness toward her, as to oblige her to believe he intended some time to release her, and that he would not run so hard a course against her, as some of them would had him to do.

Another part of the said Lords (that did still bear a great love unto the Queen, and had compassion upon her estate, and who had entred upon that enterprise only for safety of the Prince, and punishment of the *king's murther,* as the Earl of *Mar,* the Earl of *Athol,* the Secretary *Lidingtoun,* the Lairds of *Tullibardin,* and *Grange,*) sent their instructions with me to my Lord of *Murray,* praying him in their name to behave himself gently and humbly unto the Queen, and to procure so much favor for her as he could. Not that they would advise him to forget any part of honest duty to the Lords, so long as they kept touch with him; but that in cafe they, or any part of them would be offended at him afterwards, for the refusal of some casuality, benefice, or the like, they would come to themselves again, seeing the Queen and him in so good tearms, lest he should set her at liberty upon accompt of their misbehaviour. And further, That her Majesty being now free of ill company, and of a clear wit, and Princely inclination, was beginning already to repent her of many things past, and time might bring about such occasions as they should all wish her at liberty to Rule over them. and that in that cafe, he would lose by his discreet and friendly behaviour to her. He appeared much to relish this device, but he feemed somewhat refractory of accepting the Government, refusing it plainly at first, albeit I was informed by some of his company, that he was right glad when he understood first that he was to be Regent. There came home with him a *French* Ambassadour of my acquaintance, who was sent to see how matters past, to comfort the Captive Queen, and to intercede for her, but he did it very slenderly: For he said to the Lords, he came not to offend any of them, alledging that the old Band and League betwixt *France* and *Scotland* was not made with any one Prince, but betwixt the estates of the two Kingdoms, and with those who were Commanders over the Country for the time.

After that my Lord of *Murray* had met with all his friends, he granted to accept the Government. But when he went to see the Queen in *Lockleven,* instead of comforting her, and following the good counfel he had gotten, he entred instantly with her Majesty in reproaches, giving her such injurious language, as was like to break her heart. We who found fault with that manner of procedure, loft his favor. The injuries were such, that they cut the thread of love and credit betwixt the Queen and him for ever.

You

You have heard how that the Lords, who were in *Hamiltoun* were cast off, and refused to be accepted into Society with the rest, against the opinion of the fewest in number, though the wifest men, and least factious. But the worst inclined, and manyest votes obtained their intent. Whereupon the Lords who were refused to be taken into friendship, drew themselves together in *Dumbartoun*, under the pretext to procure by force of Arms the Queen their Sovereign's liberty, and landed themselves. together against the king's Lords, which they would not have done, if they could have been accepted in Society with the rest. Albeit their publick profefling their intention of fpending their lives for the Queens liberty, put her Majesties life in greater danger, fo long as she was Captive in the hands of the contrary Party, and was at length her Majesties utter wrack. For the hope that she had to get friends and favourers, caufed her to use means to efcape out of *Lockleven* too haftily, e're the time was ripe enough to recover again the hearts of the Subjects, who were yet alienated. For albeit my Lord Regent was rigorous, he was flexible, and might have been won through procefs of time by her wifdom, and the interest of her friends. The tenour of their Bond was as followeth.

Forafmuch as confidering the Queens Majefty our Sovereign, to be detained at prefent at Lockleven in Captivity, wherefore the moft part of her Majefties Lieges cannot have free accefs to her Highnefs ; and feeing it becomes us of our duty to feek her liberty and freedom, We Earls, Lords, and Barons under fubfcribing, promife faithfully to ufe the outmoft of our endeavours by all reafonable means, to procure her Majefties liberty and freedom, upon fuch honeft conditions as may ftand with her Majefties honour , the common weal of the whole Realm, and fecurity of the whole Nobility, who at prefent have her Majefty in keeping. Whereby this our native Realm may be governed, ruled and guided by her Majefty and her Nobility, for the common quietnefs, the adminiftration of Juftice, and weal of the Country. And in cafe the Noblemen who have her Majefty at prefent in their hands, refufe to fet her at Liberty, upon fuch reafonable conditions as faid is, in that cafe we fhall employ our felves, our kindred, friends, fervants, and partakers ; our Bodies and Lives to fet her Highnefs at liberty, as faid is ; and alfo to concur to the punifhment of the murther of the King her Majefties Husband ; and for fure prefervation of the perfon of the Prince, as we fhall anfwer to God , and on our honours and credit, And to that effect fhall concur every one with other at our utmoft power. And if any fhall fet upon us, or any of us, for the doing as aforefaid in that cafe, We promife faithfully to efpoufe one anothers interest under pain of Perjury and Infamy, as we fhall anfwer to God. In witnefs whereof, We have fubfcribed thefe prefents with our hand at Dumbartoun, the   day of

St. Andrews,	Fleeming,
Arguile,	Herris,
Huntly,	Skirling,
Arbroth,	Killwonning,
Gallway,	Will. Hamiltoun *of* Sanchir, *Knight.*
Rofs,	

This

This small number were the first who banded themselves together, and afterward all those who were Male-contents, or had any particular questions, claims, or feuds with any of the King's Lords, drew to these new Confederates, hoping by time to win their intent against their adversaries, in case their faction might prevail. And some drew to both the factions, who neither desired to see the Kirk nor Country in any stablished estate.

The Court of *England* on the other hand, left nothing undon to kindle the fire, and to furnish both the factions with hope of assistance, in case of need. For oft-times by their Ambassadours ordinary, who were resident here, they upon some new occasion would send in another openly to deal with the King's faction, because it was strongest, and greatest, and under-hand to deal with the Queens faction, and alledge that their quarrel was most just and right, and that her Majesties Authority was only lawful. No man can tell this better then I, who was so long well acquainted with all the Ambassadours who were sent to *Scotland*, during their banishment in *France* in Queen *Mary's* time: as with Mr. *Randolph*, Sir *Nicholas Throgmortoun*, Mr. *Dayson*, Mr. *Killegrew*, and the *Marshal of Berwick*. Among the which number, Sir *Nicholas Throgmortoun* dealt most honestly and plainly, for he shot at the union of the whole Isle in one Monarchy. And thought that it consisted only in the persons of two for the time, to wit, the Queen, and the King her Sor'. And when he saw Mr. *Randolph* go about to sow discord, he declared the same to my Brother and me, and detested him for his divilish intent and dealing. Yea he detested the whole Council of *England* for the time, and told us friendly, what reasoning they held among themselves for that effect: to wit, How that one of their greatest Counsellors proposed openly to the rest, that it was needful for the well-fare of *England*, to foster and nourish with some help the Civil Wars, as well in *France*, *Flanders*, as *Scotland*, whereby *England* might have many advantages, and be fought after by all parties, and in the mean time live at rest, and gather great riches themselves. This advice and proposition was well allowed of by most part of the Council, yet one honest Councellor stood up and said, That it was a very worldly advice, and had little or nothing to do with a Christian Common-wealth, nor yet would it be found profitable in all points. First he said, It is worldly and not godly, for though I grant, said he, that *France* which is so potent a Kingdom, if it knew its own strength, might suppress all its neighbours, and therefore would be so handled, yet even there the fire would dye out incontinent, except the Prince of *Conde* were better furnished, and helped. As for *Flanders* he said, That the trouble was prejudicial to *England*, because by the Wars in *Flanders*, *England's* great traffick of merchandize is hindered, whereby they have greatest gain. As for *Scotland*, he said it was against their weal, to hold them in dissention, solong as my Lord of *Murray* was Regent, who was their friend, and would be ready to assist them with his power in their necessity. Another Councellor affirmed that to be true, but if my Lord *Murray* were dead, *Scotland* behoved likewise to be kept in hot Water. Which conclusion was commonly followed afterward, and was soon discovered by the wisest, who were not factious; but too late by the rest of the raging.

ging multitude, who through process of time were so battered one against another, e're the play was ended, that they would have eaten one another with their Teeth.

Now my Lord of *Murray* having accepted the Government upon him, pressed to have the strengths in his hands, as the Castles of *Edinbrugh, Dumbar* and *Dumbartoun.* The Castle of *Edinbrugh* was still in the hands of Sir *James Balfour,* who had assisted the Noblemen who had pursued the murther, and now took plain part with them, and likewise assisted the new made Regent. Yet he desired to have the Castle out of his hands, which he was content to deliver up upon condition, that the Laird of *Grange* should be made Captain thereof, upon the constancy of whose friendship he reposed most; which was easily granted by the Regent, and all the rest. After this the other Strengths were also rendred to him. Then he took great pains to steal secret Roads upon the Thieves on the Borders, tending much to the quieting thereof. He likewise held Justice *Airs* in the In-country. But was not so diligent as he might have been, in settling the differences among the Nobility, and to draw them by a sweet and discreet equitable behaviour to the obedience of the King's Authority. Which might have been easily done, if they had gotten security for their persons and estates. But such as were about him, having their own ambitious and covetous ends, counselled him otherwise, thinking by the wrack of others to make up themselves. They were so blinded by their affections, and greedy appetites, that they thought all would succeed prosperously according to their desires, without any resistance. Thus rushing forward, the Regent's rough proceedings gave occasion to many to draw to the contrary faction. And they to strengthen themselves under the name of Authority, devised how to draw the Queens Majesty out of *Lockleven* to be their head, before the time was ripe. Whereof the Regent was oft and frequently warned, even by divers who were upon the Councel, of her out-taking, who desired that way to win thanks at his hands. But he would credit nothing, but such things as came out of the mouths of those who had crept into his favour by flattery.

In the mean time the Queen was convoyed out of *Lodkleven* by *George Duglas* the Lairds Brother, and the Regents half Brother, who was for the time in some evil tearms with them. The old Lady his Mother, was also thought to be upon the Councel. My Lord *Seatoun,* and some of the House of *Hamiltoun,* and divers of their dependers, received her Majesty at her landing out of the *Logh,* and convoyed her to *Hamiltoun.*

The Regent being for the time at *Glascow* holding Justice *Eyrs,* Proclamations and Missives were incontinently sent abroad, by both sides, to convene so many as would act for them in the Country. One *French* Ambassadour was come to *Edinbrugh* ten days before, called Monsieur *de Beumont* Knight of the Order of the Cockle, whom I had convoyed to *Glascow,* and had procured to him a sight of the Queen, while Captive. He said to me, that he never did see so many men so suddenly convened, for he rode to *Hamiltoun* to the Queen, and dealt between the parties for peace, but was not heard. Her Majesty was not minded to fight, nor hazard battle, but to go unto the Castle of
Dumbar-

Dumbartoun, and endeavour by little and little to draw home again unto her obedience the whole Subjects. But the Bishop of St. Andrews, and the Houfe of *Hamiltoun*, and the reft of the Lords there convened, finding themselves in number far beyond the other Party, would needs hazard Battle, thinking thereby to overcome the Regent their great Enemy, and be also Masters of the Queen, to Command and Rule all at their pleafure. Some alledged that the Bishop was minded to caufe the Queen to marry my Lord *Hamiltoun*, in cafe they had obtained the Victory. And I was fince informed by fome who were prefent, that the Queen her felf feared the fame, therefore she preffed them still to convoy her to *Dumbartoun*, and had fent me word with the *French* Ambaffadour, the fame morning before the battel, to draw on a meeting for concord, by the means of the Secretary *Lidingtoun*, and the Laird of *Grange* : And for her part she would fend the Lord *Herris* and fome other. She had also caufed my Brother Sir *Robert* to write a Letter to me that fame morning, for that fame effect, but the Queen's Army came on fo fiercely, that there was no ftay.

The Regent went out on foot, and all his Company except the Laird of *Grange*, *Alexander Hume* of *Munderftoun*, and fome Borderers to the number of 200. The Laird of *Grange* had already viewed the ground, and with all imaginable diligence caufed every Horfe-man to take behind him a Foot-man of the Regent's to guard behind them, and rode with fpeed to the head of the Long'fid'-hill, and fet down the faid Foot-men with their Culverings at the head of a ftraight Lane, where there were fome Cottage-houfes, and Yards of great advantage. Which Soldiers with their continual fhot, killed divers of the Vaunt-guard, led by the *Hamiltouns*, who couragioufly and fiercely afcending up the Hill, were already out of breath when the Regents Vaunt-guard joined with them. Where the worthy Lord *Hume* fought on foot with his Pike in his hand very manfully, well affifted by the Laird of *Cesfoord* his Brother-in-law , who helped him up again when he was ftrucken to the ground by many ftroaks upon his face, by the throwing Piftols at him , after they had been difcharged. He was also wounded with Staves , and had many ftroaks of Spears through his Legs: for he and *Grange* at the joining, cried to let their adverfaries firft lay down their Spears, to bear up theirs ; which Spears were fo thick fixed in others *Jacks*, that fome of the Piftols and great Staves, that were thrown by them which were behind, might be feen lying upon the Spears.

Upon the Queens fide the Earl of *Arguile* commanded the Battel : and the Lord of *Arbroth* the Vaunt-guard. On the other part the Regent led the Battle, and the Earl of *Mortoun* the Vaunt-gard : But the Regent committed to the Laird of *Grange* the fpecial care, as being an experimented Captain, to overfee every danger, and to ride to every Wing, to incourage and make help where greateft need was. He perceived at the firft joining , the right Wing of the Regent's Vaunt-guard put back, and like to fly, whereof the greateft part were Commons of the Barony of *Ranthrow* ; whereupon he rode to them, and told them that their Enemy was already turning their backs, requefting them to ftay and debate, till he fhould bring them frefh Men forth of the Battel. Whither at full fpeed he did ride alone, and told

N 2   the

the Regent that the Enemy were fhaken, and flying away behind the
little Village, and defired a few number of frefh Men to go with him.
Where he found enough willing, as the Lord *Lindfay*, the Laird of
Lockleven, Sir *James Balfour*, and all the Regents Servants, who followed him with diligence; and reinforced that Wing which was beginning to fly ; which frefh Men with their loofe Weapons ftruck
the Enemies in their flanks and faces, which forced them incontinent
to give place ; and turn back, after long fighting and pufhing others
to and fro with their Spears. There were not many Horfe-men to
purfue after them, and the Regent cried to fave and not to kill, and
Grange was never cruel, fo that there were but few flain and taken.
And the only flaughter was at the firft rancounter, by the fhot of the
Soldiers which *Grange* had planted at the Lane-head behind fome
Dikes.

After the lofs of the Battle, her Majefty loft all courage, which fhe
had never done before, and took fo great fear, that fhe never refted
till fhe was in *England*, thinking her felf fure of refuge there, in refpect of the fair promifes formerly made to her by the Queen of *England* by word to her Ambaffadours, and by her own hand-writ both
before and after fhe was Captive in *Lockleven*. But God and the World,
knows how fhe was kept and ufed, for not only fhe refufed to fee her,
of whom fhe appeared fo oft fo defirous of a fight, and a meeting, but
alfo caufed to keep her Prifoner, and at length fuffered her life to be
taken away, or elfe it was fubtilly taken againft her intention. This
puts me in remembrance of a tale that my Brother Sir *Robert* told me,
The time that he was bufieft dealing betwixt the two Queens to entertain their friendfhip, and draw on their meeting at a place near *York*,
One *Baffintoun* a *Scots-man* who had been a Traveller, and was learned
in high Sciences, came to him and faid, Good Gentlemen, I hear fo
good a report of you, that I love you heartily, and therefore cannot
forbear to fhew you how that all your upright dealing, and honeft
travel will be in vain : For whereas you believe to obtain advantage
for your Queen at the Queen of *England's* hands, you do but lofe your
time and your travel : For firft they will never meet together, and
next there will never be any thing elfe but diffembling, and fecret hatred for a while, and at length Captivity and utter wrack to our Queen
from *England*. My Brother anfwered, he liked not to hear of fuch
devilifh news, nor yet would he in any fort credit them, as being falfe,
ungodly, and unlawful for Chriftians to meddle with. *Baffintoun* anfwered, good Mr. *Melvil* entertain not that harfh opinion of me. I am
a Chriftian of your own Religion, and fear God, and purpofeth never
to caft my felf on any of the unlawful Arts that you mean, but fo far
as *Melancthon*, who was a godly Theologue, hath declared lawful, and
written concerning the natural Sciences which are lawful, and daily
read in divers Chriftian Univerfities, in the which as in all other Arts,
God gives to fome lefs and to othes clearer knowledg, by the which
knowledg I have attained to underftand, that at length the Kingdom
of *England* fhall of right fall to the Crown of *Scotland*, and that at this
inftant there are fome born who fhall brook Lands and Heritages in
England : But, alas, it will coft many their Lives, and many bloody
Battels will be fought e're things be fettled or take effect, and by my
know-

knowledg. fayes he, the *Spaniards* will be helpers, and will take a part to themfelves for their labour, which they will be loath to leave a-gain.

After that the Queens Maiefty had demitted the Government, when fhe was Captive in *Lockleven* in fuch manner as is rehearfed, my Lord of *Murray* being the firft of the Regents of whom I have faid fomething already, I intend now to follow forth, and fhew a part of his proceedings, and to begin where I left at her Majefties retreat to *England*.

After the Battle of *Langfide*, the Regent went through the Country, and took up the Efcheats and Houfes of thofe who had affifted at the faid Battle, and caufed to caft down divers of their houfes, diftributing their Lands to his Servants and dependers.

The Council of *England* being crafty, and in fpecial the Secretary *Cicil*, they knew what kind of men had moft credit about him for the time; and thereupon took occafion to deal with the leaft honeft, moft ambitious and covetous of that number. and Society, who had joined and banded themfelves together to affift each other, whereby to advance themfelves, and to difgrace all fuch true and honeft men as had affifted, and helped him in all his former troubles. This fort of Men were foon perfwaded and corrupted, to move the Regent to pafs unto *England*, and accufe their native Queen before the Queen and Council of *England*, to the great difhonour of their Country and Prince. For the Queen of *England* who had no juft caufe to retain our Queen, who had fled to *England* in hope of getting fhelter, and the affiftance which had been fo oft promifed her both before and after her Captivity in *Lockleven*, was very defirous to have fome colour and pretext whereby fhe might make anfwer to the Ambaffadours of fundry Princes who reproached her for her unkindly and unprincely proceedings therein.

Becaufe the moft part of thofe who had the Regent's Ear were gained to this opinion, and the number few who were of a contrary mind he went forward to *England*, accompanied with the Earl of *Mortoun*, the Lord *Lindfay*, the Laird of *Lockleven*, the bifhop of *Orkny*, the Abbot of *Dumfarmling*, Mr. *James Macgil*, Mr. *Henry Balnears*, Mr. *George Buchanan*, the Laird of *Pittarrow*, *George Duglas* Bifhop of *Murray*, Mr. *John Wood* the Regent's Secretary, a great Ring-leader, Mr. *Nicholas Elphinftoun*, Secretary *Lidingtoun*, *Alexander Hay*, *Alexander Hume* of *North-Berwick*, the Laird of *Cleefh*, with divers other Barons, and Gentlemen, who went there to fee the fafhion, fome to wait upon the Regent and Lords, and fome who could not get the Regent diffwaded from this extream folly at home, went with him to *England* to fee if by any affiftance of fuch as were friends there to the Union of the Ifle, and to the Title of *Scotland*, he might be ftayed from that accufation. For thofe who were the Queens Lords, who came there to defend the Queens part, had no credit nor familiarity with the chief faction in *England* concerning the Title, nor durft open their minds but to fuch as by long acquaintance they were well affured of their honefty and fecrecy. The names of the Queens Lords were, the Lord *Herreis*, the Lord *Boid*, the Lord *Fleeming*, the Lord *Livingftoun*, the Bifhop of *Rofs*, and fome others, with my Brother Sir *Robert* who attended to do all the good he could.

The

The Duke of *Norfolk*, the Earl of *Suffex*, and feveral other Councellors were fent down to *York*, to hear the Regent's Accufation, and to be as Judges between the King and Queen's Lords.

The firft day of meeting, the Duke of *Norfolk* required that the Regent fhould make Homage in the King's Name to the Crown of *England*, thinking he had fome ground to demand the fame, feeing the faid *Regent* there to plead his Caufe before the Councel of *England*. Whereat the *Regent* grew red, and knew not what to anfwer; but Secretary *Lidingtoun* took up the Speech, and faid, *That in reftoring again to* Scotland *the Lands of* Huntingtuon, Cumberland, *and* Northumberland, *with fuch other Lands as* Scotland *did of old poffefs in* England, *that Homage fhould gladly be made for the faid Lands*; *but as to the Crown and Kingdom of* Scotland, *it was freer than* England *had been lately, when it payed St.* Peter's *Penny to the Poor.*

It appeared ftill that the *Duke* drave off time with us, as having no inclination to enter upon the terrors of Accufation. What was in his head, appeared afterward, but he was long in a fufpence with whom to deal. For he thought (as he afterward faid) he neither did fee honeft men nor wife men. At laft he refolved to enter in Conference with Secretary *Lidingtoun*, to whom he faid, *That before that time he had ever efteem'd him a Wife man, until that now he came before Strangers to acoufe the Queen his Miftrefs, as if England were Judge over the Princes of* Scotland. *How could we find in our hearts to difhonour our Kings Mother, or how could we anfwer afterward for what we were doing, feeing it tended to hazard the King her Sons Right to* England, *intending to bring his Mothers honefty in queftion? It had been rather the Duty of you his Subjects,* fayes he, *to cover her Imperfections, if fhe had any, remitting unto God and Time to punifh and put Order thereto, who is the Only Judge over Princes. Lidingtoun,* as he might well do, purged himfelf, and declared he came there to endeavour to ftop the faid Accufation, which the Laird of *Grange*, and divers others, had endeavoured to do in vain, before the *Regent's* coming out of *Scotland*. And that now he would be glad of any help to hinder that fhameful deliberation of the *Regents*, pufhed thereto by a company of greedy, rafh, and carelefs Councellors, the moft part of them his Enviers and fecret Enemies; praying the *Duke* not to conceive fuch an Evil Opinion of him, but requefting him to draw the *Regent* apart, and enter with him upon thofe Terms which afterward the *Regent* would fhew him, and he fhould amplifie and fet it out the beft he could. The *Duke* asked *if the Regent would keep fecret?* and being thereof affured by *Lidingtoun*, the next day he took occafion to enter into difcourfe with the *Regent*, about their firft Friendfhip and Familiarity contracted at *Lieth*, during the Siege, and helping to put the *Frenchmen* out of *Scotland*. Then after that the *Regent* had promifed Secrecy, and affured him that their firft Friendfhip fhould ftand till the end of his Life, the *Duke* began to declare, how " that he would be a Faithful Subject to the *Queen* his " Miftrefs fo long as fhe lived ; but that fhe was too carelefs what might " come after her about the well and quiet of her Country : tho it " was the Intereft of the Kingdom of *England*, more to notice the " fame, by determining the Succeffion to prevent Troubles that might " otherwife enfue. That tho they had divers times effayed to do fome-
                                                                    " thing

"thing therein at every parliament, but that their *Queen* had thereat
"evidenced a great difcontent, and hindred the fame, fhewing thereby
"that fhe cared not what Blood was fhed after her for the Right and
"Title of the Crown of *England*, which confifts only in the Perfons
"of the Queen and King of *Scotland* her Son; which had been put out
"of doubt e're then, if matters had not fallen out fo unhappily at home,
"and yet he and other Noblemen of *England*, as fathers of the Coun-
"try, were minded to be careful thereof, watching their opportunity.
"But that they wondred what could move him to come there and ac-
"cufe his *Queen*; for albeit fhe had done, or fuffered harm to be done to
"the *King* her Husband, yet there was refpect to be had to the *Prince*
"her Son upon whom he and many in *England* had fixed their Eyes,
"as Mr. *Melvil*, who had been late Ambaffadour there could teftifie.
"He therefore wifhed that the *Queen* fhould not be accufed, nor difho-
"noured for the *King* her Sons caufe, and for refpect to the Right
"they both had to fucceed to the Crown of *England*. And further the
Duke faid, "I am fent to hear your Accufation, but neither will I, nor
"the *Queen* my miftrefs, give out any Sentence upon your Accufa-
"tion. And that you may underftand the verity of this Point more
"clearly, you fhall do well the next time that I require you before
"the Council to give in your Accufation in Writing; to demand again
"my Miftrefs's Seal and Hand-Writing (before you fhow your folly)
"that in cafe you Accufe, fhe fhall immediately Convict and give out
"her Sentence according to your Probation ; otherwife, that you will
"not open your Pack : Which if her Majeftie fhall refufe to grant unto
"you, which undoubtedly fhe will do, then affure your felf that my
"Information is true, and take occafion hereupon to ftay from further
"accufation.

The *Regent* took very well with this Advice of the *Dukes*, and kept
it fecret from all his Company fave Secretary *Lidingtoun*, and me, to
whom that fame Night he imparted it, fhewing us his inclination to
follow the fame ; in which Refolution we confirmed him. at the
next meeting with the Council, when the *Duke* demanded the Accufation to be given in, the *Regent* asked for his Security the Queen of
Englands Seal and Hand-Writing, as was before advifed; of which the
reft of his Faction gave *Lidingtoun* the full blame, becaufe it drew on
a delay until the Poft was fent to the Court, and returned the Queens
anfwer. Being come, it was told that fhe was *a true Princefs, her
Word and Promife would be abundantly fufficient. The* Secretary *Cicil*,
and Mr. *John Wood* Secretary to the *Regent*, thought *ftrange of this*
manner of Procedure, therefore it was advifed to defire the Lords on
both fides, to go from *York* toward the Court, that the matter might
thereto be treated, where the Queen was able to give more ready Anfwers and Replies.

In the mean time the *Regent* finding the Information the *Duke* of
Norfolk gave him concerning the Queen of *Englands* Anfwer to be true,
he entred further into Communication with him, and in prefence of
Lidingtoun, it was agreed betwixt them as followeth ; That he in no
wayes fhould accufe the *Queen* ; That the *Duke* fhould obtain to him
the Queens Favour with a confirmation of the *Regency*. The Duke
and He were to be as fworn Brothers of one Religion, fhooting continually

nually at one mark, with the mutual intelligence of one anothers minds, the one to Rule *Scotland*, the other to Rule *England*, to the Glory of God, and well of both the Countries, and their Princes, so that Posterity should report them. the happiest two Instruments that ever were bred in *Brittain*.

The *Duke* was then the *greatest* Subject in *Europe*, not being a free Prince. For he ruled the Queen, and all those who were most familiar with her. He also ruled the Councel, and ruled two Factions in *England*, both Protestants and Papists, with the City of *London*, and whole Commons. The Great Men who were Papists, were all his near Kinsmen, whom he entertained with great Wisdom, and Discretion; the Protestants had such proof of his Godly Life and Conversation, that they loved him intirely.

The *Regent* being arrived at the Court of *England*, which was for the time at *Hampton Court*, he was daily pressed to give in his accusation, especially by those who were about him, when all thought strange that he was so slow in doing thereof, until they were advertised by one of the Lords of the *Queens* Faction, of all that had past betwixt the *Regent* and the *Duke* of *Norfolk*. For the Duke by a secret hand had advertised our *Queen*, and she again shewed it to one of her most Familiars, who advertised the Earl of *Mortoun* thereof. He took this very ill, that the *Regent* had done this without acquainting him, or any of his Society of his design. But e're he, or any of his Company, would seem to understand any thing of the matter, they laid their heads together, and caused Mr. *John Wood* to inform Secretary *Cicil* of all that had Past, desiring him to press forward the Accusation, wherein of himself he was abundantly earnest. They again left nothing undone for their part, to effectuate the same, putting him in hope that the *Queen* would give him her Hand-Writing and Seal, that she should convict the Queen in case he accused her. Others of the finest of them, persuaded him that she would never give her hand-Writing or Seal for that end, putting him to a strait to see what he would do in case he obtained his desire. Mr. *John Wood* said, *That it was fit to carry in all the Writs to the Councel, and he would keep the Accusation in his bosom, and would not deliver it till first the thing demanded of the Queen was granted. The rest of the Regents Lords and Councellors* had concluded among them, That so soon as the *Duke* of *Norfolk* as chief of the Councel would inquire for the Accusation, they should all with one voice cry and persuade the *Regent* to go forward with it.

Secretary *Lidingtoun* and I minded the *Regent*, how far he had obliged himself to the *Duke* of *Norfolk*. He said, *He would do well enough, and that it would not come to that length.* So soon as he with his Counsel were within the Councel-House, the *Duke* of *Norfolk* asked for the Accusation; the *Regent* desired again the assurance of Conviction by Writing and Seal, as is said. It was answered again, *That the Queens Majesties Word, being a true Princess, was sufficient.* Then all the Councel cryed out, *Would he mistrust the Queen, who had given such proof of her friendship to Scotland. The Regents* Councel cryed out also in that same manner. Then Secretary *Cicil* asked if they had the Accusation there? *Yes*, sayes Mr. *John Wood*; and with that he plucks it out of his Bosom, *but I will not deliver it*, says he, *till her Majesties Hand.*

Hand-Writing and Seal be delivered to my Lord Regent *for what he demands.* Then the Bifhop of *Orkny* fnatcheth the Writing out of his
hand, *Let me have it,* fayes he, *I fhall prefent it.* Mr. *John Wood* run
after him, as if he would have taken it again. Forward goes the Bifhop
to the Council-Table, and gives in the Accufation. Then cryes out
the *Chamberlain* of *England, Well done Bifhop, thou art the frankeft Fellow among them all, none of them will make thy leap good*; fcorning his
leaping out of the Laird of *Grange's* Ship. Mr. *Henry Balneavs* only
had made refiftance, and called for Secretary *Lidingtoun,* who waited
without the Councel Houfe. But fo foon as Mr. *Henry Balneavs* had
called for him, he came in and whifpered in the *Regent's* Ear, *That he
had fhamed himfelf, and put his Life in danger, by the lofs of fo good a
Friend as the* Duke *of* Norfolk, *and that he had loft his Reputation for
ever.*

The *Regent,* who by his facility had been brought to break with the
Duke of *Norfolk,* repented himfelf thereof, fo foon as *Lidingtoun* acquainted him with the danger, and defired the Accufation to be rendred up to him again, alledging he had *fome more to add thereto.* They
anfwered, *They would hold what they had, and were ready to receive any
addition when he fhould pleafe to give it in.* The *Duke* of *Norfolk* had
much ado to keep his Countenance. Mr. *John Wood* winked upon Secretary *Cicil,* Who fmiled again upon him. The reft of the *Regent's*
Company were laughing one upon another only Secretary *Lidingtoun*
had a fad heart. The Regent came forth of the Council-Houfe with
Tears in his eyes, and went to his Lodging at *Kingftoun,* where his factious friends had much ado to comfort him.

The Queen of *England* having obtained her intent, received thereby great contentment through the advantage fhe thereby received.
Firft, fhe thought fhe had matter for her, to fhew wherefore fhe detained the Queen, when fhe was challenged by the forreign Ambaffadours upon that accompt. Then fhe was glad of the Queens difhonour, but in her mind fhe detefted the Regent, and all his Company,
and would notice him no more. She fent alfo incontinent to the
Queen to comfort her, praying her to look on her felf in a better cafe,
albeit for a while reftrained of her liberty, then to be in *Scotland,* among
fo unworthy Subjects, who had accufed her falfly and wrongfully, as
fhe was affured ; and that neither fhould they be the better, nor fhe
the worfe for any thing they had done: For fhe would neither be Judge,
nor give out any Sentence thereupon, nor fhould any part of the faid
falfe Accufation be made known by her, or her Council to any, praying her to take patience in her gentle Ward, where fhe was nearer to
get the Crown of *England* fet upon her head, in cafe of her deceafe,who
was but the eldeft Sifter.

Thus the *Regent* won no other thing for his labour, but to be defpifed by the Queen and Council of *England,* detefted by the Duke of
Norfolk, and reproached by his beft and trueft friends, fuffered to lye
a long time at *Kingftoun,* in great difpleafure and fear, without Mony
to fpend, and without hope to get any from the Queen. In the mean
time, the agreement betwixt him and the Duke of *Norfolk,* was told
the Queen. For the Earl of *Mortoun* caufed a Minifter called *John Wil-
lock,* to declare what had paft betwixt the Regent and the Duke of

O *Norfolk*

Norfolk to the Earl of *Huntingtoun*, who caufed my Lord of *Leicefter* to tell it to the Queen.

The Duke of *Norfolk* finding himfelf difappointed by the Regent, and his purpofes difcovered to the Queen, began to boaft and fpeak plain Language, *That he would ferve and honour the Queen his Miftrefs fo long as fhe lived, but after her deceafe he would fet the Crown of Eng-land upon the Queen of* Scotland's *head, as lawful Heir.* And this he avowed to Secretary *Cecil,* defiring him to go and prattle that langu-age again to the Queen. The Secretary *Cecil* anfwered, *That he would be no Tale-teller to the Queen of him, but would concur with him in any courfe, and ferve him in any thing wherein he would imploy him.* He threatned alfo Sir *Nicholas Throgmorton,* who he fuppofed would be a true and devoted Servant to the Queen ; So that Sir *Nicholas* was ne-ceffitated to feek after his favour by the means of the Earls of *Pembroke* and *Leicefter ,* who was alfo his friend , albeit he durft not conceal from the Queen that whereof the Earl of *Huntingtoun* had advertifed him, feeing he had defired him to declare the fame to her Maje-fty.

The Duke of *Norfolk* underftanding that his whole purpofes were difcovered, ftood not to acknowledge to the Queen, *That during her life-time he would never offend her, but ferve and honour her, and after her the Queen of* Scotland, *as in his opinion trueft Heir , and the only means for efchewing of Civil Wars, and great blood-fhed that might other-wife fall out.* Now albeit the Queen of *England* liked not that language, yet fhe would not appear to find fault with it for the time.

Now matters being caft loofe in this manner between the Regent and the Duke, and the Regent in great diftrefs ; Sir *Nicholas Throgmor-ton* being a Man of a deep reach, and great prudence and difcretion, who had ever travelled for the Union of this Ifle, after that he was agreed with the Duke, and perceived that the Earls of *Leicefter, Pem-broke,* Secretary *Cecil,* and the reft of the Court and Commons were all for the Duke, and that the Queen durft not find fault with him, he devifed and effectuated a new friendfhip betwixt the Regent and the Duke, who was unwilling again to enter with the Regent, yet at length he fuffered himfelf to be perfwaded. The Lord Regent, on the other hand, being deftitute of all friendfhip in *England* for the time, and indigent of mony, thought he would be very fortunate if again he could obtain the Dukes friendfhip and pardon, fo he was brought eafily and fecretly unto the Duke by Sir *Nicholas.* At which time he granted his offence, excufing himfelf the beft he could, by the craft and importunity of fome of his Company. The Duke helped him to frame his excufe, alledging, *That he knew how his gentle nature was abufed by the craft and concurrence of fome of the Council of* England, *who had joined with fome about him. That if he would for the future keep touch and be fecret, they fhould take a courfe with all thofe who had drawn on that draught.* The Regent promifed as far as could be devi-fed, fo that a gaeater friendfhip was packed up between them then ever. The Duke had before told him, " That he was refolved to marry the Queen our Miftrefs, and that he fhould never permit her to come to Scotland, nor yet that he fhould ever Rebell againft the Queen of England, during her time. Alfo that he had a Daughter, who would
                                                                    " be

" be better for the King, then any other for many Reasons. Now the Duke took in hand to cause the Queen his Miftreſs to give unto my Lord Regent Two thouſand pound ſterling, for the which Sum he became Cautioner, and was afterward compelled to pay it.

After that the Regent had got this mony, and had taken his leave of the Queen, he was adviſed by ſuch as had great credit about him, to tell the Queen all things that had paſt again betwixt the Duke and him. And to do it the more covertly, it was deviſed, That the Queen of *England* ſhould ſend for him, pretending to give him ſome admonition about ſome order to be obſerved upon the Border. This being done, and all things diſcovered to the Queen, with a promiſe ſo ſoon as he came to *Scotland*, and had received any Letters from the Duke, by Cyphers or otherwiſe, he ſhould ſend them to *England* by an Expreſs. In the mean time the Duke wrote unto our Queen, advertiſing her again of the new friendſhip between him and the Regent, who was become very penitent, and had been formerly deceived by craftier men then himſelf, deſiring her to let him paſs by without any harm done to him, or any in his company by the way.

At that time the Duke commanded over all the North parts of *England*, where the Queen our Miftreſs was kept, and ſo might have taken her out when he pleaſed. And when he was angry at the Regent, he had appointed the Earl of *Weſtmorland* to lye in his way and cut off himſelf, and ſo many of his company, as were moſt bent upon the Queens Accuſation. But after the laſt agreement, the Duke ſent and diſcharged the ſaid Earl from doing us any harm, yet upon our return the Earl came in our way with a great Company of Horſe, to ſignifie to us that we were at his mercy.

After the Regents ſafe return to *Scotland*, Mr. *John Wood* his Secretary procured, upon the firſt occaſion, to be ſent to *England*, with all the Letters that had been ſent from the Duke of *Norfolk*, which could tend to undo him. He deſired Mr. *Henry Balneavs* to cauſe the Regent to give him the Biſhoprick of *Murray*, void for the time, though he pretended it was neither for ambition nor covetouſneſs of the Rents, but that he might have an honourable Style, to ſet out the better his Ambaſſage. The ſaid Mr. *Henry* being indeed ſuch a man as Mr. *John* would appeared to have been, was very angry, and never liked him after that my Lord *Lindſay* vented himſelf, That he was one of the number who gave the Regent counſel ſo to do, alledging, that ſuch promiſes as were made to the Duke of *Norfolk* for fear of life, ought not to be kept.

A little after that Mr. *John* was come back to *Scotland*, well rewarded for his pains, the Duke was ſent for by the Queen to come to Court. Whereupon firſt he poſted in haſte to Secretary *Cicil* to demand his counſel, for he repoſed much upon him, they being joined in one courſe. The other made anſwer, *That there was no danger, he might come and go at his Pleaſure, no man would or durſt offend him.* Which made the Duke ride up quietly, only with his own train, whereas otherwiſe he would have been well accompanied. In the mean time, Secretary *Cicil* informed the Queen, *That the neceſſity of the time obliged her not to omit this occaſion, but to take the matter ſtoutly upon her ſelf, and incontinent command her Guard to lay hands upon the Duke, or elſe no other durſt do it, which if ſhe did not at this time, her Crown would be in peril.* The Queen following this counſel, the Duke was taken and ſecured, when he thought all *England* was at his Devotion, who after long Captivity was Executed, ending his Life devoutly in the Reformed Religion.

Shortly after *Mr. John Wood*'s returning out of *England*, there was a great Convention held at *Pearth*, where the Regent was reſolved to accuſe Secretary *Lidingtoun*, as being of Council with the Duke of *Norfolk*, but he had ſo many friends for the time, that they durſt not lay hands on him, albeit from that hour forth, he retired from the Court, and remained with the Earl of *Athol*, where the Regent enter-tained him with friendly Letters. And upon a time being at *Sterling*, he wrote for him to come and make a diſpatch for *England*, whither being come, Captain *Crauford* was directed to accuſe him before the Privy Council of the late King's murther, and being accuſed of ſo odi-ous a Crime, he was committed to Ward. Sir *James Balfour* was alſo taken out of his own Houſe, when he expected no ſuch thing.

Then My Lord of *Doun* wrote to the *Laird* of *Grange* to be upon his guard, for the *Regent* was reſolved to take the *Caſtle* of *Edenbrugh* from him, and make the *Laird* of *Drumwhaſel* Captain thereof. Which ad-vertiſement he had formerly given to *Grange*, as alſo of the deſign to take the *Secretary*, and Sir *James Balfour*. But at the firſt he would not give credit thereto, but now when he did ſee the Advertiſement take effect, he began to think that the *Regent* was ſtrangely miſled, he would have been ſatisfied to have wanted the Caſtle, and to have left the Court, were it not for the deſire he had to ſave the Lives of *Secretary Lidingtoun*, and Sir *James Balfour*, having upon his Honour engaged to protect the ſaid Sir *James* upon his rendring up the Caſtle to him. He knew they were wrongfully purſued, only by the Malice and En-vy of their Enemies for their offices. Sir *James Balfour* being taken, ſent unto the *Laird* of *Grange*, minding him how he had joyned with the *Lords* and *Regent* upon the Truſt he repoſed on his Fidelity, more than on all their Seals and Hand-writings which he had to produce. Whereupon the *Laird* of *Grange* ſent a Gentleman to the *Regent*, but the *Regent* purged himſelf, and alledged the Council were ſo banded together againſt the *Secretary*, and Sir *James Balfour, That it conſiſted not in his power to preſerve them from Priſon, ſeeing they were accuſed for the King's Murther againſt his will, but* Grange *ſhould know his honeſt part thereof at meeting ; praying him in the mean time to ſuſpend his judgment,* Neverthelefs the *Regent* and his Council were determined to proceed to procefs the two Priſoners upon their Lives, till *Grange* ſent again and deſired the like Juſtice to be done upon the *Earl* of *Mor-toun* and Mr. *Archibald Douglas*. For he offered to fight with Mr. *Archibald,* and the *Lord Herries* with the *Earl* of *Mortoun* upon that head , *That they were upon the Council, and conſequently airt and part of the King's Murther.* This ſtayed their Procefs at that time. And the *Regent* ſtill alledged, That the Lords had taken them againſt his will, and that he ſhould ſend Sir *James Balfour* to the Caſtle of *St. Andrews,* and ſhould bring Secretary *Lidingtoun* to *Edinbrugh,* and deliver him unto the *Laird* of *Grange* to be kept. So the *Regent* came to *Edin-brugh,* and brought the Secretary with him, intending, as *Grange* was
informed,

informed, to make the Secretary an Inſtrument to draw *Grange* out of
the Caſtle to the Town the next morning to receive the *Secretary* to
be carried up to the Caſtle; and then to retain *Grange* alſo till the Caſtle
ſhould be delivered unto the *Laird* of *Drumwhaſel* to be Keeper
thereof, and to ſend *Grange* home to his Houſe and reward him with
the Priory of *Pittenweem.* But the *Earl* of *Mortoun* had appointed four
men to ſlay *Grange* at the entry of the *Reg:nt*'s Lodging, without the
Regent's knowledg. But *Grange* was loath yet to believe the worſt of
the *Regent*, and being of opinion that the *Regent*'s gentle Nature was
forced by the Lords, as he had ſent him word, underſtanding that they
intended to carry the Secretary to *Tantalloun*, he came down out of the
Caſtle with a Company, and took the *Secretary* out of the hands of
his *Keepers*, and convoyed him up to the Caſtle. For he thought if
it were true that the *Regent* ſaid, That he was forced by the Lords
againſt his will to let the *Secretary* be retained after that he was accuſed, the *Regent* would be glad that he had revenged his quarrel upon
the Lords, by taking the Secretary out of their hands, whereof he
might juſtly pretend ignorance. And if the *Regent* would be diſſatisfied with his carriage therein, it would be a certain token of his diſſimulation. In that caſe *Grange* thought he did a good deed to ſave his
Friends Life, and ſo he would have good ground to believe divers Intelligences which formerly he would not credit, and therefore he would
be upon his guard in Time coming.

The *Regent* and his Councellors when they underſtood that *Grange*
had taken the Secretary to the Caſtle, were in great perplexity, ſuppoſing all their Counſels to be diſcloſed. They knew not how to help
the matter, but they adviſed the *Regent* to cover his anger until a fit
opportunity, cauſing him to go up to the Caſtle the next morning.
For he durſt truſt *Grange*, tho *Grange* would no more truſt him. At
meeting the Regent gave him more fair words than he was wont to
do, which *Grange* took in evil part.

After this there were many devices how to intrap *Grange*, ſometime in his down-coming to the *Regent*; but he was ever advertiſed
and upon his guard, ſo as the *Regent* loſt dayly of his beſt Friends, and
the number of his Enemies increaſed. For the Duke of *Chattellerault*
(who was agreed with him by the interceſſion of the *Lord Herreis*)
when the ſaid *Duke* and the *Lord Herreis* came to *Edinbrugh*, as was
appointed at the agreement, to concur with the *Regent* in Councel and
otherwiſe for the quieting of the Country, they were both warded in
the Caſtle, againſt promiſe. Which when the Laird of *Grange* found
fault with, Mr. *John Wood* ſaid, *I marvel at you that you will be offended at this ; for how ſhall we who are my Lords dependers, get Rewards, but
by the wrack of ſuch men. Yea,* ſaid *Grange is that your holineſs, I ſee
nothing among you but Envy, Greedineſs, and Ambition, whereby you will
wrack a good* Regent, *and ruine the Country.* This was long before the
taking of the Secretary, and increaſed the hatred of a wicked Society
againſt *Grange*, who upon all occaſions evidenced his deteſting their
ſelfiſh Deſigns, who were dependers upon the *Regent* ; which was one
of the faults alſo they had againſt the *Secretary*, as alſo becauſe his
Wit ſo far excelled theirs. The Captivity of the *Duke* and my *Lord
Herreis*, made many Enemies to the *Regent*, who took the greater
boldneſs

boldnefs to confpire againft him, when they perceived him to lofe and
caft off his beft Friends.

It was a grievous thing, to fee that good *Regent*, of himfelf fo well
inclined to do good offices in Religion and Commonwealth, fo led after
other mens vain pretences, and affections, to his own wrack, to the
wrack of many worthy Perfons, and to their ruine at length who led
him in thefe wayes.

He grew to give great ear to Flatterers, and would not fuffer his
true Friends to tell him the verity. The obfervation hereof, made many conjecture that his Ruine was at hand ; and I among others devifed
a prefent remedy for his prefervation, which was this :

I knew that the taking *Lidingtoun* to the Caftle, funk deepeft in the
Regent's heart ; and that the falfe practifes and wrackful fetches of fuch
as had taught him to diffemble, moved *Grange*, who had been his greateft Friend, to be jealous of him ; the noticing whereof gave ground to
his Enemies to confpire againft him.

Firft, I requefted the *Regent* to remember the falfe Practifes, that
fome about him had fundry times ufed formerly to his great difpleafure, and to confider that they occafioned all the jealoufies and fufpi-
tions that were fallen out between him and his Friends, which might
encourage his Enemies to take fome wicked enterprife in hand againft
his Perfon. To remedy this, I propofed it as fit, That *Lidingtoun*
fhould go unto *France*, finding Caution not to return to *Scotland* under the penalty of Twenty thoufand pounds, and withal giving his Son
in pledg for further Security, and that he fhould practife nothing againft
the Quiet of the Country. And that Sir *James Balfour* fhould be fet at
liberty, or banifhed after that fame manner. For he had already won the
Regent's Familiars with great Sums of Gold, which had ftanched their
wrath againft him ; which *Lidingtoun* would not do, albeit Sir *James*
had fent him his advice to do as he had done. Thefe two being freed and
out of the way, The Laird of *Grange* fhould deliver to him the Caftle
of *Edinbrugh*, to make Captain thereof whom he pleafed. That fo the
whole Country might fee, that all was in his power, and at his command. This I thought the beft way to reduce again the opinion of the
People and to fcare all his Enemies from their defperate enterprifes.
His anfwer was, *That he did bear no ill will to* Lidingtoun *, that he
would not prefs him to go out of the Country* ; *as for Sir* James Balfour,
he would fet him at liberty ; and for Grange, *he had too many Obligations
to him, and too great proofs of his Fidelity to miftruft him* ; *That he was
never minded to take the Caftle from him* ; *and if it were out of his hands,
he would give him the Keeping thereof before any other.*

He denyed that he had any fufpition either of *Grange*, or the *Secretary*, and thereupon went up to the Caftle and conferred Friendly with
them of all his Affairs, with a merry Countenance, and cafting in many
merry purpofes, minding them of many ftraits and dangers they had
formerly been together engaged in. So far was he inftructed to diffemble : yet the violence he did himfelf herein was eafily perceived by
fuch, who had been long acquainted with him, and had been his chief
advifers under God. The *Secretary* by his Wifdom, and *Grange* by
his Valour and Fidelity, who had both fuch notable Qualities as procured them the Envy of wicked men, who by their continual Flattery
and

and falſe Reports put them out of his Favour, and then like a weak Houſe wanting his ſuſtaining Pillars, he fell.

Himſelf was at the firſt of a gentle Nature, well inclined, good, wiſe, ſtout. In his firſt upriſing, his hap was to light upon the beſt ſort of Company ; his beginning was full of adverſity, true honeſt men ſtuck by him, becauſe he was Religiouſly educated, and devoutly inclined. But when he became *Regent*, Flatterers for their profit drew near him, and puſt him up into too good an opinion of himſelf. His old true Friends, who would reprove and admoniſh him, thereby loſt his Favour. I would ſometimes ſay to him, *That he was like an unskilful Player in a Tennis Court, running ever after the Ball ; whereas an expert Player will diſcern where the Ball will light, or where it will rebound, and with ſmall travel will let it fall on his hand, or racket.* This I ſaid, becauſe he took very great pains in his own Perſon to ſmall effect. After that he had gotten divers advertiſements of his Enemies Conſpiracies, yet he would credit nothing, but what came from his own Familiars, who told him nothing but of fair weather, and of the beſt Government that could be, and ſo rendred him careleſs and ſecure, which encouraged the Good man of *Bodwelhaugh* called *Hamiltoun*, to lye in his way as he was paſſing thorow *Lithgow*, who ſhot him, whereof he dyed that ſame Night ; all his Councellors and Familiars, were alſo well advertiſed as he was, both of the man, the place, and the time, and yet were ſo careleſs of him, that they would not be at the pains to ſearch the houſe where the man lay to ſhoot him, but ſuffered him to eſcape upon a ſpeedy Horſe. I have written thus far of him, becauſe every one knows not the verity how he was led away ; and becauſe St. *Auguſtine* ſayes, *That all kind of Ignorance is neither worthy of pardon nor excuſe, but only ſuch as have not the means to be inſtructed, nor to get knowledg.* I was ſometimes compelled to recite divers Sentences of *Solomon* to this Good *Regent* ; for ſo he was, and will ever deſervedly be called : How that *an heavy Toke was ordained for the Sons of* Adam, *from the day they go out of their Mothers Womb, till the day that they return to the Mother of all things ; from him who is clothed in Blew Silk and weareth a Crown, even to him who weareth ſimple Linnen ; wrath, envy, trouble and unquietneſs, rigor, ſtrife, and fear of death in the time of reſt. Again, Be diligent to know the ſtate of thy Flock ; for there are ſome who ſee but with other mens eyes, who hear but with other mens ears, theſe muſt needs be ignorant ; ſuch a man is commonly made a wicked Inſtrument to fulfil the appetites of envious, vengeable and greedy Councellors.* And *Solomon* ſayes, *That for the tranſgreſſion of ſuch wicked Councellors, the Land changeth many Princes. And again, The Prudent man ſeeth the Plague and eſchews it ; but Fools go on ſtill and are puniſhed. Wiſdome, Knowledg and Underſtanding of the Law is of the Lord ; Error, Ignorance and Darkneſs are appointed unto Sinners for Puniſhments and Plagues. The fooliſh will believe every thing, and the mouths of fools are fed with fooliſhneſs.* So the Prudent will conſider his paths, and can perceive that ſome are Councellors for themſelves : Therefore ſayes *Solomon, I Wiſdome dwell with Prudence,* and can find forth the right knowledg of Councellors ; as if he would ſay, Who have Wiſdome purified with Prudence, will not be ſo eaſily carried away with Flatterers, as a number of facil Princes, who promote them above faithful Friends and true

Servants,

Servants, who reprove them for thei unfeemly proceedings. Againſt the Rule of *Iſocrates*, who admoniſheth the King to love and retain as his trueſt Friends, ſuch as lovingly and modeſtly will correct his Faults. And as *Plutarch* ſaith unto *Trajan, Follow the Counſel of theſe who loves thee, rather than of thoſe whom thou loveſt.* And as *Thepompus* being demanded *how a Prince ſhould beſt Rule ?* anſwered, *In permitting his beſt Servants to tell him the verity of his Eſtate.* As the King of the People is, ſo are his Officers. If the Officers be wicked, ſo is the Ruler thought to be. *How are Flatterers,* ſaid I to the *Regent, flown away with your wonted humility , and who hath puſt you up, ſo that you will not ſuffer a Friendly Reproof ?* Says not Solomon, *If thou ſeeſt a man wiſe in his own conceit, there is more hope to be had of a fool than of him ? Exalt not thy ſelf in the day of honour, for pride goeth before deſtruction, and an high mind before a fall. Yet hear Counſel, and receive Inſtruction, let Reaſon go before every enterpriſe, and councel before every action. When you follwed the Counſel of your old experimented Friends, your Affairs proſpered. Since you left them, to follow the flattering fetches of your wonted Foes, (who are now become your chiefeſt Councellors ſince you have been made Regent) your Credit decayes, and all your buſineſs goes back.* I did ſhew you lately coming from Dumfries, *in what Danger your Eſtate and Perſon were ;* to which you have taken little notice; which Danger appears to me to be ever the longer the greater, without ſpeedy repentance, *and the haſty imbracing of ſuch Remedies as I mentioned for the time. Therefore take this better to heart, and in good part of his hand of whoſe Fidelity to you, you have had ſo good proof in all your adverſities.* Solomon *ſayes more,* Receive Inſtruction, *that thou mayſt be wiſe in thy latter end ; And above all this, pray to the Moſt High, that he may direct thy way in truth,* which I pray God grant you the grace to do.

The moſt part of theſe Sentences drawn out of the Bible, I uſed to rehearſe to him at ſeveral occaſions, and he took better with theſe of my hands, who he knew had no by-end, then if they had proceeded from the moſt Learned Philoſopher. Therefore at his deſire I promiſed to put them in writing, to give him them to keep in his Pocket ; but he was Slain before I could meet with him.

After the Deceaſe of the *Regent, England* ſent the *Earl* of *Suſſex* to *Berwick,* whither the Earl of *Lennox* came alſo at that ſame time, as being ſent for by the Lords of the King's Faction, to be made *Regent* in place of the Earl of *Murray.* The Earl of *Suſſex* had with him the Forces of the *North,* as if he had ſome enterpriſe to do, and to take ſome advantage at this time, when the Country wanted a *Regent.* About that ſame time, ſo many of the Lords as were banded, and profeſſed the *Queens* Authority, cauſed to proclaim the ſame at *Lithgow.* As yet they of the Caſtle at *Edinbrugh* profeſſed the *King's* Authority, albeit there were ſecret jealouſies betwixt them and ſo many of the reſt as had counſelled the late *Regent* to apprehend the *Secretary Lidingtoun,* and Sir *James Balfour,* and who would alſo have ruined *Grange,* becauſe he appeared concerned in them two, and alſo becauſe his Vertues were envied, and his Charge coveted by others.

They

They who were within the said Castle for the time, were my Lord
Duke of *Chattellerault*, and my Lord *Herris*, warded wrongfully as I
have said, therefore the Laird of *Grange* obteined a Warrant from the
rest of the King's Lords to set them at liberty. The Lord *Hume* was
there to assist with those of the Castle, with the Laird of *Grange*, the
Secretary *Lidingtoun*, his Brother the Prior of *Condingham*, three of
my Brothers Sir *Robert*, Captain *David*, and Sir *Andrew Melvil*, the
Lairds of *Drylow* and *Pittadrow*, Sir *James Balfour*, the Lairds of *Fernihast, Buccleugh, Wormistoun, Parbroth*, and divers other Noblemen and
Barons, who came there at all occasions, and were ready at a call when
they had to do.

This Company directed me to *Berwick*, toward the Earl of *Suffex*,
to know what he intended to do with his Forces; whether to assist any
of the two Factions, or to agree them? I was friendly received by
him, well lodged, and my expences by him defrayed, wanting nothing.
He sent me his own night-Gown, furred with rich furrings, to make
use of so long as I abode there. Albeit I knew him to be a great Enemy to all *Scots-men*, he appeared desirous to enter in great familiarity
with me, and as if he was desirous I should believe he had communicated to me his most secret thoughts, alledging his plainness to me, was
upon the report he had heard by sundry of his Country men to my
advantage. He said, " That his coming with his Forces, was not to
" assist any faction, nor to decide Questions and Titles that were among
" us, but to serve the Queen his Mistress, in obeying her Commands :
" That if he did any enterprise at that time against any *Scots-man*, it
" would be against his heart. That of all *Scots-men*, he liked best of
" those who were within the Castle of *Edinbrugh*, and their depen-
" ders, especially because he knew them to have been friends to the
" Duke of *Norfolk*, his near Coufin, whose part he said he would plain-
" ly have taken, if the said Duke had out of his own mouth communi-
" cated his enterprise to him, as he had foolishly done by a Gentleman
" of his, to whose credit he durst not commit the secrecy of that mat-
" ter, being of it self of so great concernment, as stood him upon his
" life and heritage. And that albeit he with his Forces came not to
" set out, nor to fortifie any Faction in *Scotland*, yet he durst be plain
" with me privately, as with a true friend, to declare that he did esteem
" the Queen of *Scotland* and the Prince her Son righteous Heirs to the
" Crown of *England*, which his judgment he had shown to few of his
" own Country-men.

So I returned with no direct answer, but with a firm opinion, that
he was sent to appear to set forward the Earl of *Lennox* to be Regent,
and to send word to the Lords of the King's side, that he would assist
them, and send in Mr. *Randolph* thither with the Earl of *Lennox*; and
yet to deal with the Lords of the Queens Faction, to encourage them
to hold forward their factious course, because the said Mr. *Randolph* had
a great dealing with the House of *Hamiltoun*, as he who convoyed the
Earl of *Arran*, now visited with the hand of God, out of *France* through
England home to *Scotland*, to assist the Congregation. He knew also
what old and long hatred had been betwixt the Houses of *Lennox* and
Hamiltoun; and was deliberately directed, secretly to kindle a fire of
discord betwixt two strong Factions in *Scotland*, which could not be

eafily quenched, and to conform the Lord *Hume*, who was not yet
refolved to take part with the Queens Faction, which *England* thought
had not money enough yet to fuftain long ftrife againft the King's Faction.

The Earl of *Suffex* entred the *Merfe* with his Forces, and took the
Caftle of *Hume*, and *Falbaftle*, full of riches and precious moveables,
that way moving the Lord *Hume* to take plain part with the *Hamil-*
touns, and the Queens Faction. Whereby it may be feen, that the conclufion was to hold Countries in difcord, by the craft of the Council
of *England* for the time, as I have before mentioned ; and which was
now put in practice, incontinent after the deceafe of the Earl of *Mur-*
ray. For albeit the Earl of *Lennox* had his Lady, Children, and Eftate
in *England*, they would not credit him, fuppofing he would be a true
Scots-man, as he proved indeed afterwards.

I being in *Berwick*, when the Earl of *Lennox* was fo far toward *Scot-*
land to be Regent, I thought it my duty to vifit him. For at his firft
in-coming before the marriage of his Son the Lord *Darnly* with the
Queen, he fent this prefent Colonel *Stuart* for my Brother Sir *Robert*
and me, and becaufe my Brother was abfent, I went to him alone. At
which time he told me, " That his long abfence out of the Country
" had made him as a ftranger to the condition of the Country, and
" that his Lady at his parting from her, had defired him to take my
" Brother's counfel and mine in all his affairs, as her Friends and Kinf-
" men. So that being familiar enough with him formerly, I vifited
him at this time, and told him the ftate of the Country. I diffwaded
him from taking upon him the Regiment, fearing that it might coft
him his life, as matters were like to be handled, as I fhould inform him
more at length, being once at home. As for my felf, I promifed to
ferve and affift him, albeit I could not find that fame refolution in thofe
of the Caftle of *Edinbrugh*. He thanked me, promifing me to be
my friend, fo far as lay in his power, upon which he gave me his hand.
Then he inquired, *What was the Caufe, that thofe who were in the Ca-*
ftle would oppofe him ? I anfwered, *For no particular prejudice they had*
againft himfelf, but becaufe the Lords who had fent for him, without ac-
quainting them therewith were not their friends, and they fufpected that
in procefs of time, they would move him to be their Enemy. He faid,
That the Laird of Grange *had been always his great friend, and had done*
him formerly great kindnefs. I faid, *I hoped he fhould yet be his friend,*
after that he had fetled himfelf in the Regiment, and might have time to
be rightly informed of every mans part.

Returning back from *Berwick*, I met the Abbot of *Dumfarmling*,
fent by the King's Lords to *England*, to meet with the Earl of *Linnox*
in his paffing by. His chief Commiffion was (fo far as I could afterward inform my felf) to defire the Queen of *England*, to deliver the
Queen of *Scotland* to be kept by the King's Lords here at home, feeing
that fhe would not proceed otherwife, according to the Accufation
given in againft her, the time my Lord *Murray* was there. Whereto the Queen of *England* made anfwer, *If they would find her fufficient*
Pledges for the fecurity of the Queens life, fhe would deliver her to be kept
by them. The Abbot alledged, *That would be hard to do, for what in*
cafe the Queen dye in the mean time ? She anfwered, *My Lord, I believed*

you

you had been a wife man, you would prefs me to fpeak what is no ways ne-
ceffary : you may know, That I cannot but for my honour require Pledges
for that end, I think you may judge alfo of your felf what might be beft
for me. Her meaning in this, might be eafily judged and underftood.

The Earl of *Lennox* came to *Edinbrugh* fhortly after me, and after
he had accepted the Government, his firft enterprife was to take *Bree-*
chin, which was kept by fome Companies of Foot men, lifted by the
Earl of *Huntly* to affift the Queens faction. Thefe Soldiers being advertifed, that the new Regent was coming to purfue them, fled, except a few who kept the Kirk and Steeple, who were all hanged. I
had made my felf ready to ride with the Regent, but Mr. *Randolph*
the *Englifh* Ambaffadour, who came with the Earl of *Lennox,* appearing to fet him forward with his power, hindred me from profecuting
that intention, fearing that I would be an inftrument of perfwading
the Laird of *Grange,* and thofe in the Caftle, to come to an amicable
agreement with the Regent. For if thofe of the Caftle, and their de-
fenders had affifted the Regent, the Queens faction were fo few and
weak, that they would not have been able to make a party anfwerable to the King's faction, who were greateft in number, and had the
hearts of the Subjects on their fide. I was very loath to ftay behind the Regent, both becaufe I had promifed to affift him, and alfo
becaufe I had obtained a promife of the Bifhop of St. *Andrews,* of the
Lands of *Lethem,* given by the Earl of *Murray* to Mr. *Henry Balneavs,*
whereof I had no Leafe, but Poffeffion, by reafon that the Bifhop was
for the time in *Dumbartoun,* forfaulted, fo the faid Lands were in the
Regent's power to difpofe to any other, yet he had promifed that I
fhould enjoy it. I told Mr. *Randolph* that the faid Land might be in
danger to be difpofed, in cafe I were abfent from the Regent. Tufh,
fays he, *I am Tutour at this time to the Regent, I fhall not onely warrant*
you that, but fhall caufe you get a better gift. In the mean time, he
promifed to write a Letter unto the Regent (who had already taken
journey) to fecure the fame to me, and to let him know that he had
ftayed me, to draw on an agreement between my friends in the Caftle
and him, therefore defiring him not to difpofe the faid Lands to any
other. But though I knew him to be a double dealer, and a fower
of difcord, yet I could not believe that he would abufe me in any thing,
having received fo great obligations from me during his banifhment
in *France,* for Religion, during the Reign of Queen *Mary.* Neither
would I blot Paper with this much concerning my particular, were it
not to declare the ftrange practifes of Princes in matters of State. Now
at Mr. *Randolph*'s defire, I ftayed. His firft propofition to me, was
to defire the Captain of the Caftle to agree with, and affift the Regent.
I told him, *That I fuppofed he might be brought to that through time, but*
not fo haftily. And that fame anfwer I brought to him from him,
with a requeft from the Laird of *Grange,* That he would be plain with
him : for there had been alfo great friendfhip betwixt them in *France.*
After fome Ceremonies and Proteftations of Secrecy, he faid. "Tell
" your friend this from Mr. *Randolph,* but not from the *Englifh* Am-
" baffadour, That there is no lawful Authority in *Scotland* but the
" Queens, fhe will prevail at length, and therefore it is his intereft, as

" the fafeft courfe, to join himfelf to her Faction. This was the help
he made to the Regent, who believed that his only Ambaffage was to
advance his Authority. I appeared to be very well fatisfied with this
wholefom advice, and went up to the Caftle, and told the Captain and
his affociates no more then I affured them of, at my return from *Ber-*
wick.

    The Laird of *Grange* was ftill refolved to own the King's Authority,
feeing to be factious under pretext of owning the Queen, during her
abfence and captivity, might do her more ill then good, and occafion
great bloodfhed among the Subjects, by the malice of the Ring-leaders
of the Court of *England*, and partialities of a few in *Scotland*, and was
therefore expecting a fit opportunity of making agreement betwixt
the parties. In the mean time, I went up and down betwixt thofe
of the Caftle, and Mr. *Randolph*, who gave me another Commiffion,
to wit, In cafe the two Queens of *England* and *Scotland* agree betwixt
themfelves, to appoint an *Englifh-man* Captain of the Caftle of *Edin-*
brugh, and fend unto him a Letter fubfcribed by both their hands to
him, to render up the fame to him whom they Commiffionate him
to deliver it, whether he would for great advantage to himfelf give
it to the perfon who fhould be appointed. This in great anger he refufed to hear: and this was all the good agreement that Mr. *Randolph*
and I made during the Regent's abfence. And inftead of minding the
Regent not to difpofe the forefaid Lands, he dealt with the Tutor of
Pitcur, that he might feek a gift of the faid Lands from the Regent,
informing him that I wanted a right thereto. When the Regent was
returned to *Edinbrugh*, I remembred Mr. *Randolph* of his promife, and
informed him a way how I might get them. He anfwered, That he
found the Regent fo ftubborn, and of fo ill a nature, that he could not
deal with him. Then I told him, That I was abundantly fenfible of
his practifes, and that whereas it appeared that he would caufe me not
only to abandon the Regent, but to be inftrumental in perfwading
the Laird of *Grange* to be upon a contrary Faction, I would not be
that inftrument, neither would I defert the King's intereft, though he
fhould caufe all the reft of my Lands to be taken from me.

    Seeing that *Grange* could not be moved to join with the Queens
Faction, according to the defire of the Court of *England* (for the reft
of that Kingdom was forry to fee this kind of dealing) the *Englifh*
Ambaffadour perfwaded the *Regent* to irritate and incenfe him, by
all manner of flights done to himfelf, and his dependers. In the
mean time my Lord Duke, the Earls of *Arguile* and *Huntly* addreffed
themfelves unto him, making their moan, "That they being Noble-
" men of the Country, of confiderable Intereft, were refufed to be
" admitted in the Society of the reft, who fought their ruine under
" pretext of the King's Authority, by the *Regent*, the Earl of *Mortoun*,
" and others, not their friends, requefting him to be their Protector,
" and to affift them during the King's minority. Telling him how
" that they at firft would gladly have joined with the Kings Lords,
" for maintaining the King's Authority, but could not get place, nor
" be admitted. Thus *Grange* finding himfelf neglected with the King's
Lords, and fought after by the Queens, he was compelled to declare
with that fide at length, having with him the Lord *Hume*, male-con-
                                               tent.

tent. Alſo Secretary *Lidingtoun*, and Sir *James Balfour* ſpurring him on to take that courſe, he was reſolved to take that ſide for his next refuge, he having been among the reſt ſummoned to be forfaulted.

Now the two furious Factions being in this manner framed, their hatred and rage grew greater and greater. For Mr. *Randolph* knew the animoſities which were among the Nobility, and the nature of every one in particular, by his frequent coming, and his long reſidence in *Scotland*. And among the Ladies he had a Mother, and a Miſtreſs, to whom he cauſed his Queen frequently to ſend Commendations, and Tokens. He alſo uſed his craft with the Miniſters, offering Gold to ſuch of them as he thought could be prevailed with to accept of his offer, but ſuch as were honeſt refuſed his gifts. He gave largely to all ſuch, as he knew were able to ſerve him in his deſign of kindling this fire, and his endeavours were ſo ſucceſsful, that the two parties were not only ſtirred up to fight, and ſhed one anothers blood; but would revile each other with injurious and blaſphemous words, and at length fell to the down-caſting of each others Houſes, to which *England* gave no ſmall aſſiſtance, having ſent in a number of Men of War to throw down *Hamiltoun*. This was occaſioned by ſome probability that appeared of a Reconciliation of the two Factions, by the endeavours of ſome of the moſt prudent Miniſters, who did all they could to prevent the enſuing troubles. And they foreſaw that this prejudice was done to the *Hamiltouns*, to inrage them, ſo as there might be no hope of agreement when they ſhould ſee themſelves ſo far injured.

Now as *Nero* ſtood upon a high part of *Rome* to ſee the Town burning, which he had cauſed to be ſet on fire, ſo Mr. *Randolph* delighted to ſee ſuch a fire by his craft kindled in *Scotland*, which was in all probability like to burn it up. And in his Letters to ſome of the Court of *England*, he gloried that he had kindled a fire in *Scotland*, which could not be eaſily extinguiſhed. Which when it came to the knowledge of Sir *Nicholas Throgmorton*, he wrote to my Brother Sir *Robert*, and me, advertiſing us how we were handled, expreſſing his deteſtation both at Secretary *Cicil* directer, and Mr. *Randolph* as executer. All the honeſt Men in *England* were ſorry at it, of which number there are as many within that Country, as in any other ſo much bounds in *Europe*.

My Brother and I did ſhew the Letters we had received from Sir *Nicholas*, to the Laird of *Grange*, and ſo many within the Caſtle as we knew to be ſecret, which they eaſily believed, as being Men of great underſtanding, who had noticed Mr. *Randolph*'s proceedings. Whereupon there were ſome ſecret meetings drawn on between my Lord *Hume*, and my Lord *Ruthven* as near kinſmen. The Lord *Ruthven* was in greateſt favour with the Regent for the time, being alſo Treaſurer, he was deſired to come and ſpeak with my Lord *Hume*, during the hotteſt of the Civil Wars. At which time Secretary *Lidingtoun*, and my Brother Sir *Robert*, came into communing with the Lord *Ruthven*; after that he and the Lord *Hume* had ſpoken a ſpace together, and did ſhew him how the *Regent* was uſed by *England*, and how this Kingdom was abuſed by the tricks of a few; for advancing their

ſelfiſh

felfifh ends, and alſo how that the Earl of *Mortoun* had deſired ſecretly to come at midnight, accompanied with Mr. *Archibald Douglas* to the Caſtle of *Edinbrugh*, and had entertained long conference with them, deſiring their affiſtance, and he ſhould chace the Farl of *Lennox* back to *England*, if they would accept and acknowledge him for Regent in his ſtead, which they of the Caſtle would nor grant, looking upon the Earl of *Lennox* as a true *Scots-man*. And they declared that their denying to affiſt him at firſt, was his being ſent for and brought in by them. That therefore they feared at the firſt, that he would have been too much at the devotion of the Court of *England*, as being an *Englifh man* ; and having yet his Lady. Children, and Lands in that Country, and moreover that he ſhould be ſo led by the Earl of *Mortoun*, and their factious Enemies, that he would ſeek their utter ruine, both becauſe that Captain *Crawford* who had accuſed the Secretary, was for the time Servant to the Earl of *Lennox*, and alledged that he had a Commiſſion from the ſaid Earl to give in the ſaid Accuſation. And that which gave matter enough to my Lord *Hume*, was the bringing in of the Earl of *Lennox*, by the Earl of *Suſſex*, and the taking of his two Houſes of *Hoome* and *Falcaſtle* all at one time, which he ſuppoſed not to have been done without the Earl of *Lennox* his knowledge and conſent. But ſince they underſtood that the Earl of *Lennox*, and the whole Country was abuſed by *England*, Mr. *Randolph* the Agent, and the Earl of *Mortoun*; they were reſolved both to agree themſelves, and to cauſe all *Scotland* agree with the *Regent*, if he would grant them reaſonable conditions.

My Lord *Ruthven* was very glad of this offer, and ſaid he hoped to bring them a good anſwer from the *Regent*; and the rather, becauſe the Earl of *Mortoun* was abſent, being malecontent, for denying to him the grant of the Biſhopprick of St. *Andrews*, which the King's houſe and the Regent's might ill ſpare. So he returned with this offer to the *Regent*, who much relliſht it, and after twice or thrice paſſing betwixt the *Regent* with the Lord *Ruthven*, had concluded a Peace quietly in their minds, none being as yet made privy thereto. But as Ambaſſadours are great Spies, and commonly ſuſpitious, Mr. *Randolph* who lay at *Lieth*, having his own Jealouſies of an intention of accommodation, knew the only way to ſtop it, was to bring again the Earl of *Mortoun*, who he knew would violently oppoſe it, and uſe the utmoſt of his endeavours to render that Deſign ineffectual. He therefore dealt earneſtly with the *Regent*, to give the ſaid *Biſhoprick* of St. *Andrews* to the Earl of *Mortoun*, alledging to her, *That the Queen his Miſtreſs had written to him for that effect, and that ſhe would recompence it to him with greater advantage. That he would cauſe her hand-writing to come to him thereabout, and that ſhe would be much diſſatiſfied if he refuſed that her deſire.* When the *Regent* had upon Mr. *Randolph's* deſire granted this, he incontinently advertiſed the Earl of *Mortoun* thereof, who immediately came to Court, and ſmelling the foreſaid deſign of agreement, he uſed all the contrary practices he could to hinder it. For as he had fiſhed that Benefice in troubled Waters, he hoped by ſuch means to fiſh much more. And finding that I was much inclined to draw forward the accommodation, óne of his Devices was to cauſe the Councel to Vote and direct the Earl of *Buchan* to take me Priſoner out of my own houſe, houfe. But I was at a Marriage in *Fordel*, where the faid Earl came, with whom I went willingly, tho I had as many Friends there, as offered to chace him back again without his Errand; but I would not prejudge my juft Caufe. For the Earl of *Buchan* was of a gentle and difcreet Nature, and affured me they had nothing to lay to my charge, but to fee if I could be a good Inftrument of Concord. He defired me when I was in *Lieth*, to fend up to the Caftle of *Edinlrugh*, and alledg that my Life was in hazard, in cafe they would not render up the Caftle to the *Regent*. I anfwered, *It was a Childifh thing in them, to propofe fuch a thing to me, feeing they could not but know that my Friends in the Caftle were angrier at me than they were, becaufe I did not take part with them.* However, the Laird of *Grange* was diffatisfied, when he heard that I was taken. For he knew how far I was Injur'd, feeing I had feveral times perfwaded him to take part with the *Regent*, and how far I had reafoned againft the *Secretary* and Sir *James Balfour* in their proceedings with the *Queens* Faction. For feeing fhe was Captive, fo that neither could fhe help them, nor they her, it would but occafion her to be the ftronglier guarded, and kept more ftraitly in *England*. For hearing that there was a Faction rifen up in her Name, it would caufe them to fuppofe that fhe was in hope of fudden liberty, by fome Practices with the Subjects of *England*. Sir *William Balfour* alledged, That her Majefty had Friends in *France*, and other Parts, who would be more encouraged to do for her, if they underftood that a number of the Nobility did own her Authority. I faid, That her only Friends were in *England* and *France*; that thofe who were in *England* durft not as yet appear, feeing there would be a fpecial Eye held over them, and her *French* friends would do her no good; the *Queen Mother* who had the chief Rule of that Country being her great Enemy, and the Houfe of *Guife* neither able to help her, nor yet were they her fure friends, as I fhall fhew more at length anon. I was declaring that the Laird of *Grange* was angry at my taking, I being fo frank for the Regent, and he fo willing to join with him. That fame night he fent down a Woman from the Caftle to *Lieth*, with a Ticket to me, *That he was refolved to come that fame night at mid-night, and relieve me out of their hands; that he had fent that Woman to know how I was kept, and where I was lodged.* The Regent's Camp lay between *Lieth* and *Edinbrugh*, and many of the Noblemen and Barons lodged in *Lieth*, for every one had not Pavilions to lodge in the Camp. The Laird of *Grange* had appointed a Boat to lye at *Grantoun*, and had refolved to come failing up to *Lieth* Harbour, as if it had been a Boat come from *Fiffe*, and thought without ftroke to come to my Lodging, and take me out of my Keepers hands, and go up the water again to a part where he had Horfemen in readinefs, to carry me up to the Caftle with him. But I would upon no accompt condefcend thereto, affuring him, *That I was in no danger ; and that my Lord* Bughan *had promifed, when I pleafed, to let me flip away, which I would not do, but defired daily to come to a Tryal.* Many of the Lords marvelled wherefore I was taken, feeing they knew, That fince the Regent's entry to *Scotland*, I had ever affifted him. The Regent himfelf was much therewith diffatisfied; fo that after inquiry, it was found, that few of the Councellors knew of my taking. The Earl of *Mar*, a true Nobleman,

faid,

said, *That the Earl of* Buchan *for embracing such a Commission, was mad-
der than the former Earl his Father, who was known not to be very wise.*
But the Earl of *Mortoun* sent me word, *That nothing should ail me more
then his own heart.* For the fashion they desired me to find Caution,
that I should serve the King's Majesty, and his Regent, and so I was
dismissed, and never brought before the Council. Of a truth I could
see no reason to set up two Factions to destroy the Country, seeing I
knew, That though the one party professed to be for the Queen, it
was so far from conducing to her advantage, that I knew it had a
quite contrary effect so long as she was Captive, nor yet could I see
any out-gate for those who professed her Authority, and who were
compelled thereto for their own defence. For whereas they would
gladly have assisted the King's Lords, if they would have accepted of
them; finding themselves refused, necessity drew them to defend
themselves under the name of some Authority, not true love to the
Queen. And therefore I thought them the less to be relyed upon.
The rest of my reasons, why the Queen could expect no help out of
France from her own friends, nor yet from the *Queen Mother*, were
these, "The *Queen Mother* had not been well used, so long as our
"Queen's Husband *Francis* the Second lived. The Council and States
"of *France* desired not the Union of this Isle. For a proof hereof, af-
"ter that my Brother Sir *Robert*, (when he returned the first time of
his Ambassage out of *England*) brought the hand-writings of twenty
five principal Earls and Lords in *England*, to set the Crown of *England* upon the Queen of *Scotland*'s head. For the Captains in the particular Shires were ready named, and by those Lords set down in
that Paper, who were to be in alreadiness to march forward, whenever
they should be charged, only they waited the Queens opportunity,
and advertisement when to stir. Upon this intelligence, the Queen
incontinently did write to *France*, to her Uncle the Cardinal of *Lorrain*, desiring him to send to her one of his most secret Servants, to
whom she was to Communicate matters of that weight and importance, that she could not hazard to send them in Writing or Cyphers.
And accordingly the said Cardinal sent hither one of his most familiar Secretaries, to whom the Queen caused my Brother and me to
declare the state of *England*, and the great party she had there to es-
pouse her interest, as is above specified, desiring her said Uncle to
send his advice what time would be most fit for her to stir, and to
send what help he and all his friends could procure. This Secretary
being returned to his Master, informed him of the whole matter.
The Cardinal again to insinuate upon the *Queen Mother*, and to appear
to be a true *French man*, acquainted the *Queen Mother* how prejudicial
to the Crown of *France*, the Union of this Isle of great *Britain* would
be; that therefore it was her interest all she could to oppose it. He
therefore advised her to advertise the Queen of *England* of the said intended Plot, as the only and most effectual means for preventing it,
which the *Queen Mother* failed not to do. But whatever the Queen
of *England*'s thoughts of the truth thereof was, she appeared to give no
credit thereto, as if she looked upon it as an *Italian* fetch to put her in
suspicion of her Nobility. This accompt I had from the Queens Majesty her self, complaining to me one day of the Cardinal's unkind
dealing

dealing towards her. Therefore I thought I had good ground to say, *There was no help to be looked for out of* France. And the Duke of *Alva* who was in *Flanders*, had plainly refused to give her any help, till the King his Master would command him; *Seeing,* as he alledged, *he had work enough to do to settle his Master's own Subjects in* Flanders.

These were the arguments which I used to move my friends to agree with the Regent, and my indeavours wanted not success, they having come very near a point by the dealing of the two Lords above-mentioned, *Hume* and *Ruthven,* assisted by Secretary *Lidingtoun* : For the Lord *Hume* would then do nothing without his advice.

But after that the Earl of *Mortoun* was returned to the Court, and had by *Randolph's* means obtained the Bishoprick of St. *Andrews,* these two suspecting the probability of the apparent agreement, which had been kept secret from them; they fell a plotting some way to hinder the same, and concluded to hold a Parliament; wherein to forfault all the Queens Lords, whereby the Regent should utterly ruine his ancient Enemies the *Hamiltouns,* and there would be a bait to every one of the King's Lords; seeing they should be made sharers of the spoil and so each of them get wealth enough. Mr. *Randolph,* for their encouragement, gave them assurance of assistance from *England,* so that they needed fear no resistance from their adversaries. The Earl of *Mortoun* had made a great Faction in the Council, partly by representing the Queens Lords as intending to re-establish Popery (upon which allegiance he knew he would make them odious to the generality of the People) but especially by promising each of his party a share of the forfaulters of the Queens Lords, so that they were easily brought to consent to a Parliament, to be held at *Sterling* for the foresaid effect.

The Queens Lords to be equal with them, held another Parliament at *Edinbrugh* both at one time, upon that very same design of forfaulting the King's Lords. The Laird of *Grange* in the mean time took great displeasure to see *Scotsmen* so furiously bent against each other, set only by the practices of *England* and the extream avarice of some particular men, for their selfish designs, who intended to augment their Estates, and raise their own Fortunes upon the ruines of their Neighbours. Therefore he sent for the Laird of *Fernihurst* his Son-in-Law, the Laird of *Buccleugh* Father to this present Lord, who loved the Laird of *Grange* better than any of his own kindred ; which Laird of *Buccleugh* was a man of rare qualities, wife, true, stout, and modest. These two Gentlemen were desired to come well accompanied, and arrived at *Edinbrugh* in an Evening late. The Laird of *Grange* had already devised an enterprise, to wit, *That same night after they had Supt themselves, and baited their Horses, to ride all night foribard with them to* Sterling, *to be there early in the morning before any of the Lords who held the Parliament were out of their Beds, hoping by the intelligence he had received, assuredly to surprise them before they could be advertised.* All the Lords and Council found the advice exceeding good, but they would in no ways grant that he should ride with them, alledging, *That their only comfort, under God, consisted in his preservation.* He on the other hand alledged, *His presence would be necessary, for he was acquainted with difficult*

difficult enterprises, and feared that they would not follow rightly her carefully his directions. But they ingaged to follow it moſt ſtrictly, and would not ſuffer him to ride with them, but the Earl of *Huntly*, my Lord *Arbroth*, and divers others went forward with the Forces. Theſe two Gentlemen had brought them, and were at *Stirling* before Four of the Clock in the Morning, and entred the Town of *Stirling* at a little paſſage, led by a Towns-man called *George Bell*, which entry of theirs was immediately after the Night-watches had retired to their reſt. They divided their Men, and appointed ſuch as they thought meeteſt to await at every Lord's Lodging, and a Company with Captain *Hackerſtoun* to wait at the Market-Croſs, to cauſe good order to be kept, and to preſerve the Town-houſes from being ſpoiled, only they appointed the Stables to be cleanſed by *Buccleugh* and *Fernehaſt's* men, giving them commands not to leave one Horſe in Town uncarried away with them, which Commiſſion the South-land Lads forgot not punctually to execute : But becauſe Captain *Hackerſtoun* came not in due time with his Company to ſtand where he was appointed, a number of unruly Servants broke up the Merchants Booths, and run here and there in diſorder after the ſpoil, leaving their Maſters all alone. After they had taken out all the Lords from their Lodgings, and were leading them Captives down the ſteep Caſſway of *Sterling* on foot, intending to take their Horſes at the nether Port, and ride to *Edinbrugh* with their Priſoners. But thoſe within the Caſtle being allarumed with the noiſe of the Towns-men, crying out, becauſe of the ſpoil taken from them, imagining what ſhame they would indure, if they did not ſhew themſelves Men, and perceiving the diſorder of their Enemies, they came down fearleſly upon them, and reſcued all the Priſoners ſave the Regent, whom one came and ſhot behind his back, commanded as was alledged by my Lord of *Pacly*. The Laird of *Wormiſtoun* was the taker of the *Regent*, and had been ordained by the Laird of *Grange* to wait upon him, to ſave him from his particular Enemies. For they all had ingaged to him, e're they went from *Edinbrugh*, not to kill one man, elſe he would not have left them. *Wormiſtoun* was alſo killed againſt the *Regent's* will, who cryed continually to ſave him, who had done what he could for his preſervation. The *Regent* dyed not ſuddenly, but ſome days after, and made a very godly end. They who had loſt this fair enterpriſe for want of *Granges* conduct, had enough to do to ſave themſelves, and had been all taken had not thoſe in *Stirling* wanted horſes to purſue after them. For thoſe who had taken the horſes, did ride forward with all poſſible ſpeed, leaving their Maſters in danger to do for themſelves.

When they were returned back to *Edinbrugh*, they were very unwelcome gueſts to the Laird of *Grange*, who greatly lamented the *Regent's* ſlaughter. He ſaid openly, *If he knew who had done that foul deed, or had directed it to be done, his own hand ſhould have revenged it.* And whereas before he uſed to be meek and gentle, he could not now command himſelf, but burſted out in harſh language, calling them diſorderly Beaſts: For he knew the Regent was inclined to Peace, and was only ignorantly driven on by the Earl of *Mortoun*, and Mr. *Randolph's* practiſes to hold the ſaid Parliament, to the hinderance of concord and agreement, therefore his intention was to bring all the

King's

Kings Lords to the Caftle of *Edenbrugh*, and to have made an agreement betwixt them and the other faction before they had parted. But God in his providence would not permit this, for further punifhment of our wickednefs. For the Parliaments held forward, and each one of them forefaulted others, the Kings Lords came and lay at *Lieth*, and the *Queens* within the Town and Caftle of *Edenbrugh*.

Mr. *Randolph* would have had *Mortoun* made *Regent* inftead of *Lennox*, but the *Lords* liked better of the Earl of *Marr* and chofe him.

For a little time there was hot skirmifhing betwixt *Lieth* and *Edinbrugh*, and extream hatred betwixt the two factions, and great cruelties exercifed, where they could be Mafters of one another. And frequently the Marfhal of *Berwick* came to *Lieth* to affift Mr. *Randolph* privately, tho publickly to find fault with him for his proceedings, which my Lord of *Marrs* friends perceived, and himfelf at laft, whereupon he began to grow colder in the quarrel, and withdrew himfelf to *Stirling*, advifing with his friends what was meeteft to be done. Alledging that he could fee nothing but the wrack of the Country, under pretext of owning the *King* and *Queens* Authority, while neither *Kings* nor *Queens* was in any of their minds, but only put on by their own partialities of ambition, greedinefs, and vengeance, *England* kindling up both the Parties, and then laughing them all to fcorn.

After this Conference, Captain *James Cunningham*, fervant to my Lord of *Marr*, a difcreet Gentleman, defired a fecret meeting with my Brother Sir *Robert*. In the mean time the moft part of the Kings Lords went to *Stirling*, where the *Regent* was living. My Lord of *Mortoun* went to *Dalkieth*, my Lord *Lindfay* lay in *Lieth*. When the Wars grew colder, and notice thereof taken by the Court of *England*, a new Ambaffador was hafted to *Scotland*, to wit, Mr. *Henry Killegrew* an old acquaintance of mine. For Mr. *Randolph* was returned home, becaufe he had not fuch Credit with the Earl of *Marr* as to do fervice to thefe he ferved, and had loft the favour of both the Factions. For his double dealing was difcovered, he having no Credit but with the Earl of *Mortoun*.

This new Ambaffador being Arrived at *Lieth* upon his way toward *Stirling*, where the *Regent* remained for the time, he fent up to the Caftle of *Edenbrugh* to fee if I was there. For they had told him in *Lieth*, that I was newly come from *Fiffe*. He defired that I would come and fpeak with him, which I did, and convoyed him unto *Cramond* reafoning together all the way upon fuch matters, as he faid he had in Commiffion, chiefly how he might be a good inftrument to agree the differences that were between the two Parties, albeit I knew there was nothing lefs in his mind, at leaft in his Commiffion. He faid, He had the *Queen* his Miftrefs commands to deal with both Parties for Concord, but that he was moft concerned in thefe of the Caftle, albeit that outwardly he behooved firft to go to the *Regent*, being in civility engaged to give him the prerogative, yet in effect he faid my friends in the Caftle were thefe, to them he was chiefly directed, that they fhould be preferred both by his firft falutation by me to them, and by two familiar Letters, the one from my Lord of *Leicefter*

to

to the Laird of *Grange*, and the other from Secretary *Cicil* to Secretary *Lidingtoun*, defiring me to intreat them to follow the good counfel given therein by the faid Lords, who loved them intirely for their vertue, and old acquaintance. He willed me to tell them, that after he had declared his Commiffion to the *Regent*, he would come back again to them and at length declare his Commiffion to them from Her Majefty.

It appeared to me that he had intelligence how that Mr. *Randolph*'s double dealing had been difcovered, therefore he feemed to find fault with him in many things, though in general he excufed him as far as he could, until I adjured him upon the long and great familiarity that had been betwixt us, to deal plainlier with me. I told him he might ferve his *Miftrefs* truly enough, without cafting me and my friends upon a wrong fide, which might be afterwards our ruin who deferved better at his hands, then to put us in fuch dangers as if we were untoward, difhoneft, or uncounfellable, as Mr. *Randolph* had done; forgetting the fraternity of Religion fo well grounded among us during his banifhment in *France* for Religion. There he was compelled to confefs to me, that his Commiffion and his mind went not one way, and that he was imployed againft his will, tho as a Servant he durft not difobey his Princefs, he faid he would give me his loving counfel, and warning very freely.

He faid that the Council of *England* neither built their courfe here upon the late *Regent*, nor yet upon this, but intirely upon the Earl of *Mortoun* as well of their own Plot laid down long fince, as by the Information of Mr. *Randolph*, who hath confirmed them in that Opinion, fo that they will not alter for no contrary perfuafion. Willing my friends and me to joyn our courfe and band with the Earl of *Mortoun*, or elfe to expect no friendfhip from the Court of *England*, but hurt and ruin fo far as they might. For albeit he was not *Regent*, they knew that he had a great Faction in the Country, which they were refolved what they could to encreafe, fo that whoever was *Regent*, he fhould get little or nothing done without his confent. In this I thought he dealt plainly, my friends of the Caftle were of that fame Judgment, yet they could not find in their heart to joyn with him, albeit he fought their friendfhip, offering to hold up the *Queens* Authority, for they thought his courfe unfure for the King, and fetling of the Eftate, he being too much addicted to *England*.

After that this Ambaffador had been with the *Regent* in *Stirling*, and was come back again to *Edinbrugh*, he told the reft of his Commiffion to them of the Caftle, to whom he ufed himfelf but like an Ambaffador as he was directed. He faid that he found them more reafonable, then the *Regents* Party. Then he went to *Dalkieth* to meet with the Earl of *Mortoun*, and thereafter returned to *Edinbrugh*, to wait all fit occafions and informations how to proceed conform to the tenor of his inftructions. He had Commandment to ftay in *Scotland* for a time, to fee if he could obtain as much Credit, as to ferve their turn who fent him. And becaufe I was of his greateft acquaintance, he came with me to my Houfe in *Halhil*, and ftayed a few dayes there to refrefh his Spirits, and after that I convoyed him back again to *Edinbrugh*, he fhewed me fome Articles of his Inftructions one of the which was.   *Item,*

" *Item*, If the *Captain* of the *Caſtle* will condeſcend, that all the
" differences now in queſtion among the *Scots*, be referred to be de-
" cided before us and our Councel, as the reſt of the Kings Lords
" have granted already, we ſhall be his good friend, maintain him in
" his Office, and give him an honourable Penſion.   But he plainly
" refuſed to comply with this; ſaying, he would prejudge his *Prince*
" and Country, ſo that this, and his other former refuſals coſt him his
" life afterwards.

About this time my Lord *Regent* ſent a Letter to me, with all diligence to come to him.   At my coming, he made a heavy moan for
the civil troubles that were kindled in the Country, by the Craft
and Malice of ſome in *England*, and ſome in *Scotland*, taking the colour of this or that authority, and yet were only moved with their
own particularities to the hurt both of *King*, *Queen* and Country, deſiring me that I would go unto the Caſtle of *Edinbrugh*, and ſhew
them as of my own head and not as from him, that I underſtood he
perceived albeit too late, how that we were all led upon the Ice, and
that it was the Intereſt of all true *Scotſmen* to agree, that the State
may be ſetled.   And ſays he, you may deſire them to ſeek to treat
with me thereabout which you may aſſure them they will obtain, if
they will ſeek the ſame.   And offer your ſelf to be the inſtrument to
bring on a good agreement between them and me, which ſhall by
Gods Grace take good effect upon your return with their reaſonable
offers and anſwer.   Whereupon I went to *Edinbrugh*, and found them
all inclined to peace and quietneſs, with little need of perſuaſions thereto, for they were near a point before with my Lord of *Lennox*,and ſome
former Conference had been betwixt my *Brother* and Captain *Cunningham* thereabouts.

At my return to the *Regent*, he was very glad, ſaying, he knew
that theſe honeſt Gentlemen were ever willing to ceaſe from civil diſcord, ſeeing the *Queen* was Captive, to whom their owning her authority could do no good but evil; but that they had been by crafty
practiſes caſt againſt their wills upon a contrary courſe.   Then he inquired upon what conditions the Captain and his friends would agree;
I ſaid that the Laird of *Grange* would not ſell his Duty to His Prince
and Country for advantage, but would ſerve the King and his Country to ſettle the Eſtate ; ſo long as the *Queen* was detained in *England*,
and if God pleaſed to grant her liberty, they doubted not but ſhe and
her Son ſhould agree betwixt themſelves, to which all honeſt and
good Subjects would conſent.   They for their parts deſired no Mans
Lands nor Goods, but only Liberty peaceably to enjoy their own Li-
vings.   Only *Grange* deſired that the *Regent* would cauſe to pay certain Debts contracted for repairing of the Caſtle and Artillery, which
conditions the *Regent* promiſed to fulfil, and to be an aſſured friend to
Grange, and thoſe in the Caſtle.   And without any other Ceremonies
he called the Laird of *Tillibardin*, and after he declared unto him how
far we had proceeded, he put his hand in mine and did ſwear the Peace
in preſence of the ſaid *Tillibardin*, who had alſo been a good Inſtrument in the ſaid agreement, together with Mr. *Clement Little* afterwards Provoſt of *Edinbrugh*.   No man was privy thereto, but my
Lady *Mar*, and Captain *James Cuningham*.   After.

After this, the *Regent* went to *Edinburgh*, to Convene the Lords of Councel, to shew them the Calamities that the Civil-Wars produced, and to let them see how necessary an agreement would be to the whole Country.   In the mean time, until the appointed Councel-day, he went to *Dalkieth*, where he was nobly treated by the Lord of *Mertoun*, shortly after which he took a vehement sickness, which caused him to ride suddenly to *Stirling*, where he dyed regrated by many. Some of his friends, and the vulgar, suspected he had gotten wrong at his Banquet.

The Earl of *Mortoun*, after the deceafe of the Earl of *Marr* was made *Regent*, *England* helping it with all their might ; so soon as he was chosen he sent for me, declaring how that againſt his mind and inclinations, the Lords had burthened him with that troublesome Office, whereof seeing he behoved to accept, he could wish that he might ſtand the Country and Common-wealth in some ſtead.   Firſt he would defire the help of all good and honeſt men, to draw on Peace and Concord to the quieting the State, praying me as one for whom he had ever entertained special favour, to travail with my friends of the Castle for that effect, and to persuade them to go forward with him, as they were minded to do with the Earl of *Marr*, assuring me that none of the former *Regents* had at any time been more willing, then he was presently to put an end to the civil troubles, nor that I should remember lefs the partialities paſt, and that the *Regent* should not revenge the Earl of *Mortoun*'s quarrels.   But whoever would serve the King and be his friend, he would embrace them upon what faction soever they had formerly been.   And he was willing to give whatever conditions the Earl of *Marr* had offered, that I should have the Priory of *Pittenweem* for my pains, the Laird of *Grange* the Bishoprick of *St. Andrews*, and Castle of *Blackness*, and every one within the Castle should be reſtored to their Lands, and Poffeffions as before.

It was very hard to bring on this agreement with the Earl of *Mortoun*, for the evil opinion which was conceived of him, and the hurtful marks they suppoſed by proofs and appearances that he would shoot at, being by nature covetous and too great with *England*, and ever Jealous that the King would be his ruine, concerning which a Lady who was his Whore, had shewn him the answers of the Oracles.   Yet the Laird of *Grange*, who was ever willing to see Concord in the Country, was eaſily persuaded, the Lord *Hume*, and *Lidington* made some reſiſtance at the firſt, but were alfo at length content.   So that after I had paſt twice or thrice between them, they appeared to be agreed in their hearts, and the Laird of *Grange* said, he would cause all the reſt of the *Queens* faction to agree with the *Regent*, but he refuſed to take the Bishoprick of *St. Andrews* and Castle of *Blackness*, defiring nothing but his own Lands.

When I returned to the *Regent* with this answer conform to his defire, he was marvellouſly glad ; but when I declared that the Laird of *Grange* would be a good inſtrument to cauſe all the reſt of the *Queens* faction agree alfo with him ; he answered, that was not meet.   And when I reaſoned againſt him, and shewed him how that I had ſpoken in his name, that he was reſolved to have agreed all *Scotland*, and that *Grange* had no quarrel of his own, but to help a number of No-

ble-

ble men who required his Protection during the Kings Minority, and had requested the *Regent* once to agree with them altogether, for *Granges* honour, and afterwards he and all these of the Castle should band with him and lay aside all other bands. The *Regent* answered, and said, *James* I will be plain with you, it is not my Interest to agree with them all, for then their faction will be as strong as ever it was, thereby they may some day circumvent me if they please, therefore it is my game to divide them. And moreover there have been great troubles in this Country this while by-gone, and during them great wrongs and extortions committed, for the which some fashion of punishment must be made, and I would rather that the Crimes should be laid upon the *Hamiltouns*, the Earl of *Huntly*, and their Adherents, then upon your Friends : and by their wrack I will get more profit, then by that of those in the Castle, that have neither so great Lands to escheat to us, as the reward of our labours. Therefore shew *Grange* and your friends, that either they must agree without the *Hamiltouns*, and the *Earls of Huntly and Arguile*, or the said Lords will agree without him, and these of the Castle. To this I answered, That I understood him, his Speeches being very plain, with this I went again to the Castle, and rehearsed our whole reasoning, *Grange* said it was neither godly or just dealing, to lay the blame upon those who were richest for their Lands and Goods, and not upon them who were guiltiest, seeing these Noblemen had been ever willing to agree, after that the *Queen* was kept in *England*, but could not be admitted. And yet if now they would abandon him, and agree without him, and those in his company, he had deserved better at their hands, yet he had rather that they should leave and deceive him, then that he should do it unto them.

When I had given this return to *Mortoun*, and that he perceived that *Grange* stood stiff upon his honesty and reputation, he appeared to like him the better, and seemed as if he had been resolved to go forward with these of the Castle. He sent up *Carmichael* at my desire, to hear out of their own mouths so far as I had spoken in their name ; they of the Castle likewise sent *Pittadrow* to the *Regent* to hear out of his own mouth, so far about the agreement as I had said to them in his name. This I did for my discharge, whatsoever might come afterwards.

The *Regent* asked at what time the Castle of *Edinbrugh* should be delivered to him, I said, within half a year. What security, said he, shall I have for it ? I said, I should be a Pledge if he would accept me. Then he enquired wherefore I sought so long delay ? I answered in the first place, till all Articles and Promises might be performed, and likewise because though the Laird of *Grange* was ever esteemed an honest man, yet by wrong Reports and Practices the Ministers have been stirred up to cry out and preach against him, therefore to inable him to serve for the future, it would be some satisfaction to his mind, to let the world see that as well after the agreement as before, he should be esteemed alike honest and worthy to keep the house, and then at the time appointed the *Regent* should be intreated to receive the Castle out of his hands. He appeared to be very well content with this manner of dealing, and gave me great thanks for his

travel

travel I had made, defiring me to go home, and he in the mean time would convene the reft of the Noble-men of his fide, and acquaint them with his Proceedings, and take their advice and confent to this good work,which he doubted not to procure, and thereafter he faid, he would fend for me again and put the form of the agreement in Writing.

But he took immediately another courfe, and fent a fit man to the *Hamiltouns,* the Earls of *Huntly,* *Arguile,* and their dependers, and offered an accommodation to them, if they would be fatisfied to make an agreement by themfelves not including *Grange* and thofe in the Caftle, which condition they accepted of, without making therein any Ceremonies, whereof they by their Letters inftantly from *Pearth* advertifed the Laird of *Grange,* lamenting that the ftraits they were redacted to,had compelled them to accept that agreement which the *Regent* had offered them,praying him not to take it in evil part,feeing they had no houfe nor ftrength to retire themfelves to.They gave him many thanks for the help and affiftance he had made them, which they faid, they would never forget fo long as God would lend them their lives.

This was the recompence this good Gentleman obtained for the great help he had given the Lords, the hazard he had run upon their account, and the Charges he had been at in aiding them,not imagining that the *Regent* would be fo malitious as to caft him off, and not accept of his friendfhip which he incontinently offered, after the reft, were agreed : but from that time forth the *Regent* would hear none of his offers, perfuading the reft of his Faction that thefe of the Caftle were fo proud and wilful, that they refufed to ferve the *King,* or acknowledge him as *Regent.* And this was Publifhed and Preached, and yet the contrary was true. For they would have taken any reafonable appointment. What rage was in the *Regents* mind for greedinefs of their Lands, and Goods, or what fhould have induced him to bring an Army from *England* to befiege the Caftle of *Ediubrugh,* I know not, it being to the difhonour of his Prince and Country, feeing a little before the Caftle was offered to the Earl of *Rothefs,* to be inftantly delivered unto his hands, to be kept to the *Regents* behoof, which was refufed. So that apparently he had fome other fetch in his head, then a man efteemed fo wife fhould have had, feeing he might have obtained his intent without the help of *England,* having all *Scotland* at his Devotion, faving that few number without the Caftle,who would likewife have agreed upon any reafonable condition.

Thus the Caftle of *Edinbrugh* was ftraitly befieged with an *Englifh* Army under the Conduct of the *Marfhal* of *Berwick,* affifted by all *Scotland.* Thefe within feeing they could not be received upon any compofition, debated fo long as they had victuals and water. For their Draw-well dryed by the drouthy Summer, and they had no other water but what they fetched, letting men with Cords down o're the Walls and Rock of the Caftle to a Well on the weft fide, which was afterward poyfoned,whereby fo many as efcaped the Shot dyed, and the reft fell deadly fick. Yet the Laird of *Grange* undertook with Eight perfons to keep the Caftle untaken by force, of the which number, were the Lord *Hume,* my two Brothers, Sir *Robert,* and Sir *Andrew,* the Laird of *Pittadrow,* and his Brother *Patrick.* This refolution being taken, the Laird of *Chefh,* and *Matthew Colvil* his Brother
ther

ther were fent to the Caftle, under the pretext of making offers of
agreement, but their defign was to get intelligence of the State of the
Houfe, and to feduce the Soldiers who were yet alive, which they
did, fo that fome fled out over the Walls, and others were fhut forth.
For the Captain thought the houfe in a better condition both for Victuals and otherwife, when they were forth.

The Marfhal of *Berwick* feeing no appearance to fucceed, entred
into contention with the Ambaffador, alledging that the Queen his
Miftrefs would be difhonoured, and faid, he would wait no longer,
whereupon they without entred on a new communing, and fent up
again the Laird of *Cleefb* to offer them good conditions to come forth
with their Armour and Bag and Baggage, which was agreed to, and
that they fhould be reftored to their Lands, and becaufe for the time
they were in other mens poffeffion, it was referred to themfelves whether they would go to *England* with the *Marfhal* of *Berwick*, or remain in *Scotland* among their friends, until the promife made them
of reftoring them to their Lands might be fulfilled. The *Englifb*
men defired that the Caftle fhould be put in their hands, but *Grange*
fent fecretly to Captain *Hume*, and Captain *Crauford*, defiring them
to come and ly within the Bulwark betwixt the Houfe and the *Englifb*
men, and to thofe he delivered the Caftle, and his perfon to the
Marfhal to go with him to *England*, until all promifes might be kept
to him, and the reft by the Queen of *Englands* means. In this manner they came forth, after that *George Duglas* natural Brother to the
Regent, had received the Houfe, they had all their Swords and Weapons about them, and were three days at liberty. My Brother Sir
Robert lay with me at his own Lodging, the Laird of *Grange* and the
Secretary *Lidingtonn* remained yet with the *Marfhal* of *Berwick* at his
Lodging for their greater fecurity, becaufe that the people of the Town
of *Edinbrugh* were greatly their Enemies. For except a few that
tarried within the Town during the Civil Troubles between the Parties that lay in *Edinbrugh* and *Lieth*, the moft part of the richeft
Men and Merchants left the Town and went to *Lieth*, to take part
with the *Regent*, therefore their houfes were fpoiled, upon which account they did bear great hatred to thofe in the Caftle.

But at the end of three days, they were all laid hands upon, and
taken as Prifoners. For fome of their moft malicious enemies put it
eafily in the *Regents* head, and the Ambaffadors, that it was well
done to move the Queen of *England* to caufe to deliver the whole Prifoners to the *Regent* to be difpofed upon at his pleafure, alledging they
had no furety but a naked promife which they needed not to keep,
and becaufe thefe of the Caftle confided wholy on the *Marfhals* promife, the Ambaffador was advifed to prevent the *Marfhals* Writing,
fo that e're he did write to the *Queen* thereabout, her Letter came to
him to deliver up the Prifoners who had been in the Caftle, to the
Regent. And he durft not difobey her Command, the fame being
fo peremptory, tho he obeyed it with much regret, and great re-
luctancy, by reafon of his promife, and returned malecontent to
Berwick. And they in the Caftle were Committed to ftrait ward, and
thereafter new Letters were purchafed by the *Regent* from the Queen,
that he might execute them, which fhe willingly permitted, for fhe

R   would

would gladly have been quit of my Lord *Hume*, and *Grange*, as being two true *Scotfmen*, unwonable to *England* to do any thing prejudicial to their *King* or *Country*, and of the Secretary *Lidingtonn*, but he dyed at *Lieth*, after the old *Roman* fashion as was said, to prevent his coming to the Shambles with the rest.

As for the Lord *Hume*, the *Regent* durst not meddle with him, he standing in awe of *Alexander Hume* of *Manderstoun*, *Coildinknows*, and the *Good man* of *North Berwick*, and the rest of that name, who boasted with very proud Language. He dyed shortly after, being warded in the Castle of *Edinbrugh*. Mr. *Killegrew* the *English* Ambassador desired no other reward for his labour, but the preservation of my Brother Sir *Robert's* life, for he was obliged formerly to him and me. The Composition, was kept to all the rest of the mean Gentlemen. The *Priour* of *Coldingham*, and Laird of *Drylaw* were afterwards set at liberty. Sundry of the Captains of *Berwick* went up to the Castle by the breach beat down in the fore Wall by the Canons, that they might say that they had won the Maiden Castle. But this was after that the house was delivered over to the *Regents* Brother, yet he would not suffer them to enter there with any number.

On this manner both *England* and the *Regent* were revenged upon that worthy Champion, whom they had sometimes in great estimation, who had done such notable service in *France*, being Captain of an hundred light Horsemen, that he was extolled by the Duke of *Vendome*, Prince of *Conde*, and Duke of *Aumale* Governors and Colonels then in *Picardy*, that I heard *Henry* the 2d, point unto him and say, yonder is one of the most Valiant Men of our Age. Also the King used him so familiarly, that he chose him commonly upon his side in all pastimes he went to, and because he shot far with a great Shaft at the Butts, the King would have him to shoot two Arrows, one for his pleasure. The great *Conftable* of *France* would never speak to him uncovered, and that King gave him an honourable Pension, whereof he never sought payment. *England* had proof of his Valour frequently against them upon the Borders, where he gave them divers ruffles. In a single Combate, he vanquished the Earl of *Rivers's* Brother between the two Armies of *Scotland* and *England*. He afterward Debated manfully the liberty of his Country against the *French* men, when they intended to erect the Land into a Province. He had lately refused the demands of Mr. *Randolph*, and Mr. *Killegrew*, as is before mentioned, and had reproached both the said Ambassadors of false and deceitful dealing. Last of all he had refused to put the Castle into the hands of *English* men, and therefore because he was true to his Prince and Country, it cost him his life. For they boasted plainly to bring down that Gyants pride, who as they alledged, presumed to be another *Wallace*. Albeit contrariwise he was humble, gentle, and meek, like a Lamb in the House, but like a Lyon in the Fields. He was a lusty strong and well proportioned personage, hardy and of a magnanimous Courage, secret and prudent in all his enterprises, so that never one that he made or devised misgave where he was present himself. When he was Victorious he was very merciful, and naturally liberal, an enemy to greediness and ambition, and a friend to all men in adversity. He fell frequently in trouble in protecting innocent

nocent men from fuch as would oppreſs them, ſo that theſe his worthy qualifications, were alſo partly cauſes and means of his wrack :
For they promoted him ſo in the opinion of many, that ſome loved
him for his Religion, Uprightneſs, and Manlineſs ; others again depended upon him, for his good fortune and apparent promotion, whereby divers of them hoped to be advanced and rewarded ſuppoſing,
that Offices and Honours could not fail to fall to him. All which he
wanted through his own default, for he had fled from Avarice, and
abhorred Ambition, and refuſed ſundry great Offices, even to be Regent, which were in his offer, as well as other great Benefices and Pen-
ſions. Thus wanting place and ſubſiſtance to reward, he was ſoon
abandoned by his greedy and ambitious dependers : for when they ſaw
him at a ſtrait, they drew to others, whom they perceived to aim at
more profitable marks. On the other hand he was as much envied
by thoſe who were of a vile and unworthy nature, of whom many
have made Tragical ends for their too great Avarice and Ambition,
as ſhortly after did the Earl of *Mortoun.* This gallant Gentleman pe-
riſhed for being too little ambitious and greedy. But ſo ſoon as the
King's Majeſty came to perfect age, and had underſtood how matters
had gone during his minority, he cauſed to reſtore the Heirs of the
ſaid Laird of *Grange,* whom he ſaid was wracked contrary to the appointment made with the Marſhal of *Berwick,* and alſo ordered his bones
to be taken up and buried honourably in the ancient Burial place of his
Predeceſſors in *Kinghorn.*

After his death the Marſhal of *Berwick* took ſo heavy diſpleaſure,
finding himſelf ſo far affronted, becauſe of the breach of his promiſe,
and that the appointment which he had made with the Caſtle of
Edinbrugh was not kept ; that he would tarry no longer in his Office
at *Berwick,* ſeeing he judged he had loſt his credit and reputation, for
he was a plain Man of War, and loved *Grange* ſo dearly, that at his
requeſt, he ſpared to caſt down the Houſes of *Seatoun* and *Nidrie,*
when he came in to caſt down the Houſe of *Hamiltoun.* Likewiſe
all the Officers of *Berwick* lamented the loſs of ſo worthy a Captain.

The Regent triumphed for a while, becauſe of the great aſſiſtance
that *England* made to him, which they had never done to any of the
former *Regents,* but rather ſtirred up factions and parties againſt them
to keep the Country in diſcord. The cauſes that moved them ſo to
aſſiſt him, were, That they believed the old jealouſies betwixt the
Stuarts and *Douglaſſes* ſhould by him be brought to an end, the young
King being in his hands, to be diſpoſed of at pleaſure ; the Queen his
Mother being already Captive in their hands, which two only could
join *Scotland* and *England* in one Monarchy. Therefore above all
others the guiders of the Court of *England* for the time, wiſhed them
out of the way, as well for the great Offices done by them both to
King and Queen, as for the deſire they had to deſtroy that Race and
Line, to place ſome of their own friends to ſucceed to the Crown of
England. So thinking that the Regent's mark in *Scotland,* and theirs
in *England* was conformable ; they eſtabliſhed and fortified him in his
Regiment, though God in his goodneſs ſuffered not their practiſes to
take effect. For the Regent wanting Heirs of his own body, and ha-

ving no Competitors to ſtay him from doing any thing that he pleaſed, when he thought the time meet, he delayed matters, and in the
mean time bent his whole ſtudy how to gather riches, and how to
ſuck out·ſubſtance both from *England* and *Scotland*, moving *England*
thereby too late to repent, that they had not preſerved the Laird of
Grange to be an awe over the Regent, as he kept the King to be an
aw over them.   And as he was crafty, ſo he was fearful and ſlow of
nature, and thought the Earl of *Angus* his Brother's Son yet too young,
and not capable to comprehend his hidden intention, and therefore
he was long of reſolving.   In the mean time ſerving his own turn
with *England*, as they did with all the World, when they were like
to have any trouble among themſelves, or with their Neighbours ;
then he compelled them to ſend him mony, which they were neceſ-
ſitated to do, though ſore againſt their heart, with a hidden deſpight
and ſecret hatred at his ſlowneſs on the one part, and covetouſneſs on
the other.

This *Regent* held the Country in an eſtabliſhed Eſtate, under great
obedience, better then for many years before or ſince.   For there
was not another Earl of *Mortoun* to ſtir up the faƈtious Subjeƈts, as he
uſed to do againſt the reſt of the *Regents*, which made him ſo proud
and diſdainful, that he deſpiſed the reſt of the Nobility.   And uſing
no Mans counſel but his own, he became ungrateful to all his old
Friends and Servants.   And being under pretext of Juſtice, uſed to
commit divers wrongs and extortions, he cauſed to begin a Proceſs
againſt the Laird of *Fentry*, becauſe many years before a Thief had
made his eſcape out of his hands, and againſt the Laird of *Seaſteld* for
a piece of Land ; and againſt Mr. *James Thorntoun* for his Benefice.   Thus
as he had loſt the favour of *England*, ſo did he by ſuch ways the hearts
of all *Scotland*, but only of *George Auflech*, and *Alexander Gerdan*. As
for the Laird of *Carmichael*, he lamented to me grievouſly of his ingratitude toward him, and was minded to leave him, until I gave him
counſel to help himſelf by the hurtful experience of the Laird of *Grange*,
and *Walter Melvil* my Brother, who was one of the Gentlemen of
the Earl of *Murray*'s Chamber, which two loſt his favour ſo ſoon as
he became Regent.   And likewiſe I told him, that very way I loſt
him my ſelf, for we had been long familiar with him, and had aſſiſted him in all his troubles, but when he was Regent, we would with
our wonted freedom reprove, admoniſh, and tell him his faults, whereby we loſt his favour.   And others who formerly had ever been againſt
him, came in and flattered him in all his proceedings, and ſtouped very
low to him, calling him *Tour Grace* at each word.   Theſe men, I ſaid,
won him, and we loſt him.   And apparently, ſaid I, to *Carmichael*,
you follow the like fooliſh behaviour as we did, therefore you muſt
take up another kind of doing.   And ſeeing your friend is become
Regent, imagine that you was never acquainted with him before, but
that you are entring to ſerve a new Maſter : Caſt never up your old
and long ſervice, cringe low, *Grace* him at every word, find no fault
with his proceedings, but ſerve all his affeƈtions with great diligence,
and continual waiting, and you ſhall be ſure of a reward.   Otherwiſe
all your former time ſpent in his ſervice will be loſt, and he will hate
you, and take a diſpight at you, which may bring on afterwards a
                                                            greater

greater wrack. *Carmichael* gave me great thanks and his hand, that he would follow this counsel, which he afterward did very punctually, and so became a greater Courtier then ever, and was employed and rewarded, and had credit to do pleasure to his friends, but I found him not thankful afterwards to me for my counsel.

Now the young King was brought up in *Sterling*, by *Alexander Areskine*, and my Lady *Mar*. He had four principal Masters, Mr. *George Buchuanan*, Mr. *Peter Toung*, the Abbots of *Cambuskenneth* and *Drybrugh*, descended from the House of *Areskine*. The Laird of *Drumwhasel* was Master of his Houshold. *Alexander Areskine* was a gallant well natur'd Gentlemen, loved and honoured by all Men, for his good qualities, and great discretion, no ways factious nor envious, a lover of all honest Men, and desired ever to see Men of good Conversation about the Prince, rather then his own nearer friends, if he found them not so meet.

The Laird of *Drumwhasel* again was ambitious and greedy, his greatest care was to advance himself and his friends. The two *Abbots* were wise and modest. My Lady *Mar* was wise and sharp, and held the King in great awe ; and so did Mr. *George Buchuanan*. Mr. *Peter Toung* was more gentle, and was loath to offend the King at any time, carrying himself warily, as a Man who had mind of his own weal, by keeping of his Majesty's favour : But Mr. *George* was a *Stoick Philosopher*, who looked not far before him. A man of notable endowments for his learning and knowledge in *Latin* Poesie, much honoured in other Countries, pleasant in Conversation, rehearsing at all occasions Moralities short and instructive, whereof he had abundance, inventing where he wanted. He was also Religious, but was easily abused, and so facile, that he was led by every Company that he haunted, which made him factious in his old days, for he spoke and wrote as those who were about him informed him : For he was become careless, following in many things the vulgar opinion : For he was naturally popular, and extreamly revengeful against any Man who had offended him, which was his greatest fault. For he did write despightful invectives against the Earl of *Monteeth*, for some particulars that were between him and the Laird of *Buchuanan*. He became the Earl of *Mortonn's* great Enemy, for that a Nagg of his chanced to be taken from his Servant during the Civil Troubles, and was bought by the Regent, who had no will to part with the said Horse, he was so sore footed and so easie, that albeit Mr. *George* had oft-times required him again, he could not get him. And therefore though he had been the *Regent's* great Friend before, he became his mortal Enemy, and from that time forth spoke evil of him in all places, aud at all occasions. *Drumwhasel* also because the *Regent* kept all the Casualties to himself, and would let nothing fall to others who were about the King, became also his great enemy, and so did they all who were about his Majesty.

The *Regent* again Ruling all at his pleasure, made no accompt of any about the King, until a discreet Gentleman called Mr. *Nicholas Elphingstoun* advertised him, That the King had no kindness for him, advising him, albeit too late, to bestow part of his Gold unto so many of the King's Servants, as were thought to be most wonable, seeing he was envyed of many, and hated of every Man, especially
by

by thofe who were in *Sterling* about the King. He gave to one that was in mean rank Twenty five pieces of Gold, at Twenty Pound the Piece ; what he gave to others I cannot tell, but fuch as had fpoken ill of him before, durft not alter their language, becaufe of the King's Wit and good Memory, who could check any that he perceived had firft fpoken evil, and then began to fpeak good again. As his Majefty had done to one of the company, alledging, That he had changed his Coat, as I was afterward informed ; fo that the *Regent* was too long in dealing part of his Gold to thofe about his Majefty, who increafing in years and knowledge, fundry Gentlemen began to look after Service, and turned On-waiters. Among others *James Stuart* Son to the Lord *Oghiltrie* a young Man of a bufie Brain,had an afpiring Spirit, and through time won great favour and credit with his Majefty. And though he was not well liked by thofe of the Caftle of *Sterling*, yet he was the more overfeen, becaufe he gave continually evil information to his Majefty of the Earl of *Mortoun*, and fo did alfo my Lord *Robert* Earl of *Orkny*, who had been warded, and hardly handled by the *Regent* for fome double dealing with *Denmark*, as was alledged.

The *Regent* being in this manner brought in difgrace with his Majefty ; when he was upon the height of the wheel, the Earls of *Arguile* and *Athol* were fecretly practifed, and drawn to *Sterling* by *Drumwhafel* with the confent of *Alexander Areskine*, Mafter of *Mar*, and Mr. *George Buchanan* ; by whofe advice and counfel, his Majefty was eafily moved to depofe the *Regent* from his Office : who yielded eafilier thereto, then any Man would have believed, againft the opinion of his friends, retiring himfelf to the Houfe of *Lockleven* within the *Logh*, for the furety of his perfon, until he might underftand what was like to follow thereupon, and what might be the next beft for him to do.

The King's Majefty having attained unto the Age of   years, ordained a Council to fit at *Edinbrugh* for ordering the Affairs of the Realm. The Earl of *Athol* was made Chancellour, becaufe the Lord *Glams* was a little before flain in *Sterling* by the Earl of *Grauford* as was fufpected, though he denied the deed, and purged himfelf thereof, as far as he could. The Earl of *Arguile*, and the Mafter of *Mar* ftayed in *Sterling* with the King's Majefty.

During the time that this new Council fate in *Edinbrugh*, the Earl of *Mortoun* who was quiet in *Lockleven*, making the walks of his Garden even ; his mind was in the mean time occupied in crooked paths, plotting how to be brought again to be Mafter of the Court, which was accomplifhed upon a night at midnight. When he came to the Gates of the Caftle of *Sterling* they were opened unto him by the two *Abbots*, and a Faction that they had drawn in there with them. Albeit the Mafter of *Mar*, and Earl of *Arguile* made what refiftance they could, where the Mafter's eldeft Son dyed in the throng, yet the enterprifers prevailed, and brought in again the Earl of *Mortoun*, and put out the Earl of *Arguile*, the Mafter of *Mar*, *Drumwhafel* and fuch others as they mifliked, and fo made a new change at Court. Where the Earl of *Mortoun* handled the matter fo difcreetly, and moderately as he could, that the alteration fhould not appear to be over fharp or violent.

violent. The new chosen Council scattered incontinently, some of them retiring home, and some joined with the Earl of *Mortoun*, hoping never to see a turn again.

About this time came out of *France* my Lord of *Aubonie*, who was afterward made Duke of *Lennox*, who was Brother's Son to the Earl of *Lennox*, and obtained afterward great credit and favour.

James Stuart of *Oghiltrie*, of whom I formerly made mention, assisted him through process of time, to perswade the King's Majesty to desire to ride out of *Sterling*, and make a progress among the rest of his Subjects, which the Earl of *Mortoun* could not resist, supposing that it lay in his power to frame the Court at his pleasure. For by his great wealth he was resolved to gain so many as he judged necessary, and so by the multitude of his friends to bear out the business; however the Court was ruled after he had obtained a discharge, and alliance of his intromission. For though during the time that he was *Regent*, he was always strongest about the King, but my Lord *Aubony* and *James Stewart* were most in favour, who by their continual rounding in the King's Ear against the Earl of *Mortoun*, ingendered at last a greater dislike in the King of him, then he had before. And as *James Stuart* was the stirrer up of the other, so afterward, when he found the time convenient, he took occasion to accuse the said Earl before the Council of the late Kings murther. Whereupon the Earl of *Mortoun* was made Prisoner, and sent first to the Castle of *Edinbrugh*, and afterward to the Castle of *Dumbartoun*, which was thought strange in respect of his many friends that were in Court for the time, who were then found to be but friends to his fortune. For he was loved by none, and envied and hated by many, so that they all looked through their fingers to see his fall.

England was also angry at him for the time, becuse of his slowness to answer their turns, which they had hoped for at his hands, having put the King and Country in his power. Yet they made some offer to assist him, which occasioned to hasten his ruin. For they sent down Seventeen Companies to the Borders, boasting to send a greater number, and to declare open War, in case the Earl of *Mortoun* was not set at liberty, and the Lord *Aubony* put out of *Scotland*. Mr. *Randolph* was sent in with this Ambassage. His Majesty again having these two young Councellors about him, who knew of no perils, raised a Taxation to pay Soldiers, and caused to make a Proclamation for every Man to be in readiness upon a call, which moved the *English* to retire, and leave off endeavouring any more his assistance, encouraging thereby such as were deadly Enemies to the Earl of *Mortoun* to ride to *Dumbartoun* with a thousand raised and hired Men, together with their own friends, to bring the Earl of *Mortoun* back again to *Edinbrugh* to undergo an *Assize*. Some of the Earl's friends convened to take him out of their hands, but found not themselves strong enough. They might have done it, had it not been the Forces which had been newly levied, occasioned by the threat'nings which *England* had made. Being brought to *Edinbrugh*, he found few friends to appear or act for him. His Gold and Silver was transported long before, by his Natural Son *James Douglas*, and one of his Servants called *John Mac-Morran*. It was first carried in Barrels, and afterward hid in some secret

cret parts, part whereof was given to be kept by fome who were lookt
upon as his friends; who made ill accompt of it again, fo that the moft
part thereof lighted in bad hands, and himfelf was fo deftitute of mony, that when he went through the Street to the *Tolbooth* to undergo
his *Affize,* he was compelled to borrow Twenty fhillings to diftribute
to the poor, who asked Alms of him for God's fake.   The *Affize* condemned him to death, as being Airt and Pairt in the *King's murther,*
and as being of Councel with the Earl of *Bothwel,* who brought him
out of banifhment, when he was abfent for the flaughter of *David
Rixio.*   He granted that he was made privy thereto, but had no hand
in devifing thereof : And as concerning the young King, he owned
that he purpofed to fend him to *England* for his weal, that he might
the rather obtain his Right to the Crown of *England,* being within the
Country, and brought up among them.   He dyed refolutely, and had
ended more perfectly, if he had declared and confeffed his Worldly
practifes and fetches to nourifh the Civil Troubles, partly at the devotion of *England,* and partly for his own particular profit, during
the Government of the firft three *Regents,* which occafioned great
blood-fheding that commonly cries to Heaven for vengeance.

During the King's young years, the partialities were fo great, and the
whole Country fo difturbed by the two feveral parties, who alledged
to fight and ftrive for the King and the Queen, being then Captive in
England, and the King yet very young ; that many perceived them
to be but factious, ambitious, avaritious, greedy, worldly, wretched
perfons.   Both parties were craftily ftirred up, and kept in trouble by
one only Faction in *England,* who had that Queens Ear, intending the
wrack as well of our King as Queen, to advance fome of their friends
to inherit the Crown of *England,* which occafioned a great out-cry
againft our foolifh contentions.

After that the Earl of *Mortoun,* the laft of the four *Regents* was depo-
fed, the King's Majefty, being young, took the Government into his
own hands, my Lord of *Aubony* being made Lord *Dalkieth,* and afterward Duke of *Lennox,* was chief about his Majefty, and *James Stuart*
formerly mentioned ; who afterward took unto himfelf the ftyle, and
then the Earldom of *Arran,* thinking that he had done great Service,
and deferved well for accufing and wracking the Earl of *Mortoun,* he
married the Earl of *March* his Relict.

The *Duke* was of nature upright, juft, and gentle, but wanted experience in the ftate of the Country.   At the firft he was wholly guided by the faid *James Stuart* and his Wife, who both began to envy
him, and therefore they endeavoured how they might caft him off,
that they might attain to the fole management of Affairs : And for this
end they gave him bad advice, and finifter informations againft fundry of his beft friends.   And being likewife Educated a Papift, and
fufpected to be at the Duke of *Guife's* devotion, and therefore a dangerous Man to be about his Majefty ; the whole Country was ftirred up
againft him ; *England* by their Ambaffadour helping to kindle the fire.
Mr. *David Macgil,* and Mr. *Henry Keer* were his chief Councellors,
both wife enough for their own profit, but carelefs of his ftanding, and
therefore not fit to counfel him who was his Majefty's greateft favourite.   At the inftigation and mif-information of the Earl of *Arran,*
and

and his Lady, he firſt did caſt off his true friend the Maſter of *Mar*
Captain of the Caſtle of *Edinbrugh*, and after that Sir *William. Stuart*
Captain of *Dumbartoun*, and then *Alexander Clerk* Provoſt of *Edin-*
brugh, and the Earl of *Gaurie* Treaſurer. The reſt of the Nobility
were alſo diſſatisfied, to ſee theſe two, young Lords, only in favour
with the King, finding that they both did aim at Noblemens lives, for
their Lands. And albeit ſome of them miſliked the Earl of *Mortoun's*
proceedings, yet they judged the taking of his life an hard preparative.
They likewiſe ſuſpected Religion to be in hazard, the one being a Papiſt, and the other a ſcorner of all Religion. They thought that from
two ſuch Counſellors,no wholſome advice could proceed for the peace
of the Country, and the eſtabliſhment of Religion. Therefore a number of them conſulted together, to diſplace both the Duke, and the
Earl of *Arran*, to ſend the one to *France*, and to remove the other from
Court. In the mean time, they reſolved to throng themſelves in about
the King, and to make a reformation of the abuſes, and to inviron his
Majeſty with their Forces, ſo ſoon as he came to *Dumfarmling*, whither he had appointed to come at his return out of *Athol*,where he was
for the time ahunting, and to preſent to him this Supplication.

" IT may appear ſtrange to your Majeſty that we your moſt hum-
" ble and faithful Subjects, are here convened beyond your expecta-
" tion, and without your knowledge; but after your Majeſty hath
" heard the urgent occaſion that hath preſſed us hereto, your Maje-
" ſty will not marvel at this our honeſt, lawful and neceſſary enter-
" priſe.

" Sir, for the dutiful Reverence that we owe unto your Majeſty,
" and for that we abhor to attempt any thing that may ſeem diſplea-
" ſing to your Majeſty, we have for the ſpace of two years ſuffered
" ſuch falſe Accuſations, Calumnies, Oppreſſions and Perſecutions, by
" means of the Duke of *Lennox*, and him who is called Earl of *Arran*,
" that the like Inſolencies and Enormities were never heretofore born
" within *Scotland*. Which wrongs, albeit they were moſt intolera-
" ble, yet when they only touched us in particular we comported with
" them patiently, ever attending when it ſhould pleaſe your Majeſty to
" give a remedy thereto.

" But ſeeing the perſons aforeſaid have plainly deſigned to trouble
" the whole Body of the Common-Wealth, as well the Miniſters of the
" bleſſed Evangel, as the true Profeſſors thereof, but in ſpecial, that
" number of Noblemen, Barrons, Burgeſſes and Commonalty,who did
" moſt worthily behave themſelves in your Majeſties Service, during
" your youth ; whom principally and only they moleſt, and againſt
" whom they uſe moſt extremity and rigour of Laws, oft-times moſt
" ſiniſtrouſly perverting the ſame for their deſtruction,ſo that one part
" of theſe your beſt Subjects are Exiled, another part Tormented, and
" put to queſtions, which they are not in Law obliged to anſwer; and
" withal execute with partiality and injuſtice all your Laws: And if any
" eſcape their barbarous fury, they can have no acceſs to your Majeſty,
" but are falſly calumniated,and debarred from your preſence,and kept
" out of your favour.

S " Papiſts

" Papifts and moft notable Murtherers are called home daily, and re-
" ftored to their former honours and heritages, and oftimes highly re-
" warded with the Offices and Poffeffions of your moft faithful Ser-
" vants.

" Finally your Eftate-Royal is not Governed by the Council of your
" Nobility, as your moft worthy Progenitors ufed to do, but at the
" pleafure of the forefaid perfons, who enterprife nothing but as they
" are directed by the Bifhops of *Glafcow* and *Rofs,* your denounced
" Rebels, having with them adjoyned in their ordinary Councels the
" *Popes Nuntio,* with the Ambaffador of *Spain,* and fuch other of the
" Papifts of *France* as endeavour to fubvert the true Religion, and to
" bring your Majefty in difcredit with your Subjects. They travel
" to caufe you negotiate and traffick with your Mother, without the
" advice of your Eftates, perfwading your Majefty to be reconciled
" with her, and to affociate her conjunctly with you in the Authority-
" Royal, meaning nothing other thereby but to convict us of U-
" furpation and Treafon.

" And fo having thefe your beft Subjects out of the way, who
" with the defence of your Authority maintained the true Religion
" as two things united and infeparable, what elfe could have followed
" but the wrack and deftruction of both ?

" For conclufion, your whole native Country, for which Sir you
" muft give an account to the Eternal God, as we muft be anfwerable
" to your Majefty, is fo perturbed and altered, and the true Religi-
" on, the commonwealth, your Eftate and Perfon are in no lefs dan-
" ger then when you were delivered out of the hands of the cruel
" Murtherers of your Father, who they were we will not infift on at
" this prefent.

" Sir, beholding thefe great dangers to be eminent and at hand,
" without fpeedy help, and perceiving your noble perfon in fuch ha-
" zard, the prefervation whereof is more precious to us then our
" own lives, finding alfo no appearance that your Majefty was fore-
" warned hereof, but like to perifh before you could fee the peril,
" we thought that we could not be anfwerable to our Eternal
" God, neither faithful Subjects to your Majefty, if according to
" our ability we prevented not this prefent diftrefs, preferving your
" Majefty from the fame.

" For this effect with all dutiful humility and obedience, we
" your Majefties true Subjects, are here convened, defiring your Ma-
" jefty in the name of God, and for the love you bear to his true Re-
" ligion, to your Country, and Commonwealth, and as you would
" fee the tranquillity of your own Eftate, to retire your felf to fome
" part of the Country, where your Majefties perfon may be moft fafe-
" ly preferved, and you Nobility fecured, who are under hazard of
" Lands, Life, and Heritages. And then your Majefty fhall fee the
" difloyalties, falfhoods, and Treafons of the perfons aforefaid, evi-
" dently proved and declared to their faces, to the glory of God,
" advancement of his true Religion, your Majefties prefervation and
" honour, and the deliverance of your troubled Common weal and
" Country, and to their perpetual ignominy and fhame.

At

At this Highland hunting, his Majefty was very meanly accompanied; The Duke of *Lennox* tarried for the time at *Dalkieth*, the new
Earl of *Arran* was at *Kinneel*, many of the Councel were appointed to
hold Juftice Airs in divers Shires of the Country. I was ordained to
hold the Juftice *Air* of *Weft Lauthian* at *Edinburgh* with my Lord *New-
bottle*, Mr. *David Macgill*, and Mr. *John Sharp*. There came to my
Bed timely in the Morning a Gentleman, alledging that I had formerly done him Courtefies, which till now he was never able to recompence, that he would make me the inftrument of faving the Kings Majefty my Mafter, out of the Hands of thofe who were upon an enterprize to take and keep him. I faid, I could hardly truft that, but I
feared that the Duke of *Lennox* might be in hazard, who was gone to
Glafcow to hold Juftice *Airs*, becaufe of the hatred which I knew was
born him, efpecially for the maintaing the two Bifhops of St. *Andrews* and *Glafcow*. He anfwered, They will lay hands firft on the King's
Majefty, and then the Duke and the Earl of *Arran* dare no more te
feen, their infolency and misbehavior being the caufe of all the prefent diforders, for there is an Enterprife to prefent a Supplication a-
gainft him to his Majefty. After he had told me this news, he defired me to conceal his name, though to tell the matter to his Majefty.
He faid, this turn would be done in ten days, and as I ftarted up to put
on my Cloaths, he flipt to the Door with a fhort farewel.

Becaufe the Duke was at *Dalkieth*, I did ride thither, and fhewed
him the whole matter, advifing him to ride himfelf to his Majefty
with this Advertifement for his own fecurity, but he chofe rather to
direct a Gentleman with all poffible diligence to his Majefty, willing
me alfo to write unto the Earl of *Gaurie*, for the Gentleman had not
named him to me with the reft of the Enterprizers, either out of forgetfulnefs, or elfe becaufe he was but lately won to that purpofe by
the Laird of *Drumwhafel*, who had affured him that the Duke of
Lennox had determined to flay him at the firft meeting, perfuading
the Earl upon this Ground to joyn with the reft of the Noblemen,
who were determined to reform the Eftate. Unto the which invented Advertifement, he too eafily gave Credit, and fo joyned with the
reft of the Nobility, who were minded to prefent the forenamed fup-
plication to the King, at his coming to *Dumfarmling*.

It is certain that the Duke of *Lennox* was led by evil Councel, and
wrong Informations, whereby he was moved to meddle in fuch
hurtful and dangerous Courfes, that the reft of the Nobility became
zealous of his Intentions, and feared their Eftates. As for the Earl
of *Arran*, they detefted his Proceedings, and efteemed him the worft
and moft infolent inftrument that could be found out, to wrack King,
Kirk, and Country. The Duke had been tolerable, had he hapned
upon as honeft Councellors, as he was well inclined of himfelf: but he
wanted Experience, and was no ways verfed in the State of the Country, nor brought up in our Religion, which by time he might have
been brought to have imbraced. But the Earl of *Arran* was a
Scorner of Religion, Prefumptious, Ambitious, Covetous, Carelefs of
the Commonwealth, a difpifer of the Nobility, and of all honeft men;
fo that every man was expecting a fuddain Change which fhould
have been made in *Dumfarling*, in prefenting the above fpecified fup-

plication

plication. But what moved the Lords to furprife His Majefty within the Houfe of *Huntingtoun*, I know not. If it was not to imbark the Earl of *Gowry*, whofe Houfe it was more deeply in their bond, or that they fearing their enterprife to be difcovered, made the greater hafte, and ftayed His Majefty in that place, which was afterward called the Road of *Ruthven*.

After that the Duke of *Lennox* was advertifed of this enterprife, he fent for the Earl of *Arran* who was peaceably paffing his time in *Kinneel*: He took in hand to ride out and fave the King, boafting that he would chafe all the Lords into Moufe-holes, but he was chafed and faved himfelf in the Houfe of *Ruthven*, where they had fhortly made an end of him, had not the Earl of *Gaurie* interceeded for his life, whofe deftiny it was to keep him alive to be his own wrack afterwards. The Duke of *Lennox* being advertifed that His Majefty was in their hands, retired himfelf to *Dumbartoun*, and His Majefty was conveyed to *Stirling* and there retained.

The King of *France*, and the Queen of *England* being informed that the King was taken and kept in Cuftody, fent each of them an Ambaffador to this Country to comfort his Majefty, to fee what the matter meant, and to offer him their beft affiftance in cafe he required the fame, and declared that he had been taken and kept againft his will. But after great thanks given unto the faid Ambaffadors, the King willed them to declare unto their Princes, that he was very well fatisfied with the Lords who were about him, and that they were all his own Subjects, willing to obey him, but that they had conceived fome hard apprehenfions of the Duke of *Lennox*, and fome others who had been about him before. Albeit his heart was full of forrow and difpleafure as he told himfelf afterward, and even then likewife to Mr. *Cairy* Coufin to the Queen of *England*, who whifpered in His Majefties Ear, requefting him to tell the plain verity, which he fhould keep fecret from Mr. *Bows* his Companion, and alfo from the Lords, and fhall only fhew his inward mind privily to his Miftrefs the Queen, yet it neither appeared by the fuccefs to have been kept fecret, nor did that Queen make any further inftance for his liberty.

The Lords in the mean time thought meet to hold a Council, to refolve what courfe to take, wherein it was determined that their enterprife was good fervice to his Majefty, the Kirk, and Common-Wealth, which His Majefty granted alfo to be true : whereupon an Act of Council was formed. At that fame time, the general Affembly of the Kirk was held at *Edinbrugh*, to the which his Majefty was moved to fend two Commiffioners, to teftify that he had allowed for good fervice the faid Lords enterprife, defiring likewife the Kirk to find it good for their parts, and to ordain the Minifters and Commiffioners of every Shire to publifh the fame to their Parifhioners, and to get the principal Gentlemens Subfcriptions to maintain the fame. Notwithftanding of all this, His Majefty took the matter further to heart then any man would have believed. He lamented his mifhandling to fundry Noblemen, and others, and at length acquainted fome of them that he intended to relieve himfelf through time out of their hands who held him as Captive. He defired fuch as he trufted in, to affift him with their counfel, and help.

The

The Lords again who were joined together for the Reformation of
the State, being rid of the Duke of *Lennox*, who had paft through
England to *France*, where he fhortly after dyed of a ficknefs contracted through difpleafure. And being alfo rid of the Earl of *Arran*, whom
they kept Captive in the cuftody of the Earl of *Gaury*, they retired
themfelves from the Court to their houfes, that his Majefty fhould
not think himfelf any way deprived of his liberty by them: for they
had got fome intelligence of his inward grief, for his taking and retaining. Whereupon his Majefty takes occafion, to appoint a Convention to be holden in *St. Andrews* for fome *Englifh* Affairs, after the
returning of Mr. *John Colvil*, and Colonel *Steward*, who both had
been fent thither, and had not agreed well concerning their Commiffion, having brought back again different anfwers. To the which
Convention his Majefty by Miffives invited fome of the Nobility, but
he called none of the Lords thereto who had lately left him, fuppofing
that perceiving themfelves fo far flighted, they would not come unwritten for, and that way he thought he might flip himfelf out of
their hands, and retain about him fuch Lords as he had written for; to
wit, the Earls of *Arguile*, *Huntly*, *Montrofe*, *Cranford*, *Rothefs*, and the
Earl of *Marsh*, who was an indweller in *St. Andrews* for the time, and the
Earl of *Gaury* of whom he judged himfelf affured, though for fome refpects he would not imploy him till afterwards, left the reft of his affociates fhould alledge that he had left them unhandfomly. For the faid
Earl had repented him, that he had fuffered himfelf to be drawn in by
Drumwhafel to join with the reft, after that he had received fure information that the Duke of *Lennox* had not laid for his flaughter, as was
alledged: Therefore he repented his folly, and offered at all occafions
to help to fet him at liberty.
So his Majefty thinking himfelf affured of all thefe Noblemen, the
day appointed for the Convention drawing near, it pleafed him to fend
Colonel *Stuart* to my houfe, fhewing me that his Majefty having fomewhat to do of great concernment, he had directed him unto me as to
one of his moft faithful Servants, of whofe fidelity and forefight he
had formerly had fufficient proof, by the true warning I had made
him before the alteration. As a fworn Gentleman of his Chamber, he
defired that I would help him to his liberty, which he was determined to
attain at his being at *St. Andrews*, whither he was refolved to go
fhortly to a Convention, to which he defired my affiftance and advice,
his Majefty being minded, as he faid, to follow my counfel fo long as
he lived, willing me not to refufe any fervice that his Majefty would
demand of me at meeting. This Commiffion was to me very unpleafant, for I had taken my leave of the Court, as being wearied with
the many alterations I had feen, both at home, and in forreign Courts,
having got great trouble and damage to my felf for other mens caufes. Therefore I had determined to be no more concerned in publick
affairs, but to lead a quiet, contemplative life the reft of my days.
This defire of my Prince and Mafter, was like to put me from this
refolution. In this perplexity I had recourfe by humble prayer to
God, fo to direct my actings as they might tend to his glory, and to
the weal of my Prince and Country. And thereafter according to
my dutiful obedience, I went unto his Majefty. When I came to
him

him at *Falkland*, he told me of his refolution, lamenting his hard ftate, and mifhandling by his own Subjects, and what difpleafure he had taken, and that he was thought but a Beaft by all neighbour Princes, for fuffering fo many indignities.

I again difcourfed unto his Majefty about the common eftate of all Countries, during their Prince's minority, the Nobility ftriving for ftate, and for the chief handling, whereby to advance themfelves and their friends. As did the Houfe of *Guife* during the young age of King *Francis* the Second: The Prince of *Conde*, during the Reign of King *Charles* the Second of *France* ; and alfo the King of *Navarr* : Likewife the Dukes of *Somerfet* and *Northumberland* during the youth of King *Edward* the fixth of *England.* And as well in the Queen his Mothers time, as in his own time, fome aiming to advance their own affairs, fome to defend and maintain their own Eftate, engaged in divers enterprifes and ftrifes, none of the parties bearing any evil will to his Majefty, but every one being in love with him, and defiring to be neareft to his perfon. And albeit fome of them be oft-times tranf-ported, either by ambition, greedinefs or vengeance, to out-fhoot themfelves, and forget their duty; yet Princes who are wife and come to perfect age, have ever found it their intereft to pardon, and over-fee all fuch faults, as have been committed at fuch times by too great a number of Subjects. Now when *Charles* the Ninth agreed with the Prince of *Conde*, all his former offences were reckoned for good Service. And as your Majefty hath done in agreeing with fo many of your Nobility, as were in fear that the Duke of *Lennox*, and Earl of *Arran*, would wrong both them, and the Country as they did alledge.

Now Sir, if your Majefty fhall flip from them, they will think their Eftate in greater danger then ever, not from your felf, but from fome of their unfriends, who may fall in again about you. And albeit they be prefently abfent, they have both a guard and fome of their friends prefently about your Majefty, and fo they will not fail to keep the Convention, and be as foon at *St. Andrews*, as the other Lords whom your Majefty hath invited by Letters. For it ftands them up-on their lives and fortunes, to be ftill chief about your Majefty. Therefore faving your Majefties own pleafure, I judge you prefently in a far better and fafer condition, then you will be by abandoning them, in cafe you get it not well effected, wherein there will be found greater difficulty, then your Majefty hath yet deeply confidered, as the importance of the cafe requires.

All their diffuafions had no force to ftay his Majefty from his former deliberation, as having taken up a great difpleafure, and a Prince-ly courage, either to liberate himfelf fully, or dye in the attempt. But for to follow the example of other wife Princes, as he had begun him-felf to allow for good fervice, the enterprife called the *Road* of *Ruthven*; fo he refolved that being at liberty, he would make a general act of Oblivion for all by-gone faults, and errours committed by his Nobi-lity, and Subjects during his minority, and from that time forth to be as a Father to the Country, and a juft and equal Prince to all his Sub-jects ; that no Man's Life, no Man's Land, Goods, nor Office fhould be taken from them. That as the fitteft and moft effectual way for fet-ling Peace in the Country, he would give fatisfaction to the Church,

in

in their defires. That he would keep about his Perfon the moft vertuous and difcreet of his Nobility, and Gentry, who could be found. His Maiefty ingaged alfo to me, to be fecret; conftant, and counfelable.

For the better management then of his Majefty's defign, it was thought expedient, that he fhould be in *St. Andrews* fome few days before the Convention, that being once there; Proclamation might be iffued out, to forbid any Nobleman or other; to come to the Convention without being exprefly called by Letter from his Majefty. For this end it was advifed, that the Earl of *March*, fhould invite his Majefty to be at *St. Andrews* two or three days before the Convention, by reafon of his preparation of wild meat,and other flefhes,that would fpoil in cafe his Majefty came not to make good chear with him fome days before. Whereupon his Majefty went forward, contrary to my opinion, and the judgment of fome others about him, who though we were fenfible of the inconveniencies which might follow, durft not be fo bold as to ftay him, though we told his Majefty our opinion, that we judged it was hazardous for him to ride till the Lords, who had been advertifed to attend him, might come forward. Neverthelefs he went on, and advertifed the Earl of *March*, the Provoft of *St. Andrews*, and other Barons to attend him at *Darfie*. Where meeting them, his Majefty thought himfelf at liberty, expreffing great joy, like a Bird flown out of a Cage, paffing his time in Hawking by the way; after his meeting them, thinking himfelf fure enough, albeit I thought his eftate far furer when he was in *Falkland*. For when he came to *St. Andrews*, he lodged in an old Inn, a very open part, the yard dikes being his greateft ftrength, few of the Lords he had written for being yet come, except only the Earl of *Crauford*, who was near.

In the mean time I perceived the folly, and went to the *Provoft* of the Town, defiring to know what forces he had within the Town at his devotion ? He anfwered, very few, and thofe not to be trufted to. I asked who was in the Caftle ? He told me, the Bifhop, with whom I dealt incontinently, to have the Caftle in readinefs to receive his Majefty, which he promifed to do. But when I returned to his Majefty, believing that the Proclamation had been made, That no Man fhould come to the Convention, but fuch as had been written for, I found that the Abbot of *Dumfarmling* was arrived out of *Lockleven*,and the Earl of *Marfhal* out of *Dundee*. The Earl of *Mar* was ftill with his Majefty, but all the Lords were advertifed with diligence from *Falkland*, that his Majefty was fuddenly gone for *St. Andrews*,defiring them to make haft to go thither, elfe they would be late. The faid Abbot for his part was foon enough there, and behaved himfelf with great diffimulation, extolling his Majefties enterprife, fo that he gain'd fo much credit as to caft down all their devices, who were upon the King's fide, though he was a fpecial doer for the contrary party; He faid it was not fit by Proclamation to ftay the Nobility, but rather to write Miffives to them, not to come accompanied with any more then two perfons with every Nobleman.

When his Majefty told me this, I was very angry, and fhewed him that this was the ready way to put him again in their hands, without thanks, from whom he had lately fled, affuring his Majefty that they

were

were coming forward very ſtrong, and in Arms, and would be ſooner there, then thoſe Lords he had written for: adding, that they might come in quietly themſelves, and cauſe their Companies to come in by two's and three's to the Town, whereas it had been better to let them come in all together, that their whole Forces might have been ſeen. Yet his Majeſty was loath to enter within the Caſtle that night for his greater ſecurity, until it was very late after Supper, giving thoſe that were there already time to adviſe, and to enterpriſe that ſame night to take him again,in caſe he had gone to the Abby yards to walk, as they had perſwaded him, till the Caſtle was prepared. And ſome were already entred the ſaid yard for that effect in Armour, whereof I had ſome ſuſpicion, and therefore inſtantly advertiſed his Majeſty, who thereupon changed his reſolution and paſt by the yard Gate to the Caſtle.

The next day the whole Lords, as well written for, as unwritten for, arrived at St. *Andrews*; the King's Lords quite without Armour, the other Lords ſtrongly Armed. The Earl of *Marſhal*, and *Mar*, and the Abbot of *Dumfarmling* lodged within the Caſtle with his Majeſty, where the crafty *Abbot* counſelled the King to let none of the Lords come within the Caſtle accompanied with more then twelve perſons. He ever appeared to favour the King's intention, and therefore this crafty councel was followed. The next morning the Caſtle was full of men, and thoſe of the contrary party being well Armed, had already taken the Stair-heads and Galleries, reſolving again to be Maſters of the King, and all the reſt, which being too late perceived, diligence was incontinently uſed, to bring within the Caſtle all the Earl of *March* his Gentlemen, with the Lairds of *Dairſy*, *Balcomy*, *Segie*, *Forret*, *Barns*, and others, with ſo many of the Town as were at the Provoſts devotion, which for that night prevented the foreſaid deſign.

The Earl of *Gaury* was alſo a great ſtay in that matter: for albeit he came thither as ſtrong, and as angry as any of the Lords, yet he was advertiſed of the King's good will towards him, and ſo was drawn from the reſt. That dangerous day being thus paſt without any harm done, the next day ſuch order was taken, as his Majeſty was Maſter of the Caſtle, following no more the ſaid *Abbot's* counſel, but declared his moderate intentions to all the Lords, to the *Fiffe* Barons, and Towns upon the Coaſt ſide, who had been ſent for, and likewiſe to the Miniſters and Maſters of the Colledge: Namely, *That albeit he had been detained againſt his Will for ſome time, yet he intended not to impute it as a Crime, nor to remember any thing done in his minority, but that he would paſs an Act of Oblivion as to all that was paſt; ſatisfie the demands of the Church; agree parties among whom there were differences, and to carry himſelf to all his Subjects equally,knowing none of them to bear him any evil will, and that they had been driven to enterpriſe the thing they had done, by the force of their Factious partialities:* uſing many other ſuch words of clemency and diſcretion, to all their contentments. Thereafter he ordained four Lords, two of every faction, to retire them for a while, to wit, The Earls of *Angus*, *Bothwel*, *Huntly* and *Crauford*, retaining all the reſt about him as indifferent for his ordinary Council, by whoſe advice he was reſolved to ſettle his eſtate, and thereafter

to

to bring again to Court the whole Lords above-named. Then his Majesty called for me before a number of the said Lords, and gave me greater commendation and thanks then I had merited, as being the only instrument, under God, of his liberty. His Majesty caused also to make a Proclamation, conform to his former promises, and moderate intention : But I took no pleasure to be praised in presence of so many, answering to his Majesty, *That I had already displeased all Those who were upon the purpose of his detention.*

Now matters being settled in appearance, and this design successfully ended, some of the King's Lords, who had been slow in coming (and when they were come finding the Lords of the contrary Faction strong and in Armour) denyed that they knew any thing of his Majesties enterprise, laying the whole burthen upon Colonel *Stuart* and me. But when they saw appearance of a prosperous success, they took the matter stoutly upon them, and began in plain Council to tell how long they had been upon the counsel of that enterprise with his Majesty, and how long waiting for his advertisement.

Of a truth his Majesty was of a merciful mind, an I gently inclined toward all the Nobility, intending to win all their hearts by his own discreet behaviour, and to that effect he went first to the House of *Ruthven*, to let the Country see that he was entirely reconciled with the Earl of *Gaury*. Where after he had Royally entertained his Majesty, he fell down upon his knees, lamenting that his Majesty should have been retained in that unhappy house at his last being there, which he said, fell out rather by accident, then deliberation, only for the safety of the Earl of *Arran's* life. Alledging that he knew no other thing, then that at his Majesty's being at *Dumfarmling*, they were minded to present him an humble Supplication, asking pardon for that accidental fault, which his Majesty graciously promised never to impute to him, knowing how blindly he was brought upon it by the practises of others.

In the mean time *James Stuart* Earl of *Arran*, had obtained the favour to be warded in *Kinneal*, his own house, and sent and Congratulated his Majesties liberty, begging that he might have access to come and kiss his hand, which was plainly refused. Then he sent daily his opinion, and advices to his Majesty, how to proceed against divers of the Nobility, and others ; advising to bring back to Court the Earls of *Huntly*, and *Craufurd*, which was too easily condescended to by the Earls of *Arguile*, and *Montrose*, only the Earl of *Gaury* resisted, alledging that the Earls of *Bothwel* and *Angus* were put in hopes to be brought in with them, or as soon as they. But the equality expected, was soon forgot, which moved the Earl of *Marshal* and others to retire to their houses. The *Abbot* of *Dumfarmling* remained still at Court, and to curry favour of Colonel *Stuart*, then Captain of the Guard, he gave him a Purse and thirty pieces of Gold at four pound the piece, which pieces the Colonel distributed to so many of the Gaurd who bored them, and set them like Targets upon their Knapsacks, and the Purse was born upon a Spear point like an Ensign. The *Abbot* shortly after was warded in *Lockleven* ; Mr. *John Covil*, the Laird of *Clesh*, and *Drumwhasel* were also warded by the advice of the Earl of *Arran* and his Wife, who continually solicited his Majesty,

T   that

that they might come to Court. And at length I was requested by
his Agent *James Stuart* to deal with his Majesty to permit the said
Earl to come again to the Court: For he said, that his Majesty was
favourable enough, and that the Earls of *Arguile, Huntly, Crauford*, and
Montrose, had not only given their consent, but that the Earls of *Arguile* and *Montrose* had said unto his Majesty, that they would ride
themselves and fetch him ; only the Earl of *Gaury* resisted ; and that
the King had shewn him, that he would do nothing therein without
my consent and advice. I answered, That his Majesty needed not my
consent, if himself and so many Noblemen were content. He replied
again, That his Majesty reposed more upon me at that time, then upon all his Councel, as his Majesty had shewn him; and that he would
not bring him without my consent. Whereupon I went unto his Majesty, and shew'd him what language the Earl of *Arran's* Servant had
to me, concerning his Master's coming to Court, and that his Majesty laid too great a burthen upon me, to say that he would do nothing
therein without my consent. Thereupon his Majesty took me to the
Gallary of *Falkland*, lamenting as he had been informed the loss of
many of his best friends, as the Earls of *Lennox, Athol*, and Duke of *Lennox* : And now, says he, They will not permit the Earl of *Arran*, who
hazarded his life to relieve me, to come and see me ; he desired me to
acquaint him, what might be the occasion they hated him so much.
My answer was, That to tell the verity perilled my self, to conceal
the truth indangered his Maiesty. He would needs know my meaning therein. I said, The Earl of *Arran* is one of the worst instruments
can come about you, whereof your Majesty hath had too sure a proof,
his mis-behaviour being the only occasion of the late interprise, and if
he ever be again admitted about your Majesty the like or worse will
follow. Thereupon its dangerous to my self to acquaint your Majesty
herewith, seeing it will occasion him to be my deadly Enemy, if he
ever get notice thereof. Then his Majesty desired only to let him
come and kiss his hand, promising he should not tarry, intreating me
to deal with my Lord of *Gaury* ; that he would also grant that he
might but once come to Court, and he should incontinently return
to his house without any stay. I said, I should cause him to yield to
his Majesties pleasure.

In the mean time I took occasion to declare unto his Majesty, how
that many great Princes are wracked by their Ambitious Counsellors,
who will rule all alone, taking upon them a greater burthen then they
can bear : for remedy whereof his Majesty should spend every day
but one hour to hear a chosen number of honest Councellors reason
upon his affairs, then himself to give his opinion what he thinks fit-
test to be done, as the King of *France* used to do. Which his Majesty granted very willingly, and so long as he kept that order, by the
ordinary Council days his turns went rightly forward. The whole
Lords who assisted his Majesty were of his Council, Sir *Robert* my
Brother, Colonel *Stuart*, the Laird of *Seigie*, and my self.

But as soon as the Earl of *Arran* got access to his Majesty, he not
only stayed at Court against promise, but also within a short time
altered all this way of procedour, with a design to draw the management of all publick affairs to himself. At his first entry, he carried
himself

himfelf very humbly, for after he had kiffed his Majeflies hand, he em-
braced me and kiffed my cheek, giving me many thanks in his Majeflies prefence, alledging, That the whole name of *Stuarts* was obl -
ged to me, for the notable fervice, he alledged, I had done his Majefty.:
As for him, he faid, he fhould never take any thing in hand, but he
therein directed by my *Brother* and *me.* But Colonel *Stuart* and be
fpoke not together, until his Majefty defired me to agree them; which
after much travel I did at length. At firft the Colonel fwore a great
Oath, *That if his Majefty fuffered that villain to remain at Court, he
would yet again undo all.* For a little time he kept himfelf quiet, but
there was no appearance of his home-going. Sometimes he would
reprove my gentle kind of procedure in his Majefties affairs, and could
not endure to fee them handled by a number. He infinuated to his
Majefty, That he would find it a troublefome bufinefs, to be incum-
bred with many contrary opinions. He defired him to recreate himfelf at hunting, and he would attend the Council, and report again
at his Majefties return, all our Opinions and Conclufions. This he
obferved two or three times, and fo in a very fhort fpace changed the
former order laid down to have been followed: So that he gave accompt of no Man's advice but his own; yet he made his Majefty believe that it was all our Opinions, and that it was his intereft to follow a
violent courfe. And though the fame was directly againft his Majefties firft Deliberation, Intention, and Proclamation of Clemency, yet
he caufed to make contrary Proclamations againft thofe of the *Road*
of *Ruthven,* ordaining them all to take remiffions for that which before was allowed for good Service, moving divers Noblemen and
others to withdraw from the Court, for fear, to fome place of Security. When he caufed to be read before the Council his new invented
Proclamation, I down-right oppofed my felf to it, faying, That I knew
it was directly againft his Majefties mind and promife. Whereupon
he leapt out of the Council-houfe in a rage, and faid I would wrack
the King by my manner of doings. I anfwered, either you or I, my
Lord, with other fharp pricking language, fo that for that time it was
ftayed. Afterward he waited a meet occafion to get it paft, having
procured a flattering Faction to affift him, in expectation to be made
fharers of the fpoil he hoped to make, a part whereof he had promifed
them, to gain their Votes to his defire. And fo all things were turned
up-fide down, a great number of Noblemen and others being put
thereby in fear of their Lives and Eftates. And when any of us who
were defirous of his Majefties quiet and profperous eftate, would acquaint his Majefty with the danger of thefe proceedings of the Earl,
he would be very forry, faying, The Earl made him believe that he
did nothing but by common confent of the Council. And when his
Majefty underftood the contrary, he was very earneft and willing to
amend the diforder, but was ftill Circumvented by the faid Earl, and
fuch as for fear, flattery, or expectation of profit, advanced all his
defigns.

About this time there came a fharp Letter from the Queen of *England* unto his Majefty, who thought the Noblemen who were aimed
at; and were abfent from Court, fitteft inftruments to be about his
Maiefty. And for entertaining of Amity and Concord betwixt their

Majefties and Kingdoms, fhe was not content to fee them fo hardly
handled. The Copy of which Letter I have here inferted.

" **A** Mong your many ftudies, my dear Brother and Coufin, I wifh
"   *Ifocrates's* noble Leffon were not forgotten, that wills the Em-
" perour his Soveraign, to make his Words of more accompt then other
" men do their Oaths, as meeteft Enfigns to fhew the trueft Badge of
" a Prince's Arms. It moveth me much to moan you, when I behold
" how diverfly fundry wicked Spirits abftract your mind, and bend
" your courfe to crooked Paths, and evil illufions, wrapt under the
" Cloak of your beft good. How can it be that you can fuppofe an
" honourable and fatisfactory anfwer can be made unto me, when all
" your actings gainfay your former Vows. You deal with one
" whofe experience will not take drofs for good payment, and with
" one who will not be eafily beguiled. No, no ! I mind to fend to
" School your craftieft Councellors. I am forry to find you bent to
" wrong your felf, in thinking to injure others. Yea thofe, who if
" they had taken the opportunity in their hands, they might have
" done you more prejudice, then a thoufand fuch mens lives be worth,
" who perfwade you to avow fuch deeds ; as to oblige the beft defer-
" ving of your Subjects to demand a faultlefs Pardon. Why do you
" forget what you wrote to my felf with your own hand, fhewing
" how dangerous a courfe the *Duke* was entred in, though you feemed
" to excufe him, as if he had intended no evil therein ; and yet you
" would not make them guilty who delivered you there-from. I hope
" you more efteem your honour, then to give it fuch a ftain, fince
" you have fo oft protefted,that you was refolved to notice thefe Lords
" as your moft affectionate Subjects, in the full perfwafion, that all
" they had done was by them intended for your advantage. To con-
" clude, I befeech you proceed no further in this courfe, till you re-
" ceive an exprefs Meffenger, a trufty Servant of mine, by whom I in-
" tend to deal as an affectionate Sifter with you, as one from whom
" you may fee you fhall receive honour, and contentment, with more
" furety to your Self and State,then by following the pernicious Coun-
" cels of thefe crafty diffembling Councellors, as knows the Lord, to
" whofe fafe keeping I do commit you.

*Your moft Affured and Faithfulleft Sifter
and Coufin,*

ELIZABETH.

Unto this Letter his Majefty commanded me in his name to write
an anfwer, that he might write it over again with his own hand.
For the Secretary for the time was in fufpicion to have been upon the
contrary courfe. The anfwer was as followeth.

MADAM,
" **I** Have received a Letter of yours, containing in the entry, that
"   fentence of *Ifocrates,* which willeth Princes Wordsto be more in-
" tirely obferved, then other Mens Oaths ; as though fome finifter
" report were made unto you of fome forgetfulnefs in me, or that you
                                                              fear

" fear that in time coming I fail in keeping fuch promifes unto my
" friends, as may be made upon juft and convenient occafions.

" For anfwer unto that head, I remember another faying of *Ifocrates*,
" where he would not have them repute friends, who allow or praife
" whatfoever we fay or do, but rather fuch who modeftly reprove our
" faults. So that I take your fharp admonition at this time, as pro-
" ceeding from a Sifterly love, albeit upon wrong information, hoping
" that fo foon as you fhall truly underftand of my hard handling, and
" patient behaviour, you fhall be fo well fatisfied as to deem me to
" have done nothing, but that which you would have done your felf
" in the like condition.

" Firft, When I was detained Captive under a fair pretext, it plea-
" fed you to fend your Ambaffadors (like as did the King of *France*)
" friendly to vifit me, offering me great kindnefs, and help, in cafe I
" needed any, for the time, for which I do yet render your Majefty
" hearty thanks : Which offer I did not think fit to embrace, alledging
" that I was well content, and had good friends about me, which was
" very true. For one part of thefe fame Lords, who were then about
" me, perceiving my grief and mifcontent, offered even then to relieve
" me, whenfoever I would defire to be at greater liberty. Whereup-
" on I made you then that anfwer, whereof you make mention in your
" Letter, as I gave the like anfwer to the *French* Ambaffadour. Ne-
" verthelefs I was ever refolved at a fit time to relieve my felf, for my
" honour, as I have done lately ; following another faying of *Ifocrates*
" willing Princes to hazard rather to dye honeftly, then to ring fhame-
" fully, for how I did ring for the time, you might know by your Cou-
" fin Mr. *Cairo* in whofe ear I rounded my familiar inward grief, be-
" caufe he faid you defired him to require it at me apart, promifing that
" it fhould be fecretly kept from all others, albeit I ufed not fuch free-
" dom with Mr. *Bowes*. Indeed I fubfcribed fuch Writs and Letters
" as the faid Lords prefented to me, for the time was unfit to difpute
" too precifely upon Circumftances, that were determined by thefe
" who were Mafters of me and the State.

" This Anfwer I fuppofe will fatisfie your own reafonable and equita-
" ble Judgment, difcreetly confidering the fame with your felf apart,
" I doubt if it will be fo interpreted by others of your Councel, who
" have particular defigns of their own, to whom becaufe I impute the
" whole hard Language contained in your angry Letter, and not to
" your felf, and gentle inclination, I think it not needful now to write
" an Anfwer unto every part of the fame. So attending patiently upon
" your better intelligence and information in thefe matters, I will ra-
" ther retain in my memory your former fruitful friendfhip, then now
" ftart at any wrong fet Syllable, or fowre fentence placed in your paper
" at the partial inftance of others.

" As concerning that which toucheth the *Duke* of *Lennox*, his godly
" end hath declared his honeft meaning. Whofe death I might juftly
" lay upon fuch as forcibly removed him from my prefence ; never-
" thelefs I refolve to put all by-gones in Oblivion, neither to compel
" any man to take a faultlefs Pardon.

" Where you defire that I proceed no further, until a trufty
" Meffenger may come from you, I intend to ftay from doing any
" thing

" thing till then, that you may juſtly be offended with) Albeit *Iſo-*
" *crates* adviſes Princes ſpeedily to execute ſuch turns, as good Coun-
" cel thinks neceſſary to be done,) wiſhing that he who, ſhall be ſent,
" may be as willing to work the effects of true love and friendſhip be-
" twixt us, as I am aſſured it is both our hearts deſire, and intention,
" whereto I pray the Lord to grant increaſe, continuance, and happi-
" neſs to his glory, and to the well peace; and quiet of both our
" Realms.

The Secretary *Walſingham* was he of whom mention is made in her
Majeſties Letter to be ſent in here, but he was long by the way by
reaſon that he was ſickly. In the mean time Mr. *Bowes* who was Ambaſſador reſident at *Edinbrugh* had received this Letter by the ordinary Poſt, and returned the Anſwer. He declared many Commendations from my Lord *Burly,* and ſeveral of the Council of *England* to
my Brother Sir *Robert,* and me, alledging that they were glad to
hear that ſuch men were about His Majeſty that were of their Religion, and with whom they were long acquainted, wiſhing many ſuch
to be in Court.

About this time the Earl of *Arran* obtained the keeping of the
Caſtle of *Stirling,* and inſinuated himſelf ſo far upon His Majeſty, that
he took upon him the whole management of affairs, and cauſed ſundry
Noblemen to be baniſhed, as the Earls of *Mar, Angus,* and the Maſter
of *Glains,* and divers others.

And by his inſolency, he drove the Earl of *Gaurie* from Court,
far againſt his Majeſties intention, who ſent me for him to his houſe
to bring him again to Court, which was for the time at *Coupar* in
Fyffe, where His Majeſty agreed him and the Earl of *Arran.* But
no conditions promiſed were kept to *Gaurie,* ſo that he was ſo vexed,
that he reſolved to leave the Country.

I have already declared how loath I was, that either His Majeſty
ſhould leave the Lords who were about him, or that I ſhould in any
wiſe be a medler again in publick affairs, conſidering the many alterations I had ſeen by long and hurtful experience, yet the affection I
had for his Majeſty, engaged me not to refuſe his Commands, being
my native Prince and Maſter, and I his humble Subject, and ſworn
Servant, firſt as his domeſtick as being one of the Gentlemen of his
Chamber, and a Member of his Privy-Council. But after his Majeſty being taken, I was no more admitted by his Keepers, who thought
fit for their ſecurity, to place ſuch men about him as were intirely at
their Devotion. As for my part, as I was ſorry that His Majeſty
ſhould be uſed any other way then at his own pleaſure, ſo I was much
ſatisfied to be permitted to live quietly at home the reſt of my days,
yet being called again by His Majeſty, I waited upon his Commands.
Now again perceiving His Majeſties moſt acceptable Proclamations,
ſlyly and cunningly changed contrary to His Majeſties merciful intentions, by iſſuing out contrary Proclamations, and intending violent
perſuits againſt theſe concerned in the *Road* of *Ruthven,* whereby too
great a number of Noblemen and Gentlemen deſpaired of their Safety,
and Lives, in a lamenting manner I remembred his Majeſty, how he
was abuſed, and what great inconveniencies were like to enſue.
Thereupon His Majeſty upon my relation, appeared very ſorrowful,
and

and assured me of his resolutions to amend these disorders, but it was his misfortune to advise thereabouts with these who underhand were chief instruments therein: Believing that because he loved them, they also loved him and the well of his affairs. They again making some appearance of intentions of satisfying his expectation, indirectly by means of too many who depended upon the *Earl* of *Arrans* extraordinary Credit, and Favour, the contrary to his Majesties princely and upright meaning was brought about, so that many Noblemen left the Country, and all honest men left the Court, to the great satisfaction of the *Earl* of *Arran* and his Wife, who had the greater opportunity of guiding all. And that they might the easier set forward this course, they perswaded His Majesty to pass to *Stirling*, whither they knew few or none durst repair, who were not at his Devotion, he being Captain of the said Castle, and Provost of the Town; after I had frequently warned His Majesty, of the storm I did foresee coming, I retired my self from Court.

His Majesty being at *Stirling* asked frequently for me, regretting that I was not continually with him. Whereupon the Earl of *Arran* advised that I should be sent ambassador to the Queen of *England* upon some pretended affair, as well to absent me from His Majesty, who he perceived had some favour for me, as to take occasion upon my return, to bring me in disgrace, as if I had been guilty of some mismanagement, because he knew that as matters stood I could do no good at that time. And commonly when Mens Commissions take no good effect, they are calumniated by their Enemies, and envyers, as unfit instruments, unskilful, and undiscreet. Which Calumnies get oft-times too much Credit, when matters succeed not conform to the desire of the Master. For this end he had engaged His Majesty to write for me, but before his Letter came to my hands for the said Voyage, I had indited a long Letter to have sent unto His Majesty, as a remembrancer of his former promises, intentions, and Proclamations; shewing what inconveniencies were like to ensue the setting forward of a contrary course, together with such remedies as I could judge meetest for the time.

The tenour of His Majesties Letter unto me was, That he had some matters to communicate to me, wherein he resolved to imploy both my advice and pains, and therefore he desired me to come to *Stirling* with all convenient expedition after the sight of the said Letter, where I should understand more amply the occasion of my being sent for, as I would do him accomptible pleasure and good service. Written from the Castle of *Stirling* the 22 *d* of *Octob.* 1583.

After the receipt of this Letter, I did ride unto His Majesty, and took with me the Letter which I had penned before, whereof the Copy followeth,

" Sir, as it hath pleased your Majesty heretofore to accept of my
" will for agreeable service, even so I hope that your Highness's con-
" stant favour shall continue toward me now, and in time coming, not-
" withstanding my present absence. For albeit that during your Maje-
" sties young Age, I was suffered to live happily at home, from the
" handling of publick affairs, yet I found my self obliged to bear my
" proportionable

" proportionable burthen in your Service, fo foon as it fhould pleafe
" your Majefty to lay your Commands on me for that effect,being then
" moft affured, to walk in a juft and lawful vocation, which to give
" continual teftimony of my dutiful obedience, not prefuming to give
" your Majefty Counfel, I have only taken the boldnefs to prefent to
" you in thefe few lines, my fimple opinion of things that are appa-
" rently to fall out upon your Majefties late proceedings.

" For when it pleafed your Majefty at your firft going to *St. An-*
" *drews,* to take upon your felf the free Government of your Affairs,
" your Majefties Gracious intention and propofition then, was not
" only moft agreeable to all the *Lords, Barons,* and *Minifters* there
" prefent for the time, but alfo to the reft of your good Subjects, when
" as they underftood of your merciful inclinations. Which being now
" otherwife overturned, then was either firft intended, or determined,
" is able to breed cumber and diforder, unlefs your Majefty by wifdom
" and dexterity prevent the apparent inconveniencies. For it pleafed
" your Majefty then openly to declare, how that you only fought
" with your own reputation, and fafety, the well and fafety of your
" whole Subjects, as being willing to give fatisfaction to the demands
" of the Church, to agree all parties, to blot out of memory the name
" of Factions, and put in perpetual Oblivion all Crimes committed in
" your Majefties Minority, acknowledging all fuch as chanced to be
" done during the fame, but to have fallen out betwixt Subject and
" Subject, for fuch particular refpects as your Majefty never purpofed
" to impute to any of their Charges,but to Reign over them all in times
" coming as a Gracious Father,and that by the advice of the leaft Facti-
" ous,and beft affected of the Nobility,Barons and other fufficient Sub-
" jects. No man to be placed about or proferibed from your Majefty
" by favour or furname, kin, friend, or allye, but for fufficiencie, ver-
" tue,and loyalty. As alfo if any were to be abfented,or fent home for a
" time, it fhould not be done at the inftance of any envious fuiter of
" his Office, or particular Party, but for your Majefties honour and
" fafety, during your pleafure, leaving them ftill in hope through
" good behaviour to obtain again familiar accefs about your Majefty
" as formerly.

" If this Calm Courfe had been followed, there was appearance of
" a quiet State. But the altering and changing this gentle kind of
" dealing to a fharp and violent perfuit of fundry, by feeking out over
" many faults in the perfons of fo many Great and Active Men, hath
" bred fuch difcontent and fo furious a Faction, that if fudden remedy
" be not provided, civil diffention and defpaired interprifes ought to be
" looked for by all fuch as have fufficient experience of the nature of
" *Scotfmen,* and feemly intelligence of the deportment of divers,which
" the neceffity of their unfure Eftate may well drive them honeftly to
" take in hand.

" It is true, that the flourifhing of Commonwealths, confifts much
" in the rewarding of the good, and punifhing of the wicked. No
" doubt but faults enough have been done during your nonage, but
" to feek them out narrowly, and to punifh them feverely in fuch ca-
" fes, and at fuch times, in matters wherein many have dipped, is no
" fafe Courfe. Yea, though your Majefty were willing, as I know

" you

" you are not, I cannot fee how you can get it done againſt ſo great a
" number, having ſo ſmall ſubſtance and few Forces, and ſo potent
" and mighty Neighbours lying ſtill, at wait upon all ſuch controver-
" ſies, and occaſions, to take advantage thereof, whereby to ſerve
" their own turn. This Conſideration alſo ought preſently to be no-
" ticed, that the wonted reverence born by the Subjects unto the
" Princely Authority of their Soveraigns, is much decayed in this
" Kingdom, by reaſon of the Queens Youth and long abſence, and e-
" ven ſo in your Majeſty (time for the like cauſes, but chiefly becauſe
" that your Majeſties being yet young) have been accompanied this
" time paſt with the youngeſt, and meaneſt ſort of your Nobility.
" Who albeit they may be faithful and honeſt, to ſet forward your
" ſervice, yet the reſt of your Subjects alledging them to be factious,
" ignorant and covetous, doubt of their diſcreet behaviour, ſeeing
" their intentions are to Rule by force ; hardly may a Prince aſſure
" himſelf at all occaſions, to chooſe a ſure courſe wherein there ſhall
" be no peril. For commonly thinking to eſcape out of one in-
" conveniency fall oft-times into an other. Therefore prudence conſiſts
" in underſtanding the quality of dangers, and in chooſing the leaſt
" evil for the beſt.

" Some Kingdoms and Countries are Governed by force, ſome by
" fairneſs, on the other part Subjects obey either for awe, or love.
" That Prince is reputed of no value, who cannot win the hearts of
" his Subjects by one of theſe two. For either muſt the means be ta-
" ken at once from ſuch as are ſuſpected deſervedly, whereby they may
" do harm, or elſe they muſt be ſatisfied in ſuch ſort as in reaſon they
" may be content, and ſo ſerve for love, and not for awe. So that it
" is eaſie to judge which of theſe two Governments may be meeteſt
" for your Majeſty.

" The Emperor *Trajan* being demanded, wherefore his Subjects
" loved and honoured him above his Predeceſſors, anſwered, becauſe
" I forgive them who offend me, and never forget any who have done
" me ſervice. *Julius Pollux* Maſter to *Cæſar* points out a true Prince
" to be of Divine Countenance, Godly, Merciful, Juſt, Equitable, Care-
" ful of his Affairs, Conſtant in his Deeds, true in his Promiſes. Sub-
" ject unto reaſon, Maſter over his Affections, fatherly towards his
" Subjects, of eaſie Acceſs, gentle to be ſpoken to, ready to forgive,
" ſlow to puniſh, princely, liberal, ſubtil, ſecret, and ſharp of in-
" geny.

" Now becauſe it appeareth your Majeſty in youth hath been ſuffi-
" ciently verſed in many of theſe vertuous precepts, I wiſh from my
" heart that ſuch impreſſions may be as well taken of them that are
" preſently about you, ſeeing that Princes are commonly deemed to
" be like thoſe whom they make moſt their familiars.

" Therefore Sir, for eſchewing all thoſe evils, and to put the near-
" eſt Remedy unto all the appearing inconveniencies, it is fit ſo ſoon
" as it may pleaſe your Majeſty to paſs to *Edinbrugh*, to convene the
" moſt ancient of your Nobility, and Barons of beſt reputation, by
" whoſe advice together with thoſe that are already in Court, your
" Country may be quieted, and your Subjects ſatisfied. For now as
" matters are handled, to ſpeak of Clemency by cauſing them to take

" remiffions, it will want Credit, and be ill interpreted, as not con-
" form to your Majefties firft Declaration.

  " The Emperour *Adrian* inquired after men of great age and expe-
" rience, and helped himfelf by their many perils:

  " *Alexander Severus* would perform no matter of importance, but
" with advice of the moft ancient and beft experimented. He never
" went out of *Rome*, unaccompanied with four or five of moft ho-
" nourable, ancient and grave perfonages, that none fhould need to
" fear that he would commit any Error. He never fuffered the Se-
" nate to conclude any weighty, purpofe, unlefs Fifty of them had
" been prefent. He caufed all his Counfellors to put their Opinions
" in writing, to fee if any were poffeft with paffions, or partialities. He
" changed oft his familiarity with fundry of the Senate, left he who
" had always his ear, might be overcome with importunate purfuits,
" or partiality.

  " The urgent neceffity of the time, moft Noble and Excellent
" Prince, caufeth me to be fo tedious. Humbly craving pardon, and
" heartily kiffing your Majefties hands, I pray the Eternal God grant
" you long and happy life.

From *Halhil* this 15*th*   *Your Majefties moft Humble,*
of *October* 1583.   *And Obedient Servitour,*

                                             James Melvil,

    When I came to *Stirling*, and fhewed his Majefty this Letter, he
not only liked well of it, but ingaged to follow the advice therein
contained. He lamented to me the partial dealing of thofe
about him. Only he faid, that my Brother Sir *Robert* was upon a
found courfe for quieting of the Eftate, and that fome Noblemen, againft
whofe partialities he had oppofed himfelf, had difcorded with him in
his Majefties prefence. It pleafed his Majefty alfo to tell me that the
caufe why I was written for, was to be fent to *England*, to travel
with the *Queen* there for entertainment of mutual Amity, and encreafe of her favour and good will, concerning the Title and Succeffion to the Crown of *England*, and affiftance to help to eftablifh his
troubled Eftate, perturbed by the infolence and partialities of his Subjects, bred and ingendered among them during his minority.

    I anfwered, that I judged it was a very unmeet time, feeing I knew
as matters ftood in *Scotland*, that *England* would make no account of
him, nor of any that would be fent from him, until firft he would let
it be feen and heard, that he could fettle his own Eftate, and by his
wife and prudent management, render his own Subjects obedient to
his Commands, this being done they would honour and efteem him.
And that the beft and readieft way to obtain alfo one day the Crown
of *England*, was to guide *Scotland* fo well, that they might find
ground fome day to wifh to be under the Government of fuch a
Prince. By this kind of Language, and his Majefty pondering what
ground I had to ufe the fame, he was fatisfied that my Voyage fhould
be ftayed till a more convenient time. So I returned from Court, to
my own houfe.

                                                              It

It is mentioned here above in the *Queen* of *Englands* Letter how that she was minded to send a Trusty Servant unto his Majesty, willing him to stay from any strict proceeding against the Lords, who were prickt at for the *Road* of *Ruthven*, until the Arriving of the said Ambassador, who was the Secretary *Walsingham*, a Counsellor of worthy qualities, who had great Credit with the Queen of *England*. But he was of a sickly Complection, and was not able to endure riding Post, therefore he was long by the way, being carried in a Chariot. So that during his longsome Voyage, the Earl of *Arran* went ay forward, forgetting the tenour of the Queen of *Englands* Letter.

So soon as his Majesty was advertised of the Arrival of Sir *Francis Walsingham*, I was sent for to come to Court, and directed to ride and welcome him in his Majesties name, to bear him company, and Convoy him about by *Stirling* to *St. Johnstoun* where his Majesty thought fit to give him Audience. Desiring me also to say unto him that his Majesty was very glad of the coming of such a notable Personage who was known to be indued with Religion, and Wisdom, whom he had ever esteemed as his special friend, being assured that his tedious travel in his long Voyage, (being diseased as he was) tended to more substantial points for the confirmation of the amity between the Queen his Sister and him, then had been performed at any time before.

The Secretary *Walsingham* answered me again, that the great desire he had to establish an assured Amity betwixt the two Princes, and Countries, moved him to undertake the Embassage himself, his Majesty being the Prince in the World, that he loved next unto the Queen his Mistress, and wished most to see and be acquainted with. And that he hoped his Commission should succeed the better, that he had met first with me his old friend, and only acquaintance in *Scotland*. For we had been Companions abroad upon our Travels, and divers times when I was sent to or passed thorow *England*, he would have me to lodge and lye with himself at *London*, which occasioned that we had more familiar Conferences. Whereupon I did write two several Letters, that his Majesty might be the better provided to make answer to such heads as I knew he would propose. Then we took our Journey thorow *Lithgow* to *Stirling*, and from that to *Pearth*. He had heard that my Lord *Seatoun* and *Livingstoun* were written unto to Convoy him, but he requested me to stay them, that he might have the more Conference by the way with me, otherwise he would be compelled to entertain the Noblemen. I judged it probable that his design in this, was to let see his own Train, For he was Sevenscore Horse in Company. Being near the Court, his Majesty sent out two of the Council to meet him, to wit, my Lord of *Doun* and my Brother Sir *Robert*.

The next day his Majesty gave him Audience, accompanied with Mr. *Bowes* Ambassador Resident in *Scotland*. Their first reasoning was upon his Majesties Liberty, and wherefore he had left the Company who were about him, being the best and most religious sort of the Nobility, and of his Majesties best acquaintance, and by whom she would deal in her affairs more friendly, then she could do with others, whom she could not so well Credit. Whereunto his Majesty made answer, so gravely and directly, that *Walsingham* wondred. The next day his Majesty appointed four of the Council, and my self to be with

them, to reafon with him, and to found what he would be at.   But
he refufed to deal with any, but with his Majefty who heard him a-
gain without Mr. *Bowes.* .Where he difcourfed long with his Majefty,
and when he came forth from his Majefty he took me by the hand,
and faid, that he was the beft content man that could be, for he had
fpoken with a notable young Prince, ignorant of nothing, and of fo
great expectation, that he thought his Travel well beftowed. The
Earl of *Arran* defired to enter into familiar Conference with him, but
he refufed to fpeak with him. Making no longer ftay, but took leave
of his Majefty who commanded me to accompany him to the Ferry.
At our parting, he promifed at all occafions to write to me,
and much lamented that the Earl of *Arran* was again in Court, and in
fuch Credit with his Majefty. Which he faid if he had underftood
before he took his Journey, he would have fhifted the fame, and fuffered fome other to have been fent. For he could fee no fure courfe
could be taken between their Majefties, fo long as fuch inftruments
had fuch Credit about him. For he efteemed the faid *Earl* a fcorner
of Religion, a fower of difcord, and a defpifer of true and honeft
men, and therefore he refufed to fpeak with him, or enter into acquaintance. For he was of a contrary nature, religious, true, and a
lover of all honeft men. Therefore *Arran* to be revenged upon him,
fpared not to do a great difhonour to his Majefty. Firft for defpite,
that he refufed to fpeak with him, he caufed refufe to permit the Captains of *Berwick*, and divers other honeft Gentlemen, who came to Convoy the Secretary *Walfingham*, the entry of his Majefties Chamber door.
And then he caufed to prepare a fcornful Prefent for him at his departure, to wit, a Ring with a ftone of *Cryftal*, inftead of a rich *Diamond* which his Majefty had appointed for him, valued at 700 Crowns
which he was oftimes minded to fend back again unto his Majefty,
rather to let him fee how he was abufed then how he was ufed.
Some promife was alfo made unto him, about the repairing fome
wrongs done by *Scotfmen* upon the borders, which he alledged was
not kept. For *Arran* did what he could to difpleafe him, and to
render his Commiffion in all points ineffectual, and his Travel in vain.
Neverthelefs he made fo good report of his Majefties vertues, and
qualities, that it put him in fome fufpition at his return to the Court
of *England*, where fhortly after he took ficknefs and dyed. My opinion is, that if God had granted him longer life, he would have
been found a great friend to his Majefty, who marvelled that the chief
Secretary of *England*, burthened with fo many great affairs, fickly,
and aged, fhould have enterprifed fo painful a Voyage without any
purpofe. For it could not be yet perceived, what was his Errand,
fave only that he gave his Majefty good Counfel. But he be being religious, and of a good confcience, was defirous to fee and underftand affuredly fuch qualifications to be in his Majefty, whereof he had frequently
been informed.   He returned with great contentment in his mind for
that part, but very forrowful for the company that he found in greateft favour and credit about his Majefty.   Which was the more unexpected, by reafon of a Letter that his Majefty had fent unto the *Queen*
his Miftrefs, promifing not to bring in again to Court the Earl of
Arran without her advice, and confent. For my part I never faw
                                                        fuch

such appearance of a prosperous Estate, for his Majesties honour, surety, love and obedience of his own Subjects, increase of the number of his friends in *England*, to the advancement of his Title, neither before that time nor since; if the said *Arran* had not been brought again to Court, which I left not undeclared to his Majesty divers times, not without some danger.

Indeed his Majesties intention was not that he should stay at Court, but onely to come and kiss his hand. But he again being once entred, won some of the Lords, whose particulars he promised to set forward, if they would concur with him, and shew his Majesty that his presence about his person was necessary, and that my Gentle proceedings would ruin the Kings interest, and them all. Managing thus the matter, he remained at Court, and minded to make himself and his assistors rich, by the wrack and spoil of others, who had taken his Majesty at the Road of *Ruthven*. And then he and they, were to guide all at their pleasure. So many of them, who shot at particular marks, ran a strait Course with him, because they thought by his Credit to make up themselves. They feared to lose his Majesties favour, in case *Arran* was not their friend. And some of them did what they could, to persuade me to do the like, alledging that otherwise I should be shut out. Which came to pass shortly after; because I would not yield nor concurr to cast all loose, to the peril of his Majesties Estate and Reputation, remembring what was intended, promised, and proclaimed at his Majesties obtaining his Liberty.

It is certain, that the Lords who made that interprise had great occasion given them to be discontent, but no sufficient cause to oblige them to compel their Soveraign Prince to remove from him these, he so well liked. Which rebellious proceeding, compelled them also for their surety to retian and hold the King as Captive, His Majesty again being advertised, and admonished, that the dangerous proceedings of the Duke of *Lennox*, and Earl of *Arran*, were like to breed disorder, took too litte care to prevent the apparent inconveniencies, and used too little diligence to get sure intelligence and information thereof, which brought him to that strait of being taken, and kept. For it had been less pains to have taken good notice in due time, how his Country was Governed, then to put order or remedy thereto afterward. For it is no little Error, to render the most part of the Nobility and Subjects malecontent, nor no great wisdom after his Majesty was in their hands, to slip from them without their consents. The interprisers, assisters and allowers of the deed, being so considerable a number, as could not be overcome, but by patience, nor punished but by subversion of the State, and endangering of the Prince his own person. Yet it pleased God to guide his Majesty to his liberty (albeit not without some peril) with honour at the first, and with the universal contentment of all his Subjects so soon as they understood his honest meaning, and gracious deliberation as well by Promise, as by Proclamation, as is already specified. For my part, I forget not at all occasions, to remember his Majesty I refused the Office of Secretary when offered by his Majesty in reward of my service, because it was promised that no man should want his Offices, Benefits, Lands or Escheats. I opposed my self in full Council against the Earl of *Arran*,

becaufe

becaufe he had formed a Proclamation againft the Lords of the *Road* of
Ruthven, contrary to His Majefty's former Proclamation of Grace and
Oblivion : For which he leapt out of the houfe in a great rage at me,
and for defpight he made a Lift of the Names of fo many as fhould be
upon the Privy Council, and left out my name. Likewife he named
fo many of his dependers, as fhould ferve in every Office, which his
Majefty was refolved not to acquiefce to, without my advice. Yet
he prevailed with His Majefty to fubfcribe the fame, affifted by the
forefaid Lords, who took plain part with him. So I was fhut out of
door, and had no more place to do good. His Majefty gracioufly
excufed the matter, and faid, That the Lords had no will of two Brothers being upon the Council. But when he fhould get a Wife, I
fhould be her Councellour, and chief about her. So that if they were
glad to be quit of me, I was as glad to be free of them, and not to be
partakers with them in advices tending directly to indanger the Prince
and the Country.

Yet his Majefty affured me, That he would go to *Edinbrugh*, according to the advice I had given in my forementioned Letter, and
Convene the Nobility, Barons, and others whom I had named, in order to the fettling of the Country. And in the mean time he told
me, That the Earl of *Arran* thought fit to fend to *England* the Bifhop
of St. *Andrews*, alledging, That he was paffing to the *Spaw* for recovery of his health : Who paffing through *England*, might have Commiffion to deal with that Queen in his Majefties affairs. And in cafe
he found her willing to difcoufe friendly and freely, he fhould then
fhew her that his Majefty would fend me thither, to fatisfie her more
fufficiently in fuch things as fhe would require. And to that effect
the faid Bifhop fhould fend back word by a Gentleman, Captain *Robert
Melvil*, who went thither exprefly to be fent back with the faid anfwer.

I was commanded to write in the Bifhop's favour, but he was too
well known in *England*. For Mr. *Bowes* who remained long in this
Country, had informed them fufficiently of the faid Bifhop's qualities,
who was difdained in *England*, and difhonoured his Country by borrow-
ing of Gold and pretious Furniture from the Bifhop of *London*, and divers
others, which was never reftored, nor prayed for. His Majefty neverthelefs would have me to grant to go to *England*, and to be in ready-
nefs. He defired me to make my own Inftructions, alledging, That I
knew what was meeteft for him to require at that time.

I would not take upon me to make my own Inftructions, but I promifed to pen the Speech that I would think moft proper to recite to
her Majefty, in cafe I went thither, and which I would judge to be
the fitteft language that any fent thither could fpeak for the time.
After his Majefty had perufed the fame, he much relifhed it, and declared
it was fully conform to his own intentions. It was in thefe words.

M A D A M,

" A Lbeit that your Majefty be as fufficiently certified of the King
   my Sovereign's conformable mind to fatisfie your Majefty,
" as well by Sir *Francis Walfingham* your Secretary, as by the Bifhop of
" St. *Andrews* his Ambaffadour, granting the one his whole defires
" by mouth, and declaring by the other how ftrictly he hath obfer-
                                                              " ved,

‘ ved, and performed the fame ; in effect more to fatisfie your mo-
“ therly mind, by fhewing the tokens of a thankful and obedient Son,
“ then for any great advantage he perceives you thereby feek for your
“ felf. So that it is his Majefty's intention, chiefly feeing he hath ta-
“ ken the Rudder into his own hand to difcover to you ay the lon-
“ ger the more the perfect fruits of his hearty affection.

“ For now having attained unto fome years of knowledge, and dear
“ bought experience (by that which hath been oft beat in his Ears)
“ he is not ignorant how that your Majefties favour and affiftance will
“ be more contributive for his advantage and advancement, then can
“ be any; or that he can obtain from all the other Princes in *Europe.*
“ Your Majefty being to him fo dear a Mother, and fo near a Neighbour,
“ both your Subjects appearing to be but one People. Efpecially fince
“ your prudent Government began, the effects whereof hath not only
“ been found by your own, but by your neighbours. The fame having
“ extended it felf to the advantage of other Kingdoms, efpecially over-
“ fhadowing this whole Ifland to your Majefties everlafting honour.
“ For never in any Princes days, hath been feen fo much reft; fo great
“ riches and felicity in *England*, which likewife might have been in
“ *Scotland*, if the particularities of fome of the Subjects had fuffered
“ them to have followed your Sage, Charitable and Loving admoniti-
“ ons. As the confideration thereof is the reafon which induced his
“ Majefty, whom the matter moft toucheth, to direct me to your Ma-
“ jefty after ripe deliberation, and upon the fure ground of the good
“ information of fuch as were beft inclined, and have greateft experi-
“ ence, to feek the affiftance which he hath fo oft feen fent unto him,
“ help and wholfom advice where he hath fo oft found it, and Salutary
“ Plaifters to be laid unto the Sores, that yet daily breed and arife in
“ his Realm as remains of the Canker, and diforder ingendred during
“ his Minority.

Seeing then the thing that he craves, is your accuftomed Kindnefs
“ and Counfel, which becaufe the ftrength of your conftancy will
“ compel you to continue towards him, he is the more humbly to fuit
“ the fame, as moft feemly for his neernefs of Kin, Age and Eftate to
“ do. Perfwading himfelf, that fuch friendly Offices might be ufed
“ between you, as may tend to both your contentments, and weal of
“ your Kingdoms, which for lack of fure intelligence of others minds
“ by fecret and mutual conference, of devotious and difcreet inftru-
“ ments, might otherwife turn to the contrary.

“ The King my Mafter knows that a mighty Man cannot ftand
“ upon one fide, he grants that he hath now greater need of your help
“ then you of his in many things. But he thinks himfelf as able, and
“ is as willing to deferve favour at your hand; as any who can contend
“ with him for the fame, or would prefume to found the Bell of Suc-
“ ceffion in your Ears. For his part, he requires no inftant Declara-
“ tion thereof, but will continually crave by his behaviour all fuch pre-
“ ferment, as an humble Son ought to feek at the hands of a loving
“ and hearty Mother. Becaufe he believes, that a word of your Ma-
“ jefties mouth, at a convenient time will fufficienly ferve his turn,
“ being yet young enough to await upon any benefit you fhall be
“ pleafed to beftow upon him. Acknowleding the Prorogation of
                                                                    “ your

" your Years, moſt profitable to ſupply his Youth. And conſidering
" the neceſſity he hath now of your aſſiſtance, in the ruling of this his
" troubled Eſtate, he believes that he would have double need of your
" help, if over-early he had any greater handling. •

" Therefore, Madam, he deſires as yet to recreate himſelf with hun-
" ting and paſtime, until he be of greater ripeneſs and maturity. Wi-
" ſhing in the mean time unto your Majeſty a long Life, a proſperous
" Reign, and as good ſucceſs in your proceedings hereafter, as you
" have had hitherto, that having ſo happily and ſo honourably in a
" manner ruled both the Realms, theſe many years by-gone, you
" may be as able to leave them ſo joined together in a cordial and ſta-
" ble Monarchy. And that the bleſt and perfect end of your prudent
" project may Confirm and Crown the worthineſs of your Reputation,
" in finiſhing the work which ſo many had ſo oft in vain enterpriſed,
" as the only Prince that ever obtained the whole handling, and hearts
" of all *Britain* without Blood. The firſt thereof begun and appro-
" priate in your perſon, ſo pleaſantly and peaceably ruled in your
" time; and ſo juſtly and righteouſly diſtribute and left after you, not
" only to the worthieſt, as did *Alexander*, but alſo to the neareſt of
" your friends and kinsfolk, as did *Cæſar* to avoid blood ſhedding; then
" as before, like a kindly Mother to the King, the Country, and Com-
" mon-wealth, to the great pleaſure of God, the perpetual praiſe of
" your memory, and to the univerſal weal and pleaſure of this whole
" Iſland.

If the Queen of *England* could have credited His Majeſty, ſhe might
have an aſſured friendſhip and concurrence of him for the time.
Certainly his Majeſty was ever minded to keep this kind of friendly
and diſcreet Correſpondence with her. For he was informed how
little ſpeed the Queen his Mother had, for ſuiting continually to be declared Second Perſon of *England*, as may be ſeen in that which I have
written before, touching her proceedings with the Queen of *England*,
who I knew would never grant to declare a Second Perſon, but with
force and compulſion, which was never in the power of *Scotland* to
do, during the rich and peaceable Reign of that Queen. Yet fair and
diſcreet language and behaviour, gave place and acceſs to His Majeſty's Ambaſſadours, to paſs to and fro, to gain friends, and get intelligence.

Now the Earl of *Arran* perceiving that by no perſwaſion he could
get His Majeſty ſtayed from executing the reſolution he had laid
down of going for *Edinbrugh*, and calling a Convention of ſuch Noblemen, Barons, Burgeſſes and Miniſters, as were meeteſt to ſettle the
troubled Eſtate of the Country, by taking up again, and following
forth his former gracious intention and promiſe, both by Proclamation
and Speeches unto divers Noblemen, Barons and Miniſters. The ſaid
Earl perceiving that he could not directly ſtay that good purpoſe, ſo
contrary to his intentions, he firſt made his intereſt to be made Chancellour, and then Captain of the Caſtle of *Edinbrugh*, that by his great
Offices, beſides his credit with His Majeſty, he might terrifie all ſuch
as durſt oppoſe themſelves to his Courſes, or Propoſitions. Then he
uſed his craft, to pervert and draw the effect of the Convention, clear
contrary

contrary to His Majefty's intention. For he dealt and fpoke with every Lord and Baron apart at their coming, fhewing them how gracioufly his Majefty was minded toward fuch as had taken him at the *Road*
of *Ruthven*; that he was refolved to grant every one of them a particular remiffion, fome of them to be a while abfent out of the Country, and
others to remain at home in their own houfes abfent from Court. Alledging, that whoever would fay that this form of punifhment was not
great clemency, they would lofe His Majefties favour, and be reputed.
as Men who have no refpect to his honour, and furety, it having been fo
odious a Crime to have laid hands forcibly upon their native Prince.

This matter being fo fet out, and declared by him, who it was
thought knew moft of his Majefty's mind, and had moft of his favour,
evidenced by his having the greateft Offices of the Kingdom in his
hand; it was Voted by them all, *To be great Clemency ufed by his Ma-*
jefty towards thofe who had committed fo odious a Crime. His Majefty
not conjecturing the trick hereby put upon him, in rendering his gracious intention ineffectual, was very glad to hear them all conclude
in one Opinion, not imagining they had been preoccupied by the
Earl of *Arran*, part for fear, part for ignorance, others for flattery, to
obtain favour of him who they faw guided both King and Country.
Few or none of them, for the time, confidered the apparent danger of
rendering thefe plainly defperate, who were ordained to take Remiffions, for that which before was allowed for good Service, in refpect of
their great number who could not yet be punifhed, nor quafhed without hazarding His Majefty's own Princely Eftate and Credit, which
all difcreet and wife Princes are loath to bring into Queftion. This
allowance of good Service hath been oft practifed in *France*, during
the time of their Civil Wars, when their late Princes were but yet
young, and where the Malecontents and Pretenders to Reform the
Eftate where fo many and mighty, as to make a Party anfwerable to
that of their King.

Becaufe I was not yet come to the firft day of the faid Convention,
His Majefty told me that fame night at my coming, what had been
Voted at their firft meeting, which he thought would be to my great
contentment, defiring me the next day to be prefent. I anfwered, I
was forry from my heart for what had been concluded, feeing it was
in effect clean contrary to his intention. For whereas he thought to
have fettled his Eftate, it was caft loofe, the Die was now caft, and
the Diffention fo increafed to the kindling of new enterprifes, that
chance would bear away the Maftery and Victory. For thofe who
were compelled to take Remiffion, would take it as their ditty, and
that finding their former fecurities altered, there was not any more
place left for any fort of agreement.

This language of mine being contrary to the Opinion of fo many,
did not a little difpleafe his Majefty. He asked me, if I thought not
the *Road* of *Ruthven* Treafon? I anfwered, That I thought it fo indeed,
yet fince not only his Majefty himfelf and his Council, had not only
wifely and circumfpectly allowed it for good Service, but had written the fame to the Queen of *England*, and had fent his Commiffioners to the General Affembly holden for the time at *Edinbrugh*, willing the Minifters at their return to their Parifhes to caufe the princi-

X   pal

pal Gentlemen of each Shire to ſubſcribe a Signature, or the Copy
wherein the *Road* of *Ruthven* was allowed for good Service, and to be
ready to defend the ſame. I declared alſo unto his Majeſty, that there
was a common Clauſe contained in all Remiſſions; to wit, *Except
the laying hands upon the King's perſon* ; ſo that how little ſecured they
were by their preſent Remiſſions, His Majeſty might eaſily judge. He
anſwered, That ſeldom or never was any Remiſſions ſeen broken, and
wondered what made me think or ſpeak contrary to the reſt of the
Council. I ſaid, if I had alwayes ſpoken as the reſt, I had not been put
off the Council by the Earl of *Arran*, whoſe qualities I had before de-
ſcribed unto His Majeſty, and what inſeparable inconveniencies would
attend his being again brought into Court. I requeſted His Majeſty
for his own weal, to ſend him home to his own Houſe. For by his
underhand dealing, I underſtood that his Convention would ſhortly
bring on new deſperate enterpriſes. His Majeſty ſaid, That I was in
the wrong to the Earl of *Arran*, and that there would never be more
deſperate enterpriſes. I affirmed that there would be continually, ay
and while the Lords who were in deſpair might mend themſelves, or
find themſelves in a better ſecurity. I ſaid moreover to His Majeſty,
that the Earl of *Arran* would yet again put his Perſon and Crown in
hazard, ſo that His Majeſty left me in anger. And yet he turned about
again, and asked who ſhall then remain about me, if I put away the
Earl of *Arran*? I anſwered, Who but your ancient Nobility, the Earls
of *March*, *Arguile*, *Eglintoun*, *Montroſe*, *Marſhal*, *Rotheſs*, *Huntly*, and
Crauford, with ſome Miniſters and Barons, known not to be factious.
But ſo many of the Noblemen, and of their Friends, as were yet remaining within the Country, after they had heard of their Remiſſions, they Combin'd together and gained divers Lords, who were about
His Majeſty to make a new enterpriſe, and were minded to ſlay the
Earl of *Arran*, Colonel *Stuart*, and ſome others that were about His
Majeſty, whom they knew to have been moſt inſtrumental in carrying on this deſign, though it ſhould be in his Majeſty's preſence, and
that way to become Maſters again of the Court. Whereof I not only was advertiſed by ſome, to whom I had formerly done kindneſſes,
but I was adviſed to abſent my ſelf from Court four or five days, till
the firſt fury of the alteration was over : For the Earl of *Arran's* hatred to me, procured me many friends. I again to ſave his Majeſty
from peril, and diſhonour, thought it my duty to advertiſe him, intreating him to ſend home the ſaid *Earl.* I cannot tell what moved
the Earl, but that ſame night he invited me to Supper, which I refuſed. The next day again he took me by the hand before His Majeſty, ſaying, That I ſhould Dine with him in his Majeſty's preſence.
He ſhewed me a very favourable countenance, for the King had forbidden him to offend me in any ſort, as he would retain his favour. If
he had got any word of my contrary Opinion to his, I cannot tell,
or that I had deſired him to be ſent home, but there was ſome appearance of this by his behaviour and paſſionate Speeches unto me, ſoon after
that I had told my judgment unto his Majeſty, as men may judge,
for leading me by the hand to dine with him in His Majeſty's preſence,
which I could not evite. Before we did ſit down to Dinner, he askt
Me how all would be? I told him very freely, all I had ſpoken unto

His

His Majefty. Then, faid he, you would place about His Majefty the Earl of *March*, who is a Fool guided by the Laird of *Compie* and *Robert Sives.* I faid, he behoved to be one with the reft of the Noblemen already named. He faid it fhould pafs my power, or any Man's to caufe him leave his Majefty, fo long as he was in fuch danger. I anfwered, That the King was in danger for no other caufe, but becaufe he was with him. I perceived he entertained a great difcontent at me in his heart, which burft out afterward, Threatning to put me out of the Gates, if I fifhed any more in his Waters. I anfwered, if I pleafed to tarry, it would pafs his power, feeing I would get more honeft Men to take my part, then he would get Throat-cutters to affift him. So foon as his Majefty heard of this language, he fent the Earl's Uncle, the Laird of *Caprintoun* to reprove him very fharply. Whereupon he retired in great difcontent to the Caftle of *Edinbrugh*, whereof he was Captain, declaring he would not come near his Majefty, till I was fent home, to give him place; which I perceived His Majefty was fatisfied I fhould do to pleafe him. For his Wife came daily to His Majefty, and faid, That her Husband was highly difcontent, finding His Majefty to take my part againft him. Whereupon I refolved to retire. At my leave-taking, His Majefty faid, he doubted not but I would return when called for. By which I underftood, that I fhould not come back, till fent for. Which fuited very well with my former intentions, being refolved to attend no longer then the forefaid Convention was ended.

Now the Earl of *Arran* triumphed, being *Chancellour*, and *Captain* of the *Caftles* of *Edinbrugh* and *Sterling.* He made the whole Subjects to tremble under him, and every Man to depend upon him, daily inventing and feeking out new faults againft divers, to get the gift of their Efcheats, Lands, Benefices. And to procure Bribes, he vexed the whole Writers, to make fure his gifts. Thofe of the Nobility who were now unfure of their Eftates fled, others were banifhed; he fhot directly at the Life and Lands of the Earl of *Gaury.* For the Highland Oracles had fhewn unto his Wife, that *Gaury* would be ruined, as fhe told to fome of her familiars. But fhe helped that Prophefie forward, as well as fhe could. For *Gaury* had been his firft Mafter, and defpighted his infolent Pride, Oppreffion, and Misbehaviour plainly in Council; which few others durft do, therefore he hated his Perfon, and loved his Lands, which at length he obtained.

For *Gaury* being unable to be a Witnefs of the Oppreffion of his Country, obtained His Majefties confent to go out of the Country. But as he was making his preparations too longfomly, and flowly in *Dundie* (as he was of Nature over flow) where his Ship was to receive him, he was advertifed by fome Factioners that the Earls of *Angus*, *Mar*, and Mafter of *Glams*, had an enterprife in hand, *viz.* To come out of *Ireland*, and take the Town and Caftle of *Sterling.* Having correfpondence with divers Nobles, and others their Friends, who were in the Country Malecontents, fo that they were in hope to make a party fufficient againft the Earl of *Arran.*

The defpight the Earl of *Gaury* had againft the Earl of *Arran*, moved him to ftay to make part with them. There was at this time an univerfal mifcontent in the Country, and great bruits of an alteration. Whereupon a Letter was written to me by Colonel *Stuart*, at His Majesty's Command, ordaining me with all diligence to repair to Court; or in case I was not recovered of my Ague, whereof I had been long sick, that I might write my Mind and Opinion to my Majesty in a Letter, what was like to fall out concerning the great Rumour and Bruits of an apparent alteration. And being by reason of my foresaid Distemper, unable for Travel, I sent my return in Writing, shewing His Majesty, that there was an universal miscontent, with great bruits, not without appearance of probability of a sudden change, occasioned by the misbehaviour of such as were managers at Court; and by the great straits, and desperate Estate of those who were pursued, being men of Quality, Active and Experienced. And a greater number then could be born down or Mastered, as I had frequently shewn His Majesty before, without respect of feud or favour, but simply for His Majesty's Service. Intreating His Majesty again to set forward his former acceptable intentions, which he had resolved to do when he went to St. *Andrews*. Seeing there was no other course advisable, for setling his troubled Estate. This kind of language was the better liked, because of so many Advertisments that came daily to His Majesty's Ears.

These bruits made His Majesty be upon his Guard, and to use means to get intelligence. The lingring of the Earl of *Gaury* in *Dundie* gave ground of suspicion. His Majesty had also been advertised, That he had laid aside his intentions of going abroad according to his former resolutions, and that he was designing to wait upon the in-coming of the banished Lords. His Majesty also dreamed a Dream, that he saw the Earl of *Gaury* taken, and brought in Prisoner before him by Colonel *Stuart*. And he thought his Estate was thereby settled, which indeed for that time came true, because the Lords who had taken *Sterling*, so soon as they understood of the taking of the Earl of *Gaury*, fled incontinently out of *Sterling*, and at last out of the Country. Believing that the said *Earl* had been taken willingly, supposing his affection to have been so great to His Majesty, as being his near kinsman, come of the House of *Angus*, his Mother being a Natural Daughter of the said House, that he would be thereby induced to discover the whole design. He not having been upon the first design of any enterprise, but drawn in afterwards by the craftiness of others. Upon these considerations, His Majesty had compassion upon him, and had no intention of taking his Life. But the Earl of *Arran* was fully resolved to have his Lands, and therefore to make a Party to assist him in that design, he ingaged to divide them with several others, upon condition that they would assist him in the design of ruining him. Which afterwards he did, having by this means procured their Consent, and Votes. At his death upon the Scaffold, he shewed himself a devout Christian, and a resolute *Roman*, much regrated by all who heard his grave Harangue, and did see his constant End.

After his death, there was quietness for a while, though without appearance of long continuance to such as took up matters right. During this little while of fair Weather, there was a Parliament held to forfault the banished Lords, wherein these were chiefly instrumental, who hoped to raise their particular Fortunes upon the ruine of their Neighbours.   Among

Among others, it pleafed His Majefty to write for me. I was by him gracioufly received, and remembring fome of my Speeches, he took me into his Cabinet, and inquired how I now relifhed his proceedings. I anfwered, That he had reafon to thank God, and no good management, and that I was affured there would be yet more enterprifes: That they who took *Sterling*, and had retired again, would never ceafe to make enterprife upon enterprife, till they might fee themfelves in a better fecurity. His Majefty replied, That they had gained fo little by their laft in-coming, that he believed they would never commit fuch a folly again. I anfwered, That had not the accidental taking of the Earl of *Gaury* fallen out, their enterprife would have been more fuccefsful: For they fufpected, he was taken by his own defire to bewray their enterprife: That otherwife they had gained their intent, feeing fome who were then about His Majefty would have concurred with them, to lay afide the Earl of *Arran*, whom they affifted for aw; and not for love, they hating his infolency, and feeing no Outgate how to ftand by him. And that there had for that effect been fecret promifes made to them, by inftruments who went betwixt them. But feeing the Earl of *Gaury* in hands, and the faid Lords thereby fo difcouraged as to fly away, fuch as had made the faid fecret promifes, took up a new deliberation, fhewing themfelves their greateft Enemies. While in the mean time, they but waited an opportunity of advancing their intentions.

About this time the Lord *Burleigh* chief Ruler in *England*, caufed fend in one Mr. *Davifon* to be an Agent here, to fee what bufinefs he could brew, who was afterwards made Secretary: For after the deceafe of *Walfingham*, Secretary *Cicil* being advanced to be Lord *Burleigh*, and great *Treafurer* of *England*, two Secretaries were chofen, one called Mr. *Smith*, and this *Davifon*, whofe Predeceffor was a *Scotfman*. Upon which confideration, he was thought more able to conquer credit here. He had been in *Scotland* before, and was at my houfe, in company with Sir *Henry Killegrew* my old friend, when he was Refident in *Scotland*. At which time, he acknowledged to me that he was come of *Scotfmen*, and was a *Scotfman* in his heart, and a favourer of the King's Right, and Title to the Crown of *England*. He defired me to keep all fecret from Mr. *Killegrew*, promifing if he could find the means to be employed here, that he would do good Offices.

His Majefty was for the time at *Falkland*, and wrote for me, to be directed to ride and meet the faid *Davifon*. Whom I was commanded to Convoy to *Coupar*, there to remain till his Majefty had time to give him Audience. Afterward I Convoyed him to my own houfe, and from that to *Falkland*, where His Majefty found his Commiffion to fmall avail. But becaufe *Walfingham* had refufed at his being here, to fpeak with the Earl of *Arran*, albeit the faid Earl had offered me to give fatisfaction to him in all his defires, fo that he would confer with him. Which *Walfingham* ftill refufed, but Mr. *Davifon* was directed at this time to deal with the Earl of *Arran*, to fee what advantage might be had at his hand. For my Lord *Burleigh* was not content that *Walfingham* was fo precife ; therefore *Davifon* entred into familiarity with him, and was made his Goffip, and heard his frank offers, and liked well of them. For after that the Lords were fled to

England,

England, and forfaulted, the Council of *England* thought they had fome ground to build a new faction upon, to trouble the King, and his Eftate. And whereas the faid *Davifon* had promifed before to fhew himfelf a kind *Scotfman,* I perceived him clean altered, and a perfect practifer againft the quiet of this State, whereof I advertifed His Majefty.

After his return, *England* appeared not to have fuch a fear, as it had formerly had at the Earl of *Arran.* For there was a meeting drawn on at the Borders, betwixt the Earl of *Hunfdon* and the Earl of *Arran.* Who had long and privy conference together, to keep a great friendfhip betwixt the two Princes and Countries; with a fecret Plot, That the Earl of *Arran* fhould keep the King unmarried for three years; under this pretext, That there was a young Maid of the blood in *England.* who about that time would be ready for marriage, whereupon the Queen would declare His Majefty Second Perfon.

This was a deceitful Traffique and kept fecret from every Body, the defign thereof being to hinder the King to deal for any other honourable and profitable Match. The Earl of *Arran* thinking himfelf fetled, being now in friendfhip with the Queen of *England* as he fuppofed, moved his Majefty to fend thither the Mafter of *Gray,* who was entred in great favour and familiarity with His Majefty, by fome fecret dealing and intelligence he had with the Queen his Mother in *England,* by means of fome of her friends in *France.* For being there at his Travels, and but lately returned, he brought fome Letters directed from Her Majefty to the King her Son; and conveyed the anfwers back again, by an intereft he had in *England,* with fome who favoured Her Majefty. He was a great dealer alfo, between Her Majefty and fome Catholicks in *England.* He was a proper Gentleman, of a Noble Spirit, and fair Speech, and fo well efteemed by His Majefty, that *Arran* thought fit to abfent him from Court by this Ambaffage. Neverthelefs he employed him alfo in the Courfe begun betwixt him and the Earl of *Hunfdean.* And yet when he was at the Court of *England,* fo well efteemed and treated as was reported by fuch as were fent back, it was alledged by fome of the Mafter of *Gray*'s friends, that the Earl of *Arran* began to envy him, and mifreprefent him unto His Majefty, as if he had difcovered unto the Queen of *England,* a great part of the Queen of *Scotlands* purpofes, and proceedings. However the faid Mafter returned again well rewarded, and commended for his behaviour, qualities, and difcretion unto the King's Majefty, to the great increafe of his Credit with the King. Not long after his return, he was informed what mifreports had been made of him in his abfence. Which he recompenced the beft he could with Court Charity at convenient times, fo that by little and little he began to Eclipfe *Arran.*

The Mafter of *Gray* alfo forewarned His Majefty of a notable Perfon who was upon the way, fent unto His Majefty by the Queen of *England,* to do him honour; and to bear him company, to entertain a ftricter friendfhip between that Queen and Him, than any had ever been intended before. And that the faid Ambaffadour called Mr. *Wotton* would not trouble His Majefty with Bufinefs, or Country Affairs, but would bear him company in his Paftimes of Hunting, Hauking,

and

and Horfe-riding; and entertain him with friendly,and merry Difcour-
fes, as one come lately from *Italy*, and *Spain*, expert in Languages and
Cuftoms of Countries ; and a great lover of his Maiefty's Title, and
Right to the Crown of *England*. So that His Majefty was ingaged
to love him before he did fee him, and caufed with diligence to write
to me to come and entertain the faid Ambaffadour.

At my return to Court, I was the better taken with, that *Arran*
was under fome Cloud. The Mafter of *Gray* was then my great
friend : For His Majefty had told him, that I had ever refifted the
Earl of *Arran*'s furious proceedings. His Majefty defired me, as I
would do him acceptable Service, to bear good company to the faid
Ambaffadour, declaring unto me all his properties, and qualifications
above fpecified ; willing me alfo to Banquet him at my houfe. But
after I had converfed certain days with him, I remembred I had formerly feen him in *France* with Doctor *Wotton*, who was their Ambaffadour Refident for Queen *Mary* of *England*, the time that fhe was
married with King *Philip* of *Spain*. During which time, there were
great fufpicions and jealoufies betwixt *France* and *England*. For tho
there was hot War between *France* and *Spain*, yet the Peace continued ftill with the Queen of *England*, who was lately married by the
King of *Spain*. She appeared ftill to keep the Peace with *France*,
though in the mean time fhe fent over to *Flanders* both Men and Mony to the help of the King her Husband. The old *Conftable* of *France*,
my Mafter, who for the time had the whole management of the Country Affairs, under King *Henry* the Second, reproached the *Englifh* Ambaffadour, for that the Queen his Miftrefs was doing her endeavour
to break the Peace. The Ambaffadour excufed his Miftrefs, alledging,
That if any of his Country-men ferved in the Wars under the King
of *Spain*, that they would be found but Soldiers of Fortune, ready to
ferve any Man for Mony. She denied that fhe knew of their paffing
into *Flanders*, or that fhe disburfed any Mony for the Wars. Albeit
that there was ground enough miniftred unto her, by reciving and retaining in *France* all her Rebels and Fugitives, giving them Penfions and
Intertainment, and ftirring them up to enterprifes againft her Life,
and Eftate. This the Conftable flatly denyed, only he faid, That out
of a general good will which was born to *Englifh-men* in time of
Peace, they were fuffered to live in the Country, which bears the
name of *France*, becaufe their fhould be Freedom and Franchife to every
Chriftian. The Ambaffadour being wife and fubtil, perceiving this
anfwer to be but a fhift, and that Wars would inevitably follow thefe
kind of fufpicions ; he intended by fome fubtilty to Circumvent the
Conftable, and for that effect had fent to *England* for his Brother's
Son, being One and Twenty years of Age, as well to employ him,
as to teach him the *French* and *Italian* Languages. This youth being
arrived in *France* with an *Irifh* Boy to be his Interpreter, who could
fpeak *French*, both apparelled in mean array, to be the lefs fufpected to have any practife or policy in their minds. Like a Forreign
young Man he addreffed himfelf to fome of the King of *France* his
Courtiers, defiring Audience of His Majefty fecretly, as having a
matter of great importance to propofe. The King again divers times
directed him to deal firft with the Conftable. At laft when he came

to

to the Conſtable, he deſired alſo of him, that he might firſt declare
unto the King his Errand, which was of great importance, although
he knew that the King ſpoke with no Man in ſuch matters, until the
Conſtable had firſt ſounded him, and then told his Opinion to the King,
what anſwer were fitteſt to make. At length he ſaid, he would declare the matter unto the Conſtable, under promiſe of great ſecrecy,
cauſing the Conſtable by this niceneſs to ſuſpeƈt ſome praƈtice. When
he gave him Audience, he cauſed me to be preſent beſide him. At
their meeting in the Conſtable's Cabinet ; his *Iriſh* Interpreter was
put forth, againſt his will, as appeared. But he was ſo inſtruƈted by
the Ambaſſadour his Uncle, to uſe ſuch forreign and rude faſhions.
Yet again e're he began to propoſe his Errand, he deſired ſecrecy. The
Conſtable being an old, wiſe, experimented Councellor, put him a little aſide, and rounded in my Ear, to know if ever I had ſeen this young
Man before. I anſwered, That I had obſerved him the preceding
day at long conference with one Mr. *Sommer* Secretary to the *Engliſh*
Ambaſſadour. Then the Conſtable thought, that he ſhould handle
the matter well enough : for he inſtantly conjeƈtured that all this
niceneſs proceeded from the Ambaſſadour, to intrap him. So calling
the young Man again, he deſired him to ſhew what he had to ſay.
Mr. *Wotton* began to declare the great miſcontentment that was in
England, not only for bringing in the proud *Spaniard* to Rule over
them, but alſo for the alteration of Religion made by Queen *Mary*,
moving ſome to Rebel, and others to remove off the Country, who
nevertheleſs were all well received and treated by the King's Majeſty
of *France*. Whereby he had gained the hearts of the third part of
England ſo devoutly towards him, that they would gladly put the
Crown of *England* on his head, (getting liberty in religion) to be
quit of the *Spaniſh* Tyranny, and terrible Inquiſition, which was feared would alſo be eſtabliſhed in *England*. And for the firſt proof of
their good will and gratitude, a number of Lords and Knights, who
durſt not write, had ſent him ſecretly with an Overture to put the
ſtrong Town of *Calis* into his hands, with the whole Earldom of *Oye*.
At this the *Conſtable* made a ſtart, and ſaid, Know you not my friend,
that there is a ſworn Peace betwixt your Queen and my Maſter ?
The other replied again, how that the Queen of *England* aided ſecretly, whith Mony and Men the King of *Spain* her Husband, in his
Wars of *Flanders* againſt *France*. Which the Conſtable alledged that
ſhe denied by her Ambaſſadour, willing him however to tell out the
reſt of his Commiſſion. Then, ſaid he, my Lord, the means how you
may get *Calis*, is this, Firſt, The moſt part of the Town is of the Reformed Religion, and are Malecontents, having refuſed to receive a
Gariſon of *Spaniards*. And they are friends to thoſe who have ſent
me, and keep correſpondence with them ; only the Towns Ship keeps
the Town, keeping Watch and Ward, being unſkilful in handling
their Arms. Therefore the King ſhall cauſe Monſieur *Senarpon* his
Lieutenant to lye in ambuſcade at ſuch a Wood within
a mile and an half of the Town, at an appointed day, then a Ship
well furniſhed with Armed Men ſhall lye at Anchor half a mile from
the Town. And ſome of them clothed like Marriners, ſhall come on
Land, and have Swords and Piſtols under their Cloaths, and ſhall
                                                                    wait

wait about two of the Afternoon, at which time the Ports of the Town are opened to let Men in, and out. Part of thofe who attend the Ports, will be at their Dinner, when one or two will come before the reſt to open the Gates. Thus the Gates being eaſily ſeiſed upon, let one of the Company ſhoot off a Culverin, that the Ship may hear, and ſhoot a Cannon to cauſe *Monſieur de Senarpon* with his Company advance. In the mean time, there ſhall be a mutiny raiſed in the Town by our friends, and partners, ſo that the Town ſhall be obtained without ſtroke.

After that the Conſtable had heard all this long diſcourſe, he ſaid, That it was a very probable deſign, and he doubted not but it might be eaſily effectuated, but in reſpect of the ſworn Peace, the King his Maſter would not, nor ſhould never have his conſent to break it. But that he was much ingaged to the Noblemen who did bear him ſo much good will, and as for him who had taken ſo great paines, the King ſhould reward him, willing me to remember to cauſe give mony to the young Gentleman. So he gained nothing at the Conſtable's hand, and never came again to ſeek his reward; but was afterward mani-feſtly known to be Brother's Son to Doctor *Wotton*, Ambaſſadour, as ſaid is.

This is he now who was ſent hither to bear His Majeſty company, as one who will not meddle with Practiſes, but with Paſtimes. But when I forewarned His Majeſty to beware of him, and told how that he being little above Twenty years old, was imployed to beguile the wiſe old Conſtable : Now he was Fifty years, and his Majeſty but Twenty, it was to be feared he would endeavour to beguile him. Yet His Majeſty would not believe me, but believed the ſaid Mr. *Wotton* to have a great kindneſs for him, and ſo he became one of his moſt fa-miliar Minions, waiting upon him at all Field-paſtimes; and in ap-pearance he deſpiſed all buſie Councellors, and medlers in matters of State ; as he was inſtructed by ſuch as ſaid, he would pleaſe His Maje-ſty beſt to appear ſuch. But he had more hurtful fetches in his head againſt His Majeſty, then any *Engliſh-man* that ever came in hither had at any time before.

You have heard before of a meeting that was drawn on at the Bor-ders, betwixt the Earl of *Hunſdean* and *Arran*; where at their ſecret conference *Arran* was required by the craft of the Lord *Burleigh*, and his faction in the *Engliſh* Council, to ſtop the King from any marriage for three years, upon many fair counterfeited promiſes; One where-of was, That he ſhould be declared Second Perſon, upon his marriage of the forenamed *Engliſh* Lady of the Blood. At which *Arran* gran-ted all that was deſired, he was ſo glad to procure the Queen of *Eng-land*'s friendſhip. About that time the Queen of *England*, by her in-telligence from *Denmark*, was advertiſed of a great and magnifick Am-baſſage, to be ſent from *Denmark* to *Scotland*, *viz.* Three Ambaſſa-dours, with Sixſcore Perſons, in Two gallant Ships. Whether ſhe ſuſpected, or had heard, that it was to draw on a marriage, I cannot tell. But this far I learned, that her Council judged it was to confirm at leaſt a greater friendſhip betwixt the two Kings, and their Coun-tries, which was one of the Cauſes that moved them to ſend this Mr. *Wotton* to *Scotland*, to uſe all his wiles to diſturb and hinder any grea-

Y ter

ter Amity, that might proceed from the said Commiffion, and Negotiation between their two Kings, and their Countries. For *England* trufted nothing to the Earl of *Arran*'s promife, for they efteemed him as an inconftant Man, as is already declared.

So foon as the *Danifh* Ambaffadours arrived by Ship in this Country, His Majefty ordered me to entertain them, and bear them company. And becaufe they were three joined in Commiffion, he willed me to choofe any other two whom I thought meeteft, to bear them company with me. I named unto His Majefty the Laird of *Segie*, and *william Shaw* Mafter of *Wark*.

Firft, At *Dumfarmling* they Congratulated His Majefty in the King their Mafter's Name, with a long Difcourfe of the old Amity, Bond, and mutual Friendfhip between the two Kings, and their Kingdoms. And laft of all they required the Ifles of *Orkny* to be reftored again to the Crown of *Denmark*, alledging they were mortgaged, to be redeemed again for the Sum of Fifty Thoufand Florins.

Their coming and demand was diverfly fcanned, fome fuppofing Wars would enfue, unlefs the faid Ifles were rendred, others thought that their intention was to bring on a marriage with the King of *Denmark*'s Daughter.

Now albeit His Majefty was determined to treat them well, and honourably, they were neverthelefs mifhandled, rufled, and delayed here the fpace of   Months, to their great charge and difcontent : for they lived upon their own expences, and were not defrayed by His Majefty, as all other Ambaffadours of that Nation have been fince. When they were appointed to part out of *Dumfarmling* toward St. *Andrews*, there to get their difpatch, His Majefty ordered to tell them, That he would fend them Horfes out of his own Stable, to ride upon. The day of their parting being come, they fent away their Baggage and Officers before them, and were booted themfelves, waiting upon His Majefty's Horfes, and becaufe they came not in due time, they went forward on foot. The King was much diffatisfied when he underftood how they were handled, and caufed his Horfes to follow faft after them, and overtake them. When they came to St. *Andrews*, divers appointed days of Council and Convention were broken unto them, which were promifed to be kept for their difpatch, for obtaining whereof they were very earneft. Then Men were appointed to deride them at their Lodgings, and before their Windows when they lookt out to the ftreet. So that nothing was left undone, which could enrage them, or ftir them up to chollor. Only Mr. *Wotton* the *Englifh* Ambaffadour vifited them frequently, and did well and favourably entertain them, comforting them at all occafions, appearing to be forry that they were fo abufed. He offered to lend them Gold and Silver largely, for the great friendfhip that he knew to be between the Queen his Miftrefs, and the King of *Denmark*. For he was affured of good payment, and thought to purchafe credit at their hands by his apparent friendly dealing. At length under great fecrecy he faid he would not conceal from them, that he had heard the King fpeak difdainful language of their Country and Cuftoms ; and alfo, That fome of his Gentlmen had heard the King fpeak evil of their King, undervaluing him as being defcended of a Race of Merchants.

chants. And he further affured them, That he and his Council were
refolved to keep them long here, without any difpatch, to affront and
weary them.

Then again the faid Ambaffadour, and two of his Gentlemen informed his Majefty of thefe hard Speeches, of the reproachful dealing
they had met with from King and Council, reflecting upon their Mafter. He informed him alfo of the rude manners, and drunkennefs
of thofe that were about His Majefty, who had the like fcornful language of the King of *Denmark*, his Country, and Ambaffadours, moving His Majefty to make the lefs of them. Whereby they were ftirred up to fuch a rage, that I had much to do to keep them two or
three feveral times from going to their Ships, to have returned to
their King without any anfwer, and to have given him an accompt of
the difdainfull ufage they had met with, and the injury thereby done
to him. The Earl of *Arran* was alfo their great Enemy, becaufe they
made no court to him, but rather flighted, fome of their Company
having known him in *Sweden* a Common Soldier. So that he was
as ready as the reft to mock and deride them; albeit at that fame time
the Ring-leaders about the Court were Combined together with the
Englifh Ambaffadour againft him.

The principal of the three Ambaffadours was a wife, grave, and ancient Councellor. The fecond was furious in his Speeches. The
third cried out, *The King our Mafter is affronted, we muft be revenged.*

I took the firft apart, requefting him to hear me patiently, for he
fpoke good *Dutch*, but mine was not fo good. Therefore I defired
that he would more notice my meaning, then my words, and be more
careful to caufe his friendly Commiffion to take effect, that he might
return home with happy fuccefs, then to withdraw, abrupely, to be
called unhappy Inftruments of difcord at the pleafure of a few fcornful Factioners, who had laid their heads together to caufe them part
diffatisfied, and to be as inftrumental in doing evil, as they were minded at their coming to do good.

I told him, how that the Queens Majefty of *England* was a wife,
well inclined, and politick Princefs, and that there were as many honeft and good Men in *England*, as in fo much bounds in the whole
World; abeit there was in it divers Opinions, and Factions, fhooting
at fundry marks, as is done in all other parts. And becaufe that their
Queen would never marry to have Succeffion of her own Body,
they were all very defirous to know who after her fhould Reign
over them.

The moft part of the Country, expects that it fhall be our King, and
wifheth his welfare and profperity, as being righteous Heir to the
Crown of *England*, both by the Father and Mother's fide. But thofe
who at prefent have a chief management at the Court, fhoot at
other particular marks of their own, minding to fet forward fome
of themfelves, or of their friends, to brook the Kingdom. And, for
that caufe, they make all the oppofition they can to our King, becaufe
of their unmerciful dealing to his Mother, for the which they fear
fame day to be punifhed, when he comes to be King of *England*. For
all thefe refpects, they endeavour to keep him from marriage; and

from all forreign Friendſhip and Alliance. This Ambaſſadour of *England*, is a very ill Inſtrument, both himſelf, and his Gentlemen, and hunting daily with His Majeſty, makes the worſt reports they can. The Ambaſſadour of *Denmark* anſwered to that, marvelling that Mr. *Wotton* ſhould make ſuch report of them, he offering them ſo great friendſhip, and giving them daily intelligence how they were ſcorned and mocked, both by the King and his Conncil, to his great regret, offering to lend them mony, and to do all other pleaſures to them that lay in his power. I replied, He knew well enough, that he would get good payment, and great thanks. For the King of *Denmark* was eſteemed a worthy Prince, and his Ambaſſadours worthy to be honoured; but the guiders of the Court of *England* deſire not that our King ſhould think or eſteem ſo of them, wiſhing him to have but few Friends, and many Enemies. Then I aſſured him, That the King's Majeſty and all his Subjeƈts, except ſome that were corrupted by *England*, were determined to entertain and increaſe a continual friendſhip with the King and Country of *Denmark*: Praying their wiſdoms couragiouſly to reſiſt, and not feebly and fooliſhly to give place to the ſaid crafty praƈtices of their ſcornful enviers, by retiring abruptly, thereby ſuffering themſelves to be made evil Inſtruments, direƈtly againſt their own Intention and Commiſſion, and they ſhould ſhortly ſee good ſucceſs to follow thereupon, to their great contentment. Promiſing unto them for my part, That I ſhould go inſtantly unto his Majeſty, and with all hazard that might be, ſhould diſcover unto him, how both he and they were deceitfully abuſed by the double dealing of the *Engliſh* Ambaſſadour, and ſuch Courtiers as aſſiſted him.

Upon this diſcourſe and promiſe, they went to council all three together, as their cuſtom was. And after long conference, they gave me anſwer, That their coming was for to do good Offices. And albeit they had ſuffered ſundry injuries, they would be ſorry to be made Inſtruments of diſcord, ſo far againſt their Commiſſion and Intention, and therefore would yet ſtay upon hope of better handling, and upon my promiſe, albeit to that hour few or none had been kept to them.

After this, I ſhewed unto His Majeſty what great inconveniencies might enſue upon the long delaying, and ill handling of the *Daniſh* Ambaſſadours. And yet that I marvelled not that he made ſo little accompt of them, in reſpeƈt of the great care, and fine praƈtices, that were uſed to make him undervalue them, by the *Engliſh* Ambaſſadour and his Aſſiſtants, who had His Majeſty's Ear for the time. At the firſt His Majeſty was impatient to hear this language ſpoken of Perſons he had ſo good liking of, and ſaid, that he was Informed, That the King of *Denmark* was deſcended but of Merchants, and that few made accompt of him or his Country, but ſuch as ſpoke the *Dutch* Tongue. For this was put in his head to prevent any of my perſwaſions in their favour, left they ſhould get place or credit. I anſwered, That neither could the King of *France*, or Queen of *England* ſpeak *Dutch*, and yet they made great accompt to the King and Country of *Denmark*. *France* having their Ambaſſadour lying there, and paying yearly to the King of *Denmark* a great Sum of Gold, to the value of Twenty

Twenty Thoufand Crowns. His Majefty faid, The more fhame was his. I faid, Rather to the King of *France*, who muft buy his kindnefs. Neither could the Queen of *England*, faid I, fpeak *Dutch*, yet fhe made much accompt of the King and Country of *Denmark*, and durft not offend him, nor none of his Ships, both by reafon of the ftraight paffage at *Elfoonure*, and alfo becaufe he had great Ships to make himfelf amends, in cafe fhe did him or his any wrong. I faid, moreover, That whereas it hath been reported to Your Majefty, the Race of their Kings not to be of Noble and Royal Blood, I fhall fhew Your Majefty that it is but manifeft invention to caufe you to defpife them. For this late King *Frederick* is defcended of an Old and Royal ftock, to wit, *Chriftianus* of *Denmark*, the firft of that name, who had two Sons, and one Daughter called *Margaret*, married into *Scotland* to *James* the Third his Eldeft Son. *John* was King after him ; his fecond Son *Frederick* was King of *Norway*, and Duke of *Holftein*. *John* had a Son called *Chriftianus* the Second, alfo King of *Denmark*, who married *Charles* the Fifth his Sifter, who did bear him two Daughters: Whereof the Eldeft was given in marriage to *Frederick* Elector Palatine ; the Second to the Duke of *Millain*, and afterward, being a Widow, married the Duke of *Lorrain*. Himfelf was taken and kept in Prifon by his Subjects, for fome rigorous Execution upon his Barons, and his Father's Brother *Frederick* was made King. After this *Frederick*, the Earl of *Altenbourg* was chofen by affiftance of the Town of *Lubeck*, but *Chriftianus* the Third, Son to the faid *Frederick*, put him out, and conquered the Kingdom. Neverthelefs this *Chriftianus* being a good Prince, would not change their old Priviledges, but caufed himfelf to be chofen, and likewife his Son *Frederick* in his time, to Reign after him ; who is now prefent King, and hath fent his honourable Ambaffage to Your Majefty, as to his good friend, and kinfman, defcended of the Kingly Race of *Denmark*. And whereas he requires again the Ifles of *Orkny*, it is for the difcharge of his Oath, becaufe every King of *Denmark* at his Election, is fworn to claim again the faid Ifles, which he hath done for the fafhion, and for no other effect, but to draw on a greater familiarity, and friendfhip. Or elfe he had not fent fo honourable a Company, but rather an Herauld of Arms, if he had been earneftly bent either to get the faid Ifles, or to quarrel about them.

After that His Majefty had heard this Difcourfe far different to his former Informations, he was exceeding glad, and faid, he would not for his head, but that I had fhewn the verity unto him ; and that fame afternoon he fent for the faid Ambaffadours, and acquainted them how near Allied he was to the King of *Denmark*. He excufed their long delay, and promifed inftantly to fee them difpatched himfelf, and that within three or four days. He called for Wine, and did drink to them, and fent them home very well content, and fatisfied to their Lodgings. He commanded a Banket to be prepared for them, which His Majefty's Controller and Officers were quietly forbidden to do, alledging the fcantnefs of Provifions. Which the Laird of *Segie* and I perceiving, we dealt with the Earl of *March*, who prepared a great Banquet for them in His Majefty's Name, to the great diffatisfaction of Mr. *Wotton*, and his Partifans, who durft not appear. And though they would not fuffer His Majefty to be prefent at the Banquet, but

to

to Dine in his own Chamber, yet his Majesty being informed by
me how matters went, he rose from his own Dinner, and went to
the Banquet house, and drank to the King, Queen, and Ambassadours
of *Denmark*, and so contented them. And he caused their dispatch
to be in readiness, conform to his promise. But when I advertised
His Majesty, That there was no Present prepared for to reward them
withal, he was wonderfully troubled, saying, They who had the management of his affairs, were resolved to affront him.

Now at this time was the Earl at Court, not so much in favour as
formerly. During the which time, there chanced a strange misrule to
fall out at a day of meeting upon the Borders, which was set between
the two Wardens : where Sir *Francis Russel* upon the *English* side was
killed. Whereupon the *English* Ambassadour took occasion to lay the
blame upon the Earl of *Arran*, alledging, That the Laird of *Fernihast*
who was Warden upon the *Scots* side had married the Earl of *Arran*'s Brother's Daughter. And that the said Earl had caused the
slaughter to be made, that the Borders might break loose. In this
complaint, the said Ambassadour was well assisted by the Master of
Gray and his Companions. So that the Earl of *Arran* was Commanded to Ward within the Castle of St. *Andrews*, and was kept strict-
ly there three or four days. So that being in fear of his life, he sent
for Colonel *Stuart*, the Laird of *Segie*, and me, and lamented to us his
hard handling, purging himself, as he might justly do, of that accident that fell out upon the Borders, requesting us to intercede for his
liberty.

He declared unto us a secret to be shewn unto His Majesty, in case
his life was taken from him, which was a promise made unto the
Queen of *England*, That the King should not marry with any, for
the space of three years, whereof I have formerly made some mention. Nevertheless he forgot not to travel for himself, for he sent his
Brother Sir *William* to the Master of *Gray* at midnight, promising to
get unto him the *Abbey* of *Dumfarmling*, so that he would obtain his
liberty at His Majesty's hand. Which was incontinently granted,
and also the said Benefice disposed unto the said *Master*. Whereupon the *English* Ambassadour was in a great rage at the *Master*, but
their discord was afterward agreed. Only Mr. *John Maitland* Secretary, and the Justice *Clerk*, and the Earl of *Arran*, were ordered to
retire home to their houses. But before *Arran*'s journey, His Majesty
was informed to desire him, with all possible diligence, to lend him a
great Gold Chain, which he had got from Sir *James Balfour*, which
weighed Fifty-seven Crowns, to be given unto the *Danish* Ambassadours. Which if he had refused to do, he would have lost His Majesty, and in delivering it he lost the Chain.

In the mean time, the Ambassadours understanding that their dispatch was in a readiness, took their leave of His Majesty, who was also ready to part from St. *Andrews*. I informed His Majesty not to
deliver them the Dispatch, because the Chain was not yet come: For
they were minded incontinently to make Sail, having stayed so long,
and that the Winter Season was at hand. Albeit that I had shewn
to one of their familiar Servants, that certain rewards were to come
within two days, praying them to stay so long. Which they
would

would not grant to do, but went to their Ships: Whither I promifed to bring their difpatch, which I requefted His Majefty to caufe deliver into my hand, to be kept till the Chain fhould come; which was divided in three parts, for it was large. When I came to their Ships, they were going to Supper. Which being done, I delivered to them their anfwer in writing, with the Chains, and fome excufes for their long ftay, and fmall reward. So they parted well fatisfied, affuring me that they would be good inftruments of Amity. Albeit by the harfh ufage they had firft met with they had once refolved otherwife. They were not commanded to fpeak of marriage, whereof there was fome groundlefs bruit. The King their Mafter had fair Daughters, with any whereof it was fuppofed the claim of *Orkny* would go. They thanked me for the good Offices, they had received from me, feeing my ftaying them from parting difcontent, had preferved the two Countries from being ingaged in War. Which, they faid, they would not fail to declare unto the King their Mafter, with whom they would not fail to make me acquainted, not doubting but that the King my Mafter would one day fay, That I had done him good Service. So I did take leave, having rewarded the *Gunners*, *Trumpeters*, and *Muficians*.

At my return to Court, I acquainted His Majefty, that the *Danifh* Ambaffadours had fet Sail for their own Country very well contented. I gave him a particular accompt of all Speeches, that paft betwixt them and me at their parting. Whereupon His Majefty took occafion fhortly after to fend one to *Denmark*, offering that Commiffion to me; which I fhifted, perceiving thofe who had His Majefty's Ear, and had moft Credit with him, to be altogether averfe from his marriage that way, holding ftill one courfe with *England*. I named Mr. *Peter Young* Almoner, as very fit for that Errand: who was fent to *Denmark*, to thank that King, and to fee his Daughters, that he might make report again of his liking of them, with a promife, That e're long His Majefty would fend a more honourable Ambaffage.

The Earl of *Arran* being fent home, as faid is, the *Englifh* Ambaffador and his *Scotch* friends (as the Mafter of *Gray*, Secretary *Maitland*, and the Juftice *Clark*) had chief credit and handling of his Majefty's Affairs. The faid Ambaffadour had procured fuch favour and familiar accefs about His Majefty at all times, that he was upon an enterprife to have brought in fecretly the banifhed Lords, to have fallen down upon their knees in the Park of *Sterling* before His Majefty, at fuch a time as they fhould have fo many friends in Court, as that His Majefty fhould have remained in their hands as Mafters of the Court for the time. But this enterprife failed him, for they durft not yet take fuch hazardous courfe, till they might lay their Plots more fubftantially.

Then the faid *Englifh* Ambaffadour interprifed to tranfport His Majefty out of the Park of *Sterling*, unto *England*. And failing thereof, His Majefty was to be detained by force within the Caftle of *Sterling*. Whether Companies of Men were fent to be there at an appointed day, of which defign my Brother Sir *Robert* got intelligence, and told it incontinently to the King's Majefty, giving him the Names of
the

the chief enterprifes. : And becaufe it came to one of their Ears, who
ftoutly affirmed the contrary, my Brother offered to maintain the
truth thereof by Combat. Which His Majefty would not permit, becaufe at laft the perfon granted it to His Majefty. Whereupon my
Brother perfwaded His Majefty with great difficulty, to depart out
of *Sterling* for ten of fifteen dayes, and hunt at *Kincairdin*, before the
enterprife were ripe. Which fo foon as the Ambaffadour underftood,
he fled in great fear and haft, without Good night, or leave-taking
of his Majefty: Well inftructed, and furnifhed with the promifes of
fuch, as had affifted him in our Court, to perfwade the Noblemen who
were banifhed in *England* to come home, where they fhould find
friends enough before them at Court, to put His Majefty in their
hands. The Mafter of *Gray* alfo abfented himfelf, and went to *Dunkel*, and there remained with the Earl of *Athol*. And upon fome
bruits of enterprifes, there was a Proclamation fet out in His Majefty's
Name, by fuch as had his Ear, to purchafe to themfelves the more
Credit, to be true and careful Councellors to His Majefty. Which
Proclamation was afterward delayed by craft, that the banifhed might
prevent the day, and come in and get the King in their hands, whereby they might difcharge the Proclamation at their pleafure.

In the mean time I received a Letter to be at His Majefty with all
poffible diligence, and another from the Earl of *Arran*, intreating me
to accompany him from *Kinneal* to the Court. But I went to His Majefty ftrait, whither alfo the faid Earl came that fame night. For
he had procured liberty to return again to Court, and remain about
His Majefty.

At my coming to *Sterling*, I had Intelligence from a very fure hand,
That the faid Lords were already at the entry of the Borders, affifted by my Lord *Hamiltoun*, my Lord *Maxwel*, my Lord *Bothwel*, my Lord *Hume*, and fundry others, who had not formerly
joyned with them. Alfo the Earl of *Athol*, the Laird of *Tillibar-
dine*, *Bucclevgh*, *Cesfoord*, *Coudingknows*, *Drumlanrick*, and others, who
were in greateft credit about His Majefty, were to join with them at
their in-coming. Whereof I advertifed His Majefty, and Colonel *Stuart* who undertook to ride unto the Borders, and overthrow them,
before they were wholly Convened together ; which might very probably have been effectuated, if the defign had not been craftily difappointed by fuch as were about His Maiefty, who appeared to fet
forward the Colonel's enterprife to pleafe His Majefty, and to conquer
credit, faying, They would write to *Coudinknows*, *Buccleugh*, *Cesfoord*,
and fuch others to affift him. Whom they knew to be upon the contrary Faction already, fo that the defign of fcattering them was rendered by that Craft ineffectual. And becaufe I perceived the crafty
intention, and that they feared I would therewith acquaint His Majefty, they caufed His Majefty to fend me a forged Errand to *Dunkel*,
that they might the better bring their purpofe to pafs without any
contradiction. The pretext of my Commiffion was to caufe the Earl
of *Athol* to ftay at home, and not to join with the Lords who were
to come fhortly to *Sterling*. And by the way I was to deliver a Letter to the Baylies of St. *Johnftoun*, to be upon their Guard, and not
to fuffer any of the King's Enemies to come within their Town. The
                                                                Bayliffs

Bayliffs inquired of me, what if the Earl of *Athol*, and Mafter of *Gray* would defire to come within their Town? I faid, They might let themfelves enter, with Ten in Company, but no more. They alledged, That their Letter fpecified not that. I told them, That was committed to me by mouth, the Conclufion of my Letter willing them to credit me.

When I came to *Dunkel*, I knew that the Earl of *Athol* would not ftay for me, who had a Thoufand Men in readinefs to take the Town of St. *Johnftoun*, and to come thence to *Sterling*, with the Mafter of *Gray*, who was yet with him. But however I told him that the Collonel *Stuart* was gone with Forces, to defeat the Lords at their entry into the Country, before they might be joyned together. And that therefore he would do well to lye at home, till he might underftand the Iffue of the faid enterprife. If that took effect, it would be folly to him to march forward, and if it did not fucceed, he might do as his heart ferved him. He thought this Counfel good, defiring me to write unto His Majefty for a Licenfe to him, and his, to remain at home; which I did. In the mean time, the Mafter of *Gray* was fent for to Court, the Ports of the Town of *Pearth* being refufed to his Men, who were come out of *Angus* to affift him. At his returning to Court, he was as great with His Majefty as ever he was, remaining with him within the Caftle of *Sterling*. Where there were two Factions, who difcovered themfelves fo foon as they faw the Malecontents, and banifhed Lords drew near unto the Town of *Sterling*. Whither they came to the number of Three Thoufand, and entred unto the Town without ftop. His Majefty inclined moft to the Faction, who brought in the faid Lords, who advifed His Majefty to fend fome down to the Town, to Commune and Compound matters. Which was at length Agreed upon, and Concluded, That His Majefty fhould remain in their hands, that no rigour fhould be ufed to thofe who were about him. So that thofe who were mediators, appeared to be good Inftruments, and ftayers of Blood-fhed. For *Arran* was efcaped, and fled at their firft entry. But Colonel *Stuart* only with Ten or Twelve, gave them fuch a charge in the midft of the narrow part of the Town, that a little more help might have put them in great diforder. For the moft part of their South-land Men were bufie, fpoiling Horfe and Goods.

The Lords, when they came into His Majefty's prefence, fell down upon their knees, humbly begging pardon. Adding, That the hard handling by *Arran*, and other partial Perfons about His Majefty, had compelled them upon plain neceffity, and for their laft refuge to take the boldnefs to come in Arms, for the furety of their Lives, and Lands, being ever humbly minded to to ferve His Majefty, and obey him

The King again like a Prince full of Courage and Magnanimity, fpoke unto them pertly, and boaftingly, as though he had been Victorious over them, calling them Traitours, and their enterprife plain Treafon, Yet, faid he, in refpect of your neceffity, and in hope of your good behaviour in time-coming, he fhould remit their faults. And the rather, becaufe they ufed no vengeance, nor cruelty, at their in-coming.

In

In the mean time, His Majesty committed and recommended the keeping of the Earls of *Montrose*, and *Cranford*, unto my Lord *Hamiltoun*. And the keeping of Colonel *Stuart* unto my Lord *Maxwel*. These three were for a time in some danger, because they had too violently espoused *Arran*'s interest. The rest of His Majesty's Servants, were over-lookt. Sir *Robert* my Brother, and his Son, were both courteously used. This moderate behaviour of the Lords, conquered daily more and more favour from His Majesty. They pressing him in nothing but in humble Intercession of such as formerly had his Ear. A Parliament was proclaimed at *Lithgow* for their restitution, whither His Majesty was convoyed to pass his time at Hunting, thereby to Recreat his Spirits.

Many Noblemen, and others, were written for, to come unto the said Parliament. Among the rest, the Earl of *Athol*, to whom I had been sent, and with whom I was, at the Lords coming to *Sterling*. Where I was waiting upon an answer from His Majesty, of the Letter which the Earl of *Athol* had desired me to write, as said is. When I came to kiss His Majesty's hand, I was gladly made welcome. His Majesty alledging, That I was *Corbie*'s Messenger. I answered, That my absence with the Earl of *Athol* had saved all my own Horse, and the Town of *St. Johnstoun* untaken, and had kept the said Earl from assisting with the rest. So that if those who had remained at *Sterling* with him, had kept the South, as well as I had done the North, their Horse had been safe as well as mine was. His Majesty said, That God had turned all to the best: For he had been before made believe, that he would be in danger of his life, in case these Noblemen had ever any more power about him. And yet thought they had both Him, and his Servants in their power, they had used no rigour nor vengeance. His Majesty remembred how frequently I had forewarned him of this, and the like accidents, that I said would follow upon the Earl of *Arran*'s rash proceedings. He acknowledged, he had been a bad Instrument, and declared he should never have more Place, or Credit about him. He desired me to wait at Court, and help to do all good Offices betwixt him and his Nobility. And to tell them the truth, who was to blame for their trouble, as having occasioned the same; seeing he had great prejudice, and no advantage thereby; it being far from his inclination to seek any Man's Life, Lands or Goods, but only the peace and quiet of the Country and the settling of the Subjects among themselves. Which I could testifie for a truth, the verity thereof consisting within my knowledg. His Majesty told me also, how he had shewn unto the Noblemen my honest and friendly advices toward them, and that I opposed my self continually to the Earl of *Arran*'s proceedings. He desired me also to help to satisfie the Ministers, who were seeking to be restored unto their former free Assemblies, which he had forbidden them at the advice of the Earl of *Arran*. The same being one of the occasions of all the following troubles, which were chiefly grounded upon the dissatisfaction of the Ministers, by whom the Country was influenced. So that I tarried a while at Court, till matters began to take some setling. Divers of the Lords also were earnest with me to stay, offering me great kindness : saying, That His Majesty had told them, every

Man's

Man's part, and behaviour in relation to their Banishment and Per-
fecution. And that I was ever for a moderate Courfe, defiring, and
preffing, as His Majefty's intereft, an Act of Oblivion to be Paft for
all by-gones during his Minority. The faid Lords therefore caufed
me to propofe fome of their fuits to His Majefty, whom in nothing they
would prefs beyond his own pleafure.

But the Council was of different opinions concerning the reftoring
of the Minifters to their former Priviledges, and Freedoms, where I
was brought in to give my Opinion. The greateft part thought fit
to delay them for a time, chiefly fuch as had remained about his
Majefty, and had faid too much before to the contrary. But they had
yet fome private defigns hatching in their heads, which could not be
brought about, if the Country were wholly in Peace. Which they
knew would be, were the Minifters fatisfied. My Opinion was,
That His Majefty was not to be blamed, that the Noblemen were banifhed, or the Minifters Priviledges taken from them, feeing all thefe
infolencies were committed by evil Inftruments, who ruled over His
Majefty's good mind. to fatisfie their own Ambition. Who now being fled and abfent, I knew no reafon why the Minifters fhould not
be reftored to their former Priviledges, as well as the Noblemen to
their Lands, and Honours; the one being no lefs contributive to the
fetling of the Kingdom, as the other. Seeing if this were omitted,
the blame would ftill lye upon His Majefty, and the Country would
be ftill in trouble. The Secretary *Maitland*, was againft this Opinion; for he had formerly fpoken too much on the contrary. But the
reft of the Noblemen, and the Council, thought my Opinion beft.
But yet at that time it was not followed, nor granted at that Parliament. Yet fhortly after, it was found His Majefty's intereft, and conducing for fully Eftablifhing Peace in the Country, that the Minifters
fhould be reftored to all their former Priviledges.

It is above-mentioned, That the Mr. *Almoner* was fent to *Denmark*.
Shortly after Colonel *Stuart* took occafion to go thither about his
own affairs; for he had a Penfion of the King of *Denmark*. He obtained alfo fome writing, whereby he was Commiffioned to fpeak of
the Kings marriage with the King of *Denmark*'s Eldeft Daughter.
And they both returned with fo good and friendly anfwers, that
there was little more mention made of the reftitution of the Ifles of
Orkny. The King of *Denmark* was alfo put into hope by them, that
His Majefty would fend the next Summer an honourable Ambaffage
to *Denmark*, to deal further in thefe matters.

I have fhewed already the dangerous practices of the *Englifh*
Ambaffadour Mr. *Wotton*, and a part of their effects, but the principal
is yet behind.

The Council of *England* having concluded to take the Life from
the Queens Majefty his Highneffes Mother, after fhe had been many
years kept Captive in *England*, thought firft to get the King her Son
in their hands, and to put him in hope that he fhould obtain the Crown
of *England*, the rather that he was within their Country. And in
the mean time to be fure, that he fhould not be able to revenge his
Mothers death, but might be as a pledge among them, in cafe his
Country-men, or his Forreign and *French* friends, would pretend to

menace

menace them, or to make war for his Liberty, or in revenge of her'
death.   For in that cafe they might threaten to cut him off, if for his
Caufe they fhould be troubled. 'And however it were, through time
it was fufpected that they intended to take his life alfo, after that they
had laid their Plots how to make him odious to the People by falfe
counterfeit Letters, and alledged practices, (as they had craftily and
deceitfully alledged upon his Mother) againft the State. But finding
this their defign of carrying him to *England*, difcovered by my Brother's intelligence, the faid Ambaffadour fled as faid is.   And for the
next beft, thought fit to fee His Majefty put in the hands of the moft
part of the Nobility, who were banifhed for the time, and during their
banifhment had been fheltered in *England*, who they thought by fit-
ted Inftruments might be ftirred up to take his Life, at leaft to keep
him in perpetual Prifon, in revenge of the injury had been done them.
But herein they were difappointed : For they ufed themfelves fo moderately, and difcreetly, that they fought nothing but their own native Country, and Lands, and that they might have accefs to ferve
and obey their Prince, without any further vengeance, or rigour
againft their particular Enemies.' As their actions and proceedings have fufficiently declared fince, to the great increafe of their favour with His Majefty, and eftimation of the whole Country.
    It hath been rarely or never feen in any Country, that there have
been fo great alterations, with fo little bloodfhed, as hath been in
Scotland in this Kings time.   Now thofe who are Enemies to our
Queen, and King's Title to the Crown of *England*, feeing fome of their
fetches to fail them, entred in deliberation what way to proceed to
take the Queen's life. The Council of *England*, a great part of the
Nobility, and States, fell down upon their knees, humbly requefting
Her Majefty to have compaffion upon their unfure Eftate, albeit fhe
fhould flight her own.   Alledging, That her life was in hazard by the
practices of the Queen of *Scotland*, and their Lives and Fortunes.
She alledged, That her heart would not fuffer her to let any Sentence
be given forth againft the Queen her dear Sifter, and Coufin, fo near
of her Royal Blood.   Yet fhe was at laft moved for very pity of their
conditions, to let Sentence of Death pafs againft her, upon this exprefs
condition, That it fhould rather ferve to be a Terrour to her, to oblige
her to ceafe from making any more practifes, then that fhe really intended to fee the Blood of fo noble a Princefs fhed.   And in the mean
time, the written Sentence was given to be kept to Mr. *Davifon* one
of her Secretaries, not to be delivered without her Majefties exprefs
Command.   Neverthelefs the faid *Davifon* being deceived by the
Council, delivered unto them the faid written Sentence of Death.
Whereupon they gave the Queen warning a night before, to prepare
her for God.   Which fhort warning fhe took very patiently, and lay
not down that night to fleep, but wrote fome Letters unto the King
her Son, the King of *France*, and fome other Princes, her friends. And
after fhe had made her Teftament, fhe put the Gold fhe had, in as many little Purfes as fhe had Servants, more or lefs in every Purfe, conform to their qualities, and defervings. The reft of the night fhe employed in Prayer, and being in the morning conveyed out of her
Chamber to the great Hall where the Scaffold was prepared, fhe took
                                                                    her

her death patiently, and conftantly, couragioufly ending her life, being cruelly handled by the Executioner, having received divers ftroaks
of the Ax. Which execution was the boldlier performed, becaufe
that fome *Scotfmen* affured them, that the King her Son would foon
forget it. Albeit His Majefty when he underftood this forrowful
news, took heavy difpleafure, and Convened a Parliament, wherein
lamenting the mifhandling of his Mother by his Enemies, who were
in *England*, he defired the affiftance of his Subjects to be revenged.
Where all the Eftates in one voice cryed out in a great rage to fet forward: Promifing that they fhould all hazard their Lives, and fpend
their Goods and Eftates largely to that effect, to revenge that unkindly, and unlawful murther. Which put the Council of *England* in great
fear for a while, but fome of our Country-men comforted them, and
fo did fome *Englifh* that haunted our Court, alledging it would be
foon forgot. Others faid, That the Blood was already faln from His
Majefty's heart, and if it were not, they doubted not but to caufe the
matter fall out to their fatisfaction.

Firft when the King's Majefty heard that they were about to Accufe and Convict his Mother, he fent the Mafter of *Gray*, and Sir *Robert* my Brother, to deal for her Majefty. Where my Brother fpoke
brave and ftout language to the Council of *England*. So that the
Queen her felf threatned his life, and afterward he would have been
retained Captive, had not the Mafter of *Gray*'s Credit prevented it,
and the promifes he made, whereby they were both fuffered to come
home together.

Four Months before His Majefty caufed fend for me, that I might
prepare my felf for *England*, to confirm a Band of Alliance Offenfive
and Defenfive with the Queen and Crown of *England*; and to take
the Queen of *Englands* Oath for obferving the faid Bond. And Mr.
Randolph who was here, was to take the King's Oath, and ufe the like
Ceremonies here.

At my coming to Court, I did what I could to be fhifted of the
faid Commiffion, being a matter of fo great confequence, as an indirect breaking of the Bond with *France*. Yet His Majefty would
take no excufe, but thought fit to fend me thither, that I might get
him fure knowledge of fundry things, which His Majefty fuppofed an
other would not get. By reafon that all his Mothers friends, and his
own that were in that Court and Country, were beft and longeft acquainted with my Brother and me. But fo foon as Mr. *Randolph* had
heard that I was to be fent to *England*, he defired Audience of His Majefty, and ufed all the perfwafions he could, to get me ftayed, and
another fent that might be found meeter for the time. After this His
Majefty had reafoned long with him thereabout, he called upon me,
and told me how that Mr. *Randolph* had fpoken fo much good of me,
whom he loved better then any *Scots* Subject, upon accompt of our
old acquaintance, but had faid that I would not be acceptable to the
Queen his Miftrefs at that time, becaufe Sir. *Robert* my Brother had
been always, and was yet upon his Mothers Faction, and alfo that my
Brother Sir *Andrew* of *Garvock* was for the prefent in *England* her Majefties Mafter of the Houfhold. His Majefty faid, he replied again,
That I was never efteemed a Factious Perfon, and fo would not yield
at

at the firft. But I requefted His Majefty to grant him his defire. For I had no will of that Commiffion, knowing that there was nothing meant, but fraudful dealing by *England* with him at that time. It is for that caufe, faid he, that I would have you there. And it is for that fame caufe, Sir, faid I, that I would gladly fhun the fame with Your Majefty's favour.

His Majefty faid, he wondered that *Randolph* fhould feem to like fo well of me, and yet defire another to be fent. I anfwered His Majefty that in *France* and *Italy* we liked each other very well, but in the handling His Majefty's affairs we fhot at fundry marks. His Majefty would ftill have me to accept that Commiffion, and asked whom I believed that Mr. *Randolph* would defire to be fent. I anfwered, either the Mafter of *Gray*, or Mr. *Archibald Douglas*. For the Mafter of *Gray* had made moyan for Mr. *Archibald*, and had brought him home out of *England*, and had fummoned an Affize of his own friends to cleanfe him of the late King's Murther. And being cleanfed, he haunted the Court familiarly with His Majefty. It was he indeed whom Mr. *Randolph* defired to be fent, or the Mafter of *Gray*, or both in a Commiffion. But His Majefty would not confent thereto. Then the Laird of *Coudinknows* Captain of the Caftle of *Edinburgh* defired the Commiffion. But Mr. *Randolph* would have none other, caufing the Queen his miftrefs to write back, that it was unneceffary to fend any Ambaffadour for that Errand at that time. Only defiring that the King would write with his own hand, that one fhould be fent when fhe thought time, affuring by his faid Letter that it was in effect already concluded in his mind, as if the Ceremony were preformed. Which Letter was fent to the *Englifh* Ambaffadour, who was refident in *France* for the time, to be produced before the King of *France*, and the Queen Mother, to let them know that albeit the King of *Scotland* was fuiting her Majefty for an Alliance Offenfive and Defenfive (which would be a clear breach of the old Bond with *France*) yet fhe would not put them in fufpicion and jealoufie of her in confenting thereto, as not much valuing the *Scottifh* King's fickle friendfhip, or feud, fo long as *France* and fhe kept their Peace and Friendfhip together, Which was done only to difgrace and difcredit the King with the King of *France*. So that there proceeded no more from the faid intended Bond. And I was not a little fatisfied that my hands had been free thereof.

Likewife when the bruit was of the *Spanifh* Navy in the year 1587, that they were coming to thefe parts, I was ordered to be fent to *Spain*, which Voyage I happily alfo efchewed.

Now to return again to Mr. *Archibald Douglas*, he returned back to *England*, to remain Ambaffadour there for His Majefty. By the which means he obtained the greater Credit with the Queen His Majefties Mother, to her no fmall prejudice; the fame contributary to her ruine, he having difcovered feveral paffages betwixt her and himfelf, and other Catholicks of *England*, tending to her liberation. Which were made ufe of againft Her Majefty, for taking her life. So foon as my Brother Sir *Robert* was fent there to ufe fharp and boafting Language to fee if it might fave the Queens life, he difcharged Mr. *Archibald* of the Office of *Ambaffadour*. This I fet down in a parenthefis,

to

to fhew how far a good King was abufed, and milled, by minions, whom he liked well to his great hurt and difhonour. In the mean time for fome diforder upon the Weft Border, betwixt the *Maxwels* and *Johnftouns*, His Majefty went there to reform the difobedience. But fome Houfes were kept out, and would not render unto him. Whereupon, Mr. *John Martland* being made *Chancellor*, the *Mafter* of *Gray*, and other Favourers of the *Englijh* Faction, did counfel His Majefty to fend to *Berwick*, becaufe it was alledged to be neareft to borrow Cannons to befiege the faid houfe. Which Guns were readily and gladly lent by the Governour of *Berwick*. Which apparently he durft not have done, without knowledg and confent of the Queen and Councel, who judged thereby that His Majefty had forgot the great boaft that was made at the fore named Parliament concerning the revenge of His Mother's death. For after His Majefty had riply confidered the beft and worft of that deed, remembred himfelf of the many Friends he had in *England*, who had no hand in his Mother's Death, he thought it not juft to trouble the Peace and Quiet of the Kingdom for the deed of a few who guided the Queen and Court, he being thereof himfelf apparent Heir. And alfo becaufe the Queen was of good years, and not like to live long, he was refolved to abide his time to be revenged upon his Enemies. As for the Queen his good Sifter, fhe had fworn and purged herfelf of the death of his Mother, being deceived by her Council, and Secretary *Davifon*, whom fhe committed to the Tower of *London*. This was the way of conveyance of that ugly unkindly Murther.

Shortly after this, there was a great Bruit of the *Spanifh* Navy bound to land in *England*, *Scotland* or *Ireland*. And then alfo were entred about His Majefty a new Faction, whereof the Earl *Huntly* was chief; who had lately married the Duke of *Lennox's* Sifter. This new Faction afpired by little and little to fhoot out the Mafter of *Gray*, the Chancellour, and others their dependers, and to retain part of thofe who were in Court before, where there were divers confpiracies to kill the Chancellour. And fuch as had affifted him, were to be removed, becaufe they did ftick too long by the Court. The Earls of *Huntly*, *Bothwel*, and others, thought to have taken the King and kept him. And albeit two of their Enterprifes had failed, yet they were defirous to be neareft His Majefty at the in-coming of the *Spaniards*. And in the mean time they refolved to caufe the King fend Sir *John Scatoun* to *Spain*. But His Majefty would have none to be fent but me. Whereupon the Chancellor, and my Brother Sir *Robert*, did write to me, defiring me to refufe the imployment, becaufe they faid his Majefty would have one there of his own Religion, who would not be corrupted, in whom he could truft. Yet His Majefty had inclination to deal with *Spain*, and I had as little defire to undertake the Voyage, albeit Sir *Gorge Douglas* defired the faid Commiffion, as one who had affifted His Majefty's Mother, yet it took no effect. The Earl of *Huntly* in the mean time procured a Gift of the Benefice of *Dunfarmling*, which was lately taken from the Mafter of *Gray* now decourted, and given to him. How that the *Spanifh* great Navy was three years in making their preparations, and were fufficiently and fubftantially furnifhed with Men, Ammunition and all forts of neceffaries, is now manifeft to all *Europe*. What was their intent and purpofe was fo fecret, that the

Chieftains

Chieftains of the Army knew no more, but as they fhould underftand
by the opening of their ftamped inftruftions at every appointed landing
Place. Many were of opinon, that they wear firft difappointed by the
Duke of *Parma* Governour of *Flanders*, who had behaved himfelf in
his Charge fo circumfpeftly, in his promifes fo truly, in enterprifes fo ftoutly, that he won the hearts of his Soldiers, and the favour of
his Enemies, fo that he was fufpefted by the King of *Spain* to entertain
defigns of Ufurping the Eftate of *Flanders*. And therefore he was minded to remove him out of that great and rich Government. He being
hereupon difcontent, as was alledged, neither furnifhed the faid Army
Viftuals, nor affifted them with Ships, nor would he fuffer them to
land in his bounds. At laft they were fo jealous of him, that they
landed not, but were lying at Anchor, where Sir *Francis Drake* by a
ftratagem fubtilly devifed of a Ship full of powder with a burning Link,
which kindled up the Powder fo foon as the the *Englifh* Ship was driven
by a direft vehement Wind within the midft of the *Spanifh* Ships, burning thereby feveral of the greateft of them, and caufing the reft to
cut the Cables of their Anchors for haft, to efchew the fury of the fire.
And in the mean time God fent fuch a vehement ftorm of Wind, that
the whole Navy was blown and broken upon divers Coafts of our Ifles,
and of *Ireland*, and their Wreck was the greater, that they wanted their
Anchors.

It is before mentioned, That Mr. *Peter Young* Almoner to His Majefty, and Colonel *Stuart* were returned from *Denmark* well rewarded,
and contented with every thing that they had feen, and chiefly with
the fair young Princefs; and alfo how they had put the King of *Denmark* in hope, that the King fhould the next Summer fend thither an
honourable Ambaffage, to deal further to the increafe of a greater Amity. And for this effeft, the Bifhop of St. *Andrews*, the Liard of *Segie*,
and I were named to be fent: But I was retired, and had no will to
medle, perceiving His Majefty's affairs fo retarded by fuch as had
greateft handling about him. Therefore upon my refufal, the Chancellour advifed the Laird of *Barnbarrow*, and the faid Mr. *Peter*, to be
again employed in that matter, with uncertain and irrefolute Inftruftions to propofe marriage, and with divers fair allegiances concerning
His Majefty's fufficient Right to the Ifles of *Orkny*, which the King of
Denmark was minded to ufe the more fharply, but for the hope he was
put in, of the apparent marriage of the Kings Majefty with his Eldeft
Daughter.

Thefe Ambaffadours were not well imbarked, when Monfieur *Dubartus* arrived here to vifit the King's Majefty, who, he heard, had him
in great efteem, for his rare Poefie fet out in the *French* Tongue. He
would not fay that he had a fecret Commiffion to propofe the Princefs
of *Navarre* as a fit Marriage for His Majefty, but that the King of *Navarre*'s Secretary willed him, feeing he was to come this way, as on his
own head, to propofe the faid marriage. Monfieur *Dubartus*'s Qualities were fo good, and his Credit fo great with his Majefty, that it appeared if the Ambaffadours had not already made Sail, that their Voyage fhould have been ftayed for that Seafon. The Chancellour affured
Monfieur *Dubartus*, (as he fhewed me) that the marriage of *Denmark*
fhould not take effeft. For our Ambaffadours had indeed fuch ftrait
Inftrufti-

Inſtrudions, and ſo ſlender a Commiſſion, that it was enough to have caufed the King of *Denmark* to ſtart,and to quarrel with our King,were it not that they dealt above their Commiſſion. Which kept that King in ſome Temper, albeit they returned without fruit, full of difpleaſure, thinking themfelves fcorned, as they were indeed. .

In the mean time that they were in *Denmark*,Mounſieur *Dubartus* being in *Falkland* with his Majefty,came to my houfe,to perfwade me to take a Commiſſion in hand, which he ſaid His Majefty would lay to my charge, which was to be ſent unto the King of *Navarre*, and to be acquainted with Madam the Princefs, his Sifter. And becaufe His Majefty knew that I would be loath to go, he named alfo my Lord *Tungland*, my Brother, who undertook the journey, and became well acquainted with the ſaid Princefs, and was well treated and rewarded by the King her Brother, now King of *France*, and brought with him the Picture of the Princefs, with a good repott of her rare qualities.

The Laird of *Barnbarrow*,and Mr. *Peter Young*,being returned back from *Denmark*,declared that the King of *Denmark* thought nothing of their Commiſſion, judging it but fruitlefs dealing, and delaying of time, and fair language, without any power to conclude. I am uncertain, whether he got intelligence of His Majefties ſending my Brother to the King of *Navarre*. But the marrying of his Eldeft Daughter with the Duke of *Brunfwick*,gave ſome appearance that he had got ſome notice thereof from the Court of *England*, who were abundantly well informed of all our proceedings.

After this,Colonel *Stuart* defirous to ſee the marriage with the King of *Denmark's* Daughter take effect,went thither upon his own expences divers times. And ſeeing the Eldeſt Daughter already married, he excuſed the King's Majefty, and laid the blame upon thofe who had the handling of his Affairs. So that the King of *Denmark* promifed yet to give his ſecond Daughter unto the King, upon conditions that Ambaſſadours ſhould be ſent there the next year, before the firſt day of *May*. In the mean time, the King of *Denmark* took ſicknefs, and departed this life, leaving the ſame Commiſſion with his Council, and ſuch as were appointed for Regents of the Realm.

Now the King being ſuited in marriage by many great Princes, and his Ambaſſadours being come back both out of *Denmark*,and *Navarre*, with the Pictures of the young Princeſſes ; His Majefty determined firſt to ask counfel of God by earneft Prayer, to direct him where it would be meeteft for the weal of himfelf, and his Country. So that after fifteen days advifement, and devout Prayer, as ſaid is, he called his Council together in his Cabinet, and told them how he had been advifing about that matter of ſo great concernment to himfelf, and his Country, the ſpace of fifteen days, and that he was now refolute to marry in *Denmark*.

The Council appeared all to relifh his refolution, requiring meet Inftruments to be imployed to compleat the marriage, and to make the Contract. Then His Majefty ſaid, That he had already chofen me in his mind for one, defiring the Council to choofe another ; which they did, to wit, The Lord of *Atry*,Uncle to the Earl of *Marfhal*. We two being written for, and come to Court, found not ſuch earneftnefs

A a   with

with the Council as with the King: Which my Lord of *Atry* perceiving, he drew home again, excufing himfelf upon his Age, and Sicklinefs. His Majefty ufed many perfwafions, and reafons, to induce me to undertake the Voyage, declaring how he had many times fent for me to be imployed in Ambaffages, and could never tell why I went not. I anfwered, That His Majefty would have done me that honour many times above my deferving, which he would not have done, if he had known my infufficiency for fuch matters of fo great import, as I did my felf. His Majefty faid, That this bufinefs concerning his marriage, was the greateft matter that ever he had to do, and that he would take no refufal. I faid, That my Lord *Tungland*, my Brother, was far meeter than my felf, being a good Scholar, who could perfectly fpeak the *High Dutch*, the *Latine*, and the *Flemming* Languages, with the *French* Tongue. But His Majefty would ftill repofe upon me in that Errand, but at my defire was fatisfied that my Brother fhould be put in Commiffion with me.

Then His Majefty faid, Albeit the Council will form your Inftructions, yet you fhall receive mine out of my own mouth.

Firft, *If the King of* Denmark *had been alive, he would not have ftood to have given a great Portion with his Daughter, wherein it is probable the Regent and his Council will be as fparing as they can. I doubt not therefore but you will endeavour to draw from them as much as can be had, but at length ftand not upon mony to conclude the marriage.*

Second'y, *Know what friendfhip and affiftance they will make me, when it may pleafe God to place me by Right in the Kingdom of England, by deceafe of this Queen, in cafe any Country-man, or other would wrongoufly pretend to ufurp and debarr me from the fame.*

Thirdly, *Concerning the Ifles of* Orkny, *you may chufe any Man of Law that you pleafe, for that Head muft be anfwered, and debated by Form of Law. Alwife if the marriage take effect, that purpofe would not be over precifely handled. It may be that my Council will give you ftraiter Conditions, but this Inftruction of mine you fhall follow, let them fay what they pleafe.*

I told His Majefty, That I would chufe to take with me for a Lawyer Mr. *John Skeen.* His Majefty faid, he judged there were many better Lawyers. I faid, he was beft acquainted with the *German* Cuftoms, and could make them long Harangues in *Latine* ; that he was a good, true, ftout Man, like a *Dutch-man.* Then his Majefty was content, that he fhould go with me.

After that I had tarried long at Court, and could fee no preparation for our Difpatch, neither Money, nor Ship making ready ; the appointed time wherein we fhould have been in *Denmark* being paft, to wit before the firft of *May.* For it was fo ordered by the King of *Denmark* e're he died, that in cafe that day was not kept, that they might think themfelves but fcoffed. This moved me to employ my friends at Court, to caufe another to be named in my place, feeing fo many fuiting to get the faid Commiffion. And the Chancellour gave me fuch terrors as he could for his part.

Now the Earl of *Marfhal* was defirous to fupply the place of his Uncle my Lord of *Atry*, and His Majefty was content that he fhould be fent thither. Whereupon I took occafion to reprefent to His Ma
jefty

jefty, That the faid Earl was very well qualified for that imployment, and that he would go the better contented, if he might have in Commiffion with him, fome of his own friends and acquaintance. His Majefty anfwered, That it was his part.to chufe his own Ambaffadours, that the Earl of *Marfhal* fhould have the firft place as a Nobleman, but that he would repofe the chief handling with the Regent, and Council of *Denmark* upon me. Then I declared, That the appointed time was paft, and that yet there was no appearance of any preparation of Mony or Ship, wherewith His Majefty was very angry. I named the Laird of *Barnbarrow*, or Mr. *Peter Toung*, as very fit to be imployed in the Commiffion with the Earl of *Marfhal*, becaufe they had been there already. But he would not hear thereof, for the blame had been wrongoufly laid upon their infufficiency, it being alledged, That their mifmanagement, was the occafion that matters formerly took not the defired fuccefs. Would not this kind of Court dealing, fcare any man from medling in fuch weighty matters, where fuch men are preferred to have the fpecial credit about a Prince, who mind only their own defigns, and not the Prince's advantage?

Thofe who at prefent ordered Affairs, counfelled His Majefty firft to fend to the Queen of *England*, and require her advice and confent to the faid marriage with *Denmark*, who they knew would not only diffwade him from the faid marriage, but alfo ftay him from any marriage, as fhe and her Council had ever done, and dealt, both with his Mother and himfelf. When I underftood of this new delay, I obtained licence to go home to my houfe; and make me ready againft the next warning. In the mean time, the feafon of the year was well fpent. The Queen of *England*'s anfwer returned, not to marry with *Denmark*. She faid, That fhe had credit with the King and Princefs of *Navarre*, that fhe would imploy the fame for effectuating that marriage, which was much more His Majefty's intereft. In the mean time fhe did write to the King of *Navarre*, to hold back the marriage of his Sifter three years, for fuch frivolous pretexts as carried no reafon. Upon this anfwer of *England*, our Council was Convened, and inticed to Vote againft the marriage of *Denmark*. Whereat His Majefty took fuch a defpight, that he caufed one of his moft familiar Servants to deal fecretly with fome of the Deacons of the Craftfmen of *Edinburgh*, to make a mutiny againft the Chancellour and Council, threat'ning to flay him in cafe the marriage with the King of *Denmark*'s Daughter were hindred, or longer delayed. This boafting and fear caufed a new refolution to be taken, that the Earl of *Marfhal* fhould be difpatched with diligence, with the Conftable of *Dundie*, and the Lord *Andrew Kieth*, whom the faid Earl requefted His Majefty to fend with him. Which His Majefty granted the more eafily, becaufe he found fo many difficulties in the matter, and fome of my friends had informed him, that it would be very fatisfactory to me that fome other were imployed. Now it was a yet long time, before the Earl of *Marfhal* could be ready, and difpatched. Then as to his dealing with the Council of *Denmark*, his power to conclude was fo limited, and his Commiffion fo flender, that he was compelled to fend back again my Lord *Dingual*, either for a Licence to come home, or for a fufficient

power

power to conclude. Where it chanced that he found His Majcfty at *Aberdeen*, and the Chancellour and moft part of the Council abfent. Which was a great furtherance to get a full power to conclude the Contract and Ceremony of the Marriage, by the Earl of *Marfl-al*, who, was incontinently difpatched by the Regent and Council of *Denm u k*, and the Queen fent home with him well accompanied. But the tempeftuous winds drave them upon the Coaft of *Norway*, where they landed and ftayed a long time for fair Winds and Weather. Which ftorm of Wind was alledged to be raifed by the Witches of *Denmark*, as by fundry of them was acknowledged, when they were for that caufe burnt. That which moved them thereto, was, as they faid, a blow which the Admiral of *Denmark* gave to one of the Bayliffs of *Copenhaven*, whofe Wife confulting with her Affociates in that Art, raifed the Storm to be revenged upon the faid Admiral.

His Majefty had heard that they were upon the Sea, and left nothing undone to make all in a readinefs to receive the Queen and her Company honourably. But in the mean time, was very impatient, and forrowful, for her long delay; laying the blame thereof upon the Chancellour, and fuch other of his Council as had plainly Voted againft the faid marriage, and thereby had delayed the difpatch of the Ambaffadours fo long, until the Seafon of Sailing upon the Seas was near paft. The ftorms were alfo fo great here, that a Paffage-Boat perifhed betwixt *Bruntland* and *Lieth*, wherein was a Gentlewoman called *Jean Kennedie*, who had been long in *England* with the Queen His Majefty's Mother, and was fince married to Sir *Andrew Melviil* of *Garvock* my Brother, Mafter of His Majefties Houfhold. Which Gentlewoman being difcreet and grave, was fent for by His Majefty to be about the Queen his Bed-fellow. She being defirous to make diligence, would not by the ftorm be ftopped the Sailing of the Ferry, where the vehement ftorm drave a Ship forcibly upon the faid Boat and drowned the Gentlewoman, and all the Perfons, except two. This the *Scottifh* Witches confeffed to His Majefty was procured by them. In that Boat alfo, I loft two Servants.

Now His Majefty remained quietly in the Caftle of *Craigmillar*, diffatisfied, as faid is, with the greateft part of his Council. He could neither fleep, nor reft. In the mean time, he directed Colonel *Stuart* to my Brother Sir *Robert*, and me, charging us to take care of his mifhandled Eftate in time coming, lamenting that he had been abufed by fuch as formerly he had too much trufted to; and that he had always found us faithful and careful of his welfare. He therefore defired us to fit down, and advife how he might beft put remedy to things by-paft, and prevent fuch inconveniencies in time coming, feeing he had determined hereafter to repofe moft upon our Council. Our anfwer to His Majefty was, That we had great reafon to render His Majefty moft humble thanks for the favourable opinion he entertained of us, which we fhould endeavour to deferve, and were very forry for the difpleafure His Majefty had taken, praying His Majefty to take patience, feeing that as he had always repofed upon God and not Man, that the fame God would mend his Eftate, as he had oft-times done before. That our care fhould be prefently, how to receive the Queen honourably, who was upon the Sea (we daily look-

ing for her landing) and next how to treat and reward the Noble
men of *Denmark*, Her Majeſties Convoy.   That being done, and they
returned back to their Country , it would be beſt time to take order
with the Affairs of the Kingdom, conform to His Majeſty's deſire ,
with the concurrence of ſo many of the Council , as His Majeſty had
found moſt faithful , and leaſt factious.   But we did not think fit to
take upon us the whole burthen, in reſpect that hath been always the
chief cauſe of the wrack of *Scots* Kings , eſpecially of all His Majeſty's
own troubles , in laying the whole burthen of his Affairs upon any·
one, or two, who moſt commonly for greedineſs and ambition abuſe
good Princes , and few or none dare controul them , for fear of their
great Authority and Credit.

The Chancellour being advertiſed of His Majeſty's diſcontent, and
diſpleaſure, as ſaid is, made preparation to go off the Country, and
cauſed it to come to His Majeſty's Ears, that he would Sail himſelf and
bring home the Queen with him :   And that they were all but Trif-
lers who were with her.· He forgot not to anoint the hands of ſome
who were moſt familiar with His Majeſty , to interpret·this his deſign
ſo favourably , that it made the King forget all by·gones, and by little
and little he informed him ſo well of the ſaid Voyage·, and the great·
charges he had beſtowed· upon a fair and ſwift ſailing Ship, that His
Majeſty was moved to take the Voyage himſelf, and to ſail in the ſame
Ship with the Chancellour, with great ſecrecy , and ſhort preparation, making no Man privy thereto , but ſuch as the Chancellour pleaſed , and ſuch as formerly had all been upon his Faction.   He had
alſo heard an incling of a word, That His Majeſty, in the time of his
high diſpleaſure , had ſaid , That he would lay the burthen of his Affairs upon my Brother, and me ; whereat he had a great envy and
deſpight , and was the cauſe why His Majeſty made me not privy to
his Voyage. He was very diſcontent , when His Majeſty had appointed my ſaid Brother *Robert* to be left Vice-Chancellour , and Convene
the Council in His Majeſty's abſence , to hold hand with the Duke of
Lennox, my Lord *Hamiltoun*, *Bothwel* and other Noblemen, with the
Officers of the Crown, and to Rule the Country in His Majeſty's
abſence.

Three other Ships ſailed with His Majeſty, wherein was the *Juſtice*
Clerk, *Carmichal* the Provoſt of *Lincludin*, Sir *William Keeth*, *George*
Hume, *Thomas Sandiland*, With all His Majeſty's Ordinary Servants.
The weather was rough enough, for it was in the beginning of Winter. But the laſt day was ſo extream ſtormy , that they were all in
great hazard , but His Majeſty landed that ſame night at   in
Norway , where the Queen was abiding the turning of the Wind, and
where he accompliſhed his marriage in perſon. But he could not be
perſwaded to return to *Scotland* that Winter, by reaſon of the raging Seas and ſtorm he had ſuſtained a little before.

The Queen and Council of *Denmark*, being advertiſed that His
Majeſty was reſolved to abide all that Winter, ſent and requeſted him
to come to *Denmark*. Whither he went by Land with the Queen his
new Bride, and behaved himſelf honourably and liberally by the way,
and at the Court of *Denmark*, where he tarried during his abode
there.

But

But the Company who were with His Majesty put him to great trouble to agree their continual janglings, strife, pride and partialities. The Earl of *Marshal* by reason that he was an ancient Earl, and had been first imployed in this honourable Commission, thought to have the first place next unto His Majesty, so long as he was there. The Chancellour by reason of his Office, would needs have the preheminence. There were also contentions betwixt him and the *Justice Clark*. The Constable of *Dundie* and my Lord *Dingwal* could not agree about place. *George Hume* did quietly shoot out *William Kieth* from his Office of Master of the Wardrobe. At length they were all divided into two Factions. The one for the Earl of *Marshal*, the other for the Chancellour, who was the stronger, because the King took his part : So that the Chancellour triumphed, and being yet in *Denmark*, devised many Reformations to be made, and new Forms and Customs to be set forward at His Majesty's return : As to have no Privy Council but the Exchequer, and the Nobility to be debarred from it : Sundry of the Lords of the Session to be put out, who he judged had no dependence upon him, and others his Creatures put in their room. He caused a Proclamation to be pen'd, which was sent home to be proclaim'd before His Majesty's return, That none of the Nobility should come to Court not being sent for, and then to bring with them six persons and no more : Likewise every Baron to bring but four. Likewise he resolved to cause Ward such as had been unruly, and disobedient during His Majesty's absence, as the Earl *Bothwel*, the Lord *Hume*, and divers Borderers and Highland Men.

The next Spring His Majesty came home, and Landed at *Lieth*, well accompanied with the Admiral of *Denmark*; and divers of the Council and many other Gentlemen. All whom his Majesty treated honourably, and after the Queens Coronation they were magnificently rewarded with more than twelve Golden Chains, and many Medals of Gold with His Majesties Picture.

His Majesty at his landing was pleased to send to me to bear them company, which I did until their parting, to His Majesties great contentment.

In the mean time, the Earl of *Worcester* was sent Ambassadour from *England*, to Welcome and Congratulate both their Majesties, with some Presents unto the Queens Majesty. Upon whom I was commanded by His Majesty to attend diligently all the time of his being here, and at his parting he was presented with a Ring of seven great Diamonds. He parted well satisfied, and so did all his Company.

His Majesty was pleased at leasure to declare unto me his whole Voyage, and proceedings during his absence. He said that he wished that I had been sent alone Ambassadour to *Denmark*, in place of the Earl of *Marshal*, and the two who were joined with him, he was so ill informed of the said Earl. I answered, That I understood that the Earl for his part had behaved himself very honourably, and discreetly, as the Admiral of *Denmark*, and divers of the company had informed me. But His Majesty had been so possessed with the Chancellour's misinformation, that for the time he believed it. He said further to me, That he had greater trouble to keep good order among the few

company

company that was in *Denmark*, than my Brother Sir *Robert* had to
keep quiet all *Scotland*, during his abfence. Which praife my Brother
indeed deferved, for he had fuch favour and credit among the Nobility, Barons, and Burroughs, that they followed his advice; believing
that he would not fay but the truth in His Majefty's Name, and that
he would give no mis-information againft them at his home-coming.
But the Chancellour envied my Brother for the great opinion His Majefty had of him, though he had been the greateft inftrument of bringing the Chancellour into Court with His Majefty firft, when His
Majefty paft to his Liberty at St. *Andrews*; and afterwards of getting
him the keeping of the great Seal, and in effect of making him Chancellour fince. The Chancellour remembred alfo of his Majefty's deliberation before his going to *Denmark*; and the direction he had fent
by Collonel *Stuart* to my Brother and me. Which the Chancellour
now went about to prevent, by taking occafion to Calumniate my
Brother in his abfence, becaufe he was not prefent in the time, when
there was to do with his Office to furnifh fome little neceffaries to
the ftrangers. He having been fent for to vifit his Wife lying at the
point of Death in *Bruntland*. The Chancellour told His Majefty,
that during his Majefty's abfence he ufed every *Saturday* fo to do,
tarrying three or four days, neglecting the common Affairs of the
Countrey. And that it was the Clerk-Regifter, *Alexander Hay*, who
had done all the good Offices; which were alledged to have been done
by Sir *Robert*. Whereby be kindled up, fo the King's anger againft
him, that he threat'ned to Ward him, and take his Office from him,
fix days after he was fo much praifed for the great and faithful Service
he had done. So ill handled oft-times are good Princes, and faithful
Servants, by crafty Calumnies. But his Majefty being thereafter fully informed of the matter foon repented his anger; and converted
the fame againft the faid Chancellour upon another occafion.

There was Emulation betwixt the Council and the Chancellour.
The Council complaining, That the Chancellour was the devifer of all
the wrongs that were done; by caufing His Majefty to fubfcribe fundry hurtful Signatures, and Commiffions; getting them paft for himfelf and his friends, taking thus the beft and moft profitable Cafuali-
ties to himfelf, and his dependers.

The Chancellour again endeavoured, to have the moft part of the
Council at his devotion, or fuch who would not be in all things ruled
by him changed, and others placed in their room, who would have
more dependance upon him. Whereupon the Council confulted, and
concluded together, to caft the Chancellour. Yet one of the Council, who had a matter of great moment to be difpatched, to curry favour with the Chancellour, difcovers the defign to him, who having
that knowledge thereof before-hand, had the opportunity of preventing the enterprife, as to the effect defigned. Yet at his firft coming to
fpeak with His Majefty, he rebuked him very forely. And leaving
him, he took me by the hand, faying, I am the worft handled Prince
in the World, as I fhall fhew you To-morrow ; for now when I go
to Bed, I defire not to enter upon fo Melancholly Subjects fo late.
Therefore fend for your Brother, and at his coming, I fhall declare
unto you both, more of my mind. I cannot forget an expreffion of
yours,

yours, That it is the greatest Art in the World to be true.

At my Brother's coming, we found that the only cause was, That the Chancellour, and some with him, would have ruined those who were His Majesty's truest friends. Yet my Brother, finding it His Majesty's interest, took up the matter betwixt the Council and the Chancellour, to His Majesty's great contentment.

After the Coronation of the Queens Majesty, and Banquetting, and rewarding the strangers, and that they returned home well contented: There was another Convention appointed, for taking order with the Affairs of the Country. To the which, many Noblemen, and Barons were written for; but very few obeyed the said Letters, or would come near the Court. Because when they were first written for to the Queens Coronation, they judged themselves slighted: For Hall, Chamber, and all doors were so straitly shut, and undiscreetly kept, that they could get no entry. Therefore many of them returned discontent to their houses, for there was no man appointed to welcome them, or to direct them, except so many as were made Knights. Which was the cause that so few came again to Court, the next time, when they were written for. Those who had been lately in *Denmark* with His Majesty, thought to retain him and the whole Government in their hands, and had given His Majesty counsel not to be over familiar, nor of too easie access. That none should be permitted to enter his Chamber, but such as were Gentlemen of his Chamber, with the Chancellour, and some of the Council. They were not content to have the whole access; and only handling at all other times, but even also at the Conventions, they continually occupied His Majesty's Ear in presence of the whole Assembly, thereby to let their great credit be seen, that they might be courted, by such as had to do with the King. None of them all had more occasion of occupying His Majesty's Ear, then I had at that time. Yet when it would please him to call upon me, to know how every stranger was treated, and satisfied, and to be informed about other things: I would give him a short answer, and instantly retire. Which was perceived by many of the Nobility, and Barons, who were come to the Convention. In the which sundry necessary Reformations were intended, though nothing was performed: Which was the more complained of, because every man was in expectation to see a settled Estate at His Majesty's home-coming, by reason of His Majesty's promise made publickly in the high Kirk of *Edinbrugh*, to be a new Man, and to take up another kind of care and doing in his own person, than ever had been seen, or used before. Which certainly His Majesty was very willing to have put in execution, but alass he lacked help and assistance. For such as he reposed most upon, had no further care of his affairs, then as they found could best serve their own particular profit, and advancement to such ambitious aims as they shot at: making His Majesty in the mean time believe, that all was well ruled and ordered. The contrary being too manifest, moved me to present unto His Majesty some Memorials, and Informations concerning his Estate and Government. The most part whereof I had set down in writing, after that Colonel *Stuart* had brought Commission from His Majesty to my Brother Sir *Robert*, and me, before His Majesty's

Voyage

Voyage to bring home the Queen, during the time that he was in great vexation in *Craigmillar*, and difcontent with the Chancellour, and fuch as were his dependers in the Council, who had been hinderers of his marriage. For at that time, he had defired my faid Brother,and me, to fit down, and advife upon fome good Rules, for the eftablifhing of fome good order in his Country,the Coppy whereof was as followeth.

SIR, your Majefty's happy return hath greatly rejoyced your whole Subjects. The expectation they have had of you ever fince your Birth, hath been great, both far and near. Your publick promife to take upon you a more Kingly care fince your home-coming through greater experience, hath augmented a good hope of a gracious Government. Your Religion pure and clean, your zeal to Godlinefs and Juftice, your chaft and fincere Life : your promptitude to fupprefs Rebellions when they arife, ravifheth the hearts of moft part of your Subjects to love you, and efteem you the beft King that hath been thefe many years in this Realm. And yet they all marvel with ftupified minds, to fee your affairs fo unluckily handled, complaining that your Country was never in greater difordur, the Kirk never worfe contented, their diffatisfaction influencing the whole Kingdom ; Your houfe fo evil at a point : The Nobility fo divided ; The Barons were never in greater poverty : The Commons never more Oppreffed ; Never more Taxations raifed, moftly applyed to the utility of private perfons: Never more Parliaments holden : Never more Laws broken ; your Proclamations and Miffives no ways obeyed ; Never was Murther and Blood fhed more increafed,then fince your home-coming, and publick promife of better Government.

Therefore, 'Sir, as in a perillous ftorm upon the Sea, or to quench fudden kindled fire on the Land, every mans help is requifite, and acceptable, fo I hope your Majefty's clemency will confider, and your prudence will take in good part, this my dutiful Declaration and Admonition, the boldlier interprifed under the Warrant of your favourable Alliance, following your Commandment before your Majefty's going to *Denmark*, that my Brother and I fhould fet down the Caufes of the evil and diforders that have been, and yet are in the Kingdom, with the meeteft Remedies for Reforming and Amending the fame.

There be Three chief Caufes of all thefe Evils and Diffordeis.

The *Firft* is concerning God's Service.

The *Second* is concerning your own Eftate, and the Provifion of your Houfe.

The *Third*, Concerning the policy and right management of the Country.

As concerning the fervice of God neglected by our fins, and carelefnefs in fetting forth his Glory, it fhould be redreffed and amended by humble Repentance, and amendment of Life, and good Example firft in your own Perfon, upon whofe carriage, every Man's Eye is fixed, as the Head to Rule the reft of the Members, with Religion, Juftice, Prudence, Temperance, and Fortitude.

Chiefly by Religion and Juftice, have all Common-wealths been Ruled. So that fuch Countries as wanted the knowledg of the True Religion, feeing the great works that God brought to pafs by his

own peculiar people obferving his Religion, they invented Religions.
Thus thinking to imitate the *Jews*, they fell into Idolatry, and Super-
ftition: yet they ftraitly obferved their faid invented Religions, and
caufed to punifh with Death fuch as defpifed or fpoke againft the fame.
Far more fhould your Majefty be careful to advance the True Religion, and to fee the fame Reverenced and Obferved. And for that effect, fhould devout and difcreet Minifters be chofen, whofe Chriftian
Lives may Preach, as well as their Doctrine. Aud fuch ought to be
provided with fufficient local ftipends, neither too much to entice them
to Avarice, nor too little to make them Indigent, and give them
ground in their Preachings to cry out of Poverty, in fuch fort as they
may have no occafion yearly to leave their flocks, to come and
make fuite for their living, with great pain and expences as they do
prefently.

Divers are the caufes of the diforders in your Court, and Houfe Officers, and Servants. For they are not chofen for their Qualities, but
at the inftance of this and that Friend, or Courtier. Then the number
of all forts of Servants are not limitted, by placing about your Majefty
fo many as are needful, but an extraordinary number, whereas two
in every Office are enough. And then your prudence will be beft
known, when you fhall be feen to make good Elections of fit Perfons
for every occupation. For the Prince is ever efteemed to be like unto
thofe fort of fervants, he likes beft to be about him. Much confifts
in this, to have in Court, difcreet, modeft Courtiers, fuch as are not
Covetous, nor unmeafurable Ambitious. Nothing wins more the
hearts of the People to the Prince: for fo long as they fee about him
fuch Perfons, they are out of fear of being unmeafurably burthened:
When they fee men, who are not greedy, nor prodigal fpenders of
the Princes Eftate, nor their own, nor ftirrers up of the Prince, to take
Men's Lives for their Lands; they are in hope that every Man may
live upon his own, and the Prince alfo upon his proper Patrimony.
Therefore fhould the Officers of the *Exchequer*, be true and honeft
Men. And the Prince fhould be frequently prefent himfelf, and hear
his own compts: for few dare controul, or find fault with the wrong
compts of his Officers, or great Courtiers. Which I have oft-times
found fault with, when upon the *Exchequer*, though afterward to
my great Prejudice.

The caufes why the Patrimony of the Crown is fo diminifhed, is be
caufe your Majefty difpofed much to the Church, for Devotion; and
to the Noblemen, and Barons, for good Service. And when Princes
were carelefs to prevent Rebellions, occafioned by their mif-govern-
ment, they were compelled to buy the Affiftance of fome, by difpofition of Lands, to help to fupprefs their unnatural Subjects. Which inconvenience, their careful and provident Government, might have prevented and efchewed.

Your Majefty alfo out of your Noble and Princely difpofition, difpofed liberally unto divers greedy and importunate Perfons, during
your minority, divers Lands, and Rents, which would have ftood in
great ftead, to the entertainment of your Houfe. And you heaped
gift upon gift to a fort of greedy cravers, and that by the perfwafions
of fuch as had your Ear, and not to thofe who deferved beft at your
hands.

hands. Now the Officers of the *Checquer* being well chosen, as said is, the Rent-Masters, and their Officers, who are accomptable, must be responsible Men; neither too mean, nor too great Men, or Courtiers; but such as dare be controuled, and whom People will not fear to offend. All vacant Benefices, and Casualities, should be retained in your own hands, till you see what you may spare.

Then the best part of the property lies in the *High-Lands*, where neither God, nor the King is served or obeyed. Your Rents may be redoubled, if the High-lands, and the Islands were reduced, as was done by your King *James* the Fifth: For the Kings of *Scotland* were never rich, since they left the High-lands and the Isles, to dwell in the Low-lands: For since that their Rents have been diminished, and their superfluous expences increased, at the unruly example of other neighbour Nations.

Then your Majesties Parks would be put to profit, and replenished, which will be found a necessary help to the keeping of your House. The rest of your store Grounds, lying in the far South parts, are in such hands, as it is not fit meddle with them yet; but some yearly number of Weathers will be easily granted by them who possess presently the said store grounds.

Also the forbidden Goods that go yearly out of *Scotland*, if they were stayed and taken according to Acts of Parliament, would be very profitable.

The best means to bring these good purposes to pass, is a Princely, Prudent and Gracious Government: Which is easiest brought to pass, when the Prince corrects himself, before he correct his Subjects: For they will be soon subdued to his Will, when they see the same made Subject unto Reason: For being Subject unto Reason, the Prince hath conquered himself, the readiest means to conquer the hearts of all his Subjects. Their hearts being conquered, the Country is easily conquered. The Country being conquered, the Prince may plant and Establish good order there at his pleasure.

Theopompus being demanded, what way a King might best rule his Realm: Answered, In giving liberty to those who love to tell him the truth.

The Senate of *Rome* writing unto *Trajan*, excuseth Princes to be negligent in many things, not so much for that they have not desire to foresee, as because few or none dare warn them of the truth; and says moreover, That it belongs to good Princes rather to have regard to the benefit of their Country, then to the delights of their Person, and rather to follow such Exercises as will increase their Reputation, then only to be taken up with their pastime, that they should be sparing in Speeches, and Prodigal in Deeds.

Plutarch saith to the same *Trajan*, If thy Government answer not the expectation of thy people, thou must necessarily be subject to many dangers. He said further, That Princes should Rule well, if they be thankful to the great God, and if they should be patient in chances of fortune, and diligent in Execution, careful of their Affairs in dangers, mild to the people, tractable to strangers, not covetous of riches, nor lovers of their own opinions, and desires. For then the burthen of their Office, will be easy unto them. As God is the Ruler and Spirit

of the World, fo ought Princes to Rule and be the Spirit of their Country. The Heaven, the Earth, the Sea, and all the Elements, obey God's
Ordinance by the ftrength of his continual Motion and Providence ; fo
fhould the Prince who is God's place-holder, by continual Care, Providence, and Motion, caufe every Lieutenant, Minifter, Magiftrate,
Judge, Officer, and Sheriffs to keep their due courfe in their Vocation.
For the which effect, it may pleafe your Majefty to confider the nature, and wrong kind of *Scottifb* Government, by a continual long
corrupted Cuftom.

  Scotland is indeed Hereditary, and a Monarchy, yet among all other
Monarchical Kingdoms, it is ofteft out of Tune, by the floth and carelefnefs of Princes, the unrulinefs and fturdinefs of the Subjects, and the
great number of the Nobility ; as alfo by reafon of the great cumber-
fom Claims, fo ready to concur together, and to Rebell for the defence
of any of their name, or to revenge the juft Execution of fome of
them for Muither, Slaughter, Theft, or fuch other Crimes. For our
King wanting hired Soldiers remaining in Garifons, as other Monarchs
have, may not at all occafions punifh and rediefs fuch wrongs, and
diforders ; except they have by Wifdom and Vertue conquered their
own paffion, opinions, and defires, and by the fame means ravifhed
the hearts of the moft and beft part of the Subjects, to affift them
with heart and hand to fupprefs the Rebels, and to punifh the offenders. Such Kings again as endeavour to command abfolutely, not caring for the hearts of their Subjects ; their Proclamation may well be
outwardly obeyed with their Bodies, but they will never help the
Prince in time of need, fave only to help to ruine him. There is nothing more dangerous for a *Scots* King, that hath not the love of his
Subjects, then when a great nnmber are Convened together. For at
fuch times, they ufe to rake fudden confultations to put order to the
Prince, and his familiar Minions. Of thefe two fort of Kings, the firft,
is more then a Monarch, and the lefs then Elective. Of the firft,
in *Scotland* too few have Reign'd, and of the laft fort too many. Which is
the caufe, that the Country is not conquered to the lawful Kings. Which
is alfo the caufe, that the corrupt Cuftoms and Diforders, have lafted
fo long, and are not to be remedied, untill it pleafe God to fend three
fuch Kings as I have named of the beft fort, granting them long life,
each one to fucceed after other. I pray God grant that your Majefty
be the firft of the three. But it appears your Majefty is not well advifed, while you are creating more Noblemen, making them thereby
the ftronger, whereas divers other Princes endeavoured to make them
lower and fewer : By reafon of the old Emulation which hath lafted
between the Kings of *Scotland*, and their Nobility, the Kings to Command abfolutely as Sovereign Monarchs ; the Nobles to withftand
their abfolute power, fometime by fecret and indirect means, and oft-
times by plain refiftance and force. Hence but few Wife, Vertuous,
and Potent Kings, or Soveraign Monarchs who have obtained the Maftery ; whereas there have been many carelefs, flothful, and fimple
Princes, that have Ruled by wicked Councellors, and have commonly
been brought to ignominious ends. The good and worthy Prince,
took upon him more or lefs abfolute Power and Authority, as he found
himfelf able by Affiftance, Subftance, and Alliance, or as he found
his Nobility feeble, foolifh, and divided.   *Eng-*

England believes it self to be in the better Estate by shedding the blood of their Nobility, and debarring them from the Council, and handling of the Princes' Affairs; *Scotland* contrariwise, by sparing the blood of the Nobility, and Barons, and by making them partakers of Honours, and Offices. For the way of taking the life of a Nobleman or Baron, breeds an hundred Enemies more or less, according to the greatness of the Clan, or Surname. Of which some will lye at wait to be revenged, albeit long after, as they can find their opportunity. For the Nobility being so numerous by long evil custom, they esteem themselves to be born Councellors. And yet will not remain at Court, nor upon the Council, unless it be at Conventions, or for some particular profit. And if the Prince intend to Rule without them, they use to make sudden enterprises against him, and his familiars, with the which Tragedies, the Chronicles are filled. Then after such a violent alteration, they find themselves odious to the Prince; so that they commonly seek to be Masters over him from that time forth, lest he should when he sees a fit time take his revenge for their contempt.

It is not best then to debar your Nobility from being upon your Council, but grant place to a number of the wisest of them, whereof they will soon be weary, and retire when their Purses begin to grow empty. Thus they will want occasion to grudge or rebel.

It is meet also to gain by good deeds, part of the worthiest of your Nobility, which may be a means to keep the rest from Rebellion, when they see so many of their number daily about you, and in your favour.

Princes are by *Homer* called *Pastors*, by the *Romans*, *Fathers of the Country*. None can be answerable to such honourable Names, without extream diligence, and fatherly care, to see every Officer about his duty, and streight accompt taken how they discharge the same, rewarding Well-doers, and punishing Offenders; reward and punishment being the Pillars, whereupon the Common-wealth stands. Especially take care, the first year of your marriage, for the reputation obtained the first year will last long afterward, whether it be good or evil.

Be earnest and liberal to get good intelligence, as well of your neighbours Estate, as your own. Of the grievances of your Subjects, and their partialities, and feuds; which will open your Eyes to see sundry out-gates in matters of State.

Give familiar access to your Nobility and Barons, when they come : Chiefly to all such, who are written for to your Conventions. Give open Audience once every Week at least, to Rich and Poor, receiving their Supplications, and Complaints, with strict Command to the Council, and Master of Requests, to give them answer with sudden dispatch.

Cause to reform the superfluity of Clothing and Banqueting, as well by your Example as Commandment.

Now supposing your Majesty to be ripe fruit, and no more green, I hope your dear bought experience hath made you apt enough to receive all profitable impressions, presented to your Majesty by your faithful proved Servants, and not to commit so easily the weighty charge of your Affairs to any one, or two, or three, seeing the same may have been

been clearly obferved, to tend highly to the prejudice of fuch, who have been, through flattery, or otherwife, induced to follow fuch courfes. Such Minions have been always obferved to fhoot at their own marks, not valuing the endangering the Eftate of the Prince, fo that they gain their own ends, by enriching themfelves, and their dependers.

No man will think ftrange that, during your younger years, you have been preffed and perfwaded to lay the burthen of Affairs of your felf upon others, who greedily courted that weighty charge above their capacity, wanting care, knowledg, and ability to bear it. But now every Man will marvell, if you fhould commit fuch a grofs Error in your perfeČt age, thinking that your pregnant ingeny, excellent memory, and hurtful experience, may compel you to exercife the Office of a King in your own Perfon. For whence hath proceeded fo many attempts, fo many enterprifes, fo many times the taking of your Majefties Perfon, fo many alterations and changes of Court-Servants, Councellors, and Laws; but by committing the charge and keeping of your Sheep, and SubjeČts, to certain ambitious and ravenous Wolfs, who choofe to bring into Court for their affiftance, fuch as they knew to be of their own qualities, that they might conquer together, firft how to put out of your favour, and debar from your Ear, all fuch honeft true Perfons, as would oppofe their pernicious proceedings, that fo your Majefty might neither fee nor underftand, but by their Eyes and Ears. Your Majefty can well enough remember, how oft for my part I have forewarned you of the ftorms which were to fall out, through the misbehaviour of fuch infolent, fuch inconftant, fuch fcornful, and fuch partial Perfons, as have ofteft poffeft your Ear, and carried the vogue in your Court. And what I thereby gained to my felf, your Majefty knows. Yet however difadvantagious to my own particular intereft, was that manner of procedure, I had this Comfort, that your Majefty confeffed that I had fhewn you the verity, but the faid confeffion was ay behind the time, with over late Repentance.

Here your Majefty may reproach me of inconftant Councils ; becaufe one year after your returning from *Denmark*, I told you that your SubjeČts were not fatisfied of their expeČtations, nor of your publick promifes, praying your Majefty yet to begin, and either be at that pains which is requifite to a right Governing King, or elfe to fubmit the whole burthen of your affairs to fuch a number as I fhould name, only for one year. In doing of any of thefe two, I engaged that you fhould find your Eftate fufficiently fetled at the years end. Then it pleafed your Majefty to demand of me the manner that I would wifh you to Rule after. Whereunto I made anfwer, that it did not become me, or any in *Scotland* to fhew you the duty of a King, which you could declare better then any of your Council, feeing you could exercife the faid Office as well as any King in *Europe*, if you were pleafed only for one year to take the pains to do it your felf. In fo doing, I fuppofed that before the end of it, there fhould enfue fuch profitable effeČts, as you fhould find the Government pleafant, and no more painful, by the which means your Majefty fhould efchew the reproach of the Poet, in one of his fayings in *French*.

Je

Je hay ; dit il entre les homes ceux
Qui font efpris dun vouloir panfheux
Et tonfiours femblet fon fy fye
Practiquer lart de la Philofophie.

Italian.

Chi non fa quel che deue, quel hafpetta non receue.

Spanifh.

Si fueras regido par razon amuchos regiras.

In four things a Prince fooneft wracks himfelf, to be carelefs and flothful in his Affairs, to forfake the Counfel of his true Servants, to give ear unto unthankful flatterers, and to fpend above his Rents.

To return again to the purpofe, it pleafed your Majefty to require for the fecond part, *viz.* What might beft fettle your Eftate within the year? I faid, to devolve the management for a year upon fuch as I fhould name, joyned to the beft inclined of your own Council. To that your Majefty once agreed, but when I came more to particulars, your Majefty judged it not your intereft, as having been otherwife advifed. Then I requefted your Majefty to exercife the Office your felf.

Yet not long after, your Majefty fubmitted your felf wholly and intirely to eight Perfons, called *Octavians*, and told me that you had followed my Opinion therein, and had fubmitted *fimpliciter* for your time to thefe eight Perfons. I replied, that I fpoke but for one year, and that I would have named fome of the faid number but not all. They were Wife Men, Learned and Politick; but the unmeeter that they were chufers of themfelves. Yet they began to do better than any had done before them, but they continued not, but divided among themfelves, after they had divided the Offices of the Crown to every man one: Whereas at the firft, they had given forth that they fhould plant mean refponfible men in the faid Offices, and they all too but Controulers of the faid Officers. So that many began to grudge againft them, feeing them become in a fudden rich. And perceiving their great backs, the whole Subjects, and His Majefty's own Domefticks to follow and depend upon them, and His Majefty to pafs through the Streets with three or four as forfaken ; becaufe none hoped any more for reward at his hands, but fo much as might be had for ferving and depending upon the faid Eight Lords. They became alfo hated and envied, partly for the Caufes fpecified ; as alfo there was great ground of jealoufie, that they were intending the eftablifhment of Popery. So that there was a Rebellion raifed in *Edinburgh* againft them, in his Majefty's prefence ; upon which they fled out of the Town, and fince durft never take upon them the whole Government, but were content to be joyned with a number of Noblemen, and others of the Council, to the number of twenty four. But the greateft part of the Noblemen did not attend, but came when they were written for to the Conventions, as formerly they ufed. So all this new device turned to the old *ficut antea.*

You

You have heard how that his Majesty was advised at his returning from *Denmark*, to imprison such as were given up to have been
most unruly during his absence. But being returned, even some of
those who had advised the said Warding, were the first who gave
advertisement to those who were to be Warded, not without some
profit for their reward, to the great discontentment of some of their
Associates. Which loosed the bond which was made at *Denmark* by
the *Chancellour* and his Faction, and caused every one of that number
to go sundry, and to do for themselves. So that all their Plots and
devises turned to change some of the Session, but there was no concurrence, and so it stopped of it self.

The Officers of the *Exchequer* continued a while to be the only
Council. And the Nobility when they came, were kept at the door,
I having at that time the honour to be one of the *Exchequer*, took
the freedom to acquaint His Majesty that the Nobility would be offended at such usage, which was so manifest a flight. I said it would do no
prejudice to cause them come in, they being great men, as my L. *Hamiltoun*, my L. *Maxwel*, and others of principal note. But His Majesty of
his own nature was not changeable from the order laid down by them
he liked, and reposed upon. Yet of my own accord I went forth of
the Chamber, and told the Noblemen, That His Majesty was upon
the ordering of his Accompts and Rents, and the daily Expences of
his House ; that he was asham'd they should see the Estate thereof,
which was the cause they were suffered to stand without. This little excuse was somwhat satisfactory to them. But that Order was also soon altered.

Concerning the reducing of the Highlands and Isles, three of the
Principals, as *Maclean*, *Macdonel* and *Donald Gorin*, were subtilly drawn
to the Court by the *Chancellour*, who understood of the differences
among them. Every one of them being by him put in hope to get
his hand above his Enemy. But at their coming, they were all three
Warded in the Castle of *Edinburgh*, to their great astonishment. For
they had each of them committed such foul murthers under trust, that
it was horrible to rehearse. Being therefore apprehensive of their
Lives, they dealt largely of their ill won Gold to those who had most
Credit, nevertheless to terrifie them the more, to draw more from
them, they were put to an Assize, and Convict of Treason. Which
caused them to redouble their gifts to the Guiders, but not to the
King. In such sort that there was an agreement betwixt His Majesty
and them, that they should give pledges that they should pay yearly unto His Majesty twenty thousand marks for the Lands, of the
property whereof they had no security. Of the which they had of
yearly Rent, as was given into the Exchequer, two hundred and fifty
thousand Marks. This was all given them for twenty thousand
Marks. And whereas before they had no right, nor security, but a
forcible possession, they obtained sure infeofments by Charter, Seisin,
and the Great Seal, and a remission of their foul Crimes. But shortly after their Pledges, who were kept in the *Blacknes* for giving a
small Sum, were released, and so the twenty thousand Marks was lost
and never payed.

Here

Here was a good Prince ill ufed, and abufed ; and the half of the Rents robbed from him ; his God offended by fparing to do juftice upon fuch bloody Tyrants, who acknowledged neither God nor the King.

I had advifed his Majefty to go himfelf to the *Ifles* to build a Fort there, and to remain two years till all things were order'd ; fhewing His Majefty that the Kings of *Scotland* were never rich, fince they left the High-lands to dwell in the Low-lands ; but have ever fince diminifhed their Rents, and increafed their fuperfluous expences in Dyet and Clothing, following the Cuftoms of other Nations : Which His Majefty, after inquiry, found to be moft true , and His Majefty was refolved to follow the faid advice, and I had promifed to go with him , but all was altered by the former mifrule. Matters thus carried on, many began to lofe hope of amendment , or to fee the Reformation promifed and expected, lamenting to fee a good King fo ill Councelled.

Yet this time His Majefty fent for me, and at my coming to *Falkland*, where the Court remained for the Summer Seafon ; it pleafed His Majefty to tell me, how that at his coming out of *Denmark*, he had promifed to the Queen and Council there, to place about the Queens Majefty, his Bed-fellow, good and difcreet Company, which he had left too long undone. That at length having advifed with himfelf, he thought me the fitteft man to commit that charge to, defiring me not to refufe the juft calling of my Prince, wherein I might ferve as in a lawful Vocation ; becaufe fuch as ordinarily fuit for Service at Court, or for any Office, do it for their own profit ; but they are more profitable for Princes that are fought after, and are chofen for their qualities. I know, fays he, That you would gladly live at home in your own houfe , with contentment of mind , which you think is not to be had in the troublefome alterations in Court. But you know that a man is not born for himfelf only, but alfo for the weal of his Prince and Country. And whereas your continual on waiting, will be chargeable and expenfive to you, and hinderfome to your own Affairs at home, I fhall ordain fufficient entertainment for your prefent relief, and recompence for this and your former faithful Service.

I anfwered, That as His Majefty's moft humble Servant and Subject, I never refufed to obey his Commandment , however prejudicial to my own intereft the fame fhould have appeared to me , and contrary to my natural inclinations : That I fhould refolve in that His Majefty's defire, to fatisfie his expectations. Then it pleafed him to tell me , That none of his Councell or Chamber were privy to this his defign of giving me that charge, but only one man, and that the Queen notwithftanding had got notice thereof, and fuppofed that I was to be put there , to inform her rightly of the Eftate of the Country, and concerning her behaviour to His Majefty, and to every Nobleman and Lady, conform to their Ranks and Conditions, and to be her keeper.

His Majefty the next day took occafion openly at the Table , to fhew unto the Queen how that fhe and all her Nation were obliged to me, for the continual good report I had made of them, and the

good will I carried toward the whole Nation; and alfo how I had
travelled many Countries, and had fo great experience that both he
and fhe might learn of me feveral things for their advantage , and
for the well and ftanding of their Eftate : And that the Queen his
Mother found her felf much relieved by my Converfation, and Service of importance , as well here at home, as when I was imployed
by her abroad. . Thus far his Majefty faid above my defervings , to
recommend me to her Majefty, to oblige her to like me the better.
Notwithftanding whereof, the Queen did fhew me no great countenance, but took coldly with me, when after Dinner it pleafed his
Majefty to prefent me unto her, to be her Highnefs's Councellour,
and Gentleman of her Chamber. Some days afterward her Majefty asked me, if I was fet to be her Keeper ? I anfwered, That her
Majefty was known to be defcended of fo Noble and Princely Parents,
and fo well brought up, that fhe needed no Keeper; albeit her dignity required to be honourably ferved with Men and Women, both
young and old, in fundry occupations. She replied that I had been
ill ufed, fhewing me that at the firft , when fhe was yet ignorant of
every mans qualities, fome indifcreet enviers endeavoured to give
her a bad Character of me. I anfwered, That I was put in her fervice to inftruct fuch indifcreet perfons , and alfo to give them good
example, how to behave themfelves dutifully, and reverently unto
her Majefty , to hold them aback, and that way to keep her from
their rafhnefs, and importunity. At length her Majefty appeared to
be well fatisfied with my Service, in which I fpent   years, keeping fometimes the Council days , and fometime waiting upon the
Exchequer, when their Majefties were together; but when they were
afunder, I waited only upon the Queen.

About this time, many Witches were taken in *Lauthian*, who de-
pofed concerning fome defign of the Earl of *Bothwel*'s againft his Majefty's Perfon. Which coming to the faid Earl's Ears, he entred in
Ward within the Caftle of *Edinburgh* , defiring to be tried : Alledging that the Devil, who was a lyar from the beginning , ought
not to be credited, nor yet the Witches his fworn Servants. Efpecially a renowned Midwife called *Amy Simpfon* affirmed, That fhe in
company with nine other Witches, being Convened in the night befide *Preftoun Pans*, the Devil their Mafter being prefent, ftanding in
the midft of them, a Body of Wax fhapen and made by the faid *Amy
Simpfon*, wrapped within a Linnen Cloth, was firft delivered to the
Devil, who after he had pronounced his Verdict, delivered the faid
Picture to *Amy Simpfon*; and fhe to her next Neighbour, and fo every
one round about, faying, This is King *James* the Sixth, ordered to be
confumed at the inftance of a Nobleman *Francis* Earl *Bothwel*. Afterward again, at their meeting by night in the Kirk of *North-Berwick*, where the Devil clad in a Black Gown, with a Black Hat upon
his Head, preached unto a great number of them out of the Pulpit,
having like light Candles round about him.

The effect of his language was to know what hurt they had done;
how many they had gained to their Opinion fince the laft meeting;
what fuccefs the melting of the Picture had, and fuch other vain things.
And becaufe an old filly poor Plough-man, called *Gray Meill* chanced

to

to fay, That nothing ailed the King yet, God be thanked, the Devil gave him a great blow. Thus divers among them entred in reafoning, marvelling that all their Devilry could do no harm to the King, as it had done to divers others. The Devil anfwered, *Il eft un home de dieu, Certainly he is a man of God,* and does no wrong wittingly; but he is inclined to all Godlinefs, Juftice and Vertue, therefore God hath preferved him in the midft of many dangers. Now after that the Devil had ended his admonitions, he came down out of the Pulpit, and caufed all the company come kifs his Arfe : Which they faid was cold like Ice, his body hard like Iron, as they thought who handled him ; his Nofe like the Beek of an Eagle, great burning Eyes, his Hands, and his Legs were hoary, with Claws upon his Hands and Feet like the *Gryphon* , he fpoke with a low Voice.

The Tricks and Tragedies he played then among fo many men and women in this Country, will hardly get credit by pofterity. The Hiftory whereof with their whole Depofitions, was written by Mr. *James Carmichael* Minifter of *Hadingtoun.* Among other things, fome of them did fhew that there was a Well-land man called *Richard Graham,* who had a familiar Spirit, the which *Richard* they faid could both do and tell many things , chiefly againft the Earl of *Bothwel.* Whereupon the faid *Richard Graham* was apprehended, and brought to *Edinburgh* , and being examined before his Majefty , I being prefent, he granted that he had a familiar Spirit, which fhewed him fundry things ; but he denied that he was a Witch, or had any frequentation with them. But when it was anfwered again, how that *Amy Simpfon* had declared, that he caufed the Earl of *Bothwel* addrefs him to her: He granted that to be true, and that the Earl of *Bothwel* had knowledge of him by *Effe Machalloun,* and *Barbary Napier, Edinburgh* Women. Whereupon he was fent for by the Earl *Bothwel,* who required his help to caufe the King's Majefty his Mafter to like well of him. And to that effect he gave the faid Earl fome Drug, or Herb, willing him at fome convenient time to touch therewith his Majefties face. Which being done by the faid Earl ineffectually, he dealt again with the faid *Richard,* to get his Majefty wracked, as *Richard* alledged. Who faid, he could not do fuch things himfelf, but that a notable Midwife who was a Witch called *Amy Simpfon,* could bring any fuch purpofe to pafs. Thus far the faid *Richard Graham* affirmed divers times before the Council ; neverthelefs he was burnt with the faid *Simpfon,* and many other Witches. This *Richard* alledged, That it was certain what is reported of the Fairies , and that Spirits may take a form and be feen though not felt.

The Earl of *Bothwel,* as I faid, was entred to Ward within the Caftle of *Edinburgh,* his Majefty not willing to credit his Devilifh Accufers, but the Council thought fit that for a while he fhould pafs his time in other Countries, and fo to be fet free upon fome Articles , and Conditions. But fome of thofe who were appointed to deal with him, endeavoured to make advantage of him to be his friends. Others who were defirous to have the State troubled, made him falfe advertifements, as if his life had been in danger. Which caufed him refolve to fave himfelf over the Caftle Wall, and retired himfelf to *Caithnefs:*

whence he was shortly after sent for by such as were male-contents, and others who were desirous to fish in troubled waters, alledging they had made him friends enough in Court, and that there was a fair enterprise devised, to take the King, and kill the Chancellour. Upon which information, he was easily perswaded to come, and make himself head of that enterprise.

He therefore not long after accompanied with *James Douglas* sometime Laird of *Spott*, the Laird of *Nidrie*, Mr. *John Colvil*, and some others, entred into the Kings Palace late, about supper time, by the passage of an old Stable, not without secret intelligence of some about his Majesty. So soon as they were all within the Close of the Palace, they cried Justice, Justice, a *Bothwel*, a *Bothwel*, and had been Masters of the whole, were it not that *James Douglas* of *Spott* after that he had taken the Keys from the Porters, entred within the Porters Lodge to relieve some of his Servants, who were kept there in Prison, and had been examined upon suspicion of the slaughter of his good Father the old Laird of *Spott*, where he met with some resistance from the Porters, the noise whereof did rise sooner than was the intention of the enterprisers. Which allarmed his Majesty, the Chancellour and others, to shut and fortifie their Chamber-doors, and to make resistance till some relief came from the Cannon-gate, conducted by my Brother Sir *Andrew Melvil* of *Garvock*, Master of his Majesty's Houshold, who knew a secret passage through the Abby Church, and entred by the same in Armour. Whereof the Earl of *Bothwel* and his Company being advertised, they stole quietly through the Galleries unto the part where they entred the Palace, and fled without any great harm as God would have it. In his out-going, he chanced to meet with *John Shaw* Master Stabler to his Majesty, whom he slew, together with his Brother, being in a rage that the enterprise had failed. But divers of his Company were apprehended by my said Brother, and by others, who were all Executed the next day.

Their manner of proceeding was, first the Laird of *Spott* with a Company took the Keys, and made themselves Masters of the Gates of the Palace; another Company was directed to the Chancellour, who was sitting at his Supper, and my Brother Sir *Robert* with him, and they had been taken, had it not been for the Laird of *spot*'s earnestness to relieve his Servants. The bruit whereof caused the Chancellour to flee out of his Hall to his Chamber, and shut the door after him. So that my said Brother got no entry, but retired himself to another void house, whither none pursued him, neither was he in any fear for himself.

The Earl of *Bothwel* accompanied with Mr. *John Colvil* and others addressed themselves unto the Queens Chamber door, where he supposed the King would be found. But the door was defended well by *Hary Lindsay* of *Kilsans*, Master of her Houshold. In the mean time, his Majesty was conveyed up to that Tower above the said Chamber, after the door of her Majesties Chamber had been broken with Hammers in divers parts, and that Mr. *John Colvil* had caused bring fire to burn it. The door of the Chancellours Chamber was manfully defended by himself. He caused his men to shoot out of the Windows continually, and through doors. Where *Robert Scot*
Brother

Brother to the Laird of *Balweary* was shot through the thigh. The Chancellour took courage when he heard my Brothers voice, and then the enterprisers fled as said is.

At their first entry within the Palace, I was sitting at Supper with my Lord Duke of *Lennox*, who incontinently took his Sword, and pressed forth. But he had no company, and the place already was full of Enemies : We were compelled to fortifie the Doors and Stairs, with Tables, Forms and Stools, and be Spectators of that strange hurly burly for the space of an hour, beholding with Torch-light forth of the Duke's Gallery their reeling, their rumbling with Halberts, the clacking of their Culverins, and Pistols, the dunting of Mells and Hammers, and their crying for Justice. Now there was a passage betwixt the Chancellour's Chamber and my Lord Duke's by a Stair, and during this fray, the Chancellour came up the said Stair, and desired entry into my Lord Duke's Chamber. My Lord Duke by my advice, desired him to cause his men debate at the nether door so long as they might, and offered to receive himself within the Chamber. Which the Chancellour took in an evil part, and suspected my Lord Duke : And so returned back again to his own Chamber, and debated the best he could, as said is. So soon as my Lord Duke saw a company of friends within the Close, he went forth to pursue the Earl of *Bothwel* and his Company, but the night was dark, and they took them speedily to their horses and escaped.

They being retired, we got entry to her Majesties Chamber, whither the King was for the time come down. Where his Majesty discoursed with me a good space, concerning this terrible attempt, and of his many hard misfortunes. Where I left not to tell his Majesty some of the special Causes of the said enterprises, and how that many of them might have been prevented by a prudent and careful Government, as may be sufficiently marked and considered by the many admonitions, and former advertisements made unto his Majesty before all the accidents that chanced unto him, and also in this. For two days before this enterprise, my Brother Sir *Robert* and I, had got intelligence, that some such design was shortly to be put in execution by the Earl of *Bothwel*, and his Complices against his Majesty, and the Guiders of Court. Whereof his Majesty made no accompt, though thereof advertised. But was the next day going to hunting, which coming to my Brother's Ears, he rose out of his Bed in his Shirt, only in his Night-Gown ; and came forth to the utter Close of the Abby, and took his Majesty by the Bridle, (for he was already upon Horse-back) using many perswasions to have stayed him, though all in vain : For we were in doubt whether the enterprise would be executed in the Fields, or in the Palace.

After this attempt, his Majesty went up to the Town of *Edinburgh* for his greater security ; where there were divers new enterprises made, whereof my Brother Sir *Robert* getting frequent advertisements, sometimes to keep his Lodging such a night, sometimes to be well accompanied such a night, as being one who had done pleasures to many, and was not hated, nor would never have been in danger, so that he could but save himself from the first fury of the attempters.

This

This hath been the hard Eſtate of this good King, occaſioned by his laying the burthen of his Affairs upon a few hated and envied for their Ambition, Covetouſneſs, and Partialities, who ſo ſoon as they had attained ſo weighty a charge, took only care how to make themſelves ſoon rich, moſt commonly by the wrack of others. So blindly tranſported by ambition and greedineſs, that they neglected both King and Common-Wealth, ſatisfying the King with fair language, though diſpleaſing the Country with foul deeds; caring only how to diſcredit and bear down ſo many honeſt men, as they knew would diſcover their misbehaviour, or who would oppoſe them in their pernicious deſigns, which I may juſtly teſtifie for my part.

Not long after this, a new enterpriſe was made, to make a great alteration in Court, by ſome Courtiers among themſelves. When as the Maſter of *Glams* was Treaſurer, Sir *George Hume* Maſter of the Wardrobe, my Lord of *Spinze* Gentleman of the Chamber, and young *Logie*; alſo Sir *John Maitland*, Lord *Thirlſtane* Chancellour, Sir *Robert* my Brother Treaſurer depute, had the principal handling of the Office by disburſing and receiving; the Provoſt of *Lincludin* Collector, and   *Seatoun* of *Parbroth* Controller, Sir *Richard Cockburn* of *Clarkingtoun* Secretary, and I was one of the Privy Council, and Gentleman of her Majeſties Chamber; my Lord Duke of *Lennox*, my Lord *Hume*, and my Lord of *Mar* were drawn upon this courſe, to reform the abuſes at Court as was alledged. There was no good liking between the Maſter of *Glams*, and my Lord of *Spiny*, chiefly for the feud between the Houſes of *Crauford* and *Glams*. At that time my Lord *Spiny* was in great favour with his Majeſty, and ſometime his Bed-fellow: And upon that accompt he was envied. And beſides the foreſaid feud, he was accuſed to have been a dealer with the Earl of *Bothwel*, and upon that was for a time decourted. Young *Logie* was alſo thought to have had much dealing with the ſaid Earl, and was accuſed, taken and warded for the ſame. But he eſcaped out of a Window in *Dalkieth*, by the help of a *Daniſh* Gentlewoman; whom he afterward married.

There was great hatred betwixt my Lord *Duke* and the Chancellour. For after the late enterpriſe in the Abby, the Chancellour cauſed cloſe up the paſſage with Stone and Lime that was betwixt their Lodgings, whereby he gave the *Duke* to underſtand that he ſuſpected him; which was too raſhly done by the ſaid Chancellour. For after that, the new alteration was intended; and called the enterpriſe made at *Dalkieth*, my Lord *Duke*, and my Lord *Hume* riding from *Dalkieth*, to *Edinburgh*, met the Chancellour well accompanied riding to Court, where the ſaid Lords made a mint to ſet upon him to ſlay him; yet the matter was at that time taken up by *Alexander Hoom* of *North-Berwick*, and my Brother Sir *Robert*, who were in company with the Chancellour for the time. But ſhortly after that the Chancellour left the Court, retiring himſelf to his Houſe, and in his abſence a great number of faults were charged upon him, and among the reſt, how he had ſo long hindred the King's marriage, whereby the Queens Majeſty was made his great Enemy. The Maſter of *Glams* alſo would fain have had my Brother out of his Office, to brook the whole Office of *Treaſurer* alone. Therefore the Laird of *Carmichall*
Captain

Captain of the Guard, was eafily perfwaded to caufe a number of the
Guard , who ftood with Culverins at the Gates of the Houfe of
D.ilkieth, to boaft to flay my faid Brother divers times in his paffing
in and out of the fame houfe, fuppofing that my Brother fhould fear
his Life, and leave the Court, as the Chancellour had done. But my
Brother made no accompt of their boafts ; for he knew the Duke was
his friend, and that he had but few enemies : Therefore he frequent-
ed the Court more frequently then formerly, but came always well
accompanied ; for they could get nothing to lay to his charge, but
faid to his Majefty that he was too lavifh in his Office to be a Treafurer, over eafie in his Compofitions, and over gentle to fuch as were
denounced to the horn. The Queens Majefty according to her cuftom, whenever fhe underftands that his Majefty by wrong information is ftirred up againft any honeft Servant, or Subject, fhe incontinently intercedes for them , and ufeth great diligence to get fure
knowledge of the verity, that fhe may the boldlier fpeak in their favour. Therefore fo foon as her Majefty underftood that they were
dealing againft Sir *Robert* my Brother, it pleafed her to fpeak far in
his favour , declaring how that at her firft Landing in this Country
his Majefty had prefented him to her, praifing him as one who had
been a true and faithful Servant to the Queen Regent his Grand-mo-
ther, to the Queen his Mother, and to himfelf, willing her to look
upon him as fuch, and to follow his advice. Alfo many of the Lords
took my Brother's part in fuch fort, as he ftill kept the Court and his
Office.

When this alteration was made I was abfent, and at my coming
again to Court, his Majefty told me of the Chancellour's fearful retreat, and that he was in no danger in his company. I anfwered
again, that the Prince's prefence fhould be a fafe-guard, albeit it was
not always fo in *Scotland.* It appeared that his Majefty was fomewhat altered upon the Chancellour, my Lord *Spiny,* and my Brother.
For as the Mafter of *Glams* would have had his Office, fo others mifliked him, becaufe he haunted the Chancellour's company, and was
lookt upon as his great friend , who was generally hated. So that
his Majefty was moved to think and fay that he was not meet for
his Office. I being prefent, anfwered , That it grieved me to the
heart, to hear and fee fo good a Prince always invironed with bad
company, caufing him fo oft without reafon or offence to caft off his
moft faithful Servants ; and that it would be feen, let men ferve never fo well , if they were mifreprefented by fuch as had his Ear, it
availed nothing. To this His Majefty replied ; That he knew my
Brother to be a true Servant, but too gentle, liberal, and eafie in his
Compofitions : he declared that he would never alter upon him nor
me, fo that he continued conftant againft the intentions of thofe who
were about him.

Here it may be feen how neceffary it is to have good friends about
the Prince , and how hurtful and dangerous it is for a Courtier,
when fuch as have the Prince's Ear are his Enemies. For in that cafe,
whatfoever his good Service hath been, he is in hazard of being cou-
ped and wracked.

About

About this time the Earl of *Arran*, who had been abfent ever fince the Road of *Sterling* came to Court, and fpoke with his Majefty, and pretended to have obtained again his Office of Chancellour. His Majefty had ftill fome favour for him, and would have been content of his company. But others held him back, and fhortly after that he was furprifed, and flain by *James Dowglas* of *Park-head*, in revenge of the death of the Earl of *Mortoun* his Uncle. Little diligence was made to revenge the fame, many thinking ftrange that he was permitted fo long to live, in refpect of his arrogant and infolent behaviour, when he had the Court at his will.

Now the Chancellour, who was decourted at the alteration made in *Dalkieth*, did what he could to procure his Majefties favour, which at laft he obtained, and was again introduced. But at firft, the Queen would not fee him; yet at length by the moyan of Sir *Robert Ker* of *Cesfoord*, who had married his Brother's Daughter his peace was alfo made with her Majefty.

About this time there did arife great ftrife and diforders in the Country, between the Earls of *Huntly* and *Murray*; between the Earls of *Caithnefs* and *Sunderland*; between my Lords *Hamiltoun* and *Angus*: for divers of them made fuits, and obtained Commiffion, with ample Priviledges over other Lands, as well as over their own, which engendred many difcords. Whereof I advertifed his Majefty, that Order might be taken therewith. Whereupon the Council being Convened, they ordered Ltters to be directed in his Majefties name, charging them all to defift from Hoftility, and to compear before the Privy-Council at prefixed days. Firft the Earls of *Murray* and *Huntly* compeared, there being a Gentleman of the name of *Gordoun* killed with a fhot out of the houfe of *Tarnua* by the Earl of *Murray*. Both the parties being come ftrong to Court, were commanded to keep their Lodgings, for preventing of trouble before their compearing. When his Majefty was advifed by the Chancellour what to do in reference to that matter, then his Majefty propofed the fame to the Council; to wit, three points, either prefent Agreement to be made, or Warding both the Earls, or Caution to be taken of both; then to fend home the one, and hold the other ftill at Court for a while. His Majefty following forth this Propofition, declared firft, That the parties could not be agreed, becaufe of the hot blood of the Laird of *Cluny*, *Gordoun*'s Brother lately flain. Concerning Warding, he alledged, That the Caftle of *Edinburgh* had enough of prifoners already; that the Abby was not a fit Prifon for Noblemen: So that it would be fitteft to take Caution of them both, and to hold them fundry; to fend home the one, and retain the other at Court for a feafon. The Chancellour was of that opinion, and fundry others who ufed to depend upon fuch who had the chief handling. Then his Majefty commanded me to tell my Opinion, which was different from this: I advifed prefent agreement, fuppofing that the Earl of *Huntly* for his Majefties pleafure, and in obedience to his command, would not refufe to compound the matter by a prefent up-taking, feeing he was come fo great a journy with his Lady and whole Houfhold, to remain all Winter at *Edinburgh*. At this the Chancellour took me up ntingly, faying, that the Earl of *Huntly* would tarry at Court all

that

that day till to morrow, and would part no fooner ; for he had promifed to the faid Earl that advantage over his Enemy, albeit I knew the Earl's intention was to tarry all Winter at Court. The *Juftice Clark* was of my judgment, but faid, that it appeared his Majefty with the Chancellour had already concluded to fend *Huntly* home, and keep the other at Court. So foon as *Huntly* went home, wanting his competitor, he triumphed and took fundry advantages upon the Earl of *Murray*'s Land, giving the Earl juft occafion of complaint, and getting no redrefs, he retired himfelf from the Court, and became fo malecontent, that he took plain part with the Earl of *Bothwel*, who was ftill upon his enterprizes.

The Earl of *Huntly* being advertifed that his Adverfary was an Out-law with the Earl of *Bothwel*, he returned again to Court, to get yet fome advantage upon him. But in the mean time the Lord *Ochiltrie* endeavoured to agree them by confent of his Majefty. He drew the Earl of *Murray* to *Dunibirfil* to be near hand, that Conditions and Articles might be added, and paired at the pleafure of their friends. The Earl of *Huntly* being alfo made privy to his coming to *Dunibirfil*, obtained incontinently a Commiffion (appearing therein to do his Majefty acceptable Service) to purfue by Fire and Sword the Earl of *Bothwel*, and all his partakers. Little knew his Majefty , that under this general, he was minded to affail the Earl of *Murray* at his own houfe, to kill him, as he did to the regret of many. But the Lord *Ochiltrie* took fuch a defpight that his friend was fo flain under communing, as he alleadged, that he took plain part with the Earl of *Bothvel*, and fo did divers others in revenge of his quarrel, incouraging the faid Earl to affail his Majefty within his Palace of *Falkland*, having divers in Court familiar enough with his Majefty upon the faid confpiracy with him, whofe Council his Majefty followed moft. So that they drew him into a Net to abide ftill in *Falkland*, notwithftanding of the many fure advertifements that had been made unto him. Such hath been his Majefty's hard fortune in many fuch ftraits.

The few number who were faithful to, and careful of his Majefty, counfelled him after the firft advertifement, to pafs the *Coupar*, and Convene with all poffible diligence the Barons of *Fiffe* for his defence. But fuch as fought his wrack, perfwaded him to tarry and delay; alledging that they had fure advertifement, that the Earl of *Lauthian* would not come out of *Lauthian*, till fuch a day, which would have been two dayes longer and behind the day which he kept ; for he came to *Falkland* two dayes fooner. This advice was given, that his Majefty might be furprized before he could either enter within the Tower of *Falkland*, or be provided with any forces to defend him. And becaufe they knew my Brother and me to be careful for him, they advifed his Majefty to fend us home to our houfes that fame night, that we underftood the Earl of *Bothwel* would be there, and had fo told his Majefty, but he believed his abufers better. We gave his Majefty counfel to ride quietly to *Bambrigh*, that there he might when he pleafed take a Boat and goe over to *Angus*, where he would have leifure to Convene the Towns of *Pearth* and *Dundie*; and the Countrey thereabouts. But this advice was alfo overthrown, by thofe who were upon the contrary part.   D d   Thus

Thus we being commanded by his Majefty to ride home, and to warn the Countrey in cafe he were befieged within the Tower, we obeyed. My Brother that fame night, by the way, was advertifed by one of the Earl of *Bothvel's* company, that he was already in *Fiffe*, and would be in *Falkland* againft Supper time. Upon which advertifement he fent his Gentleman called *Robert Anflock*, to acquaint his Majefty therewith, and to requeft him to enter within the Tower in due time. When the faid *Robert* declared the matter unto his Majefty, they all laughed him to fcorn, calling him a Fool. The faid *Robert* returning malecontent to be fo mocked, met the Earl of *Bothvel* and his Company upon the heighth of the *Lummonds*, when it was already dark night, and turned incontinently, as if he had been one of their Company. He ufed great diligence to be firft at his Majefty. Entring within the Palace of *Falkland*, he clofed the Gates himfelf, and cryed continually to caufe his Majefty enter within the Tower, who at length believed him, and mocked him no more.

The Earl of *Bothvel* at his coming had Potards to break up Gates and Doors. It was not without ground alleadged, that fome of thofe who fhot out of the Tower for his Majefties defence, charged their Culverins with Paper. But fome of his Majefties Houfhold Officers fhot out Bullets, which gave the Earl and his Company a great fcare ; as alfo his being within the Tower before he was furprized. And fuppofing that the Countrey would gather together, the faid Earl and his Company retired, and fled, none purfuing them : Whereas a few might eafily have overtaken, and overthrown them. That fame night I lay in my Boots upon my Bed, expecting word from *Falkland*, where there was one left to be ready for that effect. At whofe back-coming, I with other friends and neighbours, did ride to Convene the Countrey about *Coupar*, to have refcued his Majefty. But the King immediately fent me advertifement, that the Earl was fled, yet he defired me to bring thefe forward, whom he knew I would Convene for his relief, as they did to the number of 3000 that afternoon. Thus God miraculoufly delivered his Majefty as he had done divers times before.

About this time came to his Majefty an honeft Gentleman from *Ireland*, called   who made offers of confequence to his Majefty. Whereof the Queen of *England* was incontinenly advertifed, and defired to require the faid Gentleman to be delivered to her. Which the moft part of the Council, counfelled his Majefty to do. But the *Juftice Clark*, my Brother, and I, were of a contrary opinion. Which deed did great harm to the fettlement of his Majefty's Affairs in *England* and *Ireland*. This I fpeak with great regrate, becaufe it was fo far againft his Majefties own mind, and yet he fuffered it to be done, becaufe the chief Ring-leaders advifed it, who have been alwayes won to the devotion of *England*.

Now the Prince being born at *Sterling*, the   day of   in the year   his Majefty thought fit to fend Ambaffadours to *England*, *Denmark*, *France* and *Flanders*, to require their Ambaffadours to be fent to the Baptifm of the Prince his firft-born Son. The Council were commanded to nominate fuch as were meeteft to be fent on that meffage, as they did. Yet fome obtained that Commiffion miſſion, who were very unmeet for that Errand, as Sir *William Keith*, for he could neither ſpeak *Latine*, *French* nor *Flemings*. The Laird of *Eaſter Weems* procured to carry the Commiſſion to *France*, and alſo to *England*, becauſe he was to go thither about his own Affairs, being the King of *France* his Servant. But Mr. *Peter Young* ſped beſt, who ſent to *Denmark*, and to the Dukes of *Mecklburg*, and *Brunſwick*, for he got three fair Chains. But the King of *France*, nor the Queen of *England* gave nothing ; which they would have been engaged to do, if Ambaſſadors had been ſent to them expreſs. Neither ſent the King any Ambaſſadors here at that time. The Queen of *England* was once reſolved to have done the ſame, till ſhe was advertiſed by her own Ambaſſadour in *France*, that the King was reſolved to ſend none. Then very late ſhe ſent the Earl of *Suffex*, to let us ſee that ſhe would ever be a ready Friend, when *France* would refuſe and lye back. On the other part the Dukes of *Mecklburg* and *Brunſwick* were diſcontent that they were ſo far ſlighted, as not each of them to be thought worthy of an Expreſs. A ſpecial day was appointed for Solemnizing the ſaid Baptiſm. The Ambaſſadors of *Denmark* and *Dutchland* arrived almoſt together. His Majeſty had ſent for me to be there at their coming to receive them, and to entertain them. But the Ambaſſadours of *Mecklburg* and *Brunſwick*, would not ride out of *Leeth* in company with the *Daniſh* Ambaſſadour, when they were Convoyed up to *Edinburgh*, but deſired a Convoy apart.

A few dayes after them, arrived the Ambaſſadours of the Eſtates of the Low-Countreys, to wit, *Monſieur de Broderod*, and *Monſieur Fulk* great Treaſurer of *Holland* and *Zeland*, who landed at *New-haven* : where I was well accompanyed to receive them, having Horſe and Footmantles in readineſs to carry them up to *Edinburgh* to their Lodgings.

A little before the landing of the ſaid Ambaſſadours the day of the Baptiſm was delayed, becauſe there was neither word of an Ambaſſadour from *France*, or *Ireland*, and the King's Chappel in the Caſtle of *Sterling* which was caſt down to be built again in a better form, was not yet compleated. So that the Ambaſſadours were ordered to remain in *Edinburgh* till all might be put in good order. Therefore his Majeſty appointed the Maſter of his Houſhold, and my Lord *Tungland*, my Brother, together with me, to entertain them upon his charges, and alſo to bear them company. After that they had tarried longer in *Edinburgh* (there being no appearance of any Ambaſſadours from *France* or *England*) we were commanded with ſome others of the Council to Convoy them to *Sterling*, where his Majeſty made his excuſe that they were ſo long delayed at *Edinburgh* But they alledged, they had great contentment in our company. Which his Majeſty forgot not to declare before the whole Council, giving me thanks, alledging, that I had done him good Offices, and this among the reſt, which he would never forget, and that he had three other of my Brothers all fit for ſuch matters, and for forreign Affairs.

Now being in doubt of the *Engliſh* Ambaſſadour's, the Ceremony was to be Solemnized without longer delay. In the mean time, there came word that the Earl of *Suffex* was upon his journey toward *Scotland*, for the Queen his Miſtreſs, on whom the action ſtayed. The

day of the Solemnity, there was great bufinefs for their Honours and
Seats, that being agreed, there was an empty Chair fet before the reft
for the King 'of *France* his Ambaffadour. The order of the Banquet and
Triumph I leave to others to fet out.

When the Ambaffadours had Audience of the Queens Majefty, I
was appointed to ftand a little behind, and next unto her Majefty.
To the *Englifh*, *Danifh*, and *Dutch* Ambaffadours, her Majefty made
anfwer her felf. But though fhe could fpeak feemingly *French*, yet
fhe rounded in my Ear, to declare her anfwer to the Ambaffadour
of the States of *Holland*. Then every one of them by order, gave
their Prefents. The Jewels of Precious Stones the Queen received
in her own hand, and then delivered them unto me to put them
again in their Cafes, and lay them upon a Table which was prepared in the mids of the Chamber to fet them upon. The Queen of
England's had a great fhow, being a fair Cupboard of Silver over-
guilt, cunningly wrought, and fome Cups of maffy Gold. The Ambaffadour of the States prefented a Golden Box, wherein was written
in Parchment in Letters of Gold, A gift of a yearly Penfion to the
Prince of five thoufand   by year, with great Cups of maffy
Gold, two efpecially, which were fo weighty, that it was all that I
could lift them, and fet them down upon the faid Table. I leave it
to others to fet down the weight and value. But I fay thefe which
were of Gold, which fhould have been kept in ftore to pofterity,
were foon melted, and difpofed: But if they had been preferved, as
they ought to have been, thofe who advifed to break them would have
wanted their part.

All thefe Ambaffadours being difpatched, and well rewarded, thofe
of *Denmark* were advifed by *John Lindfay* of *Monmuire* to caufe with
all diligence fend new Ambaffadours, to require the Contraft of marriage made in *Denmark* to be fulfilled : Alledging that the Chancellour who had made it, had left out the Rents of the Abby of *Dumfarmling* fraudfully, and had taken in fee to himfelf, all the Lordfhip of *Muffilburgh*. For this end two Ambaffadours were fent from
Denmark, upon whom I was appointed to attend, to fee them well
entertained. As they were well inftrufted, fo they happened upon a
meet time, for the Chancellour was for the time decourted, and my
Brother was Ambaffadour for his Majefty in *England*. So the Chancellour was caufed to renounce his part. And becaufe my Brother
Sir *Robert* was abfent, young Sir *Robert* his Son, and I, obliged us that
his part, which was 13 Chalders of Victual fhould be alfo renounced
at his return, which was accordingly done. His Majefty promifed
to him as much heritage in another part, in refpeft that his gift was
obtained long before the Contraft of marriage. Divers others who
had portions of thefe Lands, were likewife compelled to renounce, either voluntarily, or by a new Law made for that effeft.

F I N I S.

Alphabetical Table

OF THE

Principal M A T T E R contained in this B O O K.

A

ABbot *of* Dumfarmling *is fent by the King's Lords to meet the Earl of* Lennox *in his paſſage to* England, *p.* 106. *His Meſſage to the Queen, and her Anſwer thereunto,* ibid. *Haſtens to the King at St.* Andrews, *where he behaves himſelf with great diſſimulation,* 135. *Endeavours by Gold to curry favour with Colonel* Stuart, 137. *Is after Impriſoned in* Lockleven, *ibid.*

Admiral *of* France *his death conſpired by Captain* Charry, *p.* 38. *but being diſcovered is killed by Monſieur* Chattelier, *ibid.*

Ambaſſadors *ſent from* Denmark, *three joined together in commiſſion to King* James, *arrive in* Scotland, *p.* 162. *Their Commiſſion and Demands, ill uſage and delayes, viſited by Mr.* Wotton, *who was very kind to them,* ibid. *Upon his inſtigation they inform his Majeſty of Reflections upon their Maſter by his Subjects, and of their rudeneſs, p.* 163. *The Ambaſſadors ſlight the Earl of* Arran, *having known him in* Denmark *but a private Soldier,* ibid. *Are Banquetted in his Majeſties name,* 165. *Take leave of his Majeſty,* 166. *Part well ſatisfied after they had received their Preſents on Ship-board from the hands of the Author* James Melvil, *p.* 167. *Promiſing to be good inſtruments of Amity,* ibid.

Ambaſſadours *arrive in* Scotland *from ſeveral parts upon the birth of Prince* Henry, *p.* 202. *Their ſeveral rich Preſents to the Queen at that time, p.* 204. *Are all diſpatcht and well rewarded,* ibid.

Areskine Alexander, *the Governour of King* James *during his Minority,* p. 125. *Is made Maſter of* Mar, *p.* 126.

Arran *Earl, ſee* James Stuart.

Athol *Earl, made Chancellour,* p. 126. *Hath* 1000 *men ready to take St.* Johnſtoun, *but being diſuaded from it by the Author, deſires him to write to his Majeſty for a Licenſe for him and his to remain at home, p.* 169 *Which he did, and procur'd for him,* ibid. *Is written unto to come to the Parliament at* Lithgow, *p.* 170.

Atry *Lord, Uncle to the Earl of* Marſhal *nominated by the King's Council to go Ambaſſadour to* Denmark *with the Author to Treat about the King's Marriage,* p. 177. *Comes to Court, but finds the Council not ſo earneſt as his Majeſty,* p. 177, *and* 178. *Returns home, excuſing himſelf as ſickly and Aged,* p. 178.

Aubonie *Lord, returns from* France, *p.* 127. *Being the King's Favourite,* ibid. *is made Lord* Dalkeith, *and after Duke of* Lennox, 128. *A ſhort Character of him,* ibid. *led by evil Counſel to dangerous courſes.*

courfes, p. 131. *Underſtanding that his Majeſty was in the hands of the other Lords he retires to* Dumbartoun, *p.* 132. *Paſſeth through* England *to* France, *p.* 133. *And dies ſhortly after*, ibid.

B

BAlfour *Sir* James, *Captain of* Edinburgh *Caſtle*, p. 81. *delivers the Caſtle of* Edinburgh *to the Laird of* Grange, *p.* 90. *Is taken out of his own Houſe , and committed by the Regent's order*, p. 100. *Wins the Regent's familiars with Gold, p.* 102.

Balnears Henry *turns from the Proteſtant to the Popiſh Religion, p.* 7. *And by the perſwaſion of Abbot* Pally *breaks the intended Match between Prince* Edward *and* Mary *Queen of* Scots, *ibid.*

Barnbarrow *Laird, ſent Ambaſſadour upon the Author's refuſal*, p. 176. *Returns with his Fellow-Commiſſioner, their Power er being inſufficient, having no Commiſſion to conclude*, ibid.

Baſſingtoun, *a Learned Scotsman and Travellour, his Story concerning the Affairs of* England *and* Scotland, *p.* 92.

Baſtien, *a French-man, at the Banquet after the Baptiſm of King* James, *deviſed a Machine that gave great diſtaſte and diſturbance, p.* 76, *and* 77.

Beaton David *Cardinal, makes King* James *the Fifth's Will when dying, which he dictated, which was therefore annulled, p.* 6. *is ſlain in his Caſtle at St.* Andrews, *p.* 7. *by the complotting of Sir* George Douglas, &c. *ibid.*

Bedford *Earl, one of Queen* Mary's *ſureſt Friends in* England, *p.* 76. *Arrives in* Scotland *with ſeveral other Perſons of Quality*, ibid. *departs, and they are all rewarded,* 77. *deſires the Author to beſeech*

the Queen to entertain the King as formerly, and not to ſlight him, ibid.

Bettancourt *Maſter of the Houſhold to the Queen Regent of* Scotland, *brings inſtructions to deſtroy* Hereticks, p. 24. *which ſhe obſerves being menaced*, ibid.

Biſhop *of St.* Andrews *deſigned Ambaſſadour for* England, *p.* 194. *Diſdained and diſhonoured in* England, *p.* 150. *The reaſon,* ibid. *Is nominated to be ſent Ambaſſadour to* Denmark, *p.* 176.

Biſhop Thomas, *a* Scotſman, *ſends a Letter from* England *to the Authour about the report of the Queen's marriage with her Husband's Murtherer, together with his Character, diſſwading her from it, p.* 79. *Which he ſhew'd the Queen, and was forced to flie for't,* ibid.

Bothwel Adam, *Biſhop of* Orkny, *p.* 84.

Bothwel *Earl, is ſent by the Queen to clear the Borders of Thieves upon the departure of thoſe that attended the Prince's Baptiſm, p.* 77. *He and Earl* Huntly *attempt the ſlaughter of the Earl of* Murry, *but were prevented*, ibid. *Is ſuſpected of ſome enterpriſe againſt the King, p.* 78. *The Earl of* Orkny *tells him, it would coſt him his life if he ſtayed at* Edinburgh, *ibid. Lays a Train of Powder and blows up the King's Lodgings,* ibid. *Upon a rumour of his murthering the King he calls an Aſſize of Lords, and is acquitted*, ibid. *He with a great company ſeizeth the Queen,* p. 80. *A number of Noblemen meet at* Edinburgh, *and declare it is the Queen's intereſt to marry him, which he did, having at that time the Lord* Huntly's *Siſter to* Wife, ibid. *Intends to kill Secretary* Lidington *in the Queen's Chamber, which had been effected, had not the Queen interpoſed, being married, he was very earneſt to get the young Prince into his hands,* ibid. *Flies from* Edinburgh

The Table

burgh, *and takes the Queen with him wherever he goes*, p. 82. *Convenes a great number of his Friends against the Lords, resolving to fight them*, ibid. *Challengeth to fight any one that would maintain he murthered the King, but refuseth the* Lord Grange *and* Tallibardine, *because but Barons*, p. 83. *Then the* Lord Lindsay *offered the Combat, but he coldly declin'd it*, ibid. *Flies to the Castle of* Dunbar, *and from thence to* Sheatland, p. 84. *Is pursued by two Ships of the Lord* Grange's, *and he saved himself in a little Boat*, p. 85. *Flies to* Denmark, *is kept there close Prisoner, and dies mad and miserable*, ibid.

Bothwel *and others endeavour to take the King and keep him*, p. 175. *but fail in their Enterprise*, ibid. *Labour with the King to send Sir* John Seatoun *to* Spain, *ibid.*

Bothwel Francis, *accused of a design against his Majesty; Wards himself in the Castle of* Edinburgh, *p.* 194. *Desiring to be Tried for the same*, ibid. *Escapes over the Castlewall, and retires to* Caithnesse, *p.* 195. *Is sent for by some male-contents, who design'd to take the King and kill the Chancellour*, p. 196. *With whom he joyn'd and headed them*, ibid. *He with others enters into the King's Palace by night*, ibid. *Their proceedings therein*, p. 197. *Steals away quietly, but kills* John Shaw *Master Stabler to his Majesty, and his Brother*, ibid. *He and his Party makes a second attempt on his Majesty in* Falkland, p. 202. *but finding resistance, he and his Company fled*, ibid.

Bowes Mr. *Ambassadour Resident at* Edinburgh *from Queen* Elizabeth, *p.* 142. *Attends upon* Walsingham *when he first received Audience*, p. 147. *A long time Resident in* Scotland, p. 150. *Informs the* English *of the Bishop of St.* Andrews *Qualities, when he was sent* Ambassadour *to Queen* Elizabeth, ibid.

Broderade *Monsieur, and* Monsieur Fulke *sent Ambassadours to* Scotland, *from the States of* Holland, *and arrives there upon the birth of the Prince*, p. 203.

Buchanan *Master to King* James, p. 125. *His Character*, ibid.

Buccleugh Laird, *Wife, True, Stout and Modest*, p. 113.

Burleigh *Lord, see* Cecil.

C

Cairo Mr. *Queen* Elizabeths *Cousin*, P. 141.

Calis *promised to be restored to* England *after the loss of St.* Quintins, p. 22, *and* 23.

Caraffe Cardinal, *sent Legat to* France *from the Pope*, p. 19. *The ground of his Embassy*, ibid. *Is strangled by Pope* Pius *the* 4th, p. 20. *And why*, ibid.

Cardanus *an Italian Magician, Cures the Bishop of St.* Andrews *of his Distemper*, p. 14.

Caprintoun Laird, *the Earl of* Arran's *Uncle, is sent by his Majesty to reprove the Earl*, p 155.

Carmichael James, Minist. *of* Hadingtoun *writes the History of those Tricks the Devil play'd in* Scotland, p. 195. *And the whole deposition of the Witnesses upon the acount of the Earl of* Bothwel, ibid.

Carmichael Laird, *laments to the Author the ingratitude of the Regent of* Scotland, Mortoun, p. 124. *Follows the Authors Counsel, and becomes a great Courtier*, p. 125. *But proves afterwards ingratefull to the Author, who promoted him*, ibid. *Is made Captain of the Guards to King* James, p. 199. *Boasts that he would kill Sir* Robert Melvil, ibid.

Casimire Duke, *Second Son to the Elector* Palatine, *is about the* Contract-

Contracting a Marriage with the Duke of Lorrain's *Eldest Sister,* p. 31. *But proved ineffectual,* ibid. *The reason thereof,* p. 32. *Finding no probabilty of a Match with* Queen Elizabeth, *he Marries the Elector of* Saxonies *Eldest Daughter,* p. 40. Cavatius *the Learned Mathematical Tutor of the Bishop of* Valence, *is imprisoned by the* French King, p. 13. *The reason why,* ibid.

Cecil *Secretary, promiseth rewards to* Ruxby *by Letter, but it was discovered to the Queen,* p. 69. *Pretends to be her friend, is the first person that whispered to her the News of the Birth of the Prince,* ibid. *Informes the Queen that the Duke of* Norfolk *was come to Court, and that she should seize him, which was done accordingly,* p. 99. *and* 100. *Created afterward Lord Burleigh, and causeth* Dallison *to be sent Agent into* Scotland, p. 157. *Is discontented that* Walsingham *was too precise and would not confer with the Earl of* Arran, ibid.

Charles *the* 9th *of* France *suceeds* Francis *the Second,* p. 29.

Chattellerault *imprisoned in* Edinburgh Castle, p. 101. *Set at liberty through the mediation of the* Lord Grange.

Clergy *of* Scotland *use their utmost endeavours to prevent the interview of* Henry *the* 8, *and his Nephew* King James *the* 5th *of* Scotland, p. 2.

Clark Alexander, *Provost of* Edinburgh, p. 129.

Cockburn Sir Richard, *Secretary to* King James, p. 198.

Colvil John, *and* Colonel Steward *are sent to the Convention at* St. Andrews, *and return,* p. 133. *Disagree in their Commission,* ibid. Colvil *and others imprisoned,* p. 137.

Constable *of* France *entertains the Author with design to promote him,* p. 15. *Is sent with* 16000 *Men to keep the* Spaniard *from entring upon*

the Frontiers of France, p. 20. *His Discourse and Passion with an Enthusiast who Fore-told his Misfortune,* ibid. *His Noble and Resolute Answer to the Master of his Horse, who advised him to fly,* p. 21. *He being overthrown by a Party of* Spaniards, *and his Men all slain desired to be kill'd, but was shot in the Thigh and taken Prisoner,* p. 22. *Is Commanded by* Francis *the Second,* King *of* France *to retire,* p. 28. *Yet still offers to retain the Author in his Service, which he accepts,* ibid. *Is sent for to Court, but delays coming, and in the mean time the* French King *dies, and then he Posts to Court like the Constable of* France, *Commanding all the Guards,* p. 29. *The Duke of* Guise *and the Cardinal his Brother are Commanded out of Town, and the Constable is kindly received by the Queen-Mother,* p. 29, *and* 30.

A Convention is appointed for ordering his Majesties Affairs after his return from Denmark, p. 184. *But few of the Nobility appear there, being slighted at the Queens Coronation as they supposed,* ibid. *Reformation is designed by this Convention, but nothing performed,* ibid.

Condingknows Laird, *is made Captain of the Castle of* Edinburgh p. 174. *Desires a Commission to go* Ambassador *for* England, *but is denyed,* ibid.

The Council of England *conclude to take away the life of* Mary Queen *of* Scotland, *Prisoner in* England, p. 171. *Falsly alledging that She practiced against the State,* p. 172. *Think fit to secure his Majesty in* Scotland, *in the hands of the Banished Lords; that so they might seek his life, or keep him a perpetual Prisoner, but herein prove defeated,* ibid. *Fall down upon their knees with many of the Nobility, Alledging that her life as well as their lives and fortunes was in hazard, by rea-*

son

son of the practife of Queen Mary, ibid. *Received the Summons. from Secretary* Davifon, *and give her warning to prepare for Death the Night before,* ibid.

A Council Conven'd about the diffention of feveral Lords, p. 200.

De Crook Monfieur, *is fent Ambaffador to the French King from* Scotland, *with a Letter about the foulnefs of the Murther of their King,* p. 82. *Receives an Anfwer from the Lords. with a refolution to ufe all diligence to detect the Murtherers,* ibid.

Crauford *Captain, Accufeth Secretary* Lidington *of the Murther of the late King of* Scots, p. 100. *He being at that time Servant to the Earl of* Lennox, *Alledging his Commiffion for fo doing from the faid Earl his Mafter,* p. 110.

Crauford Lord, *is Committed to the Cuftody of the Lord* Hamiltoun, p. 170.

Cunningham James *Captain, a difcreet Men, Servant to the Lord of* Marr *then Regent in* Scotland, p. 115.

D

DArnly, *Son to the Earl of* Lennox, *a Handfom, Beardlefs, Lady-fac'd Man,* p. 48. *Procures a Licenfe from the Queen of* England *to go to* Scotland, p. 53. *His intention therein,* ibid. *Propofeth a Marriage to Queen* Mary, *who refufeth a Ring he prefented to her,* p. 56. *which the Queen feems to difrelifh,* ibid. *Becomes acquainted with* Rixio, *who was his great Friend to the Queen of* Scots, ibid. *Finds the Queen cold in her favours, after her confinement upon the murther of* Rixio, p. 66. *Follows the Queen (though flighted) whitherfoever fhe went,* p. 77. *Goes to* Glafcow, *falls fick, being fufpected to have poifon given him by a*

Servant of his own, ibid. *Is brought from thence to* Edinburgh *to recover his health,* p. 78. *Dies, and how,* ibid.

Davifon *is fent Agent into* Scotland, *and afterwards made fecretary to Queen* Elizabeth, p. 157. *Profeffed himfelf a Scot,* ibid. *Remains at* Coupar *till he had Audience, which he had at* Falkland, ibid. *But proves deceitful,* p. 158. *Returns to* England, ibid. *Receives the written Summons for the Execution of Queen* Mary, *with a ftrict charge not to deliver it without her exprefs Command,* p. 172. *But being deceived by the Council of* England *delivers it,* ibid. *For which he is Committed to the Tower by Queen* Elizabeth, *for difobeying her orders upon that account,* p. 175.

Dingual Lord, *is fent to King* James *for a Licenfe to return, or a Commiffion to conclude the Match with* Denmark, p. 179. *Finds his Maiefty at* Aberdeen, *the Chancellour and moft part of the Council being abfent,* p. 180. *So that he obtained a full power to conclude the faid Match,* ibid.

Dofel Monfieur, *Lieutenant in* Scotland *for the French King,* p. 24. *a paffionate Man,* p. 25.

Douglas Archibald, *is cleanfed of the late King's murther in* Scotland, p. 174. *Frequents the Court familiarly,* ibid. *returns to* England *to remain Ambaffador there,* ibid. *Hath great reputation with* Mary Queen *of* Scotland, *yet injureth her Caufe in* England, *and is difcharged of his Embaffy upon the Arrival of Sir* Robert Melvil *in* England, ibid.

Douglas George, *the Natural Son of the Lord* Angus *enters the King's Clofet with the Lord* Ruthven, *the Queen being prefent, and with the Kings Dagger ftruck him,* p. 64. *And afterwards drew him into the outer Hall, and kill'd him,*

E e   p. 65.

p. 65. *Conveys the Queen to Lock-leven as a Captive to the King's Lords,* p. 90. *Hath the House of the Castle delivered to him,* p. 121.

Douglas *Sir* George, *desires to have the Commission for Ambassadour to* Spain, *p.* 175. *But is denied,* ibid.

Douglas James, *the Natural Son of the Earl of* Mortoun, p. 127. *Kills the Earl of* Arran *in Revenge of his Uncle's death, the Earl of* Mortoun, 260.

Drake *Sir* Francis, *by a Stratagem of a Ship full of Powder with a burning Link, fires the* Spanish *Navy, and discomfits them,* p. 176.

Drumhasel *Laird, Master of King* James *his Houshold when young,* p. 125. *Draws the Earl of* Arguile *and* Athol *to* Sterling, p. 126. *Is discharged out of Court;* ibid. *Assures the Earl of* Grange, *that the Duke of* Lennox *designed to kill him,* p. 131. *though it prov'd false,* p. 133. *Is imprison'd by the procurement of the Earl of* Arran *and his Lady,* p. 137.

Du Bartas *Monsieur, famous for his French* Poesie, *arrives at* Scotland, p. 176. *Proposeth a marriage with the King of* Scots *and the Princess of* Navarre, *ibid. Resides at* Falkland *with the King,* p. 177.

Dundee *Earl, is sent one of the Ambassadors to* Denmark *about the King's marriage,* p. 179.

Dudly, *Lord* Robert, *afterward made Earl of* Leicester, *is proposed by Mr.* Randolph, *as a fit Match for* Mary Queen *of* Scotland, p. 40.

E

After Weems, *Laird, goes with a Commission to* England, *and* France, p. 103. *Is a Pensioner to the French King,* ibid.

Elizabeth *Queen of* England *sends Instructions to Mr.* Randolf, *her Ambassadour in* Scotland, *to pro-pose the Lord* Robert Dudly, *as a fit Match for* Mary Queen *of* Scotland; p. 40. *Disrelisheth the proposal of a Match between Queen* Mary *and* Charles *the Arch-Duke of* Austria, p. 41. *which appears by her sending the Earl of* Sussex *to the Emperor's Court to draw on the marriage of the Arch-Duke with her self,* ibid. *This occasion'd grudges between the two Queens of* England *and* Scotland, p. 42. *She designs* Darnly *for Queen* Mary's *Husband,* ibid. *Creates the Lord* Robert Dudly *Earl of* Leicester, *and Baron of* Denbigh, p. 47. *Is Distemper'd with a Fever, insomuch that her life was question'd,* p. 67. *Disturbed at the Birth of the Prince, Queen* Mary's *Son,* p. 69. *Yet promiseth to be Gossip to him by proxy of Lords and Ladies,* p. 70. *Upon her fair promises Queen* Mary *flies to* England, *but she would not see her, though she often desired it,* p. 92. *Causeth her to be kept Prisoner till she lost her life, after a tedious confinement,* ibid. *Is Reproached by the Ambassadors of Foreign Princes, for her unprincely dealing with Queen* Mary, p. 93. *Having obtained her desires upon the Accusation of Queen* Mary, *received great content, having now matter sufficient to shew Foreign Ambassadours why she detained the Queen,* p. 97. *Is glad of the Queen's dishonour, yet sends privately to comfort her upon her false Accusation,* ibid. *Her Answer to the Abbot of* Dumfarmling *upon his Proposition,* p. 106. *Sends an Ambassadour to the King of* Scots, *when confin'd, offering him her Assistance,* p. 132. *Sends a short Letter to King* James, p. 139. *The Contents thereof,* p. 140. *Receives intelligence of a Magnificent Embassy from* Denmark *to* Scotland, p. 161. *by Three Ambassadours with a splendid Train,* ibid. *Upon which she sends* Wotton *to* Scot-

The Table

land *to difturb the Affairs of that.*
Kingdom, ibid. *Is intreated by the*
Council and Nobility to take away
the life of Queen Mary, *p.* 172.
which at firft fhe refufeth, but af-
terwards condefcends to, ibid. *Purg-*
eth her felf of the Death of Queen
Mary *as being deceived by her Coun-*
cil and Mr. Secretary Davifon, *p.*
175. *Is fent to for confent to the*
Marriage of King James *with the*
Daughter of the King of Denmark,
and returns her Anfwer, p. 179. *Say-*
ing, She would employ her Credit
with the King & Princefs of Navarre,
to bring his Marriage with that Prin-
cefs to pafs, idid. *Sends the Earl of*
Suffex *Ambaffador to* Scotland, *and*
upon that account, p. 203.

Elphingftoun Nicholas, *advifeth*
the Regent Mortoun *that he was in*
disfavour with the King, and ought
by Gold to purchafe friends, p. 125.

Emanuel *Duke of* Savoy, *leads*
the Spanifh Army that Invades
France, *p.* 201.

Emperor *of* Germany *retires to*
a Monaftery of Monks in Spain, *p.*
18. *Endeavours to get his Son* Philip *Elected Emperor, but is denyed,*
ibid. *Gives him all the Dominions he*
had in Spain, Italy, *and the Low-*
Countries, p. 19. *Labours for a Trea-*
ty with France *for 5 years, which*
was agreed and fworn to, but broken
by the Popes perfuafion, ibid.

Enig, *the Dutch word, admits of*
Two divers interpretations, which
was difputed by the Emperor, &c.
p. 12.

F

FErdinand *King of* Bohemia, *Bro-*
ther to the Emperor Philip *and*
Arch-Duke of Auftria, *Elected Em-*
peror by the Princes, p. 19.

Fernthaft *Laird, warden of the*
Borders on the Scots *fide,* p. 166.
Marries to the Earl of Arran's
Brothers Daughter, ibid.

Fofter *Sir* John, *warden, a ftrange*
trick of his Steed, that mounted and
hurt Mary *Queen of* Scots, *when*
difcourfing with him, p. 77.

Francis *the 2d Dauphin of* France
Married to Queen Mary *of* Scotland,
p. 8. *Succeedes his Father* Henry *the*
2d, p. 28. *Is wholly guided by the*
Duke of Guife, *and Cardinal* Lor-
iain, ibid. *Raifeth Men to fend into*
Scotland, *p.* 29. *Dies at* Orleans *in*
France, *ibid.*

Frederick *King of* Denmark, *his*
Genealogie related by the Author to
King James, *when he had Three*
Ambaffadors joyned in one Commiffi-
on in Scotland, *p.* 165. *Hath feve-*
ral fair Daughters, p. 167.

G

GAury *Earl, Treafurer of* E-
dinburgh, *p.* 129. *Intercedes*
for the life of the Duke of Lennox,
p. 132. *Keeps the Earl of* Arran
in Cuftody, p. 133. *Repents his be-*
ing drawn in by Drumhafel. *to joyn*
with the Lords that were againft the
King, ibid. *But at* St. Andrews
he turns to the Lords of the Kings
Party, p. 136. *Treats his Maiefty*
Royally at the Houfe of Ruthven,
p. 137. *Begs his Majefties Pardon*
and obtains it, ibid. *Is driven from*
Court by the Earl of Arran, *but re-*
conciled to him, p. 142. *Yet condi-*
tions being unperform'd, he refolves
to leave the Country, ibid. *Obtains his*
Majefties confent to depart, the faid
Earl of Arran *proving his mortal E-*
nemy, p. 155. *Before he goes takes*
part with the Earl of Angus *and*
others in their defign to take Sterling *in defpight of the faid Earl,*
ibid. *Is taken Prifoner in that en-*
terprize, p. 156. *Is near of Kin to*
his Majefty, hath his Lands feized,
and is Executed on the Scaffold, dy-
ing a devout Chriftian, ibid.

E e 2 Gordoun

The Table

Gordoun *a Gentleman of that name, is kill'd by the Earl of* Mur-ray, *p.* 200.

Graham Richard, *hath a familiar Spirit, p.* 195. *Is brought to* Edinburgh *and examined before his Majesty about the Earl of* Bothwel, *and burnt with other Malefactors,* ibid.

Grange *Laird, is Lord Treasurer and Favourite to King* James, *upon the Kings Command alledgeth reasons against the Prelates Proposi-tions, p.* 2, 3, *and* 4. *A stout, bold Man; p.* 4. *Pursues with two Ships* Bothwell, *p.* 184. *But he escapes, and his Servants were taken and the first discoverers of the King's Mur-ther, p.* 185. *Is made Chief of a Company of Horsemen, who came to fight against* Bothwel, *which the Queen understanding, sends for him under surety, p.* 83. *Was like to be kill'd by a Souldier appointed by* Bothwel *for that purpose, but was saved by the Queens crying out,* idid. *Offers to Combat* Bothwel *upon his Challenge, but is coldly refused,* ibid. *Promiseth upon his honour to protect Sir* James Balfour *upon his delive-ry of* Edinburgh Castle *to him, p.* 100. *Offers to fight with Mr.* Archibald Douglas *being guiltless of the Kings Muther,* ibid. *Takes Se-cretary* Lidington *into the Castle of* Edinburg, *p.* 101. *His vertues are envied by some, and his Charge co-veted by others, p.* 104. *Obtains a Warrant from the King's Lords to set the Duke of* Chattellerault *and the Lord* Herreis *at liberty, p.* 105. *Sticks close to the Kings Authority, p.* 108. *Sides at last with the Queens Lords,* ibid. *Sends for the Laird of* Fernihaft *and* Buccleugh, *who resolved to seize on the Lords at* Sterling, *p.* 113. *Which they at-tempted but failed, p.* 114. *La-ments the slaughter of the Earl of* Lennox Regent *of* Scotland, *ibid. Was ever esteemed honest, p.* 119.

Is taken Prisoner after the delivery of Edinburgh Castle *with Sir* Ro-bert Melvil *and* Lidington, *p.* 121. *Is wracked to death, p.* 123. *His Character,* ibid.

Guise *Duke, goes with a great Army into* Italy, *after the breach of the Truce between the Emperor and* French *by the Popes persuasion, p.* 19. *He and the Lieutenant of* Picar-dy *unexpectedly enters on the King of* Spain's *Dominions, p.* 19, *and* 20. *Is killed by* Poltrot *at the Siege of* Orleans, *p.* 35. *For which the Ad-miral of* France *is Accused, p.* 36. *But cleared,* ibid.

H

HAmiltoun *Laird, is advan-ced to be Governour of* Scot-land, *p.* 7. *Induced to resign the Go-vernment to the Queen, p.* 2. *Shoots the Regent* Murray *in his passage to* Lithgow, *p.* 203. *And Escapes,* ibid.

Henry *the* 8th *King of* England, *is discontented at the Popes denial of his Divorce from Queen* Kathe-rine, *and thereupon proclaims him-self Head of the Kirk, discharging St.* Peter's *Pennies here, and the Popes Authority, p.* 1. *Declares his Daughter* Mary *a Bastard,* ibid. *Obtains a Divorce from his own Clergy, and seeks amity with his Nephew* James *the* 5th, *King of* Scot-land, *desiring an interview with him at* York, *ibid. A short Chara-cter of him, p.* 3. *Is highly offended at the disappointment and affront put upon him by King* James *his not meeting him at* York, *that he sent an Army to* Scotland *to destroy it, p.* 5. *Is much afflicted at the death of the King of* Scotland, *and lays down the reasons of his warring with that Nation, p.* 6. *His wrath against the Pope is great,* ibid. *He demolish-eth Abbeys, and compells the Nobi-lity to exchange their Lands for* them,

them, that might never return to the Kirk, ibid. Endeavours a Match between Edward the Sixth his Son, and Mary of Scotland, though it brake off, and caused War between the two Kingdoms, p. 7. But it was at last agreed, ibid.

Henry the Second of France had hot wars with the Emperour, the occasion and management thereof from p .15, to p. 18. Is hurt by the shiver of a Spear, engaging with the Earl of Montegomery at the Justings of his Daughter's Marriage with the King of Spain, p. 28. And dies Eight days after, ibid.

Henry Prince, King James his first Son, born at Sterling, 202.

Herreis Lord, is Imprisoned in the Castle of Edinburgh, p. 101.

Hume George, turns William Kieth out of his place of Master of the Wardrobe, when King James was in Denmark, p. 182. Being Knighted is made Master of the Wardrobe, p. 198.

Hume Lord, takes part with the Hamiltouns and Queens Faction, p. 106. With whom the Regent Mortoun durst not meddle, standing in awe of his Party, p. 122. Dies shortly after, being a Prisoner in Edinburgh Castle, ibid.

Hunsdon Earl, hath a Conference on the Borders with the Earl of Arran, p. 158. Contrives a secret Plot, ibid.

Huntley Earl, is Chief of the new Faction about his Majesty, p. 175. Endeavours to turn out the Master of Gray, and Martland the Chancellor, ibid. Procures the Gift of the Benefice of Dumfarmling, ibid. Great disorders occasioned by the Dissention between him and other Earls, p. 200. Is sent home hereupon, p. 201. Triumphs, and takes advantage of the Earl of Murray's Lands, giving him just cause of Complaint, ibid. Kills the Earl of Murray, ibid.

I

James the Fifth of Scotland his resolute Speech to the Prelates, p. 4. Gives the Ward and Marriage of Kelly in Angus to the second Son of the Lord Grange, ibid. Gives ear to the Clergy to put off the Convention with King Henry the 8th at York, ibid. Is forced to raise an Army to defend his Country upon that account, p. 6. Is much troubled at the Defeat of his Army, and useth severe Language against the Prelates, who fearing his displeasure, poison him with an Italian Poset, ibid. His Character, p. 7.

James Lord Prior of St. Andrews, the Natural Son of James the Fifth, p. 25. Hears of Queen Mary's Resolution to return to Scotland, and goes to France to request it; p. 31. Returns to Scotland to prepare them for her Reception. ibid.

James the Sixth, King, born, p. 69. When of Age he causeth the Heirs of the Lord Grange to be restored, p. 123. Orders his bones to be taken up and honourably buried at Killingborn, ibid. Is brought up at Sterling by Alexander Areskine, and the Lady Mar, p. 125. Hath Four Masters, their Character, ibid. The Earl of Mortoun being deposed, he takes the Government into his own hands, p. 128. Is surprised by the Lords in the House of Huntingtoun, p. 132. Is conveyed afterward to Sterling, and there retained, ibid. Laments his mishandling during that Captivity, ibid. Invites by Letters some of the Nobility to a Convention, p. 133. Goes from Falkland to St. Andrews, some few dayes before the Convention, to the Earl of March, p. 155. Thinks himself there at liberty, ibid. Lodgeth in an old Inn there, ibid. Becomes Master of the Castle, p. 136. And declares

declares his moderate intention to-word all the-Lords, ibid. Orders 4 Lords to retire, and retains the rest as his Council, ibid. Causeth a Proclamation to be made according to his moderate intentions, p. 137. Returns the Author thanks, as the only instrument of procuring his liberty, ibid. Is gently inclined to all the Nobility, and Treated particularly by the Earl of Gaury, ibid. Solicites the Authority to prevail with the Lord Gaury, that the Earl of Arran might come to Court and kiss his hand, p.138. Promising he should not stay there, ibid. Sends a Letter in Answer to Queen Elizabeth's, p. 140. The Contents thereof, p.140, 141, and 142. His Majesty is taken again, p. 142. Gives Secretary Walsingham Audience, p. 147. Sends a Letter to Queen Elizabeth, promising not to bring again the Earl of Arran into Court, p. 148. Is taken at the Road of Ruthven, p. 149. And retain'd Captive, ibid. Takes little care to prevent inconveniences, yet obtains his liberty. ibid. Assures the Author that he would Convene a Council of Lords at Edinburgh, p. 150. His Dream concerning the Earl of Gaury, p. 156. Writes for Melvil the Author to come and advise him, p. 157. As also to come and entertain Wotton, being sent to him by the Queen of England, p. 159. Whom he loved before he saw, by reason of the advantageous Character, which the Master of Gray gave him, idid. Orders the Author to entertain the Danish Ambassadours, 162. And because they were three in Commission wisheth him to choose two more to accompany him, which he did, ibid. Gives them Audience at Dumfarmling, and is much dissatisfied at their ill handling, ibid. Grows impatient to hear the Author speak against Wotton, p. 164. Acquaints the Author that he was in-

formed the King of Denmark's Descent was from Merchants, ibid. But after he was informed of the truth, he sends for the said Ambassadors, p. 165. Promiseth them a speedy dispatch to their satisfaction, ibid. Orders a Banquet for them, is hindred from being present at it, but being informed how matters stood, goes thither and drinks to the King, Queen and Ambassadors of Denmark to their great content, p. 166. causeth their dispatch to be ready according to promise, ibid. Sends to the Earl of Arran for a great Gold Chain which he got from Sir James Balfour, to present it to the Three Ambassadors, which was done accordingly, ibid. Sends to agree with the Banished Lords at their coming to Sterling, p. 169. where it was agreed his Majesty should be in their hands, and no rigour used to those about him, ibid. Calls them Traytors at first, but after grants them a Pardon, ibid. Acknowledgeth the Earl of Arran to have been a bad Minister of State, and that he should never be readmitted to Court, p. 170. Hears the news of his Mothers Execution, which highly displeas'd him, p. 173. Convenes a Parliament desiring the Assistance of his Subjects, ibid. When he at first hears they were about the Conviction of his Mother, he sent Two Ambassadors on her behalf, ibid. Sends for the Author to prepare him to go Ambassador to England, ibid. Goes to the Western Borders to reform some disorders between the Maxwels and Johnstouns, p. 175. Resolves to wait an opportunity to revenge his Mothers Death, rather than trouble the Peace of the Kingdom of England, ibid. Is Courted in Marriage by many great Princes, p. 177. Asks Council of God by Prayer Fifteeen days, and then resolves to Marry the King of Denmark's Daughter, ibid. Makes choice

The Table.

choice of the Author to go Ambaffadour to Denmark, ibid. Perfwades
him to undertake that Embaffy, p.
178. Confents that his Brother, the
Lord Yungland fhould be joyned in
Commiffion with him, and gives him
Commiffion by word of mouth, ibid.
Is angry with the Author, p. 179.
Is advifed to fend to Queen Elizabeth
to defire her Confent to his Marriage
with Denmark, ibid. Her Anfwer
thereunto, ibid. Is incenfed with his
Council for Voting againft that Marriage, ibid. Deals privately with
thofe at Edinburgh, to threaten the
Council and Chancellor, menacing him
with Death, if that Marriage was
hindred, upon which he fends the Earl
Marfhal with 2 other Perfons to Denmark, ibid. Hears of their being at
Sea with the Queen, and makes preparation for her Reception, and being
impatient at their long delay, lays the
fault on his Council, p 180. Directs
Colonel Stuart to Sir Robert Melvil
and the Author, charging them to
take care of his Eftate in his abfence,
p. 180, and 181. Is perfwaded to go
in perfon to Denmark, p. 181. Sails
to Denmark in perfon to fetch the
Queen, and leaves Sir Robert Vice-
Chancellor, ibid. Three Ships went
with him befides his own, he lands at
Norway, where the Queen waited for
a Wind, and their Celebrates the
Marriage, ibid. Returns not that
winter, is fent for to Denmark, whither he went by Land with his new
Queen, where he behaves himfelf liberally and honourably by the way, and
at the Court of Denmark, ibid. Is
much troubled to make thofe Officers
of State agree that were with him
there, p. 182. Returns the next
Spring with the Admiral of Denmark and other Perfons of Quality,
ibid. Treats them all honourably, and
after the Queens Coronation difmiff-
eth them Magnificently Rewarded,
ibid. Sends for the Author at his
Landing, ibid. Repents his anger

with Sir Robert Melvil, and turns it
againft the Chancellor, who incenfed
him againft Sir Robert, p. 183.
Rewards the Strangers foon after
the Queens Coronation and Banqueting to their great fatisfaction, p. 184.
Defires Sir Robert Melvil and the
Author to advife upon fome good
Rules for the eftablifhing Affairs before his going to Denmark, p. 186.
Is abufed upon the account of Maclean and other Highlanders, p. 192,
and 193. Sends for Melvil the Author to wait upon the Queen, promifing him rewards, p. 193. takes occafion at Table to difcourfe advanta-
geoufly of the Author to his Queen,
p. 193, and 194. Secures himfelf in
Edinburgh after Bothwel's Attempt
on the Palace, p. 197. Thinks Sir
Robert Melvil not fit for his Office,
yet continues him ftill, p. 199. Is
defign'd to be feized at Falkland by
Bothwel and his Party, p. 201.
And miraculoufly delivered by God
from that Confpiracy, p. 202. Determines to fend Ambaffadors to England, Denmark, France and Flanders
about the Birth of his Son Prince
Henry, p. 203. Requiring them to
fend Ambaffadors to folemnize the
Baptifm of the firft born Son, ibid.
The Ambaffadors are fent, p. 203.

Jane Kennedie, the Wife of Sir
Andrew Melvil was a long time in
England with his Majefties Mother,
p. 180. Is Sent for by him to wait
upon the young Queen, who making
haft, was drowned in the Paffage-
Boat in a great Storm, which was
raifed by the witches of Scotland,
as appears by their own Confeffion to
his Majefty, ibid.

John de Monluck, Bifhop of Valence, is fent Ambaffador from France
to the Queen-Mother of Scotland, p.
8. Goes firft to Ireland by his Mafters Command, and why, ibid. A
pleafant ftory of his Harlot, ibid.
Was formerly Ambaffador from the
French King, to the great Turk
Solyman,

Solyman, *p. 9. After his Arrival at Paris is sent to* Rome, *p. 10. And wherefore,* p. 10, 11, 12, *and* 13. *But to no effect,* p. 11. *Learns the Mathematicks of* Cavatius *& other Sciences by* Taggot *another knowing Man,* p. 13.

K

Keer Henry, *one of the Counsellors of the Duke of* Lennox, *p.* 128.

Keeth *Sir* William, *is sent Ambassador to* Flanders, *upon the Birth of Prince* Henry, *p.* 203.

Kieth Andrew *Lord, is sent Ambassador with the Earl of Marshal to* Denmark, *at the request of the said Earl,* p. 179.

Killegrew Henry, *is sent Ambassador from* England *to* Scotland, *p.* 68. *Complains against Mr.* Raxby *as a Rebel and Papist harboured there,* ibid. *Upon which he was secured,* p. 69. *Is dispatch't with a friendly Answer some time after,* p. 72. *He carries two Letters from Queen* Mary *to Sir* Robert Melvil *in* England, *and to what intent,* p. 72, 73, *and* 74. *Is hasted Ambassador to* Scotland *after Mr.* Randolphs *return to* England, *p.* 115. *Desires the preservation of Sir* Robert Melvil's *Life as a reward for his labour,* p. 122.

King of Denmark *marrieth his eldest Daughter to the Duke of* Brunswick, *p.* 177. *Excuseth to King* James, *laying the blame upon his Ministers,* ibid. *But promiseth to dispose of his Second Daughter to him, if he would send his ambassadors thither, but in the interim dies, leaving the same Commission with the Council and Regents,* ibid.

King of Navarre, *is Governour for the time of the young French King,* Charles *the* 9*th,* p. 30. *Procures of the Three Estates assembled at Orleans, that the Queen-Mother should be Regent of the Realm,* ibid.

King of Spain *enters the Frontiers of* France *with a great Army,* p. 20.

Kings of Scotland *never grew rich since they left the* High-Lands *to dwell in the* Low-Lands, *p.* 193. *But ever since diminished, which his Majesty found true,* ibid.

Knolls *Sir* Henry, *is sent Ambassador from Queen* Elizabeth *at the Dyet Imperial held at* Franckfort, *Anno* 1562, *p.* 39.

L

Leicester *Earl,* Queen Mary's *avowed Friend,* p. 71. *And several other Persons of Quality,* ibid.

Lennox Duke, *endeavours to free the King of* Scots, *but is chased into the House of* Ruthven, *and saved by the intercession of the Earl of* Gaury, *p.* 132. *Retires to* Dumbartoun, *ibid. Afterward goes to* France *and dies,* p. 133.

Lennox *Earl, is sent for to be made Regent of* Scotland, *in the room of the Earl of* Murray, *p.* 104. *Proves a true Scotsman,* p. 106. *after he had accepted of the Regency, he takes* Breechin, *and hangs the Soldiers found in the* Kirk *and Steeple,* p. 107. *Is shot in the Back in the Enterprise of taking the Lords Prisoners at* Sterling, *p.* 114. *Dies in few days after, and makes a godly end,* ibid.

Lennox Lady, *the Mother of* Darnly King *of* Scotland, *is Committed to the Tower and kept there a long time, because he Married the Queen of* Scots *without Queen* Elizabeth's *advice,* p. 58.

Lidingtoun, *Secretary to Queen* Mary, *and of great Credit with Secretary* Cecil, *p.* 32. *He with the Prior of St.* Andrews *procures a fair Correspondence between the* 2 *Queens of* England *and* Scotland, *ibid. And* p. 33. *He retires with other persons, being in danger of their lives,* p. 65.

The Table.

p. 65. *Goes from Court*, p. 100. *Is accufed of the late King's murther, and imprifoned*,, ibid. *Is brought by the Regent to* Edinburgh, *and delivered to the Lord* Grange *to be a Prifoner*, ibid. *Is fet at liberty by the King's Lords*, p. 105. *Taken Prifoner after the furrender of* Edinburgh *Caftle*, p. 121. *dies at* Lieth *'to prevent his coming to the Shambles with the reft*, p. 122.

Logie, *a young man, Gentleman of the Chamber to King* James, *p.* 198. *Is Accufed and imprifoned for dealing with Earl* Bothwel, *ibid.*

Lords (*called the* Queen's Lords, *as the other the* King's) *meet together at* Dumbartoun *to procure their Soveraign's liberty, being againft the King's Lords*, p. 88. *Binding themfelves in a Bond*, ibid. *They iffue out Proclamation on both fides to Convene their friends*, p. 90. *Meet and fight, but the Queen's Lords are Routed*, p. 91. *The King's Lords fend for the Earl of* Lennox, *to make him Regent in the room of* Murray, *p.* 104. *They hold a Parliament at* Sterling, *and the Queen's at* Edinburgh, p. 113. *Lords all written and unwritten for arrive at St.* Andrew's, *to attend the Convention intended there by the King*, p. 136. *Defign to have the King in cuftody*, ibid. *Lords met at* Edinburgh, *pafs a Vote unanimoufly ; being preoccupied by the Earl of* Arran, *p.* 153. *Thofe Lords who defigned the attempt on* Sterling *fly to* England, *p.* 157. *Are forefaulted*, *p.* 158. *They return and come to the Borders with Affiftance*, *p.* 168. 3000 *of the banifhed Lords enter* Sterling, *fall on their knees, and beg his Majefty's pardon*, p. 169. *Which is granted*, ibid. *The Lords gain great credit by their moderate behaviour*, p. 170.

Lorrain Cardinal, *defigns to promote Queen* Mary *to the Crown of* England, *by alledging Queen* Eliza-

beth *to be Illegitimate*, p. 32. *Caufeth all Queen* Mary's *Silver Veffels to be engraven with the Arms of* England, *ibid. After the conclufion of Peace is fent Ambaffador to* Spain *to take that King's Oath, and to fwear for his Mafter's obferving the fame*, ibid. *Propofeth two Matches to the Emperor of* Germany, p. 33.

M.

Macclean *and others, chief of the Highlands is fubtilly brought to Court by the Chancellour*, p. 192. *Are imprifoned in* Edinburgh *Caftle, accufed of foul murther, but get off*, ibid.

Maitland *Secretary, is confin'd to his houfe with others*, p. 166. *Oppofeth the Author in Council*, p. 171.

Mar *Earl, keeps the young Prince, and will not deliver him to* Bothwel, *p.* 80. *Is made Regent in the room of* Lennox, *p.* 111. *Goes to* Edinburgh *to Convene the Lords in order to an Accommodation*, *p.* 118. *In the mean time goes to* Dalkieth, *and fhortly after dies at* Sterling, ibid.

Margil David, *one of the Duke of* Lennox *his Chancellors*, p. 128.

Marfhal *of* Berwick *befiegeth* Edinburgh *affifted by an Englifh Army, and all* Scotland, *p.* 120. *Contends with the Ambaffadour*, p. 121. *Is forced to deliver up the Prifoners in* Edinburgh *Caftle to the Regent, being commanded by the Queen of* England *to do it*, ibid. *Which he doth with much regret, and returns to* Berwick *difcontented*, ibid. *The Laird of* Cleech *having before offered them good Conditions to quit the Caftle*, ibid. *Takes the Death of the Laird of* Grange *very much to the heart, by reafon of the breach of his promife, and thereupon quits his Employment of* Marfhal ; *whofe lofs is much lamented.*

F f

ted, being a worthy Captain, ibid.

Marſhal Earl, and others, lodge within the Caſtle with his Majeſty of Scotland, p. 136. He and others retire to their houſes, p. 137. Deſires to ſupply the place of the Lord Atry as Ambaſſadour to Denmark, p. 178. Which is granted, ibid. But his Commiſſion is ſo ſlender that he ſends the Lord Dingual for a Licenſe to return, or a power to conclude the Match with Denmark, ibid. Which he receives, and is preſently diſpatcht for Scotland by the Regent and Council, and the Queen ſent home with him well attended, p. 180. But are driven by Tempeſt upon the Coaſt of Norway, the winds being raiſed by the Witches of Denmark, and the reaſon why, ibid. Is not well thought of by the King upon the account of his Embaſſy to Denmark, occaſioned by the Chancellour's miſrepreſentation of him to his Majeſty, p. 182.

Martland is made Chancellour in Scotland, p. 175. Threatned to be kill'd, p. 179. Hears of his Majeſties diſcontent at the Queens delay of coming from Denmark, and adviſeth him to ſail thither in perſon to fetch her home, p. 181. Who goes with him privately, ibid. Being at Denmark, he deviſeth many Reformations to be made at his Majeſties return, p. 182. Cauſeth the Lord Hume, Earl Bothwel, and divers others to be impriſoned for their diſobedience, during the abſence of the King, ibid. Miſrepreſents Sir Robert Melvil, and envies him, though a great friend to his promotion, ibid. Emulation between the Council and him, who deſign to turn him out, p. 183. But prevents it being diſcovered, ibid. Great hatred between him and the Duke of Lennox, p. 198. He retires to his own Houſe, and is accuſed of ſeveral Crimes, ibid. Procures again his Majeſties favour, and is re-introdu-

ced at Court, p. 200. And at length reconciled to the Queen, ibid.

Mary Queen of Scotland, the only Child left of King James the 5th. p. 7. Born when he lay on his death-bed, p. 7. After her Arrival in France great diſputes ariſe about her Marriage between the two Factions in France, but is at laſt wedded to the Dauphin, p. 8. Proves a ſorrowful Widdow after the Death of her Husband, p. 30. By degrees leaves the Court upon diſlike, ibid. Occaſion'd by the Queen-Mother's rigorous dealing with her, p. 31. Is adviſed to return to Scotland, and behave her ſelf moderately, ibid. At length arrives in her own Country, p. 32. Seems to approve of the Match propoſed by Cardinal Lorrain, between her and the Arch-Duke of Auſtria, ibid. Advertiſeth the Queen of England of this propoſal, deſiring her advice, p. 40. Which ſhe Anſwers by Mr. Randolph, ibid. and p. 41. Lays aſide the thoughts of that Match, p. 43. And the Reaſons why, ibid. Behaves her ſelf very diſcreetly, and gains great reputation in all Countries, p. 53. Her Character, p. 54. Is much taken with the Lord Darnly, p. 56. Determines to marry him tho oppoſed by ſeveral Lords, ibid. And is married to him accordingly, p. 57. Is kept Priſoner by Douglas and his Party upon the Murther of Rixio, p. 65. Cauſeth the King to adviſe them to withdraw the Guards they had upon her, ibid. So they went all to their home, but the Queen, King, and ſome in their Retinne went at midnight to Dunbar, p. 66. Subſcribes Remiſſions for the Lord Murray and his Dependers, lamenting the young King's folly, ibid. Goes to Sterling to Ly In, her time approaching, p. 67. She miſlikes the King, who grows melancholick thereupon, ibid. She is much troubled at that foul fact committed in her preſence, by killing

ling her Servant Rixio to the endangering of her self, and the Child in her Womb, p. 74. Keeps her Chamber sometime after the murther of her Husband Darnly, p. 78. She wonders at the reports of her marriage with Bothwel, but denies it, ibid. Is forced to marry him, the Nobility approving it, and he having first Ravished her, p. 80. Is married by Adam Bothwel, after the Reformed Religion, ibid. Resigns her self to the Lord of Grange, and conveyed to Edinburgh, p. 83. where she is respected by the Nobles, but reviled by the vulgar, ibid. Writes a Letter, wherein she calls Bothwel her dear heart, promising never to forsake him, p. 84. Which being brought to the Lords by the Treachery of one of her Keepers, they sent her to be secured in Lockleven, ibid. Upon the Lord Lindsay's coming she subscribed to the Demission of the Government to the Prince, and certain Lords named as Regents, p. 85. Is conveyed from Lockleven to Hamiltoun, p. 90. After the loss of the Battle of Langside, she quite loseth her courage, never thinks her self secure till she arrives in England, p. 92. Is kept Prisoner in the North parts here, p. 99. Endeavours to get her self declared second Person of England, p. 152. but it proves ineffectual, ibid Receives warning of her death for the Council the night before, p. 172. Her carriage and deportment thereupon, ibid. Takes her death patiently, and dies couragiously, p. 173. Receives divers strokes with the Ax through the Executioner's cruelty, ibid.

Master of Glams is Treasurer of Scotland, p. 198. Designs to get the Office from Sir Robert Melvil, and manage the Treasury solely, ibid.

Master of Gray is in great favour with the King of Scots, and why,

p. 158. His Character, ibid. Is sent Ambassador to England, and returns with great Credit and Approbation, notwithstanding he is misrepresented by the Earl of Arran, whom he begins by degrees to Eclipse, ibid. Acquaints his Majesty that Mr. Watton, a Man of great Parts, is upon his journy from the Queen of England, and upon what account, p. 158, & 159. Procures the Earl of Arran's liberty, p. 166. Is rewarded for it with the Abby of Dumfarmling, ibid. At which the English Ambassadour is enraged, but afterward reconciled to him, ibid. He retires to Dunkel, p. 168. Is sent for again to Court, p. 169. And in as great favour as ever, ibid. Is deprived of his Benefice of Dumfarmling, p. 173. And discharged from the Court, ibid.

Maurice Duke, God-son to the Landgrave of Hesse, p. 11. perswades his God-Father to come to the Emperor, who retains him Captive, ibid. Is Cousin to the Duke of Saxony, and obtains the Electorate as a gift from the Emperor, p. 12. Sollicits the Emperor for the liberty of his God-father, but in vain, ibid. Lays Siege to Magdeburgh, being the Emperor's Lieutenant, ibid. A subtile man, ibid. Surprizeth the Emperor at Isburgh, compels him to fly so clearly out of Dutchland, that he never set foot in it again, p. 13. Yet he and the Emperor is after reconciled, and lay Siege to the Town of Metz, tho to no purpose, ibid.

Maximilian, King of the Romans, by his politick carriage between Protestant and Catholick obtains the Empire, p. 33. Is skill'd in several Languages, p. 34. Proves an enemy to the Match with his Brother Charles, the Arch-Duke of Austria, and the Queen of Scots, though seemingly a friend, p. 35.

Melvil *Sir* Andrew, *one of the undertakers to keep the Castle of E-*dinburgh *p.* 120. *Is Master of the Houshold to Queen* Elizabeth, *p.* 173. *After Master of the Houshold to King* James. *p.* 180. *Marries* Jane Kennedy, *who had been a long time in* England *with Queen* Mary, *ibid.*

Melvil *Sir* James, *the Author and Brother to Sir* Andrew Melvil, *is sent by the Queen-Mother with the Bishop of* Valence *to be Page of Honour to her Daughter there Married to the Dauphin,* p. 8. *The kindness of* Odocart's *Daughter to him, promising him Marriage,* p. 9. *His pleasant discovery of the two Scotsmens Deceit, to whose care he was committed in their Journey to* Paris *p.* 10. *Is design'd to be promoted by the Bishop, but prevented and by what means,* p. 14. *Is entertain'd in the Service of the Constable of* France, *by the consent of the Bishop of Va-*lence, *p.* 15. *It commissionated by the* French *King, and afterward by the Constable to go into* Scotland, *and the purport of his Commission,* p. 25. *and* 26. *Endeavours to be inform'd of the Prior of St.* Andrews *intentions who declares his mind to him at large,* p. 27. *In his return to* France *meets with an* English *Mathematician, and the Discourse between them,* p. 27. *and* 28. *Gets licence of the Queen of* France *to Travel, the reason thereof, he takes his leave,* p. 29. *Is recommended to the Elector Palatine by the Constable his Master, and entertain'd as one of his Servants, ibid. And is thereupon sent by the Elector to Condole the death of* Francis *the* 2d. *French King, ibid. Receives great Favour from the King of* Navarre *and Queen Regent, dispatching him back with thanks and a gift,* p. 30. *Returns, visits the Queen of* Scotland, *Mary, in her return home at* Janvile, *with a comfortable Letter from Duke* Casimire, *p.* 31. *Receives thanks from the Queen for it with favourable offers when return'd from Travel, ibid. Is desired by the Duke and his Father to go into* England *about a Match with the Queen and the Duke, but refuseth,* p. 32. *And why, ibid. Receives a Letter from* Scotland *to inquire about the Arch Duke of* Austria, *p.* 33. *Is sent for by* Maximilian, *and goes with a Letter from the Elector to him,* p. 34. *The passages between them, ibid. Finds the proposition of a Match with the Arch-Duke would prove ineffectual, and therefore presseth for a dispatch, which at length he obtains,* p. 35. *Receives a Letter from* Maximilian *to the Queen of* Scots, *ibid. Is sent by the Prince Elector to the Queen-Mother of* France, *with an Answer and Picture to her propositions of a Match between her Son* Charles *the* 9th, *and* Maximian's *eldest Daughter,* p. 36. *Is introduced into her Presence by the Constable, ibid. Is profer'd very large offers of Preferment by the Queen Mother, if he would reside there,* p. 38. *Receives Letters from Queen* Mary *to return home, ibid. Parts with a Commission to the Queen of* England, *p.* 39. *Presents the Pictures of* Casimire *and his Relations to the Queen, ibid. Which she returns next day,* p. 40. *Refusing to accept of them, ibid. Writes back to his Father, and himself a dissuasive from that Marriage and receives thanks, ibid. Returns into* Scotland *and presents the Queen with Letters from Forraign Princes,* p. 43. *Receives great proffers from the Queen, but refuseth them, and upon what ground, ibid. Is sent with instructions to Queen* Elizabeth *and her Friends to procure a Reconciliation, ibid. The instructions at large,* p. *the* 44th. *and* 45th. *Being Arrived at* London, *he next morning receives his Answer from the Queen,* p. 46. *Perswades her Majesty to tear the Angry Letter she intended* *intend to send to Queen* Mary *in answer to hers*, p. 47. *Which she did,* ibid. *The private Conference between the Queen of* England *and* Melvil, *being a Character of the Two Queens full of diversion*, p. 47, 48, *and* 49.' *Takes his leave and returns to* Scotland *with many Presents*, p. 52. *Acquaints his Queen with Queen* Elizabeth's *Answer*, ibid. *After the Queens Marriage begs leave to Travel, which she refuseth*, p. 58. *Upon her promises stayes and adviseth her*, p. 59. *Officiates as her Secretary*, Lidington *being absent upon some suspicion*, p. 67. *Rides Post to* London *to give an account to the Queen of the Birth of a Son in* Scotland, p. 69. *Has a satisfactory Audience*, p. 70. *Shews a Letter to her Majesty from* Tho. *Bishop against her Marriage with* Bothwel, *and is forced to fly for it*, p. 79. *But returns,* Bothwel's *rage being allayed*, ibid. *Is afterward taken Prisoner when* Bothwel *seized the Queen*, p. 80 *Refuseth at first to be sent Commissioner by the Lords who concluded to Crown the Prince, to the Lords Assembled at* Hamiltoun, *but at last accepts*, p. 85. *Declares their Answer at* Sterling, p. 86. *Is sent to meet the Lord* Murray *at* Berwick *upon his return from* France; *to advise him*, p. 87. *Is sent by another Party with contrary Instructions*, ibid. *Deviseth with others a remedy for his preservation and brings into a good opinion with the People*, p. 102. *Is sent to* Berwick *to the Earl of* Suffex; *and why*, p. 105. *Receives an Answer*, ibid. *Visits the Regent the Earl of* Lennox *there*, p. 106. *Dissuades him from the Regency as dangerous*, ibid. *Is taken Prisoner by the Earl of* Bughan, p. 111. *Whom the Laird* Grange *would have released by force but he disapproves of it*, ibid. *Finds Bail to serve his Majesty and the Regent, and is discharged*, p. 112. *Is sent by the*

Regent Marr *to* Edinburgh *to make an Accommodation between them and him*, p. 117. *Which they were all inclinable to*, ibid. *And after* Marr's *death by the Regent* Mortoun, p. 118. *Profferreth himself a Pledge that the Castle of* Edinburgh. *should he delivered by the Laird* Grange *to the Regent*, p. 119. *Loseth the Regents favour by telling his faults freely*, p. 124. *Is ordained to hold the Justice-Eyre of* West Lauthian *with other persons at* Edinburgh, p. 31. *Is sent for by his Majesty*, p. 133. *Goes to wait upon him, though resolved to lead a contemplative life*, ibid. *Discourseth with his Majesty about the State of all Countries*. p. 134. *Prevailes with the Bishop of* St. Andrews *to entertain his Majesty in the Castle*, p. 135. *Adviseth him to go into the Castle for his security*, p. 136. *Is acknowledged by his Majesty to be the sole Procurer of his liberty*, p. 137. *His Council is much depended upon by the King*, p. 138. *Is made one of his Council*, ibid. *Opposeth the Earl of* Arran's *new invented Proclamation in the Council-House*, p. 139. *Is made Gentleman of his Chamber, and a member of the Privy-Council*, p. 142. *Is writ to by his Majesty to attend him, and obeys*, p. 143. *Takes a long Letter with him to put him in mind of his Promises, the Contents thereof*, p. 143, 144, 145, *and* 146.' *Arrives at* Sterling *and dissuades his Majesty from sending Ambassadors to* England *for that present*, p. 146. *Which his Majesty condescends to and he retires*, ibid. *Is sent for again to conduct Secretary* Walsingham *to his Audience*, p. 147. *Is appointed with four more to endeavour the understanding his intentions*, p. 147. *and* 148. *Refuseth the Office of Secretary offered him*, p. 149. *Is deprived of all employ by the Earl of* Arran's *means, though contrary to his Majesties promise*, p. 150. *Yet is ordered*

ordered to prepare for an Embaffy to England, *and Pens the Speech he Intends to pronounce to the Queen,* ibid. *The Contents,* p. 150, 151, *and* 152. *A large Conference is held between King* James *and him about his Affairs,* p. 153, *and* 154. *Is left by his Majesties manager.* p. 154. *He entertains a smart discourse with the Earl of* Arran, p. 155. *Is resolv'd upon that account to attend no longer then the end of the Convention,* ibid. *Is sent for by his Majesty, and graciously receiv'd,* p. 157. *Conducts* Davison *the English Agent to his Audience at* Falkland, *ibid. Adviseth his Majesty that* Davison *endeavours the disturbance of that Kingdom,* p. 158. *Is sent for to entertain Mr.* Wotton, p. 159. *Gives an account of his carriage and designs in* France *at the age of* 21, p. 159, 160, *and* 161. *Gives his Majesty caution to be wary of him, but is not taken notice of,* p. 161. *Is appointed with Two more to entertain the three* Danish *Ambassadors,* p. 162. *Pacifies the first of the 3 with discourse for Indignities offered them,* p. 163, *and* 164. *Gives an account of the King of* Denmark's *Genealogy,* p. 165. *Which undeceives the King of* Scotland *and satisfies him,* ibid. *Goes on Board of the Ambassadors from* Denmark, *being upon their departure, with Presents,* p. 167. *Takes leave of them, rewards the Officers, declaring the particulars to his Majesty,* ibid. *Shifts off his going Ambassador to* Denmark, *ibid. Is sent for to Court,* p. 168. *Is sent upon a framed Errand to* Dunkel *and his Commission,* p. 168, *and* 169. *At his return forewarns his Majesty of what would follow the Earl of* Arran's *rash proceedings,* p. 170. *Is for and Act of Oblivion and restoring the Banished Lords, but Opposed,* p. 171. *Sent for to go to* England *to confirm the League with Queen* Elizabeth, *p.* 173. *But endeavours to avoid it,*

ibid. *Is discharged of that Embaffy,* p. 174. *And design'd Ambassador to* Spain, p. 175. *but has no desire for that Voyage,* ibid. *Is nominated to go to* Denmark, *which he likewise declines,* p. 176. *Is desired by* Du Bartas *the French Poet to go with a Commission to the King of* Navarre, p. 177. *But refuseth it,* ibid. *Seeing no preparations for his dispatch to* Denmark, *he obtains licence and prepares himself for the next Order,* p. 179. *Is sent for by his Majesty at his landing in* Scotland, p. 182. *Is Commanded to attend the Earl of* Worcester *Ambassador from* England, *sent to Congratulate both their Majesties at their Arrival,* ibid. *Is acquainted with his Majesties proceedings in his Voyage,* p. 112, *and* 183. *He and Sir* Robert Melvil *set down some Rules for the management of his Affairs by his order, from* p. 185, *to* p. 192. *Is sent for to* Falkland *and acquaint him that he is design'd to wait upon the young Queen,* p. 193. *which he did several years,* p. 194. *He and his Brother Sir* Robert *advertised his Majesty of a design against him by* Bothwel *and his Complices,* p. 197. *which was slighted,* ibid. *Is one of the Privy Council and Gentleman of her Majesties Chamber,* p. 198. *Is appointed with others to entertain Ambassadors from Forraign Parts upon the Birth of Prince* Henry, p. 203. *Is also appointed to attend the Two Ambassadors from* Denmark *about the performance of the Contract of Marriage,* p. 204.

Melvil *Sir* Robert, *is sent Ambassador in Ordinary into* England *by Queen* Mary, p. 63. *And upon what account,* ibid. *Is taken Prisoner with others after the Surrender of* Edinburgh *Castle,* p. 121. *Is made one of the King's Council,* p. 138. *Gets intelligence of the English Ambassadors designs against King* James, p. 167. *Acquaints his Majesty therewith*

with, ibid. *Offers by Combat to ju-stifie it*, p. 168. *But is prevented by his Majesty*, ibid. *Is sent Ambassadour with another to treat about the Accusation of the Queen of* Scots, p. 173. *Speaks boldly, and had been detained Prisoner but for the interest of the Master of* Gray *in* England, ibid. *Is left Vice-Chancellor of* Scotland, *during his Majesties absence at* Denmark, p. 181. *Though calumniated and threatned to be imprisoned, and have his Office taken through the Chancellour's means*, p. 183. *Gives his Majesty notice of* Bothwel's *design against him*, p. 197. *Is made Deputy-Treasurer*, p. 198. *Is threatned with death by the Captain of the Guards*, p. 199. *But the Queen stood his Friend*, ibid. *Sends his Servant to acquaint the King with* Bothwel's *Conspiracy against him in* Falkland, *for which he is derided*, p. 202. Sir Robert *is sent Ambassadour to* England *from King* James, p. 204. Mortoun *Earl, is challenged to fight by Lord* Herreis *upon the account of the Kings death*, p. 100. *Appoints four men to kill* Grange *at the entrance of the Regent's Lodgings, without the Regents privity*, p. 101. *Has a great Faction in the Country, though disappointed of the Regency*, p. 116. *But is made Regent after the decease of the Earl of* Mar *by the assistance of* England, p. 118. *Promiseth to the Agreement with the Lords of the Castle of* Edinburgh, *but steers another course*, p 120. *Anticipates the Marshal of* Berwick, *and gets an Answer from the Queen of* England *to have the Prisoners taken at* Edinburgh *Castle, and a Commission for their Execution, before he could send*, p. 121. *Triumphs a while, being with great Assistance from* England, p. 123. *His whole study is to gain riches from* England *and* Scotland, p. 123. *Of which* England *too* late repented, ibid. *Holds the Country in a more setled Estate then it had been in for many years*, p 124. *Grows proud, dispiseth the Nobility, commits several wrongs, and prosecutes several Lords*, ibid. *exposeth the Earl of* Orkny *to great hardship*, p. 126. *Yields easily to his deposition from the Regency, retiring to* Lockleven, ibid. *But by his designs gets in again to be Master of the Court*, ibid. *Is Accused by* James Stuart *of the late King's Murther*, p. 127. *Is condemned at the Assize for it*, 128. *And dies resolutely*, ibid.

Murray *Earl, takes part with* Bothwel, p. 201. *And is kill'd at his own House.*

Murray *Lord, and* Bedford *meet at* Berwick *about the marriage of Queen* Mary *with* Leicester, p. 53. *with slenderer offers then expected from him*, ibid.

Murray *being one of the banished Lords is sent for from* Newcastle, *and re-entertain'd by the Queen*, p. 65. *Retires from Court*, p. 78. *Obtains leave to go to* France *before the Queen married* Bothwel, p. 80. *Is appointed by the Queen first Regent of the young Prince*, p. 85. *Whereupon he is sent for from* France *by the Lords*, ibid. *Accepts the Regency of the Prince, after a Refusal*, p. 87. *Enters at first sight upon such injurious Reproaches of her Majesty, as were like to break her heart*, ibid. *Takes the Forts and Castles into his hands*, p. 90. *Clears the Borders of Thieves, and holds Justice in Eyre*, ibid. *Goes to* England, *accompanied with many Lords, to accuse Queen* Mary, p. 93. *Is privately disswaded from it by the* Duke *of* Norfolk, p. 94, *and* 95. *'Tis agreed that he shall by no means proceed in that Accusation*, p. 95. *Breaks his word with the* Duke, *and comes from the Council-House with Tears in his Eyes*, p. 97. *Is despised*

sed by the Queen of England for his intention to Accuse her, detested by the Duke; reproached by his Friends, living at Kingston penyless and unregarded, p. 97. *Is reconciled to the Duke,* p. 98. *Has* 2000 l. *of the Queen, for which the Duke becomes surety, and afterward paid it,* 99. *Takes leave of the Queen, but discovers again all that ever past between the Duke and himself,* p. 99. *Promising to send the Queen those Letters he should receive in* Scotland *from him,* ibid. *Sends for Secretary* Lidingtoun, *as being of Council with the Duke of* Norfolk, *resolving to accuse him, and writes for him to come to make a dispatch for England,* p. 100. *Being come is Accused before the Privy Council of the late King's Murder, and Imprisoned,* ibid. *Is misled, though well inclined, by vain pretences to his own and the ruine of others,* p. 102. *Gives ear to flatterers,* ibid. *Dissembles with* Grange *and* Lidingtoun, *ibid. His Character,* p. 103. *Is shot by* Hamiltoun, *and dies the same night,* ibid.

N.

NOrfolk *Duke, sent with an Army out of* England *to help the Congregationists,* p. 29. *He and several other Councellors sent down to* York *to hear the Regent's Accusation of his Queen, and be Judges thereof,* p. 94. *Privately dissuades the Regent from Accusing the Queen for the King her Son's sake,* p. 95. *Is the greatest Subject in* Europe, *not being a free-born Prince,* p. 96. *Ruling the Queen and all,* ibid. *His purposes discovered to the Queen, whereby the Regent lost the Duke's favour, yet speaks boldly to her Majesty,* p. 98. *Is prevailed with to enter into friendship again with the Regent, upon promise of his future*

secresie, ibid. *Acquaints the Regent with his resolution to marry the Queen of* Scots, *and that he had a Daughter fitter for the King then any other,* p. 98 *and* 99. *Becomes Security for* 2000 l. *which* Murray *the Regent of* Scotland *received from the Queen of* England, *which he after paid,* p. 99. *Is sent for by the Queen to come to Court (being again deceived by the Regent, then in* Scotland) *applies himself to Secretary* Cecil, *who told him there was no danger, so that he rode with his Train only,* ibid. *Is seized by the Treachery of* Cecil, *and after a tedious Captivity, dies of the Reformed Religion,* p. 100.

Normand Lesly, *gains great honour in the Wars, between* Henry *the Second of* France, *and the Emperour,* p. 17.

O

OChilterie *Lord, and divers others, in revenge of the death of the Earl of* Murray, *takes part with Earl* Bothwel, p. 201. *Adviseth him to Seize on his Majesty in his Palace at* Falkland, *ibid.*

Octavians *in* Scotland, *who, and why so called,* p. 191.

Octavio *Duke, Son-in-law to the Emperour* Charles *the Fifth, is left to the Pope's discretion, and why,* p. 11.

P

PArliament. *Proclaimed at* Lithgow *for the restitution of the banished Lords,* p. 170.

Parma *Duke, Governour of* Flanders, *wins the hearts of his Soldiers, and Enemies, by his prudent behaviour,* p. 166. *Is suspected by the* Spanish *King to have a design on* Flanders, *which caused him to deny the* Spaniard *Victuals, Ships, and landing*

The Table.

landing in his Territories, ibid.

Paul *the fourth, Pope, breaks off the five years Truce between the French King and the Emperour,* p. 19.

Peace, *concluded between Scotland and England. and upon what Terms,* p. 30.

Pool *Cardinal, appointed to be Mediator between the two Princes,* p. 16.

Prelates *of Scotland endeavour to win King James by large proffers and perswasion, to their Opinion,* p. 4. *They exasperate his Majesty against the Treasurer by their insinuations,* p. 5. *But he gets well off,* ibid.

Prior *of St. Andrews, the Lord James, Natural Son to James the Fifth, King of Scotland,* p. 25. *Afterwards Earl of Murray,* p. 32.

Prior *of Pittenweem, a great debaucher of Women and Maidens.* p. 5.

Protestants *grown very numerous in Scotland,* p. 24.

Q.

Queen *Mother of France is glad at the death of Francis the Second her Son, he being wholly ruled by the Duke of Guise, and the Cardinal his Brother,* p. 29. *Whereupon she dischargeth the King of Navarre and Prince of Conde, who had a Scaffold erected for their Execution,* ibid. *Is made Regent by the Three Estates, during the minority of Charles the Nueth,* p. 30. *Seems inclinable to the Protestant Religion, intending to joyn with the Protestant Princes,* ibid. *Makes a Peace after the battle of Dreus,* p. 36.

Queen *Regent of Scotland receives the Government from Hamiltoun,* p. 24. *Issues out a severe Proclamation against Protestants,* ibid. *Is disturbed at the discourse of the*

Prior *of St. Andrew's and others, and resolves to persecute the more,* p. 25. *Sends to France about the disorders in her Country for help,* ibid. *She, during the Controversie with the Congregation, retires with Monsieur Dosel and other Frenchmen to Lieth, which is fortified expecting French supplies,* p. 29. *But being indisposed, retires to the Castle of Edinburgh, and dies with regret that she followed the advice of her French friends,* ibid.

Queen *of Scotland married to King James from Denmark, is Crowned,* p. 184. *Shews Melvil no great countenance at first,* p. 194. *But at length seems well satisfied with his Service,* ibid. *Is offended with the Chancellour for delaying her Marriage with the King of Scots,* p. 198. *Usually speaks in favour of those Officers that are misrepresented to the King,* p. 199. *Is offended with the Chancellour, but reconciled,* p. 200. *Gives the English, Danish, and Dutch Ambassadours Audience,* p. 204.

St. *Quintin, and several other Towns lost by the French to the Spaniard,* p. 22.

R

Randolph, Thomas, *Queen Elizabeth's Agent in Scotland,* p. 40. *Denies the Queen of England made any promises to those who would oppose the Marriage of the Queen of Scots,* p. 60. *Is sent with the Earl of Lennox Ambassadour unto Scotland to set him forward with his power,* p. 107. *Is a double dealer, and sower of Sedition,* ibid. *Glories that he had kindled such a fire in Scotland as would not easily be extinguished,* p. 109. *Designs to have Mortoun Regent in the lieu of Lennox, but failed,* p. 115. *Returns home, and why,* ibid. *Is sent again Ambassadour to Scotland,* p. 127.

G g

127. *Hears that the Author was designed to be sent Ambassador into* England *and opposeth it, proposing other persons in that juncture of time,* p. 173.

Rixio David, *a mean fellow, who came to* Scotland *with the Ambassador of* Savoy, *is made Secretary to the* Queen *of* Scots, p. 54. *A Musician perswaded to sing with others, the occasion of his promotion,* ibid. *Is suspected to be pensioner and Favourite to the* Pope, p. 55. *Is kill'd in the* Queens *presence to her great regret; she being with Child, by consent of the* King, p. 64.

Russel *Sir* Francis, *Warden of the* English *borders,* p. 166. *Is kill'd at a meeting between the two Wardens,* ib.

Ruxbie *sent to sift what he could get out of* Mary Queen *of* Scots, *as to her right to the Crown of* England, p. 68. *Which he is to send to* Mr. Secretary Cecil, p. 68. *Addresseth himself to the Scots* Queen, ibid. *Writes to* Cecil *in her prejudice,* p. 69. *Is promised a reward but his intrigues are discovered and he secured,* ibid.

S

Seatoun Comptroller *to* King James *of* Scotland, p. 198.

Segie *Lord, made one of the Kings Council,* p. 138. *Chosen to accompany* Melvil *in the entertainment of the* Danish *Ambassador,* p. 162.

Señarpon Monsieure, *Lieutenant in* Normandy *for the* French King, p. 160.

Shaw William, *Master of* Wark, *is chosen to accompany* Melvil *in his entertainment of the* Danish *Ambassadors with the Lord of* Segie, p. 162.

Skeen *a Lawyer, chosen to go to* Denmark *with the Author,* p. 178.

Sinclare Oliver, *promised by the* Clergy *to be made Lieutenant of the* Army *against* England, *if* King Henry *the* 8th *should war against* Scotland, p. 4. *Is proclaimed Lieutenant over the whole Army, yet the Lords disdaining so mean a person would not fight under him, but suffered themselves to be taken. Prisoners,* p. 6.

Simson Amy, *a* Midwife *and* Witch, p. 194. *Is burnt with others,* p. 195.

Smith *Is made Secretary to* Queen Elizabeth. p. 157.

Sommer, *Secretary to the* English *Ambassador in* France, p. 160.

Spanish Navy *is rumour'd to be bound for* England, Scotland, *and* Ireland, p. 175. *Is three years preparing,* ibid. *The Commanders knew nothing of the Design but what they understood by the opening of their instructions at every landing place,* p. 175 *and* 176. *A violent storm of wind dissipates the whole Navy, and many of their Vessels suffer'd Shipwrack,* ibid.

Spiny Lord, *and the Master of* Glams *at variance,* p. 198. Spiny *is in great favour with his Majesty,* ibid. *For which he is envied and accused as a dealer with* Bothwel, *for which he is displaced and imprisoned,* ibid. *But escapes out of a window in* Dalkieth *by the help of a* Danish *Gentlewoman whom he afterward married,* ibid. *Is in disfavour with the* King, p. 199.

Spinze Lord, *is Gentleman of the Chamber to* King James, p. 198.

Stuart Colonel, *is sent to* St. Andrews *with Mr.* John Colvil, p. 133. *Is made Captain of* King James *his Guards,* p. 137. *Writes to the Author to repair to Court,* p. 156. *Is one of the* Kings Council, p. 138. *Rides to overthrow the* Bannished Lords *at their entry upon the borders,* p. 168. *But his design is frustrated,* ibid. *Is committed to the care of the Lord* Maxwel, *being in danger for espousing too violently the* Earl *of* Arran's *Interest,* p. 170. *Obtains leave to go to* Denmark *about his own Affairs being that* Kings Pensioner,

Penfioner, p. 171. *Has a Commiffion to treat about the Marriage of King* James, *with the Eldeft Daughter of the King of* Denmark, *ibid.* *Goes to* Denmark *feveral times at his own charge to complete his Mafters Marriage with the King of* Denmark's *Daughter*, p. 177.

Stuart James, *Son to the Lord* Oghiltrie *a Favourite in* Scotland, p. 126. *Perfwades the King to a Progrefs*, p. 127. *Accufes the Earl of* Mortoun *of the late Kings Murther*, ibid. *Takes upon himfelf the Title of Earl of* Arran, p. 128. *Marries the Earl of* March *his Relict*, ibid. *Cafts off his true friends*, p. 129. *His Character*, p. 131. *Is kept Prifoner by the Lords in the Cuftody of the Earl of* Gaury, p. 133. *Obtains the favour of being confin'd to his own Houfe at* Kinneal, p. 137. *advifeth the King, but is oppofed by* Gaury, ibid. *Gets accefs to Court, and ftays there contrary to promife*, ibid. *Is reconciled to Colonel* Stuart *by the Authors means*, p. 139. *He and* Melvil *the Author clafh in Council*, p. 139. *His infolent carriage*, p. 142. *He and* Gaury *are reconciled by his Majefty*, ibid. *He and his wife ruling all, perfwades his Majefty to go to* Sterling, p. 143. *He is Captain of the Caftle and Provoft of the Town*, ibid. *Advifeth his Majefty to fend the Author Ambaffador to Queen* Elizabeth, *intending thereby to enfnare him*, ibid. *Defires a familiar Conference with Secretary* Walfingham, *who refufeth it*, p. 148. *At which being incenfed he puts feveral Indignities upon him*, ibid. *Endeavours to be made Chancellor and Captain of the Caftle of* Edinburgh, p. 152. *Ufeth his Craft to pervert the effect of the Convention*, ibid. *Retires difcontented to the Caftles of* Edinburgh *and* Sterling, p. 155. *His unworthy Carriage with many other particulars*, ibid. *Seizeth on* Gaury's *Lands, and divideth*

them among feveral others, upon condition they would affift him in the ruin of the faid Gaury, p. 156. *Confers with the Earl of* Hunfdon, *on the Borders, and Plots with him fecretly*, p. 158. *Grants all that is defired at the Conference with the Earl of* Hunfdon *to procure Queen* Elizabeth's *friendfhip*, p. 161. *Is not courted by the Danifh Ambaffadors*, p. 163. *Whereupon he becomes their Enemy*, ibid. *Is in disfavour at Court*, p. 166. *Imprifoned in* St. Andrews *Caftle*, ibid. *Sends his Brother to the Mafter of* Gray, *promifing a reward to procure his liberty*, p. 166. *Which he foon did*, ibid. *Is ordered to retire to his Houfe*, ibid. *Obtains liberty to return to Court*, p. 168. *Flies*, p. 169. *Comes again to Court*, p. 200. *Is fhortly after kill'd by* James Douglas, *ibid.*

Stuart *Sir* William, *is Captain of* Dunbartoun, p. 129.

Suffex *Earl, is fent from* England *to* Berwick, p. 104. *Enters the Merfe with his Forces and takes the Caftle of* Hume *and* Falhaftle, p. 106. *Is fent to* Scotland *upon the Birth of Prince* Henry *from Queen* Elizabeth, p. 203.

T

Taggot, *a Scientifical Man who prognofticated the year of his own Death by Palmeftry*, p. 13. *And dies at* Geneva *accordingly*, p. 14.

Throgmorton *Sir* Nicholas, *Ambaffador from* England *to* France, *complains to the King and Council of the Queen of* Scotland's *new Ufurped Style and Arms*, p. 23. *But without fuccefs*, ibid. *Acquaints Queen* Elizabeth *with it*, p. 29. *Is fent Ambaffador to* Scotland *to diffwade Queen* Mary *from the Marriage with* Darnly, p. 56. *Owns, when return'd, the promifes he had made to thofe who would ftop thofe proceed-*

The Table.

ings without fear of Queen or Council, p. 60. *And comes off well,* ibid. *Is incensed that he was an instrument to deceive the Banished Lords, therefore advifeth them to beg their Queens Pardon, and penn's a persuasive Letter to her Majesty of Scotland,* p. 60, 61, 62, *and* 63. *A man of a deep reach, and great prudence, studying the Union of both Kingdoms,* p. 98. *Reconcileth the Duke and the Regent,* ibid.

Tulke Monsieur, *see* Broderode.

U

Villamonte, *a French Gentleman sent to* Mary *Queen of Scotland to shew no favour to the Protestant Banished Lords,* p. 63. *A Device of Cardinal* Lorrains, *lately return'd from the Council of* Trent, ibid.

W

Wachop, *Patriarch of* Ireland, p. 9. *went several times to* Rome *by Post tho blind,* ibid.

Walfingham Sir Francis, *is sent to* Scotland, p. 147. *His Character,* ibid. *Is conveyed by the Author to* St. Johnstoun, ibid. *Refuseth to discourse with any person about his* Embassy, *but his Majesty,* p. 148. *Is much troubled at the Earl of* Arran's *Court favour,* ibid. *Returns to* England *and dies,* ibid.

William *Bishop of* Ely *and Dr.* Wotton *sent Commissioners for Queen* Mary *in the Treaty of Peace at* Cambray *between* France *and* Spain, p. 22.

Wood John, *Secretary to* Murray *the Regent of* Scotland, p. 95. *Is desired to press forward the Accusation of the Queen of* Scotland, p. 96. *Produceth the Accusation of Queen* Mary, *upon the desire of* Ce-

cil, *who delivered it upon conditions,* p. 96, *and* 97. *which was snatcht from him by the bishop of* Orkny, *who gave it in to the Council,* p. 97. *Procures all the Letters sent from the Duke of* Norfolk *to his Master, which might tend to his ruin,* p. 99. *Is well rewarded for his pains,* ibid.

Worcester Earl, *is sent Ambassador from* England *to congratulate both their Majesties of* Scotland. p. 182.

Norminstoun, *kill'd at the seisure of the Lords at* Sterling, p. 114.

Witches taken in Lauthian *who depose against the Earl* Bothwel, p. 194. *They discourse with the Devil, his form and shape described, and are burnt,* ibid.

Wotton Mr. *sent by Queen* Elizabeth *to King* James *as Ambassador,* p. 158. *His parts and qualifications,* p. 159. *His carriage in* France, *when very young,* p. 159. 160, *and* 161. *Brothers Son to Dr.* Wotten *Ambassador from* England *to* Spain, p. 161. *Fifty years old when he came into* Scotland, ibid. *Becomes one of his Majesties Favourites, tho he did more prejudice to his Majesty, as to his affairs, then any* Englishman *that arrived there before him,* ibid. *Is sent thither to use all his wiles to disturb the two Kings (namely of* Denmark *and* Scotland) *and their Countries,* p. 161, *and* 162. *Visits the* Danish *Ambassadors making large profers to lend them Gold and Silver,* p. 162. *But secretly incenseth them with the Kings mean Opinion of their Master,* ibid. *Acquaints them that King* James *designed to affront them with delays,* p. 163. *Notwithstanding his double dealing with the King, he gains his Majesties Ear,* p. 164. *Makes a complaint to the King of the killing of Sir* Francis Russel *on the Borders,* p. 166. *which occasioned the Earl of* Arran's *Imprisonment,* ibid.

ibid. *Obtains with the aſſiſtance of his* Scotch *friends, the chief management of King* James's *Affairs,* p. 167. *His deſigns againſt the King defeated,* ibid. *Flies to* England *without taking leave of his Majeſty,* p. 168. *Perſwades the Noblemen of that nation, who were baniſhed into* England, *to return to their Native Country,* ibid. *His dangerous and circumventing Practices,* p. 171.

Wotton *Doctor, Ambaſſador from* Mary, *the Queen of* England, *who was Reſident there, when ſhe was married to* Philip *King of* Spain, p. 159.

Y

YOung Peter, *King* James's *Almoner, ſent Ambaſſadour to*

Denmark, p. 167. *His Commiſſion,* ibid. *Returns with a friendly Anſwer,* p. 171. *Being very well contented with all Tranſactions there, and as well rewarded,* p. 176. *Is ſent again to* Denmark *with the Laird of* Barnbarrow *in Commiſſion,* ibid. *Returns, his Commiſſion being lookt upon by the King of* Denmark *as inſufficient,* 177. *Sent a third time with an Embaſſy to the* Daniſh *King, and the Dukes of* Mecklenburgh *And* Brunſwick, *upon the birth of Prince* Henry, 203. *Returns with the reward of three fair Chains,* ibid.

Yungland *Laird, the Author's Brother undertakes the Embaſſie to the King and Princeſs of* Navarre, 177. *Is well treated and rewarded,* ibid. *A Scholar and Linguiſt,* p. 178.

AN

AN
Alphabetical Interpretation

OF ALL THE

Scotish WORDS and PHRASES

Contained in this HISTORY.

A

Aback, *to hold or keep back.*
Acceffion, *Condefcention.*
Alwife, *although.*
Anent, *about, concerning, as there-anent, concerning the fame.*
Affize, *a Suit or Trial.*
Ay, *ftill or ever.*

B

Banded, *joyned together, combining,*
Beft, *as the next beft way or courfe,*
Bond of Alliance, *a League or Truce.*
Brangled, *Turmoiled, Involv'd in Trouble.*
Burrough, *Burghers or Burgeffes.*
By-gones, *all that is paft.*

C

Caution *or* **Cautioner,** *Bail or Surety.*
Clan, *a Tribe or Family.*
Compear, *Appear.*
Comported, *Patiently, bore Patiently.*
Compts, *Accompts.*
Conform, *Agreeable or Suitable to.*
Conquer, *Credit, to gain Credit.*
Convoyance, *Conveyance.*
Counfelable, *one that is or will be Advifed.*

D

Decourted, *difcharged from the Court.*

Demiffion, *laying down, or tranf-ferring to another.*
Devilry, *Devilifhnefs or Devilifh Tricks.*
Devotious, *addicted to, very fa-vourable to.*
Ditty, *Doom or Damage.*
Down-cafting, *pulling down, or de-molifhing Houfes.*
Dunting, *the ftunning of Hammers, &c.*

E

Effectuate, *effected or done.*
Emit, *fend forth.*
Evangel, *the Gofpel.*
Evite, *Avoid.*

F

Factioners, *People of the Faction*
Fafhion, *as done for the fafhion, that is, done as ufual and cuftomary.*
Forefault, *to find guilty in the ab-fence of a perfon.*
Forth-fetting, *Advancement, Pro-motion.*
Fraudful, *Fraudulent, Deceitful.*

G

Gain-ftand, *Withftand.*

H

Hand writ, *hand-writing.*
Home-going, *returning home.*
Hoftlaries, *Inns.*

In

I

Indwellers, *Inhabitants.*
Infeftments, *Inheritance, Eſtate or Tenure.*
Ingeny, *Ingenuity or Wit.*
Juſtice Eyrs, *Juſtice Itinerant.*

L

Leave-taking, *bidding farewel.*
Leeſings, *Lyes or Lying Tricks.*
Liberate, *free, at liberty.*
Logh, *a watry ſloughy place.*
Longſom, *Tedious.*

M

Manyeſt, *the major part, the moſt.*
Miſcontent, *Diſcontent.*
Miſconſtructed, *Miſ-interpreted.*
Miſgave, *Miſcarried.*
Miſſives, *Letters.*
Moſtly, *for the moſt part.*
Moyen, *Means or Courſe.*

N

Noticed, *Manifeſted.*

O

Octavians, *Eight Lords appointed to govern Scotland.*
Onwaiter, *an Attendant.*
Oultmoſt, *laſt or utmoſt.*
Outgate, *a Way or Means.*
Out-taking, *freeing from Priſon.*

P

Practiſed, *dealt or laboured with to be brought over to a Party.*
Perilled, *Endangered.*
Perturbed, *diſturbed.*
Prejudged, *Forejudged.*
Procedure, *Proceedings.*
To Proceſs, *to Sue.*
Proponed, *Propoſed.*

R

Refuſe, *as he cauſed refuſe,* i. e. h: *made them deny it.*
Regrated, *Regretted, inwardly lamented or grieved for.*
Righteous Heir, *True Heir.*

S

Salutary, *wholeſom, healthful, healing.*
Skittering, *skittiſh, finical, ſilly.*
Signatures, *written inſtruments to be ſigned.*
Steadable, *firm, that will ſtand one in ſtead, available.*
Stormſted, *driven by Tempeſt into a Port or Harbour.*
To Suit, *to beg or requeſt.*

T

Time-coming, *for the future or time to come.*
Timouſly, *in good or due time.*
Tolerance, *Toleration, Permiſſion.*

V

Vengeable, *Revengeful.*
Volt, *as a merry volt, a merry pleaſant conntenance.*
Unfriends, *Enemies.*
Unwonable, *not to be won or courted to ſide with a Party.*
Uptaking, *compoſing, or taking up a buſineſs or difference.*

W

Ward, *or* Warding, *Impriſonment.*
Wel of Affairs, *the good or promotion of buſineſs.*
While by-gone, *a long or conſiderable time ſince or paſt.*
Whinger, *a Scottiſh Sword, commonly called whinyard.*
Wrongouſly, *injuriouſly or wrongfully.*

A

A Catalogue of some Books Printed for, and to be Sold by Robert Boulter at the Turk's-Head in Corn-hill, 1683.

Folio.

BIshop *Reynolds*'s Works.
Calderwood's History of the Reformation of the Church of *Scotland*, from 1560 to 1625.
Rushworth's Collections, First Vol.
——His Second Volume.
Pharmacopæa Londinensis.
Sturmy's Magazine.
Curia Politia ——
Rea's *Flora.*

Quarto.

Durham on the *Revelations.*
Baxter's Saints Rest.
Owen of Justification.
Origen contra Marchionet.
Charles the Eighth, A Play.
Lesley Historia Scotorum.
Man of Sin.
Lightfoot on *Lucan.*
Dr. *Charleton's* Anatom. Lectures.
Flavel's Husbandry.
Boys's Sermons.
Prynn's Power of Parliaments.
Burnet's *Thesaurus.*
Behin's Remains.
Manley of Usury.
Brown against *Quakers.*
Seamans Calendar.
Mariners Calender.
Seamans Practise.
Norwood's *Trigonometria.*

Large Octavo.

Pool's Nullity.
Wilson's Scriptures.

Durham of Scandal.
Dr. *Trapham*'s Treatise of *Jamaica.*
Cloud of Witnesses.
Rutherford's *Examen.*
Sclater of Grace.
Bayfield De Capitis.
Danvers of Baptism.
Flavel's Two Treatises.
——His Preparation for sufferings.

Small Octavo.

Wars of *Hungary.*
History of Jewels.
Moral Gallantry.
Flavel's Saint Indeed.
——Token for Mourners.
Roma Restituta.
Curious Distillatory.
History of *Japan* and *Siam.*
Looking-Glass for Children.
Hugh's Dispensations.
Religio Stoici.
Petton on the Covenant.
Queens Wells.
Moreland of Interest.
Miltoni Logica.
Grey of Faith.
Sydenham's Works.
Rushworth's *Solomons* Remembrance.
Gale's *Idea.*
Binning's Miscellanies.
Kirkwood's *Gramatica.*
Norwood's Epitomy.
Gellibrand's Epitomy.

FINIS.

www.ingramcontent.com/pod-product-compliance
Lightning Source LLC
Chambersburg PA
CBHW030819020726
47499CB00006B/1986